CU00653119

FINDING THE END ZONE

TAM DeRUDDER JACKSON

Books by Tam DeRudder Jackson

THE TALISMAN SERIES

(Celtic paranormal/fantasy romance)

Tracker (prequel novella)
Talisman
Warrior
Prophetess (novella)
Bard
Druid
Rogue

THE BALEFIRE SERIES

(Rockstar romance)

Play For Me
Sing For Me
Wild For Me
Hot For Me
Stay For Me

Find me at *www.tamderudderjackson.com*

Editor: Bryony Leah
Cover Design: Steamy Designs
Formatting: Damonza.com

For Joni Blood

This book (and the Game Time Series that follow it)
only exists because of you.

You're the best!

In Memory of Nikki Busch

You made me a much better writer than
I ever thought I could be.

FINDING THE END ZONE

CHAPTER ONE

Jamaica

HIS EYES FLASHED blue fire as he undressed me with them layer by layer as though he planned to have me right there in the aisle of Creston Hall. My heart sputtered then raced in my chest as if I'd run a marathon for days rather than merely walked into the auditorium for the start of fall classes. The heaviness low in my belly drew my attention to my suddenly damp panties, and I clamped my thighs together. *Who the hell* is *this guy?*

"Oh my, sweetheart. Looks like you've caught someone's eye," my best friend Axel Benson said into my ear.

Tearing my gaze from the mesmerizing scrutiny of the man who commanded the attention of every person in the lecture hall, I whispered out of the side of my mouth, "Who is he?"

"Callahan O'Reilly. Starting tight end on the Wildcats football team," Axel answered, awe in his voice.

"What's he doing in a four hundred-level lit class?"

My friend's indulgent grin put my hackles

up. "Same thing we are, probably. Picking up required upper-level credits."

Hotshot stepped into our conversation. "Do I know you from somewhere?" Though he'd dialed down the heat, the banked fires in his sea-blue eyes smoldered in my heated core.

Damn it. Football players—any sports players for that matter—were *not* my type. Tightening my grip on the strap of my backpack, I said, "Doubt it."

"Jamaica works at the sweet shop in the Union," Axel oh-so-helpfully supplied. The "oof" that followed might have been from the elbow I threw to his ribs. I didn't normally resort to violence, but Hotshot's muscular, toned body combined with his intense stare overwhelmed my common sense.

Folding my arms over my chest, I said, "From the looks of you, I imagine nothing sweet has ever gone into your mouth."

His gaze flicked down my body and back up to snag mine again, his grin positively wolfish. "Shall we test that theory?"

I blinked. "What the hell? Are you *flirting* with me?"

"All right, you pretenses of scholarly pursuits. Find a seat. We don't have all day." Dr. Dair's curmudgeonly tones interrupted our stare-down.

Grinning like a lunatic, Axel shoulder-bumped me, his eyes darting between Hotshot and me.

"Miss Winslow, are you coming or going?" Dr. Dair's voice was as dry as the Sahara.

My cheeks tingled with a rush of blood at being called out by the one professor I had yet to impress in front of the hottest guy I'd ever seen. The corner of Hotshot's mouth tipped up, and his voice dropped an octave. "Yes, Miss Winslow. Are you going"—his eyes danced as if he knew exactly the effect he was having on me—"or coming?"

Gritting my teeth, I grabbed a handful of Axel's sleeve and tugged him along the row beside me, settling somewhere near the middle. Even after I'd earned A's in his last two classes, Dr. Dair didn't take me seriously. If a certain football player weren't so tall and deliciously muscular and standing in the way of me reaching my usual seat, I wouldn't have drawn Dair's negative attention before class even started. Hell, I hadn't even had a chance to ask one question, let alone my usual several. Now I'd annoyed him by not finding my seat in a timely manner thanks to some jock who was too gorgeous for my own good.

Hotshot ambled down the aisle to an open seat a couple of rows down, tossed his backpack into the chair beside him, and angled his body so he could look back at me. When he caught me watching him, he winked, and I wanted to throw something at him. The smirk on his face said he knew that too.

As a junior, I desperately wanted to impress the English Department Chair at least once before graduation. Callahan O'Reilly put paid to that dream when he stopped me with his eyes in the middle of the aisle.

"English Literature: A Cultural Study will demand your concentration and no small amount of your time." Dr. Dair ignored the little drama playing out between a certain football player and me.

Axel, the traitor, did not.

"If Callahan O'Reilly looked at me the way he looked at you, I think we'd be skipping the first day of class," he whispered as he fanned himself beside me.

"Shhh!" I stared straight ahead at our professor. "And you have a boyfriend," I reminded my best friend out of the corner of my mouth.

"He wouldn't blame me if I bailed for Callahan O'Reilly."

I shot him a censorious side-eye and concentrated on the droning of our prof.

By the time class ended, I'd annoyed our teacher with no fewer than five questions—all of them legitimate, mind you—

and endured another wink and the ghost of a grin from a certain
irritating football player. Before he gathered up his materials and
stuffed them into his satchel, Dr. Dair announced his TA would
be reading off the names of classmates he'd paired us with for our
class projects. We'd need to choose an era and focus of study that
fit one of the themes he'd outlined on the syllabus and read and
present relevant literature to support our thesis as our culminat-
ing project, which counted for half our grade.

I glanced at Axel. "It would be a miracle if he chose us to
work together, wouldn't it?"

"With the number of times he caught us whispering in our
Shakespeare class last semester, yeah. It would be a miracle." His
eyes strayed down the aisle. "I wouldn't mind if he paired me up
with O'Reilly." He shoulder-bumped me again, and I let out a
long-suffering sigh.

"If he were your partner, would you be able to stop fangirling
long enough to do any work?"

"Eventually." My friend dragged out the word with a sugges-
tive laugh.

As usual, I couldn't help the tug at the corner of my mouth
from his antics. He'd been my best friend since we met in the
cafeteria on the first day of high school, two loners who didn't
fit in with the rest of the school but couldn't be bothered to care
much. Discovering our mutual love of literature and writing drew
us close, and by Christmas that year we were inseparable. It came
as no surprise to our old classmates that we ended up at the same
college studying the same major.

"Axel Benson and Jory Bond," the TA called out.

A guy at the end of our row leaned forward and waved
at Axel.

"Better luck next time, Ace."

Axel grinned. "Nah. This is great. Jory and I worked on a

project together freshman year." He grabbed his pack from the floor and stood. "Move those pretty legs over, wouldja?"

I angled myself to let him pass and glanced around at the people already paired up. A sick feeling settled in the pit of my stomach as I saw Hotshot and I were among the last ones left without partners. Then the TA shot my semester straight to hell when he called out, "Callahan O'Reilly and Jamaica Winslow."

Fuck. A. Duck.

Chapter Two

Callahan

THAT RIOT OF chestnut curls that slipped past her shoulders drew my attention first. The way the strap of her backpack snagged her baggy Mountain State University sweatshirt and pulled it tight across her chest sent my gaze to her sweet rack. I've always been a boob man, and this girl's looked like the perfect handfuls for a guy who can palm a football. I let my eyes slide down to discover a pair of toned legs filling out black yoga pants. Bet if she turned around, I'd have an eyeful of gorgeous round ass.

Instead, her friend said something that made her snort-laugh, snapping my attention back to her face. My gaze collided with a pair of the deepest green eyes I'd ever seen, and I couldn't tear myself away from them. The two of them whispering would have made me laugh if not for how gobsmacked I was. The girl was gorgeous.

Then she opened her mouth and sassed me, which meant I had to play with her. I parked my ass in a seat with a clear line of sight both to the prof and to her, but most of my attention was on her. When I winked at her, I swear steam puffed out of her ears, so I had to do it again. By the time the professor made his announcements and turned the class over to the TA, I'd learned a few things about Jamaica Winslow. One: she was prepared. Two: she was super intelligent. Three: she irritated the prof. I couldn't figure out if she did it on purpose, but from the prof's nasally, snobby delivery, I thought maybe she did, which interested me more. Four: she couldn't keep her eyes off me. That part I liked—a lot.

Then the TA did me a solid—not on purpose, but I'd take it. He paired me up with Jamaica for our class project. Kinda felt like I'd caught the ball on the twenty behind the corner with only the safety to beat to hit the end zone.

I gathered up my pack and headed up the aisle to chat with my new "partner." Judging by the scowl twisting her perfect pillowy lips, she didn't see our pairing the same way I did. Huh. Time to change that.

"Looks like we both got lucky," I said.

She stuffed her hand on her hip and glared at me. "You did, anyway."

I hiked a brow and waited.

The exasperated sigh that escaped her disturbed the curls falling over her forehead, momentarily distracting me.

"I'm an English major. Judging by some of the other pairings, Dair put English majors with non-English majors. I hope you have something to bring to the table."

Leaning in close, I whispered, "I have all kinds of 'something' to bring to the table."

The pink stain on her high cheekbones gratified me.

"I always like to start things on a first-name basis." I stuck out my hand. "Callahan O'Reilly."

It was all I could do to stifle the laugh that tried to escape me when she bared her teeth. "Jamaica Winslow."

Her small hand was warm, soft, and surprisingly strong as she shook mine. When our palms met, a tingle feathered over my skin, and I held on for an extra couple of seconds when she tried to pull away. Her eyes widened a fraction and satisfaction coursed through me. Good to know I got to her too.

She slipped her backpack off her shoulder, setting it on the arm of a chair to fish around inside it. A second later she extracted a day planner, opened it, and like magic, pulled a pen from somewhere in her curls. The action had me leaning in for a closer look at what else she might be hiding in that mass of hair. From beneath her brows, she gifted me a long-suffering glare I met with a grin.

"When can you meet so we can figure out our project?"

"Tuesday nights after eight and some Thursday nights after eight if we have a home game."

She consulted her old-school calendar. "I might have to work on those nights. Do you have any other time?"

"Not in the mornings. I have weight-training and film from six to eight-thirty." Ticking off on my fingers, I said, "Classes from nine to noon. Lunch and meetings. Classes from two to three-thirty, Monday, Wednesday, and Friday. Practice from four to seven. Dinner." At her wide-eyed stare, I added, "Film on some Monday and Wednesday nights, depending."

"Wow. That's—Wow."

"Can you ask your boss not to schedule you on Tuesday and Thursday evenings?"

"Or we can meet on nights when I don't work. I'm sure we'll be doing most of this project independently and exchanging notes anyway."

"That's not what it says on the syllabus."

"Excuse me?"

"Tsk, tsk, tsk. Didn't you read the syllabus? It says the group project 'must show evidence of close collaboration.'" Her eyes saucered as I quoted the syllabus from memory, and disappointment put an edge in my voice. "That doesn't imply independent research and exchanging emails." I crossed my arms over my chest and enjoyed the way her pupils dilated a fraction when her gaze dropped to my arms. That was more like it.

She glanced down at her day planner again and said, "Looks like I can meet you at 8:15 p.m. tomorrow night. Does that work for you?"

"Sure."

"You don't have to check your calendar or something?"

I tapped a finger to my temple. "It's all right here."

Tilting her head, she glanced up at me from beneath her brows. "Of course it is."

The stereotyping irritated me, so I goaded her. "Your place or mine?"

She blew out an impatient breath. "How about the study tables at the back of the first floor of the library?"

The corner of my mouth drew up. "Doubt it will be as quiet as your place, but we can meet there."

Muttering something under her breath that sounded like "Lord, save me from arrogant jocks," she wrote in her calendar and shoved it into her backpack. When she straightened up, the pen disappeared back into her hair. Fascinating.

"Arrogance comes with the territory. Dumb, not so much. I'm glad you got it right."

For a second she closed her gorgeous eyes and pulled her lips between her teeth. I didn't have to hear her say "Give me patience" to know she thought it. Damn, this girl was going to be fun.

"See you tomorrow night, Jamaica." I spun my ball cap around so the bill shielded my eyes, saluted her, and headed up the aisle. I would have rather spent the rest of the morning teasing a certain curly-haired beauty, but I didn't have to check my phone to know I was already late to lunchtime film.

By the time Jamaica arrived at the library for our study session, I'd snagged a table in the back where she'd directed, my books spread across the surface to show her I was more than the best tight end ever to grace Holland Field at Wildcat Stadium. After checking the time on my phone, I raised a brow in her direction.

"Sorry I'm late. A group of girls from the freshmen dorm rolled in at ten minutes to close and spent twenty minutes deciding to buy one bag of sour gummy worms and a couple boxes of Red Hots." A massive eye roll accompanied her into her chair as she plopped down with her backpack on her lap.

Without acknowledging my outlay on the table, she began extracting notebooks, folders, and books from her bag as though it were Hermione's magic purse from *Harry Potter and the Deathly Hallows*. At last, she set her pack on the floor beside her chair, pulled a pen from somewhere in her curls, and opened one of her notebooks. "I've outlined a list of themes we could explore. I'm sort of partial to exploitation in Hardy's novels."

"Hello, Jamaica. How was your day?"

When she glanced up at me, I sat back in my chair and crossed my arms over my chest. She might have ideas about how this partnership was going to go, but I had ideas too.

"What?"

I jacked a brow. "How was your day?" Letting a little grin slip out, I shrugged. "Aside from the annoying freshmen at closing time."

Her head tilted to the side as she finally looked at me, a puzzled expression on her stunning face. "Um, it was fine. Good, actually. Yours?"

"Better now." I leaned my forearms on the table and dropped my voice half an octave. "I'm looking forward to pairing up with you."

She scolded me with her face. "Partners. We are *project partners*."

I coughed into my hand to hide my laughter at her expression and her schoolteacher tone. "The difference is—what?"

"We are not 'paired up' as in getting together. We are partners preparing a class project for our mutual advancement."

"Is that what we are?" I drawled.

A prim nod preceded her nose tipping up and her eyes narrowing. "Precision in language precludes misunderstandings." She opened her notebook, her pen poised above the page. "Our project needs a thematic focus. As I said earlier, Hardy's interest in the exploitation of the working class runs through all his books. We could use *The Mayor of Casterbridge*, *Far from the Madding Crowd*, and *Tess of the d'Urbervilles* as our anchors and bring in some modern movies and politics to show the timelessness of his theme."

Tapping my finger on the part of the syllabus I'd circled, I said, "Or we could discuss *manners*"—I cleared my throat—"in Austen's novels. We could use *Mansfield Park*, *Emma*, and *Persuasion* as our anchors and bring in modern movies and social media to show the timelessness of her theme." I may or may not have smirked at the little "O" she made with her mouth when I mimicked her, verbatim. "Precision of understanding of intelligence precludes misunderstandings." Stealing her pen from her hand, I set the tip of it on my blank notebook page and waited.

Her plump lips disappeared inside her mouth while she pulled a long breath in through her nose. That breath escaped on a puff as she reached for her pen, a pretty shade of pink coloring her cheeks. "Got it. You're not another dumb jock."

"Correct." I held her pen away from her, examining it. "This is fancy," I said as I checked out the engraved intertwining knots that ran the length of it, ending in some sort of round pink crystal at the top. Hefting its weight in my palm, I admired the obviously expensive writing implement.

"May I have that back, please?"

I gave her my best innocent face. "You don't share your pens?"

Stretching out her hand, palm up, she said, "That one's special."

"A present from your boyfriend?"

"A present from my high-school English teacher when I graduated." She wiggled her fingers.

The edge in her tone said I was on the brink of pissing her off. Relenting, I touched her precious pen to her palm but didn't let go. "No boyfriend, huh?"

"That's none of your business." She snatched the pen from me and stuffed it somewhere in her hair. Fascinated, I watched her extract a plain old generic Bic from roughly the same spot.

"I'll take that as a no." At the top of my blank notebook page I wrote: *Jamaica is fair game.*

Her hand flashed out, and she spun my notebook to read my note. Glaring at me, she said through gritted teeth, "Dr. Dair isn't running a dating service. We're partners for an academic project. That. Is. All."

"Which totally explains why your eyes keep finding their way to my mouth."

"Are you always so full of yourself?"

I let one side of my mouth turn up and held back when her eyes strayed there—again—for about the tenth time since she sat down at our table. My interest in her plump pink lips was a given. But that would have to wait till later.

Pulling my notebook back across the table, I said, "Judging by the class discussion yesterday, I bet working class exploitation is a hot topic for presentations. Which means manners will stand out, especially when we don't go for the obvious with *Pride and Prejudice* and *Sense and Sensibility*, don't you think?"

Her mouth dropped open, then she snapped it shut with an audible *clunk*. "Have you read all of Jane Austen's books?"

"Nah. My mom and sisters have a Jane Austen movie binge-a-thon every year for Christmas. They might have dragged my brother and me in to watch with them once when we were snowed in."

"Your only experience with the literature is movies, then."

If I wanted a snowball's chance in hell of keeping my GPA at or above my current 3.85, I needed to wipe that dismissive tone off her face pronto. "I'm not a fan of the way Hardy portrays women. Bathsheba Everdene is a total bitch in *Far from the Madding Crowd*, Tess is raped and shamed in *Tess of the d'Urbervilles*, and Susan and Lucetta die basically of broken hearts in *The Mayor of Casterbridge*."

She blinked. "Your family watched those movies too?"

"No. I read the books in my AP English class in high school. Not a Hardy fan." I sat back and let that sink in.

For a long minute, we held each other's eyes.

At last, she nodded and wrote across the top of her blank notebook page: "Focus—manners. Books—*Emma, Persuasion, Mansfield Park*." When she glanced up, a little smirk played over her pretty mouth. From the moment she sat down, I'd totally been checking out her mouth and wondering about how those plump lips would feel against mine. The difference between us was that I wasn't hiding my interest.

"We're going to have to read the books, you know. We can't rely on the movies for passages to quote."

I smirked back at her. "Yeah, I had that figured out."

Loud female laughter interrupted our standoff.

"Hi, Callahan," Tory Miller's breathy singsong assaulted my ears. "We didn't see you studying with the rest of the team." She sidled up to our table, stuck out a hip, and planted a hand on it while she twirled a lock of blonde hair with the other.

The girl was a walking cliché.

When I continued to say nothing, she went on. "The other guys said you wanted to study by yourself, but we thought you might like company." Though she stood right beside Jamaica, she completely ignored my study partner.

Behind Tory, her posse of freshmen giggled. Across from me, the most interesting woman in the library stiffened, her pen poised above the page where half a word awaited finishing.

"Thanks for your concern, Tory." I glanced past her. "Ladies." I touched the bill of my ball cap.

She stepped closer. "You know, a better place to study is the ice cream shop across from the Union." A sly expression slipped into her eyes. "Or the study room at Delta Chi." When she leaned her hip against the table, her short skirt hiked higher up her thigh. Out of the corner of my eye, I saw her run her fingers along her bare skin, but I didn't bite. "Or your place."

"Another time, maybe. Right now, I'm a little busy." I glanced across the table to see Jamaica writing paragraphs in her notebook. From the ferocity of her pen strokes, I was surprised the paper remained intact.

Tory tossed a gaze over her shoulder and returned her eyes to me. "Sorry. I guess we didn't realize you had company."

"Yeah, and we're busy."

Tory's pouty lip always preceded a tantrum. Usually, I blew her off, but one look at Jamaica told me she was about an inch from stuffing her books in her bag and walking away from our project—from me—for good. And we'd barely started.

"So I'll catch you later. Ask the guys where we all should meet up. I'll text 'em when I'm done here."

The pout morphed into a sunny smile that didn't quite reach her eyes. "Don't stand us up." Though she delivered the words in her annoying singsong way, I didn't miss the edge in them. From the look of her stiff shoulders, Jamaica heard it too.

With an exaggerated flounce, Tory pushed up from the table and ran her bloodred nails across the tops of my shoulders as she sashayed past me. Gritting my teeth behind a false smile, I suppressed a shiver of revulsion at her touch and watched to make sure she and her giggling entourage left the area.

When my attention returned to Jamaica, to my annoyance, Tory's interruption had broken the connection I'd worked all evening to build.

Chapter Three

Jamaica

"CALLAHAN O'REILLY, HUH? Lucky you." Chessly said, dipping whipped cream off the top of her matcha with a spoon.

I nearly gave myself a headache with how hard I rolled my eyes. "Obviously, Dr. Dair hates me." I fingered one half of my blueberry muffin into crumbs and berries. "If I'd made any kind of positive impression on him in the past two years, he would have let me work with Axel. Or maybe one of the poli-sci majors taking the class. Instead, he pairs me with the Big Man on Campus himself, Callahan freakin' O'Reilly." I stared glumly at my mangled muffin and sighed.

My friend laughed. "Big Man on Campus?"

"Gah! You should have been at the library the other night." Glancing at her, I amended myself. "On second thought, you shouldn't have been there. You probably would have experienced PTSD or something."

She licked whipped cream from her spoon and pointed it at me. "Explain."

"Tory Miller showed up with a group of giggling freshman sycophants in her wake. Their tittering and posing and twirling their hair made me ashamed for feminists everywhere. I swear, you would have thought they'd never seen a man before."

Chess stared across the table at me with eyes three times their normal size. "You're heading off into a tangent, J."

Slouching back in my chair, I continued. "From the territorial way she acted, I think she and Hotshot have something going on. The whole time she interrupted us, she ignored me, even after Callahan pointed out I was sitting right there."

I arranged blueberries in a half-circle around the intact part of my muffin and shook my head. "You deserve combat pay—or at least an additional scholarship—for putting up with that walking nightmare on your floor last fall. If she'd been on mine, I'd have lost my job for gluing her door shut with her in her room."

My friend shot me a glare from beneath her brows. "Why couldn't you have suggested that idea last year?"

Chuckling, I popped a blueberry in my mouth. "We both would have lost our jobs, but it might have been worth it." I drew a pattern in the crumbs on the plate. "What does it say of Hotshot that he has something going with her?"

Chessly's eyes glittered. "That bugs you, doesn't it?"

With a shrug, I tried to convey a nonchalance I was far from feeling. I had no interest in Callahan O'Reilly. None. Whatsoever.

"I don't understand why guys always go for clichés. Tory's superficial pretty only hides her bone-deep ugly until she opens her mouth. Apparently, guys are too focused on her bright red lips to listen to what comes out of them." I tore a hunk off the intact part of my muffin, popped it in my mouth, chewed, and swallowed. "Anyway, her appearance at our table the other night interrupted our flow. Now we're behind on planning our project." Under my breath I muttered, "Pain in my ass."

A laugh snorted out of Chess. "On the plus side, looking at

your partner across the table when you're working together is not a hardship."

I threw a blueberry at her.

Chessly Clarke and I had been friends since we were randomly assigned as roommates freshman year. Both of us needed a residence advisor job to offset living expenses since our academic scholarships didn't pay the rent. Instead of competing, we joined forces during RA candidate class, which meant we ended up being the only two sophomore RAs on campus last year. To say we had each other's backs was an understatement. The only person I trusted more was Axel.

The alarm on my phone vibrated in my pocket, reminding me of my shift at the candy store. "Duty calls." I tossed back what was left of my muffin and pushed away from the table. "See you after dinner for the RA meeting."

"See you then." Grinning, she picked up her tea and shouldered her backpack. "Don't let Callahan run through your mind too many times today."

Before I could tell her that was absolutely not a problem, she was two tables away and moving fast, her chuckles lingering in my ears.

The afternoon crawled by. It was one of those glorious cut-glass, blue-sky days that only show up in the fall, and I was stuck inside the Union at the sweet shop when no one was in the mood for sugary snacks. I finished rereading *Persuasion*, writing copious notes in the margins. It was something else Chess made fun of me for—reading old-school paperbacks rather than reading and making notes on my computer. So what if it made me seem old-fashioned? I liked the feel and smell of books. Plus, I'd read several studies proving people retained more of what they read when they read hard copy rather than digital. Since I had to read everything twice to anchor it in my head as it was, I wanted any additional advantage I could find.

At the end of my shift, I tucked my books in my backpack and was out the door before the next shift had even tied on her apron. As I stepped outside the Union into the square, I breathed in energizingly crisp autumn air. When I opened my eyes, Callahan O'Reilly was standing directly in front of me.

"Hel-lo, Jamaica." His sexy smile did inappropriate things to my insides.

"Hello, Hotshot," was out of my mouth before I could stop it. My face heated as I stepped around him.

Not taking the hint, he fell into step with me as I headed across the square in the direction of the dorms. "Hotshot, huh?" There was a grin in his voice. "Accurate, Island Girl."

My brow went up when I spared him a glance, and his grin morphed into a delighted smile.

"Where are you headed in such a hurry?"

"Home so I can grab dinner before my meeting."

"Parking lot is that way." He gestured behind us with his thumb.

"Dorms are this way." I kept walking.

He shoved his hands in his pockets and matched my stride. "Aren't you a junior? Why do you still live in the dorms?"

"Because I can't get enough of hanging out with freshman girls who spend their time simpering and giggling for the attention of upper-class athletes." Over my shoulder I gifted him the eye roll of all eye rolls. "My scholarship only covers tuition. I make up the rest working as a resident assistant."

"That mean you have a single room?"

"The one true perk of the job."

We traversed the yard between Creston and Seagram Halls. One of the pluses of living in the dorms was their proximity to the buildings housing most of the humanities classes on campus.

It meant on days when I overslept my alarm, I still made it to class on time.

"Good to know."

"Come again?"

"It's always better to have your own space when you're entertaining guests, yeah?"

I narrowed my eyes at the unholy mischief dancing in his. "That's none of your business."

"It will be."

I stopped and glared at him. "Excuse me? Outside of English class and our project, neither of us has a say in the other's business." Picking up my pace, I brushed past him. "Which is why I ended our first meeting early when your girlfriend showed up."

"My girlfriend?"

I talked over him. "Because who you date is none of my business, even if you don't know how to pick 'em."

"What are you talking about? I'm not dating anyone—yet." The warning tone in his voice drew my gaze to his heated one.

"Have you told Tory Miller? Because I had the distinct impression she thinks the two of you are a thing."

We'd made it to the block of dorms, and I cut across the empty street to the front of mine.

Callahan laughed. "Are you jealous?"

"Hardly." I infused my tone with all the disdain of *Persuasion's* Lady Russell when she referred to anything involving Captain Wentworth.

He laughed again, and it was all I could do to keep from stomping my foot to emphasize my point.

"You live in the all-women's dorm?" Under his breath I thought I heard him add, "That's unhandy."

Why would it matter to him where I lived?

"Like I said"—I shrugged—"I can't get enough of silly freshmen girls." Shooting him a smirk, I added, "Kinda like some hotshot football players, apparently."

He stopped dead in front of me. "Wait a sec. Have I been reading this all wrong? I mean, I picked up that your friend is gay, but you are too?" The only way to describe his expression was stricken, and it was all I could do not to laugh.

"Would it bother you if I was?"

"You have no idea." Something in my demeanor must have tipped him off because his massive shoulders relaxed, and the corner of his lips tipped up. "But I didn't read you wrong. You like guys."

"Not all of them."

"Callahan! Hi, Callahan!" Some of the giggling horde from the other night sang his name as they exited Hanover Hall. I let out a sigh of relief that I didn't recognize any of them as living on my floor.

"Looks like your fan club has arrived. I'll leave you to them." I didn't bother to hide my mirth at his horrified expression as four or five simpering freshman girls crowded him.

"Island Girl, you can't leave me here alone like this," he pleaded as he avoided the grabby hands of two of the bolder ones who attempted to link arms with him.

"Sorry, Hotshot. I told you I have to hustle home for dinner and a meeting. See you in class."

As I made my way to the front door of Hanover, I heard the girls inviting—or rather, demanding—he join them for dinner in the dining hall on the opposite corner of the dorm. When I stepped inside the lobby, I glanced back through the glass doors to see him walking backward the way we'd come, his hands up in front of him as he warded off their come-ons. Though I didn't stick around to watch, I had the idea he might have to make a run for it to escape them. All the way to my room, I chortled at the mental image of the big, strong football player running away from a posse of freshmen girls.

CHAPTER FOUR

Callahan

J AMAICA'S WILD CURLS overpowered the wide flower-patterned band she'd tied over them. When she slid her backpack onto her lap as she sat beside her friend Axel in the middle row of the auditorium, she blew at them. With a rough jerk, she tugged the zipper down on her backpack, pulled out her notebook, and dropped her pack on the floor beside her. Like magic, she pulled a pen from her curls.

For a second, her gaze strayed to where I sat a few rows down on the edge of the aisle. I grinned and pointed to an imaginary watch on my wrist. She wrinkled her cute little nose in my direction, and I winked, snorting a laugh when she bared her teeth at me. It tickled the shit out of me how easy it was to set her off.

Dr. Dair interrupted my fun. "Nice of you to make it, Miss Winslow. Now class can begin." The tone of his voice could have sucked all the water from every water bottle in the room.

Instead of slouching down in her seat as I expected, Jamaica sat up straighter and narrowed her eyes at the prof. No doubt from the way he was always riding her, the guy had a hard-on for my partner. It was one more thing I wanted to know about Jamaica Winslow.

Dr. Dair launched into a lecture on the excesses of the Regency, which he said were alternately lauded in the poetry of the Romantics and called out in the rise of the novel as a literary construct. He paid special attention to Austen's *Emma*. The side of my face closest to the aisle heated up, and I glanced in Jamaica's direction. Sure enough, she was glaring fire at me. It didn't take a mind reader to know what that was about. Once I'd talked her into using Austen rather than Hardy for our project, I'd had to win a second argument over which Austen books to use, putting *Emma* on the list. Didn't take a genius to know that glare heating up the side of my face was a not-so-subtle screw-you.

Even though Dair never seemed to let her up, she acted almost desperate to impress the man. I couldn't give two shits what he thought of me personally as long as he considered my work to be A quality—which it would be because that's the way I roll. From her incisive questions in class, my partner could keep up.

As I ignored Jamaica's heated stare, Dr. Dair droned on, "Following the popularity of *Pride and Prejudice*, the Prince Regent hinted strongly—demanded, actually—that Austen dedicate her next book to him. Though she didn't want to give him the satisfaction, she understood her precarious situation as an unmarried woman living off her brother's goodwill. With great reluctance, she dedicated *Emma* to the prince, which in all reality was a bold move considering the caricature of nobility Austen portrays in the titular character."

The professor tipped his head down to peer owlishly over the top of his glasses. "What is it this time, Miss Winslow?"

That long-suffering stare combined with the undisguised irritation in his tone should have put her off raising her hand in class—ever. The combination had certainly done its job with most of the rest of the class, and we were only a week in.

Not Jamaica.

I kind of admired her for it.

"In my research I discovered multiple scholars believe the Prince Regent didn't actually read any of Austen's books. Could she have been testing if that was true?"

"Ahh, if only she were here to ask."

I suddenly wanted to punch the prof's sarcasm right out of his tone. Her question had merit. It wouldn't surprise me to learn some Austen scholar somewhere had even pursued it. If Dair hadn't assigned a larger overarching theme for our project, I might have suggested to my partner that we switch our focus to chasing down the Prince Regent's response to *Emma*. As I watched Dair relax his stance, a satisfied smirk on his face at his humiliating response to Jamaica's question, an idea formed in my head. In the margins on my iPad I jotted an addition to our project focus on manners.

When class ended, I glanced up from sliding my iPad into my pack to see Jamaica angrily stuffing her notebook into hers. The hard set of her jaw as she glared at Dr. Dair's back when he exited through a door behind the lectern explained her actions. After four class sessions with her asking pertinent questions that irritated the teacher but helped the rest of us, I began to see that questioning the lecturer was her way. Even when he tried to preempt her with the derogatory way he called on her, she never backed down. Every time I'd had a conversation with her, something in it would set fire to her cheeks, but she never showed embarrassment with our professor. Her expressions consisted of genuine interest or determination. Though she didn't flare up at the public set-down today, her actions left no doubt she was hot about it.

"What's the deal with you and Dair?" I asked as I fell into step beside her and Axel on the way out of class.

"Besides that he picks someone in every grade to hate, and I'm the junior class choice?" she gritted through clenched teeth.

"What are you talking about?"

"Everyone in the English department knows Dr. Dair chooses someone from each cohort to give a hard time." Axel shot Jamaica a side-eye. "In the junior class, that would be Jamaica. She asks too many questions." Over her head he grinned at me.

"Are we or are we not in school to learn?" she demanded as she stomped up the aisle between us. "How does he expect people to learn if they never ask questions?"

"You kinda do it on purpose, yeah?" I said.

"Do what? Ask questions?" Those gorgeous green eyes rolled in her head like marbles, the "duh" in her voice loud and clear.

"No. Irritate him."

A long sigh flowed out of her. "I irritate him by majoring in English. If I had a different major—say, sports marketing"—she slid me a glance—"he'd give me a pass on the questions. Like that premed major who sits on the opposite side of the auditorium from you. That guy asks loads of questions too, but Dair is never an ass to him."

Axel shot me a "she's right" look, and I shrugged.

Stepping out into the crisp autumn air, she squared her shoulders and stopped on the steps. I'd taken the next step down, so she stood eye-to-eye with me.

"I thought we could finish up on our outline tomorrow night."

I grinned. "Sounds like a plan."

"I'll meet you in the study carrels on the second floor of the library if you don't mind." Her eyes narrowed. "Maybe we can finish our work before your girlfriend and her posse discover us."

My brow went up at the snark in her tone. "My girlfriend?"

"Tory Miller."

"Tory Miller?" I echoed.

"Sophomore? Blonde? The one who staked her claim on you at the library last week?"

The side of my mouth crooked up. "You're jealous."

Jamaica's eyes shot daggers. "You wish."

"She's a jersey chaser." I shrugged. "Not girlfriend material."

Axel puffed his cheeks and whistled out a long breath, drawing my attention to him. He made a "cut it" gesture beneath his chin, but it was too late.

"Nothing sexist about that opinion," Jamaica began.

I cut her off. "Nothing at all. It's a statement of fact."

"Yep, Dair hates me," she muttered under her breath in Axel's direction.

He shot me a smirk, and I grinned back.

"See you tomorrow night at the library. Second floor. More private." I leaned in closer to her. "I like it."

Her knuckles turned white where she gripped the straps of her backpack. "Bring some ideas, will you?" She stomped down the steps past me.

Giving me a thumbs-up, Axel trailed in her wake.

That girl was pure fire. Somewhere in the back of my mind, I knew better than to play with her, that playing with her would lead to getting burned. But as I watched her hips sway in those tight jeans as she tromped down the sidewalk, all I could think about was how hot those hips would feel in my hands when I pulled her in close.

Nothing about Jamaica Winslow was my usual type, yet everything about her intrigued me. For whatever reason, I usually went for blondes who didn't challenge me much, girls who were in it for a good time as much as I was. Nothing about Jamaica, from that mass of chocolate-brown curls to her take-no-prisoners approach to school, said casual. Her sword was always out, ready to challenge ideas—and people. For reasons I decided not to study too closely, I liked it when she challenged me. Whistling

the tune to Balefire's "Hotter Than Hell" as I headed in the opposite direction, I couldn't remember when I'd looked forward to
a study session as much as I looked forward to tomorrow night.

When I arrived at the library, I found Jamaica seated at a tiny
table in the back corner opposite the stairs and the elevator. Her
eyes tracked me from where she sat with her back to the wall,
which meant my back would be to whoever might wander by
us. The table was littered with books and notebooks, but what
caught my attention was a pen on top of one of those notebooks.
I scanned her curls for another but couldn't see one. Didn't mean
she didn't have one—or a handful of them—stashed in all that
hair. The thought made me smile.

"What's so funny?"

"I'm smiling, not laughing." I slung my backpack off my
shoulder and onto the table and pulled my iPad from it. "Hello,
partner. How was your day?"

She wouldn't let it go. "Your eyes are laughing. What's so
funny?"

"Your strategy. You think putting my back to the rest of the
room will deter a determined jersey chaser from finding me?" I
slid into the chair opposite her and set my pack on the floor at
my feet.

"Worth a shot. Maybe it will buy us enough time to finish
our outline at least." The eye roll in her tone dared me to play
with her.

"They know when we finish practice." Sliding a finger over the
surface of my machine, I woke it up and scrolled to our project notes.
"That and I don't exactly blend into this environment." I smirked.

"That man hates me so much," she said to herself.

"I don't hate you at all." Waggling my brows, I added, "I
think you're hot in a studious sort of way."

"Studious?" She glanced down at her oversize Mountain State T-shirt. "Are you serious?"

Gesturing to the books scattered over the table, I said, "It's how you present. I don't usually go for studious—"

"Why am I not surprised?" Crossing her arms over her chest only drew my attention to her rack, which her oversize sweat-shirts didn't disguise nearly as well as she probably thought.

"—but maybe that's because I haven't met the right kind of studious."

One skeptical brow lifted. "The right kind of studious?" she drawled.

"Yeah. Smart, driven"—I let my eyes take a tour of what was in front of me, then, for good measure, leaned back to glance beneath the table at her pretty legs in her yoga pants and back up to her narrowed green eyes—"and hot."

With no little amount of satisfaction, I enjoyed the pink ting-ing her cheekbones. She grabbed her pen and pulled a notebook toward her. "Don't bother flirting with me. I'm not interested in athletes." She glanced up from her notes. "And I'm not car-rying all the weight on this project, or Dair will fail both of us. Trust me."

Making a show of reading and marking her notes, she did her best to send me "back off" vibes. But the squirming on her chair told a different story. Good to know I wasn't the only one in this pairing with a not-so-scholarly interest in my partner.

"About that. Something Dair said in class yesterday had me thinking about an angle for our presentation."

As though she couldn't believe I had an original idea, she blinked up at me.

"Rather, it was the way he dismissed your question about the Prince Regent. Made me think we have an opportunity to remind him of his manners."

Blowing at a curl that slipped past the flower-patterned band on her forehead, she said, "It's not worth the chance of him lowering our grade."

"I don't know." I smirked. "It's not like everyone in the class isn't aware of his SDE problem."

"Wow. That didn't take long."

"What? That I caught onto Dair's small dick energy? He practically shouts it every time you challenge him." I leaned in. "Out of curiosity, are all his 'cohort' targets smart women?" I asked, air-quoting her friend Axel.

She shrugged. "I don't know. But it doesn't matter. We're not giving him any reason to score us below the A we are going to earn." Her stern schoolteacher tone cracked me up, and she glared at me. "I mean it, Hotshot. Your scholarship rests on what you do bashing around on a football field. Mine rests on what happens in the classroom." Pausing, she tucked her plump lips between her teeth. "I can't afford to take any chances with mine." Those last words came out so softly I had to lean forward to catch them.

Flicking my eyes down to the notes on my iPad and back up to hers, I said, "Austen is subtle in her delivery of scathing truths." Stretching my leg, I lightly ran the toe of my running shoe up the side of her calf and back down. "We'll be subtle too. That way if he dings us, we have plausible deniability when we confront him over it."

The tiny hitch in her breath at the contact going on beneath the table gratified me. Mostly because when I touched her, the contact tingled up my calf as well. Knowing Jamaica wasn't as immune to me as she pretended to be left a warm spot in the middle of my chest.

She turned on her chair, crossing one knee over the other and distancing herself from my wayward foot. I shot her a grin, and she rewarded me with narrowed eyes. "Since Dair brought up *Emma* today"—she glanced up from beneath her brows, her sardonic tone making her point for her—"maybe we should start with it. I reread it over the weekend, this time with our focus in mind, and marked some relevant passages. I was thinking we could use the scenes where Emma is instructing Harriet on the finer points of proper behavior for landing a gentleman."

"Or we could focus on her lack of manners where one of her peers is concerned. The way she treats Jane Fairfax always pisses me off."

Her mouth gaping open and closed like a guppy was so damn funny it took some of the sting out of her obvious opinion of my academic prowess.

Leaning back in my chair, I said, "I read the book over the weekend too."

"Oh. Well, great. Um—"

The way she stammered over her stereotypical athlete prejudices demanded I play with her. "You did say you expected me to pull my weight, yeah?"

"Yes. So, uh…" She cleared her throat. "Did you happen to mark any relevant passages concerning Jane?"

"No, but it won't be difficult to find them."

Seeming to recover herself, she asked, "How many times have you read *Emma*?"

I smirked at her accusatory tone. "Just the one time this past weekend on the bus ride home from the game."

Her brows shot up.

"What?" Deliberately, I widened my eyes. "It was a six-hour ride. The guys made it clear I've won a few too many poker pots recently, so I needed to occupy myself in a different way."

Her cute upturned nose wrinkled in disgust. "You gamble?"

"Only on the bus."

Narrowed green eyes stared into mine, and I shrugged.

"Some of our rides are long. It passes the time."

With a shake of her head, she doodled something in the

margin of her notes. "So, about Jane Fairfax. It's going to take a bit of time to find relevant passages." She nodded in the direction of my iPad where I'd cued up a copy of the book.

I kept my eyes on her. "We can start in chapter 34 where Emma invites Jane to the dinner party."

"Do you have a photographic memory or something?"

"Pretty close." I leaned my forearms on the table. "On the first day of class, you were wearing a tight pair of jeans—great choice, by the way—and a light red shirt with a low neck that hinted at your cleavage—which is fine. I enjoy a little mystery."

She glared.

"Your boots added about two inches to your height—another plus. I like taller women."

Her indignation came out on a gasp.

"And you had on the same headband you're wearing tonight. What I haven't been able to keep track of is exactly how many pens you keep stashed in those glorious curls of yours."

Self-consciously, she lifted a hand to the side of her head before dropping it back to her lap. "I was asking about your ability to remember passages from a book you've only read once—with the added distraction of a busload of rowdy football players, no less—not about what I wore when."

"I know."

When I treated her to my best grin, I thought steam might escape her ears. My grin morphed into a full smile, and I watched in fascination as her entire body softened.

As usual, Finn's timing sucked.

"There you are, buddy. One of the girls swore she saw you walk into the library a couple of hours ago, and we've spent the past fifteen minutes looking for you."

"Been right here studying."

"Well, the library's closing in a few, and this lot think we should hit Stromboli's for snacks." Finn McCabe, my roommate, best friend, and probably the best defensive end in the league when he wasn't jumping offsides, gestured to the posse of jersey chasers gathered around him.

Tory Miller stepped away from the pack. "Why are you up here instead of downstairs with the rest of the team?" The accusation in her tone pissed me off, but I knew better than to show any emotion with this one.

"Too many distractions."

She tossed her hair and shot me a coy smile.

One drunken slipup. One. We didn't even round first base, but she thought we were an item.

I glanced across the table to see Jamaica gathering up her things, a determinedly neutral expression on her face. But the tense set of her shoulders and the jerkiness of her hands as she stacked books and notebooks gave her away. Clearly, she thought I had something going with Tory too.

Fuck.

As if by magic, a second later, Jamaica's side of the table was bare, her backpack heavy as she lifted it in one motion and stood. "I think we have a viable start."

Guess our study time together was over, along with any strides I'd made toward cracking her tough shell.

"Are we meeting again this week?"

I powered down my iPad, stacked it on a notebook, and stuffed the whole works in my backpack. "Can't. We have another away game. But I'll catch up with you in class tomorrow."

"Sure. Whatever."

As Jamaica stepped around the table, I heard Tory's not-so-subtle "Bitch" directed at her from somewhere directly behind me. Jamaica's brow lifted, but her acknowledgment of the jersey chaser stopped there.

Classy.

Tory not so much. She slipped her claw around the crook

of my elbow and said, "I'm in the mood for cheesy fries. They're your favorite too, right, Callahan?" The simpering tone of her voice set my teeth on edge.

I shrugged my arm away from her and shot a glare in my roommate's direction. But his eyes were on Jamaica's retreat. More specifically, with the speculative grin on his face, he was enjoying the sexy sway of her sweet round ass in her form-fitting yoga pants as she wasted no time walking away from me.

Now I had another problem.

Chapter Five

Callahan

IN FOOTBALL, TIMING is everything. When the quarterback does a three-step drop and throws a slant, the receiver needs to shed the defender and hustle his ass to the center of the field to catch the throw that's coming about two seconds after the center hikes the ball.

The other night, my timing had started moving in the right direction with Jamaica. Then Finn and that bunch of jersey chasers he lets hang off his arm showed up and blew up the play. Or maybe it was only the one jersey chaser who was the problem. Jamaica didn't react much until Tory opened her whiny mouth.

Usually, I catch Jamaica sneaking peeks at me several times during the hour we're in class together. I won't lie: catching her looking at me makes my pickle puffy, as my buddy Wyatt Baxter likes to say. Yesterday in class, I didn't catch her glancing my way even once. Doesn't take a genius to figure out she thinks I have something going with that spoiled little sorority chick—and she's not impressed. Right when I dispel one of her stereotypes about me as a football player, something else comes along to reinforce a different one. In this case, that football players only date jersey chasers.

I shoved my gear into my oversize duffel bag, slung it over my shoulder, and headed out of the locker room. As I made my way up the tunnel to the exit into the parking lot, Finn fell into step beside me.

"Hey, what put that Debbie Downer expression on your pretty-boy face, 'Han? You can't look like that when we're playing the Trojans this weekend. We are going to mess. Them. Up." A joyful laugh accompanied his words as he punctuated them with three not-so-easy punches to my shoulder.

"Dude, do you get any schoolwork done when you 'study' in the library with that pack of freshman and sophomore hyenas you let hang around?"

We stepped out the doors of the sports complex and headed across the parking lot to the bus.

"Wait, is that what's bugging you?" A feral grin slid over his features. "It's that curly-haired hottie you were with. Now that I think about it, you were sitting with her in the library one night last week too."

"Knock it off, Finn. She's my partner for my lit-class project." I slung my bag into the compartment in the undercarriage of the bus, resituated my backpack over my shoulder, and headed for the doors.

"You won't mind then if I make a run at her the next time you're studying with her in the library." He tossed his duffel in beside mine and followed me onto the bus. "What's her name?"

"Don't even think about it, asshole."

His chuckling didn't stop even after we were seated in our usual spots toward the back, across the aisle from each other. "So that's how it is. You got a hard-on for your project partner. Can't say I blame you. That girl is a smoke show." He pretended to fan himself then he eased his seat back and stretched his legs in front of him.

One of the perks of playing on a winning team was we brought in enough ticket sales and alumni money to buy two buses for road trips. Everyone could stretch out, which made a difference when your best friend stood 6'5" and weighed 270. It also made a difference if you didn't want to sit across from him and listen to his razzing for a three-hour bus ride. I stood up, but Finn stuck one of those long legs of his in my way.

"Relax. I was only giving you a hard time, bro." He pulled his foot back in when I sat back down. "I should have figured something was up when you showed absolutely zero interest in that group of jersey chasers who left no doubt they wanted to take turns getting you off after we hit the ice-cream shop last week."

"That group is bad news, Finn. You should be careful with them, especially with Tory Miller."

A slow blink accompanied his raised brows. Right then, Bax made his way down the aisle between us. With a sigh, he threw himself into his seat behind me.

"What's buggin' you, Baxter?" I asked, happy to shine the spotlight on someone else.

"Coach's dress code is no fun at all," he said with a pout.

Finn and I burst out laughing. Turning in my seat, I said, "He caught you trying to sneak on the bus in a T-shirt instead of a dress shirt again, huh?"

"I even tamed it down this time." He smirked. "I had on my best tux shirt—the one with the long sleeves."

"The one that says across the back, 'Everything I want is either too expensive or won't text me back.' That one?" I laughed. "You thought he wouldn't notice all those words?"

Bax crossed his massive arms over his understated baby-blue button-down, stretching the fabric to within an inch of Hulking out. "It was worth a shot." A tiny grin tipped up the corner of his mouth.

"You keep torturing Coach like that, you'll have us all doing burpees at practice on Monday," I warned.

Finn shot Bax a glare. "If we end up doing burpees because of you, Bax, I'm dumping all my dirty laundry in your room for the next two weeks."

"Good luck with that. Especially if your dirty laundry includes a certain group of freshmen jersey chasers." Leaning forward, he directed his comment at me. "Good thing you skipped Stromboli's last night." Gesturing toward Finn with his thumb, he said, "Ole Finnegan here had five of them crowded around him in a back booth. I couldn't tell for sure, but it looked like two of them were taking turns giving him a hand job while the other three giggled and stuck out their boobs and asked if he was going to order more pizza."

I slid a glance at our roommate whose face had the common decency to look like a tomato. He should be embarrassed about letting a posse of freshmen fawn all over him like that.

Running a hand through my hair, I stared at him. "Jesus, dude, I hope they're all at least eighteen."

"They were Delta Chi sisters." Finn shrugged. "Maybe a couple of them were pledges. I wasn't checking their sorority status or their IDs. Sue me."

"That's the trouble, buddy. You step out of line with one of them—or she says you did—and poof!" I made an exploding gesture with my hands. "There goes your football career before the NFL scouts can even take a good look at you. Is a hand job in a pizza joint worth it?" Narrowing my eyes at him, I said, "Wait. Did you even consider you might get yourself kicked out of Stromboli's?"

"That would be a tragedy," Bax chimed in.

"Knock it off, already. I didn't get a hand job in Stromboli's, okay?" Finn slunk down in his seat. "We waited until we were back at the house. Consensual between adults."

It was my turn to raise a brow.

"Two sophomores." Finn crossed his arms defensively over his chest. "One of them might have been Tory Miller," he mumbled.

"I've been warning you about her since last year." I said.

"When you weren't so discerning about freshmen?" Bax teased.

"Let's just say, I learned my lesson." Aiming a stare at Finn, I added, "I tried to do my good deed of the year and pay it forward. But it seems some people can't be helped."

As we were talking, the rest of the team boarded the buses. The coaches deliberately split us up between starters and backups, offense, defense, and special teams. It was part of their team cohesion program, not that it mattered to the three of us. We had two defensive players—Bax and Finn—and two offensive players—me and a new receiver on the team, Danny Chambers—living in our rental.

Though he was a freshman, Danny was the same age as the three of us since he'd recently come off a tour in the Air Force, which meant he didn't have to live in the dorms. He'd needed a place to live, and we'd needed a roommate after Deshaun graduated last year, so we'd offered him our open room. But for some reason, he didn't ride our bus. That was too bad because if he'd been sitting with us, maybe I could have warned him about the jersey chasers Finn preferred to entertain.

Coach interrupted. "Settle down in the back, ladies. It's time to put on your game faces, think about what's important here." He swung into his seat near the front while Coach Ainsworth, the defensive coordinator, called off the roll. Satisfied we were all where we were supposed to be, Ainsworth smacked the rail behind the bus driver twice and we headed out of the parking lot.

As usual, the three of us sat back in our seats, slid on headphones, and did what we always did on the way to a game. Finn watched videos on his iPad, Bax slept, and I did homework. On this trip, I'd brought along the study guides for my Social Media Sports Marketing test next week, homework for my stats class, and *Persuasion*. Catching a glimpse of that book put me back in class with Jamaica yesterday, and the thought of her ignoring me left a sour taste in my mouth.

I got that we didn't know each other well—yet—but I also had the impression she was as attracted to me as I was to her. Those sneaky glances all through class the first week and the way her breath hitched when I ran my toe up the side of her calf under the table at the library the other night told me of her interest even if she wasn't ready to admit it. The flirty way she played me when I walked her to her dorm after I caught up to her following her shift at the sweet shop made me smile. She acted like I was only some jock her nemesis professor had stuck her with. But something else was bubbling beneath the surface, something I could sense ran hot and deep.

That all changed after Finn and his entourage showed up.

Not only did she not look at me in class, but she was out the door of the auditorium almost before I'd had a chance to stuff my iPad in my backpack. Her buddy Axel had shot me a wide-eyed stare and hustled after her. We didn't have a meeting scheduled for last night, but I looked for her at the library anyway. I knew I'd be missing class today with the team on the road—which also meant missing the chance to see her, maybe even figure out what the problem was.

Resting my head against the back of my seat, I closed my eyes. This was why I hadn't pursued a woman since I'd arrived on campus. This was why I kept everything to casual hookups and never two in a row with the same girl. Women were distractions who took too much headspace away from what was truly important: finishing school, playing hard, and landing a contract in the pros. I didn't have time to figure out what the hell weirdness was crashing around inside Jamaica Winslow's gorgeous head.

Beside me, Finn snorted a laugh at something on his screen.

That was another thing. Now we were one year closer to our goals, we all needed to distance ourselves from the jersey chasers—at least the young ones who could cause real trouble. The guys who took women with them when they went to the pros didn't take jersey chasers. Not the smart ones, anyway. Finn laughed again, and I shook my head. After his recent antics with the Delta Chi underclassmen, the jury on his intelligence remained out.

Dragging my stats book from my backpack, I flipped it open to the chapter for next week's classes, cranked up some Avenged Sevenfold on my headphones, and forced myself to think about something else. Anything besides flashing green eyes and how desperately I wanted to sink my fingers into a headful of brown curls and lose myself in kissing a pair of plump, rosy lips.

"That was one hell of a good time," Bax said as we threw ourselves into our seats on the bus. "My favorite meetup spot in the whole world is with their quarterback in the backfield." He high-fived Finn. "How many sacks did you have anyway?"

"Two and half, but I'm happy to share that last one with you, buddy. Teach that dumb fuck Prescott to run his mouth in public before games." Finn's laughter was pure evil.

I loved it.

"That sweet block you threw for Danny when Coach finally let him in the game should make all the highlight films, 'Han," Bax added, offering me a fist bump.

"Nah, the way you stuffed that corner into the turf on your way to that touchdown in the second quarter should play on *SportsCenter*. I don't think the dude stood up until our kicking team jogged out onto the field for the extra point." As a defensive end who loved to hit people, Finn's eyes glowed with appreciation for my offensive smackdown of the Trojan defender.

"That one did feel pretty sweet," I admitted. "But the pressure you guys put on their offense all afternoon was a thing of beauty. Bet the drinks are on Coach Ainsworth at the coaches' bar tonight."

Finn leaned out to look up the aisle to where the defensive coordinator sat, caught his eye, and with a massive grin on his face, gave his coach a cheesy thumbs-up. The usually staid Ainsworth returned the gesture with a grin of his own, which told me I was right about who was buying drinks for the coaching staff after we made it back to campus.

"Since we all were superstars in this one, guess we're all pitching in for beer and pizza at Stromboli's when we get home, huh?" Bax said.

"Or we could play for who's buying." I produced a deck of cards and a sleeve of poker chips from my backpack.

In the seat in front of me, our prize kicker, Dalton Sneed, groaned. "I might as well just hand you my credit card now," he said as he turned in his seat to join us.

"Or do what 'Han does when he plays—keep your cards plastered to the top of your thigh and lean down low when you need a refresher of what's in your hand," Baker, our punter, said from his seat across from Dalton. "That way we all can't see what you have." He snickered.

My roommates and I had all redshirted our freshman year, so technically we were seniors, not juniors. Dalton came in on scholarship, a blue-chip recruit who started his freshman year. We should have broken him in easy, but what would have been the fun in that? Three road trips into the season, and he had yet to win a hand.

"Didn't you ever play when you were in high school?" Baker asked.

Dalton shook his head. "Our road games were only ever about twenty or thirty minutes away, so there wasn't time to play poker." With a sigh of resignation, he said, "Deal the cards, 'Han."

I had to hand it to the kid: he didn't back down from a challenge. "Tell you what, Kicker, I'll spot you ten chips for that
fifty-yard field goal you nailed in the first quarter. That sucker
ignited the whole game."

Following my lead, Bax, Finn, and Baker chimed in that
they'd spot him five of their chips to start, so Dalton had basically won the first pot before I'd even dealt a card. In the end it
didn't matter. Luckily for him, he was too young to buy the beer,
but the mound of pizza we enjoyed after we arrived home did a
number on his credit card all the same. At least we only made him
buy for us. The jersey chasers who appeared as if by black magic
about five minutes after we ordered were on their own.

By accident—or a stroke of pure luck—I was seated smack-
dab in the middle of the semicircular booth in the back that the
team always commandeered when we hit Stromboli's together.
When the girls showed up, Tory gave the seating arrangement a
narrow-eyed once-over then aimed a snotty glare at me.

Ignoring her, I reached for the pitcher of beer Finn had set
directly in front of his plate and topped off my glass. Beer sloshed
over the rim when I went to take a drink and Bax bumped my
elbow simultaneously.

"What the hell?" I started before I clocked four girls crowding into the booth with us from both sides. Before I knew it, I
was squashed so tight between Bax and Baker I could barely lift
my glass to my mouth.

"Ladies, ladies, ladies," Finn said, laughing as Tory all but sat on
his lap. "This booth is only built for six normal-size people or five
football players. Pull up that table over there if you want to join us."

"But we want to sit with you." The way she ran her nails along
Finn's chest said one thing, and her eyes on me said another, but
her words sounded whiny rather than flirty—as usual. From my
experience with her, whine was her default tone.

"Yeah, well, we need some space to eat here," Baker said, a

FINDING THE END ZONE

growl in his voice. If I could have moved, I might have kissed him for that. "Grab that table before someone else does."

One of the freshmen hopped up from where only one of her ass cheeks clung to the edge of the booth and stepped over to the empty table. Right as she went to grab a chair from it, a group of people showed up. Two of them slid into the empty chairs and claimed the table.

"Oops. Looks like we have no choice but to join you," Tory said with a self-serving smirk.

"Don't worry about it. We'll find another table."

I glanced up to lock eyes with the pair of greens that had started haunting my sleep the last few nights. What were the odds that Jamaica and her friends were seating themselves at the table beside ours? Yet when her eyes landed on Tory and the other girls, her face clouded, and she stood up so fast she almost knocked her chair over.

"I don't think there are any other tables," said one of the guys who remained seated.

Jamaica jerked her gaze from mine and glanced around the bar, stopping on a spot toward the front. "A table's opening up by the door. I'll claim it." Without waiting for a response from her friends, she spun on her heel and marched away.

"Hey, Jamaica—"

She kept moving.

While I enjoyed the sweet sway of her ass in a pair of tight jeans, I didn't appreciate that she hadn't even acknowledged me. A hello would have been polite, at least.

"You know that girl?" Bax asked, his stare caught in Jamaica's wake.

"Yeah."

"You wanna introduce me?"

"Not even a little bit."

Bax shot me a wounded look. "What the fuck? I'm a nice enough guy."

"She's not your type." I glanced down at his T-shirt that read: "Boobs. Proof that men can concentrate on two things at once," then I stared hard into his eyes. "Trust me."

A knowing grin spread over his face. "You've got a thing for her." He waggled his brows. "Can't blame you, man. She is hot." His fanning-the-flames gesture lost some of its heat when done close to his chest in our current squished-together situation.

"Jamaica's a bitch," Tory said as though it were common knowledge.

"Takes one to know one," Axel said as he and the other two guys with him moved away from the disputed table. He shot me a "what the hell, dude?" shake of his head and headed in Jamaica's direction.

"Jamaica, huh?" Bax knocked his shoulder into mine. "Pretty name. How do you know her again?"

"Study partners." Finn smirked.

Tory's eyes shot daggers first at Axel's retreating back, then at Finn, then at me. "You can do so much better, Callahan. You know that, right?"

"I've had enough pizza." I glanced at my friends. "Anyone else up for relocating to the Slide?"

"The Slide? But they card." Tory's whine hit my next to last nerve.

Staring her straight in the eye, I said, "Guess that'll give us some elbow room to enjoy our beers then."

Chapter Six

Jamaica

"WHAT ARE YOUR plans for the weekend?" I'd asked Axel as I slid in beside him. For once, I'd managed to be first in line at the coffee hut in the Union, which meant I'd made it to class with time to spare.

My friend's surprised eyes spoke volumes about how unusual it was that I hadn't skidded in at the last possible second before our professor started his lecture. "Drake and I are probably going to hang out. Maybe catch the new John Krasinski thriller."

"I'm not on call this weekend for once. Maybe you won't mind a third wheel on your date? I'll buy the popcorn." I gave him my cutest puppy-dog eyes.

He shot me a look from beneath his brows. "Won't you have, like, six books to reread for classes?"

"It's come to my attention that perhaps I should try to read with more purpose the first time through— or, in the case of this class, the second or third time through since I read most of these classics in high school." Taking a sip of my coffee, I worked to keep from picturing Callahan's smirk when I'd stupidly commented on his photographic memory. The guy may be a jock, but he didn't fit the old "dumb jock" stereotype.

But when Axel, Drake, and I arrived at Stromboli's after the movie Saturday night, there sat Callahan with a bunch of other football players—and Tory Miller, staking her claim on him. I amended my earlier thought. He fit one jock stereotype: dating girls who clung to him purely because he played a popular sport.

Fine, maybe Tory wasn't staking a claim specifically on Callahan since she was as close to sitting in his friend's lap as possible in the confines of the booth. But the daggers she shot at me made it clear she didn't want my friends and me sitting so close to her posse and the football players they couldn't stay away from. From the looks of things, a party had started in that booth. One I didn't care to listen to.

Callahan's intense stare sealed it.

Fortunately, I noticed a table opening on the opposite side of the bar from the team and their groupies, which meant I didn't have to suggest we order takeout pizza and go back to Axel and Drake's apartment. Putting up with the inevitable teasing from my best friend wouldn't have been fun, but it would have been better than putting up with hearing those sorority girls fawning and simpering over the football team.

A dark expression marred Axel's good looks when he sat beside me.

"What?" I asked. "That one girl had already grabbed one of the chairs at that table. From the looks of things, they needed it."

"Not the problem," he said.

I lifted a brow.

"The girl Chessly had so much trouble with on her floor last year is a first class be-otch." His expression cleared as he clocked how close we were to the bar. "Good call with finding a different table." Raising his hand, he signaled a waiter rolling by us with a tray of empty mugs. "Can we get a pitcher of stout, please?"

Without slowing down, the guy nodded.

A few minutes later we were enjoying our beers and dissecting the finer points of the movie as we waited for our extra-large meat-lover's and jalapeno pizza to arrive. A shadow fell over me, and I didn't need to flick my eyes up to the mirror behind the bar to know who stood at my back. I shivered as his breath ghosted over my ear, and I wanted to kick myself. Instead, I remained rigid.

"I need the notes from yesterday's class. Can I get 'em from you tomorrow?"

Angling myself so I could pull away from the annoyingly enticing scent of clean skin and musky sandalwood, I shot him a side-eye. "We don't have a study session scheduled. You do football on the weekends, remember?"

"Come on, Jamaica. We have a quiz on Monday. I imagine something from Friday's class will be on it." With one hand on the back of my chair and the other on the table in front of me, he caged me in. "You don't want me to have more riding on our project than you have, do you?" A mischievous smirk tugged at the corner of his mouth, but the banked fires in his eyes sent a different message.

I huffed out a sigh. "Fine. I'll scan them into my laptop and send them to you." Careful not to touch him in my confined space, I tugged my phone from the back pocket of my jeans and pulled up my contacts. "What's your email?"

"That's the thing. I'm probably going to need you to walk me through them." He flicked a glance up at my friends whose eyes I could feel boring into me. "I get out of film at two. We could meet up then"—he dropped his voice a notch—"or over dinner if that works better for you."

Clenching my jaw, I held back what I truly wanted to say.

About then, the posse of giggling girls sidled up behind him. Something about the narrow-eyed glare Tory shot me made me change my mind. "I work at the sweet shop until three. I can meet in the Union after that."

"Thanks. I'll drop by and pick you up when you get off work." He ghosted his hand across my shoulders as he joined the other guys waiting for him near the door.

The gang of overly made-up freshmen all vying for his attention followed in his wake except for Tory who hustled ahead to link her arm through his. Whatever game he was playing, I had no intention of joining in. Yet my shoulders tingled with his touch long after the door to Stromboli's closed behind him.

Damn it.

Drake launched in first. "Oooh, you and Callahan O'Reilly, huh? You've been holding out on us, J." He nudged Axel with his shoulder and laughed. "Good thing for you the guy is straight."

"That's what Axel said about you after Dair saddled me with O'Reilly for our project." Lifting my beer to my lips, I took a deliberate sip, licked the foam from my upper lip, and sipped again.

Drake gifted Axel an affectionate grin. "I forgive you."

"Me too," Axel said and focused his attention on me. "Told you." He turned to his boyfriend, ran the tip of his nose along Drake's jaw, and gave him a little kiss.

I loved how my best friend since forever had found his person during orientation freshman year. They were so good for each other. Yet there were times, like right this minute, when I envied their relationship. Beneath the table, I kicked myself.

Drake eyed me over his glass. "Never took you for someone who went for football players."

Wrinkling my nose at him, I clarified, "I *don't* go for jocks. Football players especially."

His lifted brow said he didn't believe me. Now I wanted to kick someone else under the table.

"Have you ever known me to date a jock?" The tone of my voice dared him to contradict me.

"Nope." He leaned his arms on the table, a smirk on his lips. "But I saw how you reacted to that one." He waggled his brows. "There's a sizzle there, and it's not all one-sided." With a nod in Axel's direction, he added, "I'm not the only one who noticed, am I?"

Axel, the traitor, chuckled as he patted my hand in a patronizing way that made me want to smack him. Why had I begged to join them this weekend? I could be home rereading *Persuasion* and eating my own pizza right now instead of putting up with my friends' nonsense. I threw up my hands. "Men have stereotyped women as gossips, but you two prove that men are the real talkers."

Mercifully, our giant, delicious pie arrived in time to shut up the Callahan O'Reilly speculation. But I blame all the jalapenos stacked on it for the restless night I spent dreaming of Captain Wentworth, who for some weird reason, resembled a certain irritating football player.

When I stepped out of the sweet shop after work on Sunday afternoon, I almost ran over Callahan who was waiting with one shoulder leaning on the wall as he scrolled through his phone. The smile that broke over his face when he saw me stopped me dead in my tracks.

"Hello, Island Girl. How was work?"

I resumed walking, and he fell into step beside me as we headed down the hall. By a strange silent agreement, we walked in the direction of the study tables on the lower level outside the game room.

"Why do you call me that?"

"What? Island Girl?" He chuckled. "Come on, *Jamaica.*"

I could feel my face heating, and I quickened my pace.

He easily kept up. "It isn't any more obvious than why you call me Hotshot."

"Oh, really?" I drawled as I scanned the tables outside the game room for an open one. To my surprise, every table was occupied. Crap. We'd have to go upstairs to the more public ones.

Callahan trailed me up the stairs to the ground floor of the Union. "If you came to one of my games, you'd see how accurate your name for me is."

"Right." I stretched the word out like a rubber band and let it snap back on the T as I scanned the study tables for an open one.

"There's an open table at the back of the café," he said. With his superior height, he could see what I couldn't. From my vantage point, the Union was the campus hot spot on this gorgeous autumn afternoon.

Motioning me to follow, he led the way to an empty table by the windows. Anyone walking into the Union who happened to glance up would see him sitting like a display advertising sexy football players. With his ball cap spun around bill backward, a shock of dark blond hair poking out of the hole where he adjusted its size, he exuded an attractive boyishness a person would have to be blind to miss. He'd pushed up the sleeves on his gray hoodie, exposing muscular forearms that begged for a fingertip tour. His massive shoulders and back strained the fabric covering them, drawing attention to his size. His torso arrowed down to a pair of well-loved jeans that fit his ass to perfection while showing off his long legs. Axel, Drake, and Chessly were right: Callahan O'Reilly was easy to look at.

Snagging the leg of a chair with the toe of his sneaker, he tugged it away from the table and set his backpack on it, taking the seat beside it. I dropped my backpack in the other empty seat between us and pulled the chair closer so I could rummage around inside for the notebook I needed. By the time I'd gathered my materials, Callahan had his iPad booted up and was eyeing me expectantly.

"I still don't see why we had to meet. I could have scanned these and sent them to you during my break this morning. You would have had them when you finished practice." I puffed at a stray lock of my hair that had escaped my headband.

"Since this is the first time I've asked for your notes, I wanted to be sure I'd understand them. You need to walk me through them for that." Though his tone sounded sincere, when I flicked my gaze up from my notes, I caught the mischief dancing in his eyes.

"I don't believe you, but since we're here—" I turned my notebook so he could see the words right side up, sorta, with the thing resting mostly sideways between us. "I've highlighted the parts I have confidence Dair is going to ask about in green. The ideas I think he might ask about I've highlighted in orange. The rest that's plain is what he lectured on that's interesting to me that I want to remember. From experience in Dair's other classes, I'm pretty sure that info won't be on the quiz."

For a long minute, he stared down at my notes. "Do you always do this much work for class?"

"I have goals, Hotshot. Goals that require another two years beyond my undergrad at least. I'm going to need scholarships for law school, which means I need to make top grades while I'm here." With a shrug, I said, "Freshman year, I took a class on how to be a successful college student. One of the modules was notetaking and studying your notes. Rereading and highlighting class notes as soon after a lecture as possible was one of the strategies. So far, it's worked for me."

"Let me guess—you have a 4.0."

"Lucky you to be paired with me, huh?" I shot him a smug grin.

A naughty smile broke over his features, and I think his voice dropped an octave. "Oh yeah, but not for your GPA."

Beneath the table, I crossed one knee over the other and willed myself not to react to that voice. "Exactly what is that supposed to mean?"

He leaned forward on those delicious forearms. "It means I get to study with the hottest girl in class."

With a snort, I shook my head. "Save the flirting for your 'jersey chasers,' O'Reilly. I don't get involved with study partners, especially study partners who are also jocks."

What the hell? Callahan O'Reilly thinks I'm hot?

"I prefer 'football player.'" He winked. "And those were your rules before you met me."

"Cocky, much?" I intended it as an insult, but my mouth wouldn't cooperate and smiled at him instead.

For a long moment, we stared into each other's eyes.

"It's not cocky when I can back it up."

"Riiight," I drawled. But the intensity of those mesmerizing sea-blue eyes had me dropping my gaze to the pages in front of me. "What Dair was on about on Friday was the sociopolitical aspects of readers' growing access to fiction during the Regency."

"Uh-huh." Callahan leaned over the table to see where I pointed on my notes. "This will be a whole lot easier if we rearrange a few things."

Before I could ask, he stood and moved my backpack into his vacated seat, pulled the empty one around beside me, and sat close enough that I could smell the musky, rain-shower-infused scent of whatever soap he used. He set up the keyboard on his iPad and started typing in notes as if sitting together this way was an everyday occurrence. The four-top was a standard card table size, so if I tried to put some space between us, I'd have to scoot around the side, and we'd be back to square one.

I had to wonder if the guy played chess.

The side of me closest to him heated from my shoulder to my knee, and I struggled to concentrate on explaining the notes to him. Nodding and adding info to the open screen on his machine, he seemed completely oblivious to my distress. When he pointed to a line on my page that I'd marked in orange and I leaned forward to see it better, he shifted in his chair. The shift, of course, caused him to slide even closer to me. It meant I couldn't point out anything on my notes without brushing lightly along his arm. If I uncrossed my legs, my thigh would touch his from hip to knee.

Yet if I said anything about his subtle come-on, I'd play right into his game. *Damn it.* I did not want to be attracted to him. Such a dumbass move had heartbreak written all over it—highlighted in green, no less. If only he'd stop with the smart questions and insightful comments, ideas I had no choice but to write in the margins of my notes because I hadn't thought of them, and they were brilliant. Why couldn't he fit the "dumb jock" stereotype? I could ignore his sexy good looks easily then. But paired with those eyes that seemed to see inside me and that brain that could keep up with mine? Callahan O'Reilly was the whole incredible package.

Tittering giggles alerted us to the interruption seconds before it arrived.

"Hi, Callahan. We saw you in the window."

"It's Sunday, Callahan. Want to go out and play?"

"Hey, Callahan. Whatcha doing?"

The girls' singsong delivery grated on my ears worse than twigs scratching at a window pane. There it was. The one thing reminding me that football wasn't the only thing Hotshot played. The jersey chasers couldn't have timed their appearance better.

"Those are pretty much all of Friday's notes." When I uncrossed my legs to scoot my chair away from him, my thigh brushed his, and a lick of fire singed the skin beneath my jeans. At the contact I might have sucked in a tiny gasp of air. Fortunately, Callahan couldn't hear it over the cacophony of freshman fangirl noise surrounding us.

"Jamaica—"

I couldn't decipher his tone. A warning? Distress? Didn't matter. It was time for me to take advantage of the exit opportunity his fan club's timely arrival offered. Accidentally bumping one of the girls who stood directly behind me, I said, "Excuse me. I was just leaving."

She took the hint, and I stood and walked around the table to the chair where Callahan had deposited my pack. I slid my notebooks inside, shoved my pen behind my ear, and hiked the strap of my pack over my shoulder. "See you in class, Hotshot." I glanced around at the group of girls whose eyes never strayed from him.

His chair screeched against the linoleum floor as he hastily stood up from it. "Wait up, and I'll walk you to your dorm."

"You know you'd rather spend the rest of your afternoon with people who know how to have fun, right, Callahan?"

Somehow I'd missed Tory Miller in the midst of the posse. What I didn't miss was the dark expression that marred Hotshot's face when she made herself known.

"Hey, Tory." At last he gave the girls his attention. "Ladies."

"Enjoy the rest of your afternoon," I directed at Callahan. Then because I couldn't help myself, I gave a little rolling four-fingered wave to his fan club. "Toodles," I said to them and took off before any of them, especially Tory, could respond.

CHAPTER SEVEN

Callahan

"HOW WAS YOUR 'study session,' Slick?" Finn asked with air quotes when I walked through our living room on my way to the kitchen.

"I got the notes." Something of my bad mood must have come through in my tone.

"Ouch!" Finn set his game controller beside him on the couch. "She shot you down hard, huh?" He stood and followed me.

I tossed my backpack on the table on my way to the fridge, pulled out a beer, and downed half of it in one swig. Wiping the back of my hand across my mouth, I let a belch go and didn't feel even slightly better.

"Whoa! She *really* shot you down." A smirk crossed his face as he pulled two beers from the fridge. He cracked one open and set the other on the table beside me.

Narrowing my eyes over the rim of my beer can, I glared at him as I finished it, smashed it between my palms, and tossed the empty in the recycle box by the back door. I opened the second one and took a long pull. "In the few times we've studied together, I've figured out I need to be patient with Jamaica. Things were moving along fine, then your fan club showed up—again. It's like they have trackers on us or something. She took one look at that bunch of jersey chasers, shoved her shit in her bag, and blew out of the Union like her ass was on fire."

"Damn." He took a thoughtful sip of his beer. "At least you had a consolation prize."

My eyes might have bugged out of my head. "What?"

"You had a pack of adoring female admirers to hang out with, yeah?"

Cuffing him on the back of the head, I said, "Dumbass. Where in any of what I just said did you hear I wanted to spend time with jailbait instead of with a smart, hot woman?"

The back of his neck took on a shade of red I'd seen on more than one occasion when Finn fucked up. "Did you sic those Delta Chis on me?"

"Look, Coach Ainsworth wanted to show me where I'd missed a golden opportunity to rush Prescott in the first quarter, so I left film a bit after the rest of you guys. I ran into the girls outside the gym—"

"Pure coincidence, I'm sure," I mumbled.

"Tory was asking about you. I might have mentioned you were studying in the Union this afternoon." He swigged some beer and shrugged his shoulders. "The way the two of you act, I thought you had something going with her."

Shaking my head at my friend, I corrected him. "You mean the way *she* acts. Dude, that girl is nothing but bad news. I avoid the shit out of her and never give her a straight answer when she asks what I'm doing or hints at doing something with me."

Confusion furrowed his brow. "Didn't you hook up with her last year?"

I ran a hand down my face. "I might have had a few too many of these." I held up my beer. "So when she came onto me in the hallway during a rager at the Delta Nu house, I kissed her. But even in my drunken state, I sensed something about her was off." I shuddered. "Then Hyde or someone yelled for me, which made it easy to escape her. Only later did I find out she was a freshman—and the daughter of some big donor to the school." I finished my second beer, crushed the can, and sent it to join the other one I'd tossed in the recycle box. "She's entitled, related to the girl who damaged Freeman's career, and out to bag a football player. Bad news with a capital B. I don't want a damn thing to do with her." Picking up my pack and heading out to my room, I called over my shoulder, "You should keep your distance too."

After tossing my backpack onto the floor beside my desk, I shucked off my hoodie, kicked off my tennis shoes, and threw myself on my bed. Resting my head on my hands, I glared at the ceiling. Things with Jamaica had been progressing well during our study session. Her mouth said she didn't date football players, but her body said she might make an exception for me.

The cute way she'd lost her place when I inched my chair closer to hers had made me lose my place too. The blink in the side-eye she'd sent me when her arm had touched mine as she reached for a second notebook said she'd noticed as the hairs on my arm stood at attention. The way she'd sucked in air when her thigh grazed mine as she stood up told me she sensed the heat between us every bit as much as I did. Whether she was ready to admit it or not, Jamaica Winslow was interested in me. If Finn hadn't sicced that obnoxious bunch of jersey chasers on me, I might have had a chance to talk her into something more than a study session.

But the game was only in the first quarter. My mouth turned up in a grin. I had plenty of time on the clock to run a new play.

"Good morning, Island Girl," I said when I sat next to Jamaica in Dair's class on Monday. Nodding in his direction, I added, "Axel," as I unzipped my pack and pulled out my iPad.

Dr. Dair's standard "Settle down, you pretenses of scholarship" preempted the flare-up boiling behind Jamaica's glare at my audacity to sit next to her in class, and I chuckled.

"This seat is never taken," I whispered.

"My backpack sits there," she hissed back.

I gave her my best scored-a-touchdown grin. "Not anymore."

I think she might have growled, and I loved it. If I didn't get to her, she wouldn't react. Then her scent, spring flowers and musk, wafted over me, and I shifted in my seat to catch another whiff of my new favorite smell. She squirmed as she tried not to brush my arm when she raised the desktop on her chair so she could take notes in her notebook. From the corner of my eye, I caught her frown before she magicked a pen from somewhere in her curls and wrote something across the top of an empty page.

Leaning down a touch, I took a peek at her notes. She'd written the day, date, and class number across the top. When Dair launched into his lecture on Hardy's commentary on the exploitation of the working class, she added a title.

Shooting me the stink-eye, she whispered out the side of her mouth, "Take your own notes, Hotshot."

Lightly bumping her shoulder, I whispered, "We can compare after class."

The professor aimed a censorious glance in our direction over the rim of his glasses, and Jamaica sat taller in her seat. As I watched the interplay between our prof and her, I had to wonder if she acted the same way in all her classes or only in Dr. Dair's.

Curiously, Jamaica didn't ask her usual barrage of questions, instead, keeping her inquiries to two—both of them excellent since I wanted the answers too. When she asked about Hardy's reception among the working class who could read at the time, one of the other study pairs in class asked if Dair could hold off as the answer was part of their project. The interplay between students delighted the prof to no end judging by the half-smile he gifted both Jamaica and the premed student and his partner who sat together in the front row.

She blinked and turned to Axel whose I-don't-have-a-clue expression coupled with a shoulder shrug said the teacher's response was new territory. Jamaica hastily scribbled something in the margin of her notebook and highlighted it with a blue marker that materialized from the apparently endless store of writing implements hidden in her curls.

A snort escaped me. Jamaica swiveled her head in my direction so fast I feared she might have sprained her neck. "What's so funny, Hotshot?" she hissed.

With a nod toward the front of the auditorium, I lowered my voice. "I'll tell you after class."

Dair was staring over the rim of his glasses again, and we both looked down at our notes. From the corner of my eye, I caught Axel showing Jamaica something he'd written on a separate page in his notebook. What was up with these two handwriting notes anyway? She emitted a tiny growl while she furiously wrote something back. I heard his chuckle while she studiously ignored both of us, lasering her focus on the droning man behind the lectern.

When the chimes signaled the end of class, both of us simultaneously reached for our bags at our feet. Our biceps and shoulders touched, wafting a fresh round of her floral scent over me. I wanted to savor that smell almost as much as I wanted to bask in the sharp intake of her breath at our unexpected contact.

Yep, I got to Jamaica Winslow.

Good to know since she never strayed far from my thoughts either.

Taking my time, I stood and stretched, knowing full well I was holding her up when she wanted to escape.

"Do you mind, Hotshot? Some of us have another class in a few minutes."

I think she was going for snarky, but with her eyes on my abs when my hoodie and T-shirt rode up as I lifted my arms over my head, her words come out on a soft breath. Uh-huh. She was thinking of her silly rule about not dating athletes, especially football players. Grinning, I slung one strap of my backpack over my shoulder and made my way down the row.

"Where's your next class?" I asked as she and Axel joined me in the aisle and I walked them out of the building.

"In Huffine, which means I don't have time to stand around and chat."

I zeroed my focus on her. Oh yeah, that rosy tinge on her cheeks gave her away.

"Cool. That's on the way to the gym. I'll walk with you."

"Axel—"

"I'm meeting Drake at the Union. See you two later." Before Axel sauntered off, he slipped me a discreet thumbs-up, and I winked.

Seconds ticked by as Jamaica watched her friend leave her to the big, bad wolf, a panicked expression marring her gorgeous features. Then she pulled in a breath, squared her shoulders, and started walking. Fast.

"You were kinda quiet in class today. Only two questions for the man. What gives?" I asked as I fell into step beside her.

"I was distracted." She clamped her hand over her mouth, but I heard her say, "Fuck," behind her palm.

Yeah, that was valuable info I wasn't letting go of. "Distracted, huh?"

When she slid me a side-eye, I gave her my best smile. Her eyes saucered, and she tripped over a crack in the sidewalk. Being chivalrous, of course, I caught her elbow with one hand while I slid my other arm around her waist. "Careful there, Island Girl."

We walked another step or two with my hands on her before she deliberately slipped out of my grasp—and I let her. My nerves crackled and sparked everywhere my skin had come into contact with hers, sensations zinging straight to my cock. The hoodie I'd chosen to wear today wasn't long enough to cover a semi, not to mention it was damned uncomfortable walking with one. Now *I* needed a distraction.

"What class do you have in Huffine?"

She kept her eyes on the sidewalk. "The Historic Rise of Social Media."

"Yeah? Couldn't you take that one over Instagram?" I laughed at my joke.

"Ha, ha," she deadpanned. "Since I couldn't afford a phone until I was seventeen, I wasn't on any of the socials. Joining late meant I missed a crap ton of unnecessary drama—which I'm quite happy about—but I also didn't fit in with people who used TikTok slang and sent funny memes on IG or shared their latest party fail on Snapchat."

She glanced up at me, but I kept my expression neutral. If this girl was going to let me in, even a tiny bit, I didn't want to give her any reason to clam up.

"Anyway, the class is pretty interesting. What class do you have?"

"Film."

"In the gym?" Her wrinkled-nose expression was too cute.

"We're playing the Hornets this weekend. We need to know their schemes so we can counter them." A group of students stood in the middle of the sidewalk chatting, and we split to walk around them. "I told you I spend lunch watching film, remember?"

"How many hours a day do you do football, again?"

"Eight, most days."

"And go to class and study and keep your grades up?" Her voice went up with each part of the question.

"What?" I shrugged. "It's no different from you being an RA and holding down a part-time job and going to class and studying and keeping your grades up." I winked at her narrowed eyes. "We both work full-time and go to school. Our jobs are different is all." Playfully, I bumped her shoulder. "Mine's just more fun."

She shook her head, sending her glorious curls bouncing. "Bashing other men around in the grass sounds like a blast… not."

"Have you ever been to a game?"

"No." She drew the word out to about three syllables long.

"Maybe you should come watch me play before you pass judgment."

"Saturdays are for picking up extra hours at the sweet shop and studying."

"No, Island Girl. Saturdays are for the boys." I shot her a hot grin and reveled in the way her nostrils flared and her pupils dilated. "Since we're partners now, it's incumbent upon you to attend a game and watch me play."

"Incumbent? Really?" She couldn't seem to stop herself from snorting a laugh.

"Hey, I go to college." I tapped the side of my ball cap. "I know things."

This time she smiled, and the sun on this glorious autumn afternoon shined a whole bunch brighter. We stood outside the building where she had her next class grinning at each other like a pair of loons, and I swear my heart grew a size in my chest. I'd latched onto one of her curls with an intention I wasn't entirely sure of when the strident tones of my name called by someone I never enjoyed seeing split the air.

The smile dropped right off her face. "Sounds like your fan club has arrived. Did you give them your schedule or something?"

"For reasons beyond human understanding, the team posts our schedules on the website. Something about proving we're student-athletes, emphasis on the first part." I rubbed my hand over the back of my neck. "It's a fucking invasion of privacy. Are we on for tomorrow night?"

"I have to cover for one of the other girls at the shop. I won't be done before ten. Sorry."

"Then I'll see you in class, yeah?"

With a nod and a glance past my shoulder, she spun on her heel and walked away right as Tory Miller sidled up beside me and sank her claws into my bicep.

CHAPTER EIGHT

Jamaica

AS USUAL, I ended up at least seventh in line for coffee at the Union on my way to Dr. Dair's class on Wednesday. That meant I flew into Creston Hall and down the aisle with about thirty seconds to spare before my nemesis instructor glanced up from his notes to start class. I'd barely set my cup in the cupholder on my seat and said hello to Axel when a now familiar clean, masculine scent wafted over me. I squeezed my eyes closed then opened one to have Axel confirm with a smile and a nod what my nose had already told me.

Callahan O'Reilly was sitting next to me in class—again.

"Is this going to be a thing with you?" I hissed as I pulled my notebook from my backpack, pulled the side table up, and clamped it in place on my seat.

"Good morning to you too, Island Girl." He leaned forward to address Axel sotto voce, "Guess her coffee hasn't kicked in yet, huh?"

Axel, the traitor, grinned back at him. "Nah, she's always like this."

Giving my best friend a tooth-rotting saccharine grin, I said, "Would you like to trade seats?"

He leaned in close and whispered, "He's not into me."

Gritting my teeth against acknowledging his implication, I directed my attention to the professor. For once Dair was engaged in a conversation with the premed student and his partner in the front row rather than directing his displeasure at the three of us for not giving him our undivided attention.

Beside me, Callahan "casually" crossed his left ankle over his right knee so his thigh rested along mine. The contact sent waves of heat rolling over my skin even through the two layers of clothing separating us. From the corner of my eye, I watched a grin ghost over his features, and I wanted to smack him. The only way to put some space between us would be for me to lower my writing table back into its resting spot, but previous experience had already taught me how uncomfortable taking notes on my knee would be. With his sexy long legs, Callahan was apparently more comfortable without the desk, judging by the relaxed way he sat.

When I squirmed in my seat to put some air between us, he settled down further in his chair. Now not only were our thighs touching, but also our shoulders and upper arms. Subtly, I pushed against him, hinting he should stay in his seat without overflowing onto mine. Instead of taking the hint, he whispered, "Island Girl, I'm sitting as close as I can with all this hardware on our seats."

"You. Are. Incorrigible," I said through gritted teeth.

Dr. Dair launched into the day's lecture, and I did my absolute best to pay attention. But the side of Callahan's body pressed along mine took my thoughts to places they had no business going. Heat flashed over me as I pictured our naked skin pressed together side by side in my narrow dorm bed, and I had to cross my legs. The move brought marginal relief from where our thighs touched—except Hotshot noticed and angled his head so I could see his arched brow.

I shook my head and attempted to redirect my attention to our professor. The problem was, crossing my legs drew my mind to my suddenly needy clit and the damp state of my panties, and oh boy, was I ever in trouble. Why in the ever-lovin' hell was I responding to Callahan *Football Player* O'Reilly in this way?

My eyes strayed to his hands where he took notes on his iPad. His hands were works of art with their wide palms and long, tapered fingers. Hands that could wrap themselves completely over my hips and hold me close. I'd always been a sucker for beautifully proportioned hands, and now I was wondering what Callahan's would feel like on my body. I glanced back to my notebook where I was not taking notes and hissed in a disgusted breath. *Get a grip, Jamaica. He's not even your type.*

Axel lightly bumped my other shoulder, drawing my attention to his notes. Hastily, I copied his scribbles. He met my smile of gratitude with a wicked gleam in his eyes, and now I wanted to smack both of the men flanking me. But at least my friend's interruption dragged my mind back to class, and for the most part, I managed to take adequate notes for the rest of the hour. It was only at the end when Dr. Dair shot me a quizzical look that I realized I hadn't asked a single question.

On the sidewalk outside Creston, the knowing smile on Axel's face told me we'd be having quite the discussion when we met later in the afternoon for our standing coffee date. For now, he leaned in, kissed my cheek, and whispered, "Good job." At my silent, narrow-eyed question, he nodded in Hotshot's direction, and I gifted him with the mother of all eye rolls. Laughing, he said, "See ya later." With a wave, he added, "Bye, Callahan," and left me there alone with the wolf.

Without my permission, Callahan fell into step with me as I hurried off for my next class. "We're on for a planning session tomorrow night, right, Island Girl?" he asked. With his long-legged stride, he had no trouble keeping up as I attempted to speed-walk away from him. When I didn't answer, he said, "Library or Union?"

"Yes, I can meet you at the library tomorrow night. Usual time." I needed space from his too-sexy-for-my-own-good person. Couldn't the guy take a hint?

"That was an interesting class today, yeah? I had no idea how big a role Romanticism played in the Industrial Revolution." He shoved his hands in his pockets, showing off how relaxed he was in keeping up with my pace that was now almost a jog, his long legs eating up the sidewalk beside me as though he were out for a leisurely stroll.

Giving in, I slowed down. "Why have you decided to sit by me in class?"

He shrugged. "Seems like a good idea, what with us being project partners and all."

I glared at him. "Axel doesn't sit with his partner."

"The premed guy sits with his." He smirked.

"You are a giant pain in the ass, you know that?"

Bumping playfully into me, he smiled. "You like me anyway though."

It wasn't enough that he was gorgeous, athletic, and smart. Oh no. He also had a smile that melted my insides like chocolate. Damn it.

Our arrival outside the lecture hall for my next class pre-empted me having to respond to his question. "This is my stop."

The twinkle in his arresting blue eyes said he knew he was right about me liking him.

Gah!

Like clockwork the fangirls arrived, inadvertently saving me from more awkwardness or worse: having to admit he was right.

"Hi, Callahan!"

"Callahan, hi!"

So original. The poor freshmen needed a lesson in flirting. Even I could do it better than they did.

"You don't have to go straight to film, do you?" This came from Tory Miller as she sidled up beside Hotshot and tried to link her arm with his. He chose that moment to reach up and readjust his ball cap.

"See you tomorrow, Jamaica." Something resigned in his tone stopped my snarky observation about his entourage.

With a nod, I turned and walked toward my building. I didn't intend to look back, but when I did, I saw him shrug out of Tory's hold as he said something with a half-smile to the two freshmen, then he jogged off in the direction of the gym.

Maybe I was wrong about him encouraging the girls who couldn't seem to leave him alone….

As I left the sweet shop for my study session with Callahan, my phone chimed in a text.

> Hotshot: I reserved us a study room on the third floor.
>
> Me: Why?
>
> Hotshot: My roommates are studying at the library tonight.
>
> Me: So?
>
> Hotshot: We want to make progress on this project, yeah?
>
> Me: We don't need a private room for that.
>
> Hotshot: Two words: jersey chasers.

I huffed out a laugh. Then a picture of Tory Miller hanging all over Callahan invaded my thoughts, and something like jealousy clenched my middle. *WTF?* She could have him. He was a *player*, not a person I had any interest in. Another picture interrupted—a picture of Hotshot's thigh pressed to mine and the sensations that had coursed through my body for an entire hour of class.

Fine. He had my attention too. But I was above all that ridiculousness.

Even after my dad disappeared from our lives for good about five years ago, my mom still pined for him. I didn't need to do a Google search on one John Blackwood to know his stories that had kept my mom hanging on for over twenty years were pure bullshit. The fact that he missed more birthdays than made them, never spent a single holiday with us, and promised to help me with college then ghosted us a year before I graduated high school told me everything I needed to know about him. Players could play a sport or drive an over-the-road truck, but either way, trusting a man with your heart meant trusting him with your future. If Mom's experience had taught me anything, it was to stay clear of players.

Loud whispering and giggles snagged my attention as I made my way to the stairs leading to the third floor. Sure enough, there sat several members of the Wildcats football team with their dedicated fans. The big guy, Finn, shot Tory a teasing smile, and she batted her lashes in way that made me think she'd practiced in front of a mirror. Gag.

Guess Hotshot was right. If we wanted to make progress on our project, we had to meet somewhere the fan club couldn't just happen by.

Keeping my head down so as not to draw attention that might lead them to catch onto another football player lurking somewhere else in the library, I made my way to the third floor. The door to the room Callahan had reserved stood open, and I stepped inside to find him already hard at work. He was marking something on his iPad and adding to a list on a notebook beside it. The smile on his face when he glanced up flashed fire through me—a heat so intense I'm sure my skin flushed from the roots of my hair to the soles of my feet.

"Hey, Island Girl." He sniffed at the air. "Mmm, you smell like chocolate and strawberries. Were you making candy tonight? Did you bring any with you?" The hopefulness in his tone gave me a guilt complex.

By the time I finished a shift, I was sick of candy and sweet things. It never occurred to me to bring a treat for him.

Clearing my throat, I set my pack down and took the chair across the table from him. "Sorry. I didn't think athletes indulged in sweets."

He stood and walked over to close the door. "You'd be surprised." The naughtiness in his voice reminded me of my earlier personal pep talk to keep my guard up where a certain football player was concerned.

"Why did you close the door?" I asked when he sat back down.

The intimacy of being alone with the hottest man I'd ever met, especially with my new resolve not to respond to him, left me nervous about being in a closed room with him.

"Kinda defeats the point of avoiding the jersey chasers if they take a tour of the library and discover us here."

I shrugged. "I guess." Pulling my notebooks from my backpack, I said, "Do you honestly believe they'd go on a tour of the library looking for you?"

"Depends on if Tory gets Finn to slip." At my raised brow, he clarified. "My roommates and I rode over from our apartment together. If she finds out I'm in the library, she and her buddies will come looking for me." The sigh that escaped him explained more than his words could about what he thought of the prospect, and I relaxed.

Within a few minutes, he brought me up to speed on the list

he'd been composing when I walked in. Every time I wanted to write him off as a jock or a player or someone I could blow off, he surprised me with his insightfulness and intelligence. As we worked together, it dawned on me I might be the true beneficiary of our pairing and not the other way around. I peeked at him through my lashes as he bent his head over his iPad, his brow furrowed in thought.

It seemed we'd barely started working when I pulled out my laptop to look up some info on nineteenth-century manners and saw that an hour had passed. We bounced ideas off each other, laughed at antiquated notions of proper behavior we discovered, and made as much progress in this one session than we had in the past two combined. Guess working without distractions—like giggly freshmen girls—helped.

"Fannie Price's observations in the parlor when she first arrives at Mansfield Park kinda remind me of the way Dair responds to you in class," Callahan said as he pointed out a passage in the text.

"You've already finished *Mansfield Park*?"

"Long bus rides, remember." His brow drifted up. "What's the deal with you and Dair anyway?"

I shrugged. "I ask too many questions. It irritates him." Dropping my eyes to my notes, I added, "It irritates some of my other professors too, but they aren't as obvious about it. Probably because I've only taken one class from them." I hazarded a glance at him. "This is my third class with Dr. Dair."

"You ask smart questions. They help everyone." A sly grin crossed his features. "Except you didn't ask any questions yesterday in class. Weird."

Heat flared along my thigh like a phantom touch of his body against mine, and I shifted in my chair, crossing my legs like I'd done in class.

"He was more explanatory than usual, so I didn't have questions."

"That's what you're going with, huh?" Mischief sparkled in his eyes.

I readjusted in my chair and tried to ignore how hot it had become beneath my hoodie.

"We can make a point about his rudeness that will grab his attention without making an obvious slam if we discuss Sir Thomas Bertram's treatment of Fanny versus her constant decency." He slid his chair around the table to sit right beside me. "We can use these passages here." He pointed out a couple I'd marked with sticky notes in my paperback. "What do you think?"

That was the trouble. When he sat this close to me, I couldn't think.

He slid his chair closer. "You smell so good. You always smell good, like spring flowers and something musky."

The barely-there brush of his nose along my neck sent shivers through me, and I waited, paralyzed, for what he'd do next.

Without touching me, he caged me in, one arm resting along the back of my chair and the other on the table in front of me.

"What—?" I swallowed and tried again. "What are you doing?" It came out as a croak.

"Mmm." His lips hovered a mere breath over mine. "I think I'm going to kiss you."

But he didn't. He was waiting for something.

"Now?" I wasn't sure he heard the breath of sound I made.

"Yes."

Soft lips brushed over mine with the lightness of fairy wings. When he pulled back, ending the contact, I couldn't help myself. I chased him, pressing my lips to his. After a beat, his fingers plunged into my hair as he added delicious pressure to the kiss. He licked along the seam of my lips, daring me to open for him. When I gave him what he asked for, electric heat exploded through my veins, short-circuiting all my thoughts except for the one that screamed, *Closer. You need to be closer.*

The next thing I knew, I was in his lap—or rather, I was straddling it. My fingers plowed through his hair, knocking his ball cap to the floor. I held his head as we vied to see who could plunder whose mouth more thoroughly.

His hands had found their way to my ass where he smoothed and squeezed my flesh over my jeans, encouraging my center closer to his. To my shock, the moans and whimpers that broke through the sounds of my heartbeat thundering in my ears were coming from my throat as I explored the entirety of Callahan's tongue with my own.

Lined up as we were, I couldn't stay still. The friction of his hard-on pressed to my center was a siren call I couldn't resist as I rubbed up and down over him. In the back of my mind, I had a fear of setting our jeans on fire with my movements, but his mouth tasted delicious, like caramel coffee and something dark and male. All I wanted to do was melt all over his hard body.

A jiggling of the doorknob and a loud, insistent pounding on the door jerked me out of Callahan O'Reilly-induced lust.

"Hey! You were supposed to be out of this room ten minutes ago," an annoyed male voice shouted through the door.

"Sorry, dude. We'll be done in a minute." Callahan's voice was surprisingly calm considering the wild desire blazing in his gorgeous sea-blue eyes and the pronounced bulge in his jeans wedged against my crotch.

In a blink I scrambled off his lap. Standing beside the table on decidedly unsteady legs, I started shoving books, pens, and notebooks into my backpack.

"Um, that—" I gulped in a breath. "That never, uh, that shouldn't have happened," I stammered. What was wrong with me? Words were my world. I never stumbled over them.

"Correction, Island Girl. That was always going to happen." He didn't even bother to hide it as he adjusted himself behind the fly of his jeans. The wolfish grin on his face as he deliberately repacked his books and iPad into his backpack did nothing for my peace of mind.

Touching my hair, I discovered he'd dislodged my messy bun. Scanning the floor around the table, I located my scrunchie behind my chair and hastily set my hair back into some semblance of order.

Letting out a low chuckle, he said, "Sorry, sweetheart, but no matter what you do, you can't hide what we've been doing." He ran the pad of his thumb over my lower lip, setting off a new throbbing in my core. "These plump, rosy lips give us away."

I batted his hand away. "Would you stop, please? This is mortifying enough."

Hoisting my heavy backpack by the strap, I shrugged it over my shoulders as I stepped over to the door. An expectant glance over my shoulder revealed a wholly unrepentant Callahan O'Reilly on my heels. I sucked in a breath, let it out, and turned the handle on the door he must have locked when he'd closed it earlier.

Across the hallway, a tall, lanky guy leaned against the wall, his shoulders and the sole of his left foot resting flush against it, the picture of nonchalance as he scrolled through his phone. When the door opened, he flicked his eyes up from his screen, and a smirk tipped up one corner of his mouth.

"Well, fuck, O'Reilly. It doesn't take a genius to know what you were 'studying' in there. Do I need disinfectant when I go in?"

Indignation warred with embarrassment, but right as I opened my mouth to set the guy straight, Callahan reached out to shake his hand in some kind of secret bro code—palms, thumbs, one-armed-hug, fist-bump—thing. "Nah, Enriquè. You're safe." He laughed. "How's the team looking?"

"Good as yours." A grin split the guy's—Enriquè's—face. "Maybe we'll celebrate two conference championships this year." His striking green eyes danced in his dark brown face.

"That would be sweet." Callahan fist-bumped him again. "Come over to the house after the game on Saturday. No doubt we'll be celebrating."

Casually, he threw his arm over my shoulder and led me down the hallway toward the stairs. I shrugged from beneath his arm and stomped ahead of him.

"That was rude. You didn't even introduce us," I tossed over my shoulder as I trotted down the stairs.

"I'll introduce you on Saturday at the party—if Enriquè has a date. If he comes stag, I'm locking you away from him."

I stopped dead still on the second-floor landing, and he bumped into me. Without turning around, I gritted out, "You aren't the boss of who I date. Also, I don't do frat parties, Hotshot," before I jogged the rest of the way down to the ground floor.

When he fell into step beside me on my way out of the library, I shot him a warning side-eye. I crossed the street in front of the building on my way back to the dorms, and he remained beside me, his ambling steps keeping up with my speed-walking in the most infuriating way. As I traversed the campus, at last I asked, "What are you doing?"

"Walking you home." There was a "duh" in there somewhere, I was certain, but when I glanced at him, a grin turned up the side of his mouth.

"You don't need to do that."

"Yeah, I do." Though the half-grin remained on his face, there was steel in his voice.

"You expect to get your way." It wasn't a question.

"Pretty much."

A growl escaped me, and he chuckled. The sound of his mirth left an odd sensation in my chest, and for a minute the autumn air didn't feel quite so crisp.

"Are you going to the game on Saturday, see what I do besides be an awesome class partner?"

"You only read the assigned book once. How is that awesome?" It was a stupid argument, having more to do with my study methods than his contributions to our project. Grudgingly, I admitted to myself he had some pretty great ideas and insights—especially after basically skimming the material.

"Island Girl, you need to learn to work smarter, not longer. Give yourself more time for fun." He bumped my shoulder with his. "Like going to the game on Saturday."

"Hate to burst your bubble, Hotshot, but I can't imagine a more unproductive way of spending a Saturday afternoon than watching big men in helmets bash into each other."

He slammed his hand over his chest and pretended to stagger. "Damn, that's harsh, woman. You've wounded me, slashed my chest wide open with a dull knife." He staggered ahead of me and walked backward, his eyes dancing even as he faked dying.

His antics twitched half a smile out of me.

Damn it.

Chapter Nine

Jamaica

"HAVE YOU EVER watched a football game, like at your high school or on TV?" Callahan asked, his expression relaying he couldn't believe he even needed to ask the question.

"No. But I've seen commercials for games." I defended myself.

"Oh, darlin', you and your big brain are missing out." Falling into step beside me as we continued walking toward my dorm, he said, "Football is a massive game of chess. You do know chess, right?" He smirked at my exaggerated eye roll and continued. "The coaches from one team draw up offensive and defensive strategies to outplay the other team. The plays they call on both sides of the ball are their chess moves. When one team has the ball, the coaches are calling plays to advance it, while the coaches on the other team are calling plays to stop that advance."

We crunched through some early downed leaves on the sidewalk as we passed through a small stand of trees a block from my dorm.

"The one variable in this chess match is the players."

I frowned in confusion, and he went on.

"At any time during the play—the chess move, if you will—a player might see something on the other side of the line that causes him to improvise. In this live chess match, the chessmen can make changes during a play."

His explanation pulled me in, and to my surprise, being a chess nerd and all, I wanted to know more. "You make it sound like something out of *Harry Potter*."

He chuckled, and I asked the obvious question. "But why all the violent bashing into each other?"

The tone of his laughter said he knew he had me, but I was intrigued enough not to care. We stopped beneath a street light on the corner outside my building. He picked up a stick and squatted down to draw in the dirt of a fallow flower bed. Drawing two lines of X's and O's, he said, "These are linemen. Think of them as pawns." Behind the line of O's, he drew more. "This is the running back." He pointed to an O. "Think of him as the knight. These are receivers." He pointed to a couple more O's. "Think of them as bishops. This is the quarterback." He pointed a lone O in the center of the area behind the line. "Think of him as the queen. The ball is the king. In this chess match, though, once you ring the bell—or in this case, the center snaps the ball back to the quarterback—all the pieces move at once."

He glanced up to see if I was following him. When I circled my hand in the universal gesture for "go on," he continued. "The defensive players are doing two things simultaneously: trying to reach the quarterback to take the ball from him and covering the running back and receivers so he can't give the ball to them to advance it toward the goal. When the defense"——he pointed to the X's he'd drawn— "is successful, they stop the advance of the offense. When the offense is successful, they score a goal and move ahead in the game."

A lock of hair escaped his backward ball cap to fall over

his forehead as he bounced back up to stand in front of me. His enthusiasm and that wayward curl gave him a boyishness I couldn't help but smile at. Mischief narrowed his eyes.

"Admit it, Jamaica. You want to watch a game."

Tilting my head to one side, I crossed my arms over my chest. "Which piece are you in this game?"

"Tight end."

"Of course you are." The words slipped out before I could clamp a hand over my mouth.

A laugh barked out of him. "I'm that versatile piece that can be played as a pawn, a rook, or a bishop depending on the play the coach calls. I can line up here"—squatting beside his drawings, he pointed to the line of O's with his stick—"or here or here." He marked additional spots in the dirt. "Depending on where I line up, I can block for the running back or receive a pass. Either way, I'm helping to advance the ball."

In spite of myself, his description of the game grabbed my attention. Stepping a bit closer, I studied his scratchings under the light.

"When we advance the ball—a.k.a. the king—over the goal line, we score six points. Checkmate. Then the other team has their try."

The flaw was obvious. "What you're saying is basically whoever has the ball last wins."

His eyes glittered. "Nope. Whoever scores the most points wins."

"But if each team has a turn back and forth, then the team who has the ball last wins. And you still haven't explained all the bashing." Honestly, the guy played a silly game.

As if he knew my thoughts, he said, "Let's say we score." His tone was all kinds of patient. "We kick off and they field the ball to begin their drive to advance down the field. One of our defenders, say a pawn or probably a rook or a bishop—we call them linebackers since they back up the defensive line." At my raised brow, he clarified. "The line of X's in front."

I nodded.

"Let's say one of them steals the ball either by intercepting a pass or forcing a fumble. Then we're back on offense and can score again. In that scenario, we're up two scores before the other team has had a chance to advance the ball. But usually, our defense forces the other team into a stalemate, and they have to kick the ball back to us. Then we have another chance to advance the ball." He stood and grinned. "All the 'bashing' is how each team tries to force the other team away from the goal." Waggling his brows, he added, "It's the best part of the game."

His excitement drew me closer, but when I glanced up from his drawings, his eyes were on me. More accurately, on my mouth. Involuntarily, my tongue slipped out to wet my lips.

"You know you want to come." His voice dropped an octave, sending tiny tremors through me.

I blinked, and the corner of his mouth tipped up.

"To my game, you naughty girl. But after the hot way you kissed me in the library, I can see how your mind might have gone somewhere else."

My eyes nearly bugged out of my head as I huffed out a breath. "You truly think you're the BFD, don't you?"

"Come to my game on Saturday. See for yourself, Island Girl." The words were cocky, but his smile was gentle. Vulnerable. I couldn't figure out how to react.

Callahan did it for me. "What happened in that study room tonight? Hottest. Kiss. Of. My. Life." He leaned down and brushed a soft kiss over my cheek, shoved his hands in his pockets, and stepped back. "See you in class tomorrow."

He walked backward two steps, long enough to let his smile linger between us, then he turned on his heel and strode back up the sidewalk the way we came.

The next day when I walked into class, I was still thinking about how Callahan had described our ill-advised make-out session in the library. The hottest kiss of his life? Seriously? How I'd let things go so far off the rails, I had yet to figure out. Yes, he was gorgeous and smart and oddly sweet, but he was still a player. A player who could make me forget my own name when he put his talented lips on mine. I sighed.

"That was heartfelt." Axel smirked as I slouched into the chair beside his. "I heard you were a bit disheveled after your study session at the library."

I sat forward so fast I almost gave myself whiplash. "Where did you hear that?"

"Drake knows Enriquè from their graphic design classes. He comes over sometimes to play COD with us," Axel explained. "He popped in last night after he finished up at the library."

My heart tried to climb up my throat, but I shoved it back down with attitude. Crossing my arms over my chest, I said, "Your friend has no idea what he's talking about. He doesn't even know who I am."

"Jamaica, darling, this glorious mass of curls draws everyone's attention. That and the entertaining way you annoy professors with your endless questions in all your classes." He gave me a patronizing pat on the thigh. "You'd be surprised how many people on campus know who you are."

Hotshot chose that moment to slide in beside me, sandwiching me between himself and my best friend as though I needed an additional testosterone boost. Axel with his laughing eyes and that thigh pat was plenty, thankyouverymuch.

"Good morning, Island Girl. Did you have sweet dreams last night?" The wicked gleam in his intense blue eyes sent a shot of pure lust straight to my center.

Why did that part of me have to have delicious memories of rubbing up and down his length?

Turning up my nose at him, I said, "I was too busy sleeping to spend time dreaming."

Callahan chuckled and smiled his infectious smile. "It's your story, babe. Tell it any way you want." He leaned in close and whispered for my ears only, "I dreamed about kissing you all night. Woke up with morning wood hard enough to take out a brick wall."

My hand flew to my mouth to cover my snort of laughter at his outrageous description. Recovering myself, I shook my head. "That's a visual I did not need."

He winked at Axel over my head, and I had to reach into my backpack for my notebook to keep myself from smacking him. Sliding a glance at my best friend, I amended that thought—to stop myself from smacking both of them.

Dr. Dair interrupted. "If you're finished with your theatrics in the middle row, the rest of us would like to start class."

Now I wanted to add my professor to the smack fest forming in my head.

Sitting up straight, I pulled up my writing table and clicked it into place, tugged a pen from my hair and set it on a blank notebook page and zeroed my focus in on my nemesis instructor. Soft laughter, in stereo, assaulted my ears as Axel and Callahan reacted to Dair's pronouncement and my response.

For the next hour, I studiously ignored my best friend's intermittent chuckles and Hotshot's not-so-subtle touches as he all but glued himself to my side. Fine, I struggled with that second one, but I worked hard to stay in the lecture. I even managed to stop daydreaming about a certain football player's hands on my ass long enough to ask three pertinent questions, eliciting dramatic sighs from the teacher.

As we packed up to leave class, Callahan reached across me to hand a pair of tickets to Axel. "These are for you and a plus-one for Saturday's game." His eyes sparkled as he handed me a ticket too. "It goes without saying that you'll be at the game."

"Excuse me?"

"You can't argue my chess analogy if you don't watch a game." He gave my shoulder a tiny bump with his own. "We both know you want to argue it, so you'll be there." Grinning at my oldest friend, he added, "She'll probably come with a notebook and take notes, yeah?"

Axel, the traitor, laughed. "Jamaica will be there." He held up the tickets. "Thanks for these, man. Drake is going to be pumped to sit at the fifty rather than crowd into the student section as usual."

"Game time is one o'clock, but you'll want to arrive thirty to forty-five minutes early for the full experience."

My brow shot up. "Explain."

"There's a whole thing leading up to kickoff, Jamaica," Axel chimed in. "The marching band, cheerleaders, and dance team perform. Fireworks and a military flyover. Someone awesome from the music department wins the honor of singing the National Anthem. It's a big deal." If I didn't know better, I could have sworn he bounced in his seat.

"I'm sure it is a whole thing." I sighed. "You can tell me about it later. Right now, I have about five minutes to make an eight-minute walk to my next class."

Callahan led the way out of the building. "Don't worry, Island Girl. I'll break a trail for you, make sure you arrive with thirty seconds to spare."

"I'll catch you later at our usual coffee spot, J." Giving Hot-shot a salute, Axel spun on his heel and sprinted toward his next class.

Without asking my permission, Callahan grabbed my hand and started walking at a pace that forced me to jog to keep up.

When we arrived outside Huffine Hall, I was slightly winded. I was also on time.

Giving my hand a lingering squeeze, he leaned down to whisper in my ear, "You can cheer for me tomorrow if you want." He ghosted a kiss over my cheek. The contact was so light it shouldn't have even registered, let alone electrify a band of butterflies into doing the cha-cha in my belly. Straightening up, he smirked as though he knew exactly how that little move played through me. "My number is 85."

Chapter Ten

Jamaica

AXEL, DRAKE, AND I arrived at the game thirty minutes before kickoff. Since I was stuck in the dorms on call on Friday night, I'd spent the better part of an exceptionally quiet evening studying the game of football, so I knew the terminology for the start of the game, much to my best friend's surprise.

As promised, the marching band was on the field entertaining the large crowd of people already filling the stadium. On the sidelines the cheerleaders and dance team executed routines in time with the music. The jumbotron scoreboard counted down the minutes in giant numbers, alternating with crowd shots and close-ups of instrumentalists and cheerleaders.

We'd stopped at the concession stand on our way to our seats, picking up large coffees that we discreetly intensified with Jameson from a flask Drake had managed to sneak past the bouncers and their handheld contraband wands at the gate. When I'd questioned my friends with a raised brow after they dragged me into a corner behind a set of stairs, Axel had said, "Trust us. You're going to need help staying warm in the stands."

As we took our seats a few rows up from the field on the fifty-yard line directly behind the Wildcats' bench, I understood my friends' idea. A slight breeze coming off the mountains announced winter's imminent arrival even though the blue of the early October sky was sharp enough to force me to squint. Per Axel's instruction, I'd worn my insulated snow boots, my winter coat, a hat, and mittens. Still, I was glad for alcohol-laced hot coffee.

"What do you think so far? Pretty exciting, huh?" Axel asked, a wide smile splitting his face.

I shrugged. "People here are definitely excited." After another sip of coffee, I said, "This was a good idea." I saluted Drake, who inclined his head. "It's chilly here."

"You'll warm up once the game starts and you start cheering," Axel said. "Besides kickoff, what else did you learn in your football cram course last night?" His eyes sparkled over the rim of his cup. The man knew me so well.

"Following a coin toss, one team kicks the ball to the other team who starts the game on offense. If they score, their fans are happy. If they don't, they go on defense, giving the other team a chance to score." Wrapping both hands around my cup, I held it close to my body. "How am I doing so far?" With a flirty, eye-batting blink at my friend, I took another small sip.

"Rocking it, J. Now for the question of the day: what position does Callahan play?"

With a dismissive wave of my hand, I said, "Tight end. What an apt name for his… .position." I smirked.

Drake nearly spit out a drink of coffee he'd just taken.

Axel's eyes danced. "Glad to know you've paid attention to his tight end. For a minute there, I was worried you'd miss it, what with your ridiculous prejudices against athletes."

I gifted him a long-suffering glare. "Get it right, Benson. I don't have a problem with athletes. For instance, I've always adored *you*. I don't think I missed a single one of your lacrosse games in high school. It's *players* I have a problem with."

"I don't get the idea O'Reilly is playing you, J."

Before I could ask him what he meant, the crowd erupted in boos as the opposing team ran onto the field.

"This is going to be a dogfight," Drake shouted, his face lit up like Christmas.

Leaning in so he could hear me over the roar of the crowd, I asked Axel, "Who are we playing again?"

Right then, the announcer's voice rang through the stadium from the PA system. "Today's game features the Western Washington Bulldogs and your Mountain State Wildcats!"

Fireworks erupted above the stadium. The band struck up school fight song. Flash pots blew fire into the air on either side of the mouth of an inflatable Wildcat head in one corner of the field. The cheerleaders made a long tumbling pass between the two lines of marching band players. Four fighter jets screamed overhead, passing low and abruptly pulling up at the fifty yard line.

The Wildcats raced out onto the field. One player carried a pole with an American flag streaming behind him, another carried a Mountain State flag, and a third carried a Wildcat flag. The players behind them yelled, ran, and jumped while the crowd in the stands launched into a frenzy of cheers, screams, and applause. In spite of myself, my body hummed with excitement. Then I saw number 85.

Over the course of the past few weeks of studying with him and seeing him regularly in class, I'd become used to his size. Seeing him in his helmet and pads reminded me that Callahan O'Reilly was a seriously large man. Even among the other guys on the team, he stood out. Yet the way his pads fit beneath his tight jersey, he looked proportional and sleek. Powerful.

When he reached the bench area, he glanced up into the stands, his eyes finding mine, and instantly I was wet. Even at this distance, the intensity of his stare made me throb, and I locked my knees together. As if he knew exactly the effect he had on me, he winked.

The man had the audacity to wink. At. Me.

Then his face lit up with a massive grin, and before I could think, I grinned back.

His hands went up in the air in a victory salute, and he turned to his teammates who were all slapping hands, backs, and asses, and engaging in some sort of weird ritual with each other.

Beside me, Axel stopped cheering to take in the little drama playing out between Hotshot and me, a sly smirk on his face. "The two of you are working on more than your class project, I think."

"Keep your opinions to yourself," I hissed.

He was still laughing when the announcer hushed the crowd for the singing of the National Anthem. As the singer—a baritone I'd heard practicing on several occasions when I went to the music building for my piano lessons—neared the end of the song, the crowd lost its composure and started cheering again. From the smile on the guy's face, he believed that applause was for him, and maybe it was. But from the way the team started high-fiving each other and jumping around on the sidelines, I think the cheering was for the start of the game.

Somewhere along the line, I missed the coin toss. Apparently, the Bulldogs won it because they were kicking. Axel explained it was part of game strategy to defer having the ball to start the first half in favor of having it to start the second. His explanation only reaffirmed what I'd told Callahan when he was explaining the game the other night. Whoever had the ball last would win. Even the other team's coaches figured that out.

Number 85 lined up nearest the Wildcats sideline, and I

jumped when he smashed into the defender who came across the line when the center snapped the ball. The crash of pads was audible even above the noise of twenty thousand screaming fans. As the quarterback dropped back, Callahan kept pushing the other player until the guy tripped and went down, Callahan on top of him.

"Way to go, 'Han!" Axel yelled. When he turned to Drake, I heard him say, "He pancaked the shit out of that defensive end. Bet he thinks twice before coming after O'Reilly again." They high-fived each other as though they'd made the play, and I shook my head.

Meanwhile, the quarterback had handed the ball off to a running back who followed behind Callahan and sprinted up the field for several yards before being tackled. The announcer's exuberant voice echoed through the stadium.

"First down—" He dragged the word out, and the crowd finished with "Wildcats!"

The team continued running what seemed to me was the same play. In chess, a competent opponent would have put a stop to that immediately. Perhaps the Bulldogs' coaches weren't that competent? At any rate, Callahan was only blocking as the other guy kept receiving the handoff and running the ball through the line of defenders until the Wildcats were on the five-yard line. Though I tried to watch all the players, my eyes always came back to number 85 who pushed back every player he faced. After every play he yelled to the sky, his fists clenched in front of him, then bounded back to the huddle.

"O'Reilly's on fire out there today," Axel said, his face shining. "You must be inspiring him."

I rolled my eyes so hard that it took me a second to focus them on my friend. "Hardly."

The team ran the play, but this time the running back dropped in behind the guard and followed him into the end zone.

The crowd went bananas. The band played the fight song. The cheerleaders performed a complicated stunt in the end zone. The dance team did a tumbling pass across the opposite end zone beneath the jumbotron that proclaimed "TOUCHDOWN" with an old-timey Batman-style *ka-blam* graphic behind it. From the spectacle of the crowd, one would have thought the entire stadium had scored the points.

As if someone flipped a switch, the crowd abruptly stopped cheering as the kicking team trotted out onto the field. When the kicker sent the football through the goalposts, the fans erupted again.

Pointing at the scoreboard proclaiming "media timeout," I asked, "What's the deal with that?"

"You truly don't have a clue, do you, J?" Axel grinned. "The game is being broadcast over TV and radio. They need a break for commercials."

"This event is quite the production." I sipped my coffee, which was now mostly the alcohol left in the bottom of my cup. "I had no idea."

Wrapping an arm across my shoulders, he pulled me in for a rough and bouncy one-armed hug. "Admit it. You're having fun."

"It's nothing like what I expected."

By halftime the game was close, with the Bulldogs up by what Axel explained was a field goal. Callahan had caught a pass and dropped another. I couldn't help but cringe each time he was tackled. It seemed unfair that three or four monsters could grab him and jump on him as they pushed him to the ground. But each time, he bounced back up as though he'd only tripped over his feet.

When the teams went to the locker rooms, the marching band took the field. Honestly, their performance of a medley of songs from *Star Wars* was the best part of the afternoon. Yet half the fans missed it, including Axel and Drake. When the band collectively moved to create a perfect C-3PO and R2D2 together, I whipped out my phone and filmed it to show my friends when they returned.

After the band marched off the field, I headed to the concessions area in search of a restroom. On my return to my seat, I discovered the second half had already started with the Bulldogs on the move. Axel handed me a fresh coffee, and I my eyes watered at the first sip. Leaning around my friend, I tapped his boyfriend on the shoulder. "Is there any coffee in this?"

Drake grinned. "Plenty. Swirl it around a little."

I had Drake and Axel in hysterics when I wrapped both hands around my cup and did a silly swirly dance, using my entire body to mix my drink. When I took a second sip, I could taste a little something other than whiskey, but not much. Still, it was hot, which was welcome. As the afternoon moved closer to dusk, the breeze had picked up, and standing in the bleachers, even surrounded by scores of other people, was chilly.

When I chanced a visual tour of the sidelines, I caught Callahan watching me with narrowed eyes. With a nonchalance born of my second Irish coffee of the afternoon, I shrugged. The shrug he returned broadcast sarcasm like a flashing neon sign. I couldn't help but grin. Then I saluted him with my cup, and he shook his head, returning his attention to the field.

"Looks like someone noticed your absence to start the second half," Axel said, his expression speculative.

"Whatever." But as I stared at Callahan's broad back, a tiny shiver, one that had nothing to do with the weather, rippled through me and tickled my center.

An interesting aspect of the game that my friends had to explain was tailgating. We hadn't stopped at any of the tailgate parties on our way in, but apparently, we weren't the only fans in attendance imbibing in a bit of jolly-juice. It wasn't until the middle of the third quarter that the stadium returned to its sold-out complement of fans as they straggled in from the tailgates. By then we were down by ten points, and the crowd was at the top of its lungs encouraging the team to rally.

As Drake had predicted at the start, the game was a dogfight. With less than two minutes to go, the Bulldogs were up by three, but the Wildcats had the ball. Number 85 had spent most of the second half blocking for the running backs. Unlike his description of his role as more of a bishop, in today's chess game, he played as a pawn.

The crowd quieted as the teams lined up on the Bulldogs' forty on third and one. The quarterback called "Hut! Hut!" but instead of blocking someone into the turf like he'd been doing all game, Callahan pushed off the defender and ran past him. Somehow, he was behind the line of defenders when the quarterback threw the ball to him. He caught it in stride and took off at a dead run for the end zone. A defender launched himself at Callahan but only managed to catch his feet. He lost his balance and fell forward over the goal line.

When he stood up, he pointed the nose of the ball straight at me before he handed it to the ref. His teammates swarmed him, hugging him and fist-bumping him, slapping him on the helmet and on his back, and jogging with him back to the sidelines where he received more handshakes, back slaps, and hugs. The kicking team trotted onto the field where the kicker extended the lead to four points with less than a minute to go in the game.

Between media timeouts and the teams calling timeouts, that final fifty seconds of the game took up half the afternoon. But at last the clock ticked down to double zeros, the buzzer blew, and the ref picked up the ball. The stadium erupted in pandemonium. The band played a raucous rendition of the school fight song, with the team singing the words as they stood in the end zone facing the band and the students' section. Then they jogged off the field to the locker room.

"What do you say we hit Stromboli's before the crowd arrives?" Axel suggested.

Drake threw his arm over Axel's shoulder. "Excellent plan, babe."

"Um—"

Axel grabbed my wrist as the two of them started down the bleachers. "Don't even think about going back to the dorms yet."

"But—"

"You have to eat, Jamaica. Might as well share a to-die-for pizza with us rather than settle for mediocre cafeteria food by yourself." He stopped and shot me a look from beneath his brows. "The books will be there when you get home. Promise."

"You talk like you know me or something."

Ignoring my remark, he added, "Besides, you've had too much alcohol to study properly. Plus, it's Saturday. You have all day tomorrow to go over all your notes twenty or thirty times."

"Does he nag you like this too, Drake?"

"It's one of his charms." The affection in the smile Drake bestowed on Axel hollowed me out.

Wasn't that a kick in the ass? Sure, I'd noticed the deep feelings my best friend and his boyfriend shared, but I'd never envied them. Besides, they always included me whenever there was fun to be had and I wasn't buried in books. So why did that look between them leave me with a gaping hole in my chest?

Then a picture of a certain hot football player invaded my head, and for a fleeting second I wondered if I'd see number 85 at dinner.

Chapter Eleven

Jamaica

AS WITH EVERY other part of the college football game day experience, my friends were spot-on about hustling out of the stadium and heading directly for Stromboli's. We grabbed an open booth opposite the bar about halfway between the front door and the back. Behind us, people spilled in like someone had turned a faucet on high. Within minutes, the place was packed.

A harried server stopped at our table to drop off menus and grab our drinks order. When he came back about ten minutes later with a pitcher of dark beer and one of water, we ordered a jumbo meat lover's with extra jalapenos and settled in to wait for our pie.

"We probably should have ordered breadsticks too," I said as I accepted a glass of beer from Drake.

At his raised brow, I clarified, "To soak up the alcohol we already have in our systems before adding more." I indicated my brimful glass of beer.

Axel snorted. "It's okay for you to let your hair down sometimes, J."

Shaking my head, I bent down and slurped the top off my beer in an effort to keep it from spilling on me when I lifted the glass to my mouth for another drink.

"Admit it, Jamaica. You enjoyed the game today," Axel said as he slid closer to Drake across the booth from me.

With a shrug, I said, "It was fun, I guess."

"You're such a bad liar." Axel smirked. "When O'Reilly ran that last touchdown in, you were screaming your head off."

Running my finger through the condensation rings on the tabletop, I said, "It was more exciting than I thought it would be to watch a bunch of big guys bash into each other."

Drake almost choked on his beer. When he hauled himself back under control, he said, "You mean watching a certain big guy bash into the Bulldogs defenders." His sly grin had me downing a long pull from my glass.

Axel's eyes danced as he leaned forward. "Tell us, J. What's going on between you and O'Reilly?"

"We're project partners. That's all." A vision of the two of us in a private study room in the library flared in my brain, and my entire body flashed hot.

"Totally explains the color of your cheeks right now." Drake smirked.

"Just because the two of you are an item doesn't mean everyone else needs to be too," I said with a sniff.

"Stop deflecting, Jamaica." Axel's naughty grin matched his partner's, and I wanted to throw the half-full pitcher of beer at the two of them.

Instead, a big body loomed over me. The clean scent hitting my nostrils told me who it was before I looked up into a pair of sea-blue eyes that pinned me to my seat.

"Thanks for saving me a spot, Island Girl."

Without asking my permission, he slid in beside me, crowding me into the corner of the booth. Again without my permission, he helped himself to my glass, tossing back what was left in it and refilling it.

He moaned. "Mmm. Exactly what I needed."

"Hello, Hotshot. Care to join us? Drink my beer for me?" I asked and didn't hold back the snark.

Ignoring it, he smiled. "What did you think of your first football game, Jamaica? Off-the-charts awesomeness, yeah?"

I crossed my arms over my chest, mostly to keep from sliding my hand over the muscular thigh beneath his jeans. With a shrug, I said, "Chess is still better, but football was all right."

All three guys burst out laughing.

"She loved it, didn't she?" he asked my friends.

"Was totally into it from the second you stepped on the field, Callahan."

I shot my best friend a why-am-I-friends-with-you? glare, and he laughed at that too. Traitor.

Callahan leaned in close and said into my ear, "What did you think of that touchdown I scored for you?"

I narrowed my eyes. "That was for me? Really? 'Cause it sure seemed like your team needed it."

He chuckled. "We all needed it, but I dedicated it to you. For watching your first game."

The server chose that opportune moment to show up with our pizza. His eyes almost bugged out of his head when he saw who had joined our little party.

"Great game today. We watched it on TV while we prepped for this insanity." The server glanced around at the heaving mass of people crowded into the pizzeria. "You need another glass here?"

"Thanks, man. We could use another glass, another plate, another pitcher, and another pie," Callahan said.

"On it!" The server disappeared into the crowd and reappeared only a minute or two later with a fresh pitcher and a glass and plate for Callahan.

Drake poured what was left of the first pitcher into his and Axel's glasses, then he reached for the second and filled Hotshot's and topped mine off. Axel was busy dishing up slices and handing them around. Both of them were born hosts even when they weren't at home entertaining a houseful of people.

"You like the seats?" Callahan asked my friends.

"Damn, 'Han, those were excellent," Axel gushed. "Thanks again for the tickets."

"Game days are always a blast, but we only ever watch from the student section. It's a whole other experience seeing the game from the fifty." Drake saluted Callahan with his beer and took a drink.

Talk turned to the finer points of football. As a newbie, I didn't quite follow what the guys discussed. Then again, I was busy stuffing my face with meaty, cheesy goodness and surreptitiously stealing stray jalapeno slices from the pizza tray.

In the middle of Axel's observations about the weaknesses in the Bulldogs' interior defensive line, Callahan snatched a jalapeno slice out from under my wandering fingers. As I opened my mouth to voice a complaint, he popped it between my lips. "You call me Hotshot. Maybe I should call you Hot Lips."

The heat in his eyes as they strayed to my lips sent a naughty shiver through me.

"I knew it," Axel called out.

I did my level best to burn my oldest friend to a cinder with my stare alone, and he had the good sense to slide down a notch on the bench seat across from me.

"But don't worry. Your secret's safe with us." He turned to Drake who nodded and shot me a wink.

"There is no secret." I narrowed my eyes at Callahan who returned a wicked grin. I was torn between wanting to rub that smirk off his face and wanting to kiss it. *Gah!*

"So this is public knowledge?" Drake asked, waving a hand between Hotshot and me.

Throwing my hands in the air—no mean feat in the tight corner space Callahan left for me when he slid in beside me—I ground out, "There is no"—and repeated Drake's gesture. "What is wrong with you two?"

"Nothing. Our eyes work fine," Axel said. He exchanged a look with Drake, and two Cheshire Cat smiles turned in my direction.

"Hanging out with you has always been fun, J," Axel added. "But when you bring in a bonus"—he pointed his slice of pizza at Callahan—"you're even more fun."

"Oh, for the love of—"

Callahan slid his arm across the booth behind me, crowding me even further into the corner. "I'm your bonus, huh? I like the sound of that." When he gifted me with bedroom eyes again, I wanted to slide my hand between my legs and shield my clit—or give it some pressure. Neither choice was exactly a good one at the moment. Callahan's low chuckle told me he had a clue what I was feeling, which did not make my current situation any better.

"Like I've told you before, men have stereotyped women as gossips, but this right here?"—I circled my hand around the table to include all of them. "This proves starting rumors and gossip is an equal-opportunity sport regardless of gender." I shoved a bite of pizza in my mouth before I could say anything else such as, "What the hell do you think you're doing, Hotshot?"

Out of the corner of my eye, I chanced a glance his way and immediately wished I hadn't. The sly grin he directed at me made it hard to swallow the pizza in my mouth. Especially as that look accompanied the press of his thigh along the side of mine. Heat prickled over my skin, and in spite of myself, I squirmed and tried to resituate. But there was nowhere for me to go. On one side was the wall the booth abutted to and on the other side was Callahan's deliciously hard body.

The server chose that opportune moment to deliver the second pizza Callahan had ordered. Before he could whisk away the now empty pan from the first one, I reached out and snagged the last jalapeno slice left on it and popped it in my mouth. I hoped it was hotter than sin so I'd have something else to think about other than Hotshot's too-tempting body pressed along too much of mine.

Usually, one pizza was enough for the three of us, but a certain football player's presence must have brought out the guys' appetites because the three of them devoured that second pizza in a few minutes. When the server returned to see if we needed another pitcher of beer and Axel started to say yes, Callahan interrupted.

"We could have another here, but then we'll be too far ahead for the party."

"What party?" Axel asked.

"What the hell, Island Girl? You didn't tell these guys about the party?" His incredulous expression was comical.

I shook my head. "I have no idea what you're talking about."

"Sure you do. At the end of our last study session, I invited you." At my furrowed brow, he added, "You know. When you got all pissed off about me not introducing you to that fuckboy Enriquè Simms who was showing you far too much interest."

"Oh my God. You have got to be kidding." I glared at him. "You invited your basketball friend, not me."

He dropped his hand on my shoulder and pulled me even closer to his side. "Jamaica." Hearing him sound out my name in that indulgent tone set my teeth on edge. "Stop acting stubborn. I invited you." Giving his attention to my friends who were avidly watching our little drama, he added, "Now I'm inviting you guys. We like to celebrate victories at our place." He waggled his brows, and Axel and Drake cracked up.

I closed my eyes and prayed for patience. Was he seriously implying I was a victory too?

This.

This was why I kept my distance from players.

Chapter Twelve

Jamaica

BECAUSE MY FRIENDS were traitors and not real friends, after we left Stromboli's, I ended up in Callahan's truck for the drive over to his party. Axel and Drake followed behind in Axel's car. I was about to protest the arrangements—again—when Hotshot turned up the radio. The newest song from Godsmack blasted through the speakers. "I love these guys. It's kinda funny 'cause my parents love them too." His head bobbed to the beat as he glanced in my direction. "What do you think, Island Girl?"

"About your parents liking rock bands?" I was still processing being in his truck, which smelled like pine trees and him. The console separating us was its best feature. At least I had some room to breathe now, unlike in the bar. The side of my body that had been pressed to his all through dinner still tingled.

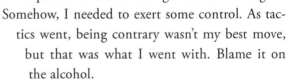

Somehow, I needed to exert some control. As tactics went, being contrary wasn't my best move, but that was what I went with. Blame it on the alcohol.

He barked out a laugh. Apparently, my snark didn't put him off in the least.

"By the way, we're alone now. You can stop pretending you don't like me."

I rolled my head on the headrest and shot him a glare from beneath my brows.

"We both know you were as into that kiss the other night as I was." He slid his hand under the front of the console and flipped it back, creating a full bench seat. The move gave him easy access to me, which he took full advantage of. He slid his palm over my knee and halfway up my thigh, resting it there. "Don't think I haven't noticed how you heat up whenever I touch you."

I pushed his hand away and crossed my arms over my chest while I stared studiously straight ahead. "I thought we established that I don't date players."

He eased up to a red light and stopped. Giving me his undivided attention, his voice dropped an octave, his gaze as serious as I'd ever seen it. "I'm not playing you."

My body flashed fire. How was I supposed to resist the oh-so-gorgeous Callahan O'Reilly, his voice resonating through me when he looked at me that way? The light turned green and he resumed our drive to his place without talking for several blocks.

At last he broke the silence between us. "Our parties tend to be massive. Like house heaving at the seams massive. But you'll know people there."

"Axel and Drake. And you. But I imagine you're going to be busy during this bash, seeing as you're one of the hosts and all."

"I'm hosting you, so yeah, I'll be busy." He shot me a grin.

"Riiight." A picture of Tory Miller and her posse of sycophants popped into my head. If they were there—and everything about their stalkerish attention to Callahan indicated they would be—chances were the two of us wouldn't see much of each other from five minutes after we walked through the door. "Have you told your fan club?"

"We have a bouncer at the door to keep the under-twenty-ones out of the house. We're football players for a conference championship contender—we don't need any bad press or run-ins with the cops." Under his breath, he mumbled, "If Finn doesn't fuck it up."

"What does that mean? What will your roommate fuck up?"

Callahan put two hands on the wheel as he drove us around a roundabout and onto a narrow residential street lined bumper-to-bumper with cars. "He can't seem to say no to jersey chasers. Hopefully, Bax has more sense and overrides him."

"Bax?"

"Wyatt Baxter, one of our roommates. Danny Chambers, our new roommate, doesn't do parties, so I know he won't be any help with the jersey chasers."

"How can he live with you and not attend a party at your house?"

"By spending the night with his best friend—who is *not* his girlfriend, despite all indications to the contrary." He snorted, giving me a good idea of what he thought of his roommate's love life.

We pulled into the driveway of a two-story Victorian. With all the lights blazing, no one could miss the party. Surprisingly, I didn't hear much sound. Then someone opened the front door, and loud music poured out into the yard. I gave Callahan a dubious look as I unbuckled my seat belt and stepped out of his ride.

Together, we waited for my friends to arrive. After several minutes, Axel and Drake walked up the sidewalk.

"For a second there, I thought I'd lost you guys at the roundabout."

"Nah, but parking around here is brutal. Did you know that?" Axel asked.

Callahan laughed. "It's not all that great even when no one on the street is throwing a party." Casually, he slipped his arm around me and turned to head inside. "Let's go have some fun."

Short of making a scene, I could do nothing about the way he laid claim to me except to throw a glare over my shoulder when my friends chimed "Ooooh" as they followed us inside.

The house was heaving with people when we walked through the front door. We'd barely managed two steps out of the foyer and into the living room when a guy rivaling Callahan in size shoved a red cup into his hand and pounded him on the back—hard. "Fuckin' A, 'Han! You're the hero of the day. About fuckin' time you showed up."

"Bax, this is Jamaica Winslow. Jamaica, this is my roommate Wyatt Baxter." He had to shout over the music and raucous laughter whose decibels rivaled a jet taking off.

My hand disappeared into Bax's giant one. "Nice to meet you."

"Likewise." He didn't try to disguise the appreciative once-over he gave me, and I raised a brow, letting him know what I thought of that. "Uh-huh. You're feisty. No wonder Callahan hasn't let go of you since you walked through the door. If you were my date, I wouldn't either." Turning to Hotshot, he added, "You're a master of hooking up with the hottest girls on campus. Just once, you could do me a solid and show me how you do it."

Callahan laughed, took a sip of his beer, then handed it to me. "All the lessons in the world won't help you, Bax." He pointed a look at Bax's T-shirt that read: "The things you do for me, girl, when you walk away."

Bax flipped him the bird. "When you get tired of this one's ego"—he gestured to Hotshot—"you can hang out with me. I'm a nice guy." The tone of his voice implied that the man whose arm was tightly wrapped around my waist was not nice. But at least he wasn't wearing an offensive T-shirt.

"This is Axel Benson and Drake Jones."

The guys all shook hands, and Bax said, "Welcome to the party. Keg's in the kitchen."

"Great game today. You owned the Bulldogs' QB," Axel said.

At the compliment, Bax lit up. "Thanks, man. Their line made me work for it."

"Yeah, well, that sack at the end of the fourth quarter is the reason this guy gets to be the hero of the day." Axel hooked a thumb in Hotshot's direction.

"Exactly," Callahan said. "It's why we're such a damn fine team."

They all nodded and chuckled in some weird bro code they all understood but I didn't have a clue. One second they were flipping each other shit, with his roommate obviously hitting on me while I was standing in the circle of Callahan's arm, and the next, Callahan was bragging on the team.

My plan had been to stick with Axel and Drake, but Hotshot kept me snuggled in close to his side as more people came up to congratulate him on the game. So many names and faces floated by me, and keeping them all straight was giving me a headache. Two I recognized were his roommate Finn McCabe and Enriquè Simms, the basketball player he wouldn't introduce me to in the library.

As usual, the football fan club gathered around Finn, so apparently the bouncer was selective about that under-twenty-one rule for the party. Tory Miller was chatting up Enriquè. If her hair flips were anything to go by, she was doing her level best to come onto him. His million-watt smile lit up the corner of the living room where they stood until she glanced away and caught my eye. The thunderous expression that crossed her features when she saw who had his arm around me wiped the smile right off the basketball player's face. When he glanced over the crowd to see who had her attention, a speculative gleam came into his eyes, and all I wanted to do was find shelter before I landed in the eye of a storm.

"I thought you said nothing is going on between you and Tory Miller," I practically shouted in Hotshot's ear over the booming bass of the music and the raucous conversation of a houseful of people.

"Nothing has ever gone on between me and Tory," he emphasized, his breath tickling my ear and sending a ripple straight down my spine.

"Does she know that?"

He rolled his eyes and shook his head, which could have meant anything. "Come on. Let's find some beer."

With a sardonic arch of my brow, I handed him the mostly full red cup. He downed it in one gulp and grinning at me added, "We're out."

Callahan and his roommates lived in one of the cool old Victorian houses several blocks off-campus. The living room, even with a full complement of furniture in it, held at least sixty people. We weaved our way through them to the equally spacious kitchen at the back of the house. Probably twenty more people filled that space, with most of them crowded near the back door where a seriously large human pumped the keg and filled red cups with a precision that implied this wasn't his first rodeo.

I glanced around, looking for my friends, but they were nowhere to be found. A frission of panic prickled through me. As though he sensed it even as he chatted with another football player, Hotshot tightened his arm around me. Weirdly, his presence and the way he seemed to be tuned into me grounded me. Relaxed me. I slipped my arm across his waist, and he leaned down to whisper in my ear, "About time, Island Girl."

I couldn't be certain, but I think he took advantage and whispered a kiss with his words. A shiver slid over me, and he grinned.

Whispering in my ear again, he said, "Patience, babe. We'll have time for that later."

Before I even had a second to sputter at the man's audacity, the guy at the keg called out, "'Han, my man! This party is almost as good as that last catch you made. Hand me that." He nodded at the empty cup in Hotshot's hand.

"Thanks, Fitz. My date needs one too, since you're pouring." Turning to me, he said, "Jamaica, this is Jeremiah Fitzgerald, but he answers to Fitz. He plays D tackle."

"A defensive lineman. Got it." I nodded to Fitz. "Nice to meet you."

"You've been studying the game," Callahan said, a note of pride in his voice. "Why am I not surprised?"

I shrugged. "Since you were so generous with the tickets, I thought I should know something before I attended a game."

"Wait. Are you saying your lady here is not a football fan?" The idea was such an anathema to Fitz that he missed the cup he was filling and splashed beer on the floor at his feet. Glancing down, he righted the spigot with a muffled, "Fuck." After handing me the cup, he reached behind him for a roll of paper towels, mopping up the mess with his foot and tossing the soiled towels in a trash can by the door.

"After today's game"—Callahan squeezed his hand on my hip—"she can't help but be a fan. Isn't that right, Jamaica?"

The cocky grin on his face dared me to respond in the negative. That, of course, required me to be contrary. With a shrug, I said, "The game might grow on me."

Callahan barked out a laugh while his teammate looked confused.

With a little nudge, Callahan said, "Let's go check how the beer pong tournament is going."

Through a door to my left, I glanced into a spacious dining room. The giggling posse of Finn's fan club entered the kitchen without their main man. Callahan returned his attention to Fitz, his expression dead serious. "Under no circumstances do you fill any of their cups. Got it?"

Fitz nodded. "Let me guess. None of them are twenty-one."

"Exactly."

"How did they get past the bouncer?"

Callahan tilted his head, his tone sardonic when he said, "Two guesses, and the first one doesn't count."

Fitz rolled his eyes. "Your roommate's a slow learner."

"You have no idea." He spun us back toward the dining room. "Let's disappear before they spot us."

It was marginally less crowded where a spirited game of beer pong was underway. On one end of the table stood a group of big, broad-shouldered guys, some of whose faces I recognized from the sideline of the game. On the other end of the table stood a group of super-tall guys. Callahan positioned us on the end nearest the stocky players and leaned in to explain, "It's football versus basketball, cutthroat beer pong. Whichever team loses has to chug that." With his cup, he pointed to the row of whiskey bottles lined up along a side table.

"Do you guys do this often?" The idea of chugging pints of whiskey horrified me.

"After every home win. It gets really ugly during basketball season though."

I blinked at him. "Worse than this?"

He shrugged. "They play more games. Like us, they're winning."

"Why do two winning teams from the same school compete against each other in drinking games?" I already had the notion athletes were over-the-top. Watching the nonsense going on in front of me cemented it.

He laughed. "Isn't it obvious? To prove who are the bigger dogs on campus." He glanced at the progress of the game. "Looks like the football team is going to retain the title." In solidarity with his teammates, he downed half his beer. "As we should."

I watched in fascination as he ran his tongue over his lips, licking the foam from them. When he caught me, his eyes heated, and involuntarily, I fisted his shirt in the hand that was still around his waist.

A roar went up around the table, tearing our gazes apart and breaking the spell. The last ball dropped, and the basketball team as a unit headed over to the line of whiskey bottles. They uncapped them, clinked them together in a salute to each other, and started chugging to the rowdy encouragement of the winning football team.

"Who cleans your house after one of these events?"

"We do."

As I watched the basketball players finish their whiskeys, I asked, "Do you draw straws for bathroom duty?"

Following my train of thought, he said, "These boys would never mess up the bathrooms, just like we never mess up at their places."

I raised a dubious brow, and he chuckled.

"It's a matter of pride, Island Girl. Losing at beer pong is bad enough. You don't want to compound it by losing your Stromboli's in front of the other team. That would be bad form." The wicked sparkle in his eyes as he glanced at the basketball players told its own tale.

It wasn't long before one by one they slipped out through the screen door leading into the back yard. Callahan fist-bumped several of the football players as they filed past him back into the kitchen.

"The beer pong 'tournament' is over, I take it," I said, raising my cup to my lips.

He stared at my mouth for a second. "That was the opening round. In a few minutes when the rest of the party sees who's returned to it, they'll know it's safe to come out here and challenge each other."

I furrowed my brow. "Does no one else take on the winner of that round?"

"It's a private event between our two teams. Since everyone here—except for you—knows the players on both teams, everyone knows who the big dogs are for this week when they return to the festivities." He grinned. "I doubt it'll take you long to catch up now that you're part of the team." He touched his cup to mine and tossed back what was left of his beer. "Come on. Let's go see what else is happening."

For the next hour or so, we mingled with the crowd. Not once did Callahan leave my side. Somehow, our chance meeting at the bar seemed to have morphed into a date or something.

Someone changed up the playlist to a dance mix, and the next thing I knew, he had me out in the middle of the living room. Our bodies were pressed together from shoulders to knees, even as we danced to a wild and sexy beat. My arms wrapped around his neck. His hands firmly cupped my ass. During the course of the evening, we'd both switched from beer to water, so I couldn't blame alcohol for the hot way he looked at me as we undulated together in synch.

What was it about Callahan O'Reilly that made me lose my common sense?

My body answered the question. We fit together perfectly, his hardness to my softness. Rubbing along each other as we danced left me hot and bothered, my core throbbing in rhythm with our movements. Where our chests met, my nipples pebbled beneath my oversize sweater. This physical connection had no business sizzling between us, yet it rendered me powerless to step away.

His eyes blazed into mine, daring me. The desire swirling in their sea-blue depths left me breathless. Involuntarily, I gave him the satisfaction of a full-body shiver. He answered me with a wolfish grin. Fortunately, the music drowned out my moan.

Or not.

Setting his lips to my ear, he made sure I heard him. "Admit it, Island Girl. You want me as much as I want you."

This time when I moaned, it was directly in his ear. Could anything be more mortifying than being so obvious about my interest in him?

"Fuck, that's sexy."

His deep voice was another aspect that drew me inexorably to him. Then he kissed the corner of my jaw, and to my everlasting mortification, I whimpered and tightened my arms around his neck.

"Thank you for being here tonight."

That did it. The man had everything: gorgeous looks, a sexy swagger, intelligence, a sense of humor—and he was grateful I'd attended his party. I melted all over him. When my lips lingered on the kiss I pressed to the side of his neck, it was his turn to shiver. His response ratcheted up the throbbing in my core to pounding.

Right then, the music changed to Lady Gaga's "Bad Romance"—the song that had cranked up the fans' frenzy between the third and fourth quarters of the game. It seemed to be a signal of some sort because the entire house shook with the crowd jumping up and down to the beat and singing "Wildcats" instead of the lyrics. Callahan laughed and let me go, the two of us jumping with the rest of the revelers. I couldn't decide if I was relieved or disappointed at the mood change. But after that, I made sure there was space between us as we danced to a few more songs.

With him being a college athlete, his fitness level was twenty on a scale of ten. Mine, on the other hand, was about a four. Who knew hours of reading didn't build cardio? At last I had to take a break. We wove our way through the throng to the kitchen for more water, but the cooling liquid didn't revive me. My day had caught up to me, and I was ready to call it.

CHAPTER THIRTEEN

Jamaica

"I NEED TO FIND Axel and Drake."

"You wanna go home already?" The disappointment in Callahan's tone tugged at me.

Glancing at the clock on the microwave, I discovered it was after one in the morning. "It's way past my bedtime."

Accepting my decision to call it a night, he laced his fingers through mine, his rough palm leaving tingles, and led me out to the back yard where a spirited game of cornhole was in full swing. From the intensity of the players and spectators, money definitely played a part. Gambling wasn't high on my friends' radar, so I wasn't surprised they weren't in the back yard. Plus, it was damn cold outside. They weren't among the beer pong players in the dining room, and we'd already established they weren't in the kitchen when we grabbed our water.

We ambled back into the living room, but with so many people dancing and drinking, it would probably take us an hour to wind our way through to find my friends. Tugging on

Callahan's hand, I halted our progress and pulled him back into the relative quiet of the kitchen. Retrieving my phone from my pocket, I gave Axel a quick call that went straight to voicemail. My text went unanswered as well.

"Follow me."

He wove us through the crowd to the stairs. When I balked, he said, "Trust me? Please?"

With a nod, I followed him up to the second story where we walked down a hallway past a couple of closed doors and one that opened right as we reached it. A pair of sweaty people stepped out of the bathroom. From his disheveled hair and her flushed cheeks, it didn't take a genius to figure out what they'd been doing in there.

"Hey, 'Han. Great party." The guy offered his fist, and Callahan bumped it.

"Glad you're enjoying it."

The girl stared at Callahan as if she'd like to haul him into the bathroom next.

After an awkward moment, the pair headed back downstairs while we continued down the hall. When we stopped at the door on the end, he pulled a key from his pocket and unlocked it. He flipped on a lamp on a table beside a king-size bed that took up most of the space and faced me.

"Is this your room?"

"Yeah."

"Why do you lock it?"

He slipped behind me and closed the door. "It's damned inconvenient when you throw a party in your own house and can't bring a girl to your own room because some other dude is banging someone in your bed."

I blinked.

"After that happened to each of us during the first couple of parties we threw last year, we all put locks on our bedroom doors." He nodded in the direction of the hallway. "There's a bathroom downstairs too, but you'll notice Buckford had a girl up here. No doubt he tried the knobs on every door along the hall before he settled on taking her to the can." A massive eye roll accompanied his words. "Anyway, it's quiet in here. You can wait in peace while I go look for your friends."

"How did you know… ?"

"That you needed a break from the masses? I pay attention, Jamaica." Something hot flashed in his eyes then he was at the door. "I'll be back in a few. If I can't find them, I'll take you home, okay?"

"Thanks."

As if by habit, he turned the lock on the door on his way out. Considering all the noise downstairs, his room was blessedly quiet. The lamp on the nightstand threw enough light to see most of the room. Curious, I glanced around. He kept his space neat. I don't know why that surprised me, but it did. A black duvet with dove-gray swirls covered his massive bed. A closet with double doors flanked the door into his room. His desk sat beneath the window facing the street. Books were stacked on one side of it, while his laptop took up the middle. In the corner of the room to the left of his desk was another table holding a forty-six-inch TV, games console, and controllers.

Open dove-gray curtains allowed the full moon to bathe the room in silver. A thick rug matching the duvet covered most of the hardwood floor. A pair of slippers tossed haphazardly in front of the closet was the only "mess." Well, that and a bulletin board affixed to the wall above the nightstand. Stepping closer to it, I noted his class schedule, workout schedule, game schedule, and something that listed "appearances," whatever that meant. Next to the schedules he'd tacked a collage of photos of him and guys from the team, him playing football, and several shots of what could only be his family.

From the looks of it, Callahan came from nice, middle-class

people—mom and dad, two sisters, and a brother. A wistful sigh escaped me. All my life I'd wanted siblings. I'd also wanted a dad who spent more than a day or two with us every month when he rolled through town in his semi and trailer. When I turned sixteen, even those days disappeared. Mom's only answer when I asked why we never saw Dad anymore was sadness. I had the feeling she didn't have a clue either. After a while I stopped asking.

Thinking about my family left me even more tired than I already was. I sat on the edge of Callahan's soft, massive bed. *He'll be back any minute*, I thought. But as the bed sagged invitingly under my weight, I decided I could chance a lie-down. After kicking off my boots, I lay on my side, intending to close my eyes only for a minute until he showed up with Axel.

A sound like a snort woke me. Between the furnace at my back and the duvet covering me, I was toasty warm even though I was only in my underwear and camisole.

Wait. *What the hell?* How was I mostly naked in Callahan's bed spooning with him? His big hand was splayed over my belly, holding me close to—Oh, fuck. Tucked up tight against the crack of my ass was his morning wood. Slowly, carefully, so as not to wake him, I eased my lower body away from his. The hand covering my belly tightened.

A sleepy voice at my neck said, "Hey, Island Girl, the alarm doesn't go off for another hour. Go back to sleep." He snuggled me closer.

Once again, I tried to scoot my ass away from his erection, but he pulled me back.

"Callahan, how did I—?"

"Go back to sleep. I'll explain in the morning," he mumbled.

"But you're—" I cleared my throat and tried again. "A certain part of you is wide-awake."

An exasperated growl rumbled on the pillow. "Jamaica, this is only our second date. I never put out before the third one." He nuzzled the back of my head and splayed his big hand fully over my belly. "Go. To. Sleep."

After a few minutes, his breathing evened out, and though he didn't let go of me, his body relaxed along my back, except for his cock. He didn't seem concerned about it or inclined to push me for sex even though we were snuggled up tight together.

The room was as dark as the inside of a cave, and I was warm and comfy in the nicest bed I'd ever lain in. Only a few minutes later, it seemed, I cracked my eye open when a shaft of light hit it at the same time as the rich aroma of fresh-brewed coffee tickled my nostrils. Groggily, I pushed myself up on my elbows, blinking furiously at the light streaming into the room from the hall. A fully dressed Callahan O'Reilly knelt beside the bed, sipped from a steaming mug of morning ambrosia, and offered it to me.

"Sleep well?" he asked, a twinkle in his eye.

I sat up against the pillows, pulling the covers over my chest. "Your bed is way more comfortable than a dorm mattress." Taking the mug from him, I sipped and savored delicious black coffee.

The bed sagged with his weight as he sat beside me, took the mug from me, and sipped from it. Sharing morning coffee was oddly as intimate as waking up in the middle of the night spooning with him.

"Um, how is it that I came into this room fully dressed and woke up in my underwear?"

He chuckled. "Funny story. When I couldn't find your friends, I came back up here to tell you I'd take you home. Only you were sacked out on top of the covers, snoring softly."

Crossing my arms over my chest, I narrowed my eyes. "I do not snore."

His eyes danced as he handed the mug back to me. "Okay, breathing audibly."

Exaggeratedly tilting my head, I conveyed exactly what I thought of his observation. Lifting the coffee to my lips with one hand, I gave him a "go on" gesture with the other.

A naughty grin tipped up the corner of his mouth. "You were *out.* I tried and tried to wake you, but you wouldn't budge. So I slipped your jeans and sweater off so we'd both be more comfortable, slid you under the covers with me, and went to sleep too." He took the mug back, drank from it, and said, "Now it's time for you to get your sexy ass out of bed so I can drive you home on my way to watch film from yesterday's game."

I nodded. "That's on your schedule."

"You read my schedule?"

"What did you expect? It was taking you forever to come back with Axel." I grabbed the mug back but was disappointed to discover only dregs left in the bottom of it. "At least I didn't go through your desk or open your closet."

"Good plan on the closet. Who knows how long it would have taken me to dig you out of the avalanche of shit I stuffed in there?" he teased.

"Hmmph. I bet your closet is as neat and organized as the rest of your room."

A slow smile spread over his face. "You really didn't snoop, did you?"

Furrowing my brow, I answered, "I told you I didn't."

Reaching out, he fingered a wayward curl, straightened it, then let it bounce back with the rest. No doubt I looked an absolute fright, but the expression on Hotshot's face said he didn't mind. "Too bad this is only our second date. And I have to be at the field in a few minutes."

"Why?" After our pillow talk in the middle of the night, I think I knew the answer, but for some perverted reason, I wanted to hear him say it.

"Because you are pure temptation sitting in my bed in nothing but sexy lacy panties and a satin cami."

His deep, sensuous laugh when I instinctively pulled the covers higher up my chest left a certain part of me tingly. I desperately wanted to cross my legs at the sensation, which would have given him far too much info about how he affected me.

"Speaking of my clothes, where are they?"

He nodded in the direction of his desk where my jeans and sweater were folded neatly over the chair.

With a shooing motion of my hand, I said, "Do you mind letting me dress?"

"Not at all." He stayed put where he sat on the edge of the bed.

Exaggerating a long-suffering sigh, I said, "You have to leave the room."

His brow shot up. "Why? I've already seen you in your underwear."

"Callahan." I drew out the full three syllables of his name through gritted teeth.

He laughed again, but he stood and took the now empty coffee mug from me. "My private bathroom is through there." He pointed to a door in the corner of the room that I hadn't noticed on my first inspection.

"Thanks."

"Five minutes, Island Girl. Otherwise, you won't get breakfast," he warned as he let himself out of the room.

As soon as the door closed, I jumped out of bed and snagged my clothes on the way to his en suite bathroom. It wouldn't have surprised me if he conveniently "forgot" something and needed to return in time to catch me hopping around on one foot as I tugged on my jeans.

Like the rest of his room, his bathroom was clean and tidy. Towels hung on a rack above the toilet beside the shower. No tub, but the shower looked big enough to accommodate a person Callahan's size. The smooth white tile in the shower extended around the room.

Razors and shaving cream were lined up beside a cup with a lone toothbrush resting in it on the tiny vanity. A half-used tube of toothpaste, which he'd squeezed in the middle like a barbarian, lay beside the cup. On the opposite side of the sink was a hairbrush. Rather than the medicine cabinet one would expect in an old house, an oval mirror hung above the sink. Out of curiosity, I opened the cupboard below the sink to discover extra toilet paper and bath linens and nothing else.

From what I could see, Callahan didn't hide anything. For a second I thought about his closet, but that five-minute warning to avoid missing breakfast changed my mind. After using the facilities, I hastily dressed in yesterday's clothes and wrinkled my nose at the faint stink of beer on my sweater. I stared longingly at his toothbrush, but in the end I stuck my mouth under the faucet and settled for rinsing it out. Without a shower and my pick, my hair was a lost cause. Still, I finger-combed it the best I could and exited the bathroom.

I found my boots beside his desk. Parking my ass on the chair, I was tugging them on when he rapped once on the door and walked in. Good thing I was dressed.

"Damn. You're quicker than I thought you'd be." His eyes danced.

I bared my teeth at him. "Because I didn't trust you not to pull something like walk in on me without warning."

His unabashed laughter twitched a grin out of me.

Extending a hand, he said, "Breakfast is ready. If we hustle, we can beat Finn and Bax to it."

Without thinking, I slipped my hand into his big, warm one and instantly regretted it as tingles raced up and down my arm. I did not need to react to this man. I absolutely did not.

But I couldn't seem to help it.

We tripped down the stairs into the living room. A slight stench of spilled beer permeated the air, but the space was stunningly clean. No red cups, no aluminum cans, no sign the house had been heaving at the seams with partygoers until only a few hours ago. The kitchen was spotless. The keg had disappeared, along with the chips bags and takeout pizza boxes that littered the counters and the table in the breakfast nook. Plus, the room smelled like heavenly bacon and toast.

I stared at Callahan in wonder. "Where's the mess?" slipped out before I could think.

The grin on his face said he wasn't offended. "It's how we roll, babe. The soberest members of the team who are still at the party at the end help usher out the stragglers and clean up the big stuff." Cuffing the back of his neck with his free hand, he glanced away. "I might have done a bit of scrubbing after I came downstairs while you still slept."

A smile stretched my lips. "I appreciate the effort." My stomach chose that moment to react to the scent of breakfast. Clearing my throat, I said, "You said something about breakfast?"

He let me go to grab a hot pad and open the oven door to reveal a platter of bacon, a massive bowl of scrambled eggs, and a mountain of toast on a plate. Over his shoulder, he said, "Plates are in the top cupboard to the right of the sink. Utensils in the drawer directly below it."

In a jiff, I had the table set for two while Callahan laid the food out on trivets in the middle of it. He told me to sit while he gathered hot sauce, jam, and salt and pepper. Next, he poured two generous glasses of orange juice from a pitcher in the fridge and brought them over to the table.

"Um, this is a lot of food for two people."

A snort escaped him. "It won't be the two of us for long. Dig in."

As if he'd conjured them with his words, Finn and Bax crashed down the stairs and fought for who would come through the kitchen door first. It would have been comical except for the real possibility one or both of them might land face-first in the middle of the table. Callahan cleared his throat, and the two of them clued in that I was in the room. In slow motion, they disentangled from each other and straightened their T-shirts then Bax graciously stepped aside to let Finn precede him into the room at a more sedate speed.

As he helped himself to coffee, Finn said, "Good morning, Jamaica." A smirk followed. "I thought the two of you were only study buddies."

Bax nudged him with an elbow. "Callahan takes his studies serious. You know that." He turned away, suppressed laughter at his joke almost choking him. When he managed to regain a bit of control, he turned back and said, "Good morning, Jamaica."

Gesturing toward his T-shirt with my empty fork, I said, "I see you believe in truth in advertising."

He glanced down at his shirt which read "My brain is giving me the silent treatment today."

"Ha, ha." Focusing on Callahan, he added, "Your girl is hilarious."

"I'm not his girl."

"Yeah, you are," Hotshot said.

Ignoring his nonsense, I continued. "I accidentally fell asleep here last night when my friends disappeared on me."

"We'll discuss your confusion later," Callahan said. "When we don't have an audience."

I glanced at his friends whose eyes followed the conversation between us like a tennis ball during a match. When my gaze found his again, his brow raised in challenge while a hint of desire lurked in his eyes.

His girl? What the hell was he talking about?

I guess my lack of immediate response gave his roommates the green light to gather their own plates and utensils since the show was apparently over. The two of them crowded around the table and wasted no time mounding eggs, bacon, and toast on their plates. Good thing I dished up my plate before they arrived. In a few short minutes, and without conversation, breakfast concluded. Only half a piece of toast remained on the plate as well as the eggs and toast I was still eating. I was normally a slow eater, but Callahan's words swirling in my head had slowed me down even more than usual.

Three pairs of eyes stared at me and then at my plate. "What?"

"Are you going to finish that?" Bax asked, his tone hopeful.

"I planned to, yes."

"Oh." He conveyed a world of disappointment in that one syllable.

"Just because I like to taste my food rather than vacuum it up like an industrial-size machine doesn't mean I don't want to finish it." I pointed to the toast still on the plate in the middle of the table. "That's up for grabs."

"But it's better if it has some eggs on top." Bax gave me puppy-dog eyes as he slowly reached a hand toward my plate.

I stabbed that sneaky hand with my fork. "Make more eggs then. I'm eating the ones on my plate."

"Ouch!" Rubbing his hand, he addressed Hotshot who was cracking up. "Why do you have to like a feisty one?"

Callahan caught my eye. "Because she's fun."

Chapter Fourteen

Callahan

AS I PULLED into the horseshoe drive in front of Jamaica's dorm, I wished for the hundredth time that I didn't have to go to film this morning. While the coaches would certainly praise us more than ride our asses after our performance yesterday, I'd rather have stayed home, let my girl sleep in, and shared a leisurely breakfast with her instead of that embarrassingly rushed event we'd left a few minutes ago.

"Thanks for the ride, Hotshot." Without looking at me, she unclipped her seat belt and opened the door. "You didn't have to make me breakfast, but I appreciate it."

"Don't I get a kiss goodbye?"

"Callahan." The way she sounded out my name implied I should know better than to ask.

"Jamaica." I sounded out her name to remind her I wanted that kiss. Emphasizing my request, I slipped a hand into her curls and deliberately brushed the pad of my finger along the shell of her ear.

She grasped my wrist but didn't resist

when I gently pulled her toward the middle of the seat in the cab of my truck.

When our mouths were only a breath apart, I whispered, "Thanks for coming to see me play. And for coming to the party." I brushed a kiss over her lips, and I swear a shock of electricity leaped between us.

A tiny gasp escaped her, telling me she felt it too. As I increased the pressure, her hand slipped from my wrist to the side of my jaw. Accepting that invitation, I tasted her lips with the tip of my tongue. Giving me what I wanted, she opened her pretty mouth and let me in. In a flash the kiss went from a chaste "see ya later" to "fuck, I can't get enough of your hot, sweet mouth." I plowed my fingers into her mass of curls, holding her head with one hand while I gripped her hip with the other. One soft palm cradled the side of my face while the other clung to the top of my shoulder. Our tongues played a spirited game of tag that made me wish I could fool around with her all day.

From some distant place a car horn honked. Only when we came up for air on a series of short, lippy kisses, did the sound intensify, alerting me it was coming from directly behind us. Jamaica straightened up so fast she almost fell out of the open passenger door.

Wide eyes stared at me. "That should never have happened." On a whisper I think was supposed to be to herself, she added, "Why does this always happen with him?"

"Like I told you before, this was always going to happen, Island Girl." With a grin, I tugged one of her curls and let it spring back with the others. "See you tomorrow in class."

The guy behind me blared his horn again, and I flipped him the bird through my back window.

"Callahan." She gritted my name through her teeth, her eyes on my upturned finger. "I'm already doing the walk of shame. Don't make it worse."

"Zero shame, Jamaica." When she tossed me a look, I added, "You're too classy for that. Trust me."

That stopped her. She blinked and a tiny smile tugged up the corner of her lips. "See you tomorrow, Hotshot."

She slipped out of my truck, shut the door, and sashayed into her dorm, throwing me a wave over her head. There was absolutely zero shame in Little Miss Super-Cool's walk. Laughing, I put my truck in gear and rolled out of the drive.

Ten minutes later I arrived at the practice facility in a great mood. I was also a few minutes early. Double bonus. I'd scored a sizzling-hot goodbye kiss from a girl who intrigued me in a way no other girl ever had, and my early arrival for film meant earning brownie points from the coaches. Breezing through the front door, I waved hello to the equipment manager and headed straight for the film room.

At MSC, Wildcat football ruled. The administration and staff treated the players like kings. The film room was more a movie theater than a practice space, right down to the cupholders in the seats big enough to comfortably accommodate a 350 pound lineman. An array of fruit waited on a back table, and I snagged a banana and a cup of pineapple chunks on my way to my usual seat.

Early in my career I'd learned the players who stood out on the team stood out first in the locker room, leading by example. That meant no hiding in the back for any aspect of practice, including watching film. After a bad game, sitting in the front of a film session put a guy square in a coach's sights and wasn't any fun at all. Conversely, after playing a great game—and scoring the winning touchdown—sitting in the front meant having all the positive attention. I smiled to myself as I set my pineapple cup in the cupholder and peeled my banana.

As I took my first bite, naughty fantasies starring a certain curly-haired brunette flashed through my head, and I almost choked. Finn announced his presence with a solid smack in the middle of my back as he took the seat next to mine.

"What the fuck, dude?" I demanded when I regained my breath.

"You were dying. I brought you back to life." He smirked. "You're welcome."

The heavenly aroma of coffee wafted from a to-go cup he placed in his cupholder. "You happen to bring two of those?" I asked.

"Uh, no." A sarcastic crinkle of his brow punctuated his response. "You left the house with plenty of time to pick up your own, so why didn't you?" His eyes gleamed with an unholy light. "Too busy making out with your girl?"

"I took Jamaica back to her dorm. There wasn't a coffee shop en route." Not that I'd cared about coffee at the time. Now after only about four hours of shut-eye, I wished I had some to ensure I stayed awake through three hours of dissecting yesterday's game.

"She's not your usual type."

"Meaning?"

"You usually go for blondes with long legs. Like Tory Miller."

The mention of that girl's name turned the sweet pineapple in my mouth sour. "That jersey chaser is one hundred percent *not* my type. Is that why you keep inviting her over, because you think I need help hooking up with her?"

He shrugged. "You're always kinda weird around her, so I thought maybe you actually liked her." His eyes darted to a door at the front of the room where Coach Ellis and his staff were filing in.

"She's all yours, man. But I'd think twice about hooking up with that one if I were you."

"Yeah? Why is that?"

"Tory Miller is a calculating little bitch. I'd hate to see you in a jam over that girl." I finished off my fruit and was debating grabbing more when Coach spotted us.

"You two are early." He fist-bumped each of us. "Does this mean you used common sense and didn't spend last night drunk?"

"Nah. We were drunk," Finn stupidly admitted. "But our mad skills extend off the field too, Coach. Superman wishes he had our strength." Flexing his bicep, he grinned.

I couldn't elbow him to shut him up without being obvious.

"You too, O'Reilly?" Coach asked with a shrewd narrowing of his eyes.

"I switched to water fairly early in the evening, sir."

"Don't give him any credit, Coach. He was trying to impress a girl." Finn laughed when I gave in and slapped him upside the head.

Coach grimaced. "Ah, Jesus. I thought you were smarter than that."

"In 'Han's defense, you should see this girl. She's got sweet—"

"Do not finish that sentence, Finn," I growled.

Coach smirked.

"—curls. It was all I could do not to reach over and sproing them during breakfast." He made a tugging gesture like he had one of Jamaica's curls between his fingers.

My fist found his thigh and he yelped, but at least he shut his damn mouth.

"Make sure you focus on what's important, O'Reilly. We have a real shot at the National Championship this year, but it will only happen if all of you"—Coach glanced in Finn's direction—"keep your eyes on the prize."

In unison we said, "Yes, Coach."

With his laptop tucked under his arm, he headed up the aisle to the projection box.

Loud laughter preceded the running backs, Johnson and Taylor, as they entered the room, followed by the shuffling of heavy feet, which meant Dally, our all-conference center, was on his way in. Within a few minutes of their arrival, most of the rest of team had filled the room in various states of awake.

Bax and Danny slid into the row behind us. Danny leaned forward and poked me in the shoulder. "Are the rumors true? You're hooking up with someone?"

Making a quarter-turn in my seat, I shot him the stink-eye.

His brows waggled as he grinned at me. "From the expression on your face, I'd say the rumors are true. You gonna bring her around when the house isn't full of rowdy, drunk-ass people so I can meet her too?"

"What the fuck is wrong with you guys? You act like you've never seen me with a girl before."

"That's not it," Bax said. "We've never seen you make breakfast for one before." He turned to Danny. "Plus, the kitchen was spotless when we came downstairs. 'Han even mopped it, and it wasn't his turn." Returning his attention to me, he added, "Thanks, man. I owe you one."

"It's fine with me if you assholes don't make a big deal out of me getting to know Jamaica."

"So that's what the kids are calling it these days, huh?" Danny asked.

The guy was our age, but his four years in the military before he started classes this fall gave him the idea he was our elder. Most of the time, he did act older. I would have appreciated if now were one of those times.

"Okay, ladies, finish grabbing your food and find your seats. Film starts in one minute," Coach Ainsworth called out.

I checked my phone. 9:59 a.m. Our coaches lived for punctuality.

Last call gave me an out with my roommates, so I bounced out of my chair and headed to the food, grabbing another cup of pineapple and one of melons, and returned to my seat right as the opening kickoff appeared onscreen. For the next hour, we studied what we'd played right during the game against the Bulldogs. The high-fives were flying along with "atta boys" and "fuckin' A's" as we congratulated ourselves on our prowess.

After a five-minute break, we came back to enjoy our screw-ups, of which there were surprisingly few considering how evenly we matched the Bulldogs and how close the game had been. Still, the two key blocks I missed had irritated me when I'd missed them and thoroughly pissed me off when I watched myself miss them on the big screen.

"How could you have read that inside linebacker better, O'Reilly?" Coach Wiley, our offensive coordinator asked.

"I misheard Patty's call, so I didn't shift like I should have. I stepped left when I should have paid attention when the outside backer put his weight on his inside foot." Turning to Mick Patterson, our QB, I said, "Sorry for letting him through on that one, Patty."

Patterson nodded, a smirk lifting the corner of his mouth. He had avoided a sack on that play by tossing the ball into a team meeting on the sidelines. We lost a down but no yards. Plus, we both knew I made up for letting that linebacker through when I caught the pass that padded the hell out of Patty's stats for the game—not that Coach Wiley would see that as a win.

After dissecting offense and defense, we switched over to special teams, and I kinda zoned out as thoughts of Jamaica Winslow filled my head. When I'd come back to my room a lot later than I intended after I left her, I discovered her curled up in a ball on the edge of the bed, fast asleep. I nudged her shoulder and told her to wake up, but she waved a sleepy hand in my direction and rolled over. With her sweater riding up the way it was, she didn't look comfortable, and I knew from experience that sleeping in jeans was not great. So I took it upon myself to help her be comfortable.

She muttered something incoherent when I told her I was going to take off her jeans. When I undid the fly and pushed them down over her hips, revealing pretty white lace bikini panties, my cock twitched in anticipation. But I ignored it. Sitting beside her, I lifted her torso into my arms and tugged her sweater over her head. That sexy satiny camisole showed off her gorgeous rack, but I forced my eyes from lingering the way they wanted to. When she let out a sleepy protest but still didn't wake up, I had to chuckle. The girl apparently was a hard sleeper. I tugged the covers down and slid her under them, then undressed down to my boxers and slipped in behind her, spooning her close. In seconds I was out.

When she woke up to discover us in bed together, I was as surprised as she was at the state of my dick. I had no idea I could have the mother of all hard-ons while sound asleep. Then again, I'd never fallen asleep snuggled up with a woman as sexy as Jamaica before either. If not for early film today, I might have broken my three-dates-before-sex rule for her.

As it was, when my alarm went off at stupid o'clock and I dragged ass away from her and into the shower, I had to be especially quiet as I jerked off to fantasies of how sweet it would be to enter her from behind while we spooned in the middle of the night.

"'Han, pay attention," Finn hissed with an elbow to my ribs.

I blinked and readjusted myself in my seat as Coach Wiley said, "Those pancake blocks you laid on the D-end were textbook, O'Reilly. Yours too, Elliot," he said to our all-purpose fullback.

"Thanks, Coach."

"All right, that's it for today. Coach Larkin will see all your shiny faces in the weight room at 6:30 a.m. sharp tomorrow morning."

After the way my roommates worked me over at the start of film, I was glad I'd driven to the facility alone. Then Bax invited himself to join me for the drive home, reminding me it was our week to buy groceries. At least he let me up about Jamaica. Sort of.

"I was serious last night about you helping me meet someone hot like your girl," he said as he strapped himself in.

"Take an English class," I said. "Maybe don't hang out with Finn and the jersey chasers."

"Jesus, I thought you'd give me some useful tips."

I shot him a side-eye.

"I mean, shit, I still want to get laid."

That cracked me up. "Make up your mind, dude." As we rolled up to the store, I said, "Do you have the list?"

"Nah. I thought you did."

"Guess we're making it up as we go."

CHAPTER FIFTEEN

Jamaica

THE GIGGLING FRESHMEN who followed me into the lobby of the dorm upended my attempt to sneak past the front desk unnoticed.

"Jamaica." One of them trilled my name. "Was that Callahan O'Reilly you were kissing?"

"You're so lucky," another one added in a dreamy voice.

"Hey, Jamaica, didn't you leave here yesterday morning in that exact same outfit?" Chessly called out from behind the desk, mischief dancing in her eyes.

Flipping her a discreet finger, I said, "I thought we were friends," and kept walking.

She slipped out of the side door, intercepting me as I headed down the hall. Falling into step with me, she grinned. "Spill it, babe. I want all the juicy deets behind your first ever walk of shame."

Glancing over my shoulder, I clocked the two freshmen walking close behind us and nodded to my friend. Chess linked her arm

through mine and subtly increased our pace. In two minutes she'd hustled me to my room. After I let us in, she threw herself into my reading chair and waved her hand at my clothes. "Explain this and why you were kissing Callahan O'Reilly in the front seat of a pickup a few minutes ago."

I dropped to my bed, toed off my boots, and threw myself back on the mattress. "I don't have a clue." Turning my head on my pillow, I caught her eye. "He gave Axel, Drake, and me tickets to yesterday's game as a dare after I told him I'd never seen one. After the game, Axel, Drake, and I went to Stromboli's. Our pizza had just arrived to our table when Callahan appeared as if by magic, as though Axel and Drake had conjured him with their fangirling over his play in the game. He slid in beside me, and for the rest of the night, he stayed right by my side."

"You didn't spend the night at the bar, so what happened after Stromboli's?"

"A party at his house—one he'd mentioned after our last study session. At the time I thought the invite was for his friend who showed up to use the study room after us. Turns out, he meant it for me and for me to extend it to Axel and Drake." I blew a breath at my curls. "Somewhere in the evening I lost those two, and the next thing I knew, I was waking up in Callahan's bed."

Her eyes took up her entire face. "You slept with Callahan O'Reilly?" She fanned her face with both hands. "Oh, babe, I knew you were lying when you said you didn't think about him, but then you went and broke all the rules."

"No, I did not. We *slept*. That's it. He was a complete gentleman." Even though she was one of my closest friends, she didn't need to know the rest.

"Which absolutely explains the hot kiss in the front seat of his truck." She smirked. "From where I was sitting, it looked like you climbed right into his lap and made yourself at home."

A long sigh escaped me. "I don't know what to do, Chess. We're paired up for the whole semester in Dair's class. Both of us want to ace the project, which is good. What's bad is this bizarre attraction I have for him. One he reciprocates."

"Come again? One of the absolute hottest guys on campus is interested in you and that's a bad thing?" She slid down in the chair. "What is wrong with you?"

Turning on my side, I propped my head on my palm and returned her stare. "He's a football player with an entire entourage of sorority pledges following him everywhere he goes. From the way she acts around him, he had something going with Tory Miller at some point."

Chessly wrinkled her nose in disgust.

"He's a *player*, Chess." Yet even as I uttered those words, a little voice in the back of my mind contradicted me.

"You spend your time studying, working, or doing some campus community service project. It's perfectly fine for you to have some fun." She winked. "Especially when that fun comes in a six-foot-five package of solid muscle and heart-stopping gorgeousness."

"Are you serious right now?"

"As a heart attack. If someone like Callahan O'Reilly paid me the kind of attention he pays you, I'd soak up every last drop." She bounced up from the chair. "Now, grab a shower, change your clothes, and meet me in the lobby in an hour."

"What's in an hour?"

"Our planning meeting for fall dorm relays." With a grin, she added, "After your wild evening, it must have slipped your mind." She opened the door and stood half in and half out of my room. "Good thing I have your back."

I wrinkled my nose at her, her answering laughter echoing in my room after she closed the door.

Not once during my Hotshot-filled weekend had I thought

about work, school, or my programming responsibilities in the dorm. But when Chessly reminded me about our meeting, thoughts of all three crashed down on me. My plan had been to finish writing my paper for my Women and the Law history class before I went to the planning meeting because I had the late afternoon shift at the sweet shop. Now I could look forward to burning the midnight oil because I'd spent the better part of the morning in Callahan's bed, followed by a weirdly fun breakfast with his roommates.

One plus from upending my meticulously planned schedule was that now I'd have no time to think about the wickedly hot kiss he'd laid on me before he drove away.

After the short night following a long evening of finishing my paper, my alarm blared at way-too-early o'clock. It didn't help my mood that the first thing I thought of when I dragged myself from beneath the covers was Callahan O'Reilly. After I'd wasted what little sleep I'd had dreaming of him and that kiss, I couldn't believe I was looking forward to seeing him in class.

Everyone else's Monday must have started the same way mine did because the line for coffee stretched to the back of the Union. Checking my phone, I calculated the time it would take to race to the coffee hut near the gym, grab a cup of liquid energy, and still make it to class on time. I had a better than even chance of snagging a brew if I hit the gym than if I stayed in the tortoise-slow line at the Union.

My decision made, I took off for the gym at a sprint, which was quite a feat for a non-athlete with twenty pounds of books and other necessities strapped to her back. I was sure I looked ridiculous with my hair bouncing in rhythm with my backpack against my body, but I was on a mission with no time to care.

When I reached the coffee kiosk, only three people separated me from my lovely brew. My breath sawed in and out of my lungs as I planted my hands on my hips and bent at the waist.

Behind me, a deep voice I recognized all too well, said, "You'll catch your breath quicker if you stand tall and put your hands on your head."

I stood up and spun so fast I almost lost my balance, but not before I caught Callahan's eyes lingering where my ass had been sticking out from beneath my pack. Shooting him a narrow-eyed glare, I replied, "Is that so?" It would have sounded as tough as I'd intended if not for the breathiness from my sprint across campus.

"Hello, Island Girl." The smile stretching his lips said he was all kinds of happy to see me. When he deepened his voice that way, coupled with that killer smile, he stole all my indignation at him for staring at my ass.

I couldn't help the grin that twitched at the corner of my mouth. "Good morning, Hotshot."

"Is there a reason you sprinted to this coffee hut rather than grab your usual cup at the Union?" The playful expression in his eyes told me he already had his answer.

"Half of the college was in line at the Union this morning." Responding to his dubious arched brow, I added, "Seriously. When I arrived, I ended up standing by the windows at the back, and after five minutes I'd only shuffled forward one person." I tossed my hair away from my forehead with the back of my hand. "I can't face Dr. Dair's class without a shot of caffeine, and we all know how he feels about students showing up late."

He stuffed his hands into the front pockets of his low-slung jeans, briefly drawing my eyes to his impressive-looking package before I hastily blinked them back to his face.

"Huh. Here I thought you hustled over here because you couldn't wait to see me."

"Miss? What can I get you?" the barista interrupted.

It took me a second to tear my eyes from Hotshot's. *Why had*

I chosen this coffee spot so close to the gym? The barista's raised brow teased me from my thoughts. "I need a triple-shot flat white, please," I said as I shrugged off my backpack and swung it around so I could pull out my wallet.

Callahan covered my hand with his. "I got this."

His big warm hand on mine sent tiny ripples over my skin, momentarily distracting me.

At his touch, my voice caught. "You don't have to buy me a coffee."

"I want to." Turning his attention to the barista, he said, "Add a mocha grandè to the order, please." He fished his wallet from the back pocket of his jeans, extracted a card, and paid for our coffee.

"Thank you," I said as we stepped aside to wait for our drinks.

For a long moment, he gazed at me with a closed-mouth smile. I pushed my hair off my forehead again and huffed out, "Why are you looking at me like that?"

Those gorgeous sea-blue eyes of his twinkled. "Like what? Like I'm happy to see you?"

I furrowed my brow. "Why are you happy to see me?"

He took a step closer, leaned down, and whispered, "Second-hottest kiss of my life. I haven't stopped thinking about it since I dropped you at your dorm yesterday."

My face heated even as a shiver stole over me.

Callahan chuckled. "Good to know I get to you too, Island Girl."

Another shiver stole over me, followed by tingles rippling through me at the heat in his gaze. For a second, I wondered— worried—he might try a repeat of that kiss right here on the sidewalk in front of crowds of people making their way to class. My eyes strayed to his full lower lip and sculpted upper one and a tiny sigh escaped.

The barista called out our drinks.

Mercifully, Callahan let the whole kissing topic drop as we headed to class. "We had a good film session yesterday, and after the way we played the Bulldogs on Saturday, Coach is backing down on practice a bit this week."

I glanced up at him. "Which means…?" I asked and sipped my first taste of fortification for the morning.

"We can slide in an extra study session tomorrow night."

The second sip of coffee threatened to go down the wrong way. Was he suggesting we spend extra time together this week?

He went on as though I hadn't choked on his words. "I've been thinking more about Anne's inability to stand up to Lady Russell and how her good manners are a direct contrast to Lady Russell's poor ones."

"Wait. Have you already finished reading *Persuasion*?" My voice might have squeaked on the question. "Or did you get bored and decide to switch books?"

With an indulgent shake of his head, he said, "I thought we already established that I'm an Austen fan. I finished *Mansfield Park* after class on Friday and read most of *Persuasion* yesterday after film." At my incredulous stare, he added, "I needed something to do to keep my mind off a certain hot brunette who lights me on fire every time she lets me kiss her."

"Hotshot—"

He preempted what I was going to say when he wrapped his free hand around mine, lacing our fingers together. Then he picked up the pace, and I had to double-time to keep up with his long strides.

"Come on, Jamaica. We don't want to be late."

I wanted to be annoyed by his regular references to kissing and how he helped himself to my hand as if we were an item or something. But to my growing consternation, I discovered I liked the feel of his warm, calloused fingers entwined with mine. Knowing that he couldn't stop thinking about kissing me leveled the field between us too, showing me I wasn't the only one affected by our improbable chemistry.

Axel's eyes almost bugged out of his head when he saw us walk up the steps together where he was waiting for me outside Creston Hall. "You've been holding out on me, sweetheart," he said for my ears only.

"Did you even try to look for me the other night before you and Drake left the party?" I demanded.

He fell into step with us. "You two looked like you were having a blast dancing together, so we figured 'Han would make sure you made it home."

"You could have asked."

At my response, Callahan tightened his hand around mine. When I glanced up at him, he shook his head, clarifying what Axel and Drake had apparently understood: from the minute we split up outside Stromboli's that night, I was with Callahan. The current hand-holding only solidified that notion with my best friend, and once again I was scrambling to keep up with the unspoken code between men.

Chapter Sixteen

Jamaica

I WAS WORKING AT a study table near the windows across the hall from the café in the Union when Callahan tossed his backpack in one of the empty chairs with a chuckle. "You don't trust yourself not to climb into my lap when we're studying, huh?"

Narrowing my eyes, I retorted, "I don't trust *you* not to initiate shenanigans." With a shrug, I returned my attention to the books I'd laid out on the table in front of me rather than stare at his effortless hotness. I swear, in the past I'd never paid one iota of attention to any guy who always wore a ball cap backward, but the style gave him a boyish sexiness I had a hard time ignoring. Never mind the way his chest filled out his Wildcats hoodie or those low-slung jeans that emphasized his muscular thighs and tight ass. "Plus, we have a lower probability of being interrupted by your fan club if we meet here rather than at the library."

He dropped himself into the chair opposite mine and pulled his iPad from his pack. "For the record, I enjoy shenanigans with you." The wicked gleam in his eyes set a full battalion of butterflies loose in my belly.

Then the toe of his shoe slid along the outside of my calf, and I shoved both feet under my chair so fast I nearly lost my balance and face-planted the table.

His rich laughter played over me. "You can pretend all you want, Island Girl, but we both know you have a thing for me."

"Careful with that ego, Hotshot. Wouldn't want your head to get stuck in the double doors on your way out of here tonight."

Dancing eyes met mine. "I'm not worried about my ego."

Somehow we managed to do some work in spite of Callahan's repeatedly finding ways to touch me even with a table between us. Two hours flew by as our project started taking shape in a way that excited both of us. It still surprised me how much he genuinely seemed to love classic British literature as much as I did. That and the fact that if he didn't have an eidetic memory, he had the next closest thing. How he could read a book once, especially one as dense in detail as *Mansfield Park*, and have complete recall of events stunned me. I had to read a book at least twice, usually three times, to cement all those details in my head.

After we called it a night and packed up our books, I headed to the front doors of the Union. When I reached the bottom of the stairs, he was right behind me.

"You don't have to walk me home."

"Yeah, I do. It's after dark."

"It's two blocks, Hotshot. On a well-lit sidewalk through the heart of campus. I walk this route by myself all the time."

A cloud passed over his features. "Tonight, you don't have to." He had that same stubborn expression as the last time he walked me home.

With a nonchalant shrug, I said, "Suit yourself."

Shoving his hands into his pockets, he fell into step beside me. "You coming to the Homecoming game this weekend?"

"I wasn't planning on it."

"But you are now, right?" An almost vulnerable hopefulness colored his tone.

"I think it's too late to get tickets."

"It's never too late to get tickets when you know the right people." He grinned.

"Well, then, I might go to the game. What's Finn's number? 94?" I smirked.

He rolled his eyes. "You're hilarious, Island Girl."

In minutes, we were standing outside the lobby to my dorm. "Thanks for walking me home. Even though it wasn't necessary," I couldn't help but add.

"You gonna invite me in?"

I furrowed my brow. "Why would I do that?"

Rocking on his heels, he said, "I invited you to my place. Thought you'd return the favor."

Shifting my backpack higher on my shoulder, I said, "You invited me to a party at your place. Totally different deal."

Wicked mischief glittered in his sea-blue eyes. "I bet you're too embarrassed for me to see how messy you are."

My brows did their best to meet my hairline. "Excuse me?"

He didn't even slow down. "Coffee cups overflowing your trash, dirty jeans and socks piled askew under your study chair, a pair of lace panties haphazardly flung over your desk lamp where you tossed them at the dirty clothes basket and missed. The covers mounded in the middle of your bed from you reading there right up until you had to sky out to class this morning."

"You have one hell of an imagination."

"From your response, I'm pretty close, yeah?"

"You think I'm a slob?" My voice might have risen an octave with the question.

His shrug was noncommittal. "Since you won't invite me to your room, I have nothing to go on except for my imagination."

"For the record, your imagination sucks."

Slowly, his brow lifted, giving him a rakish expression. "So you *are* a messy roomkeeper."

Crossing my arms over my chest, I let a ghost of a smile dance over my lips. "Haphazardly? Askew? You're using some quarter-size words there, Hotshot."

"What?" He threw a hand over his chest in mock indignation. "I don't skip class, and I study. Stop trying to deflect attention from the cyclone that is your room you don't want me to see."

"You are such a pain in my ass," I growled. "Do you know that?" I spun on my heel and stomped toward the front door. When he didn't fall into step with me as usual, I stopped and turned to see him standing on the sidewalk with his hands in his pockets. "Well? Are you coming in or not?"

I couldn't help but return the smile that broke over his face as he jogged over to me. The front desk clerk did a double take when I waved to her with Callahan O'Reilly in tow. When I keyed us into my room and flipped on the lights, a low whistle sounded from his lips.

"Whoa. Not at all what I thought. Did you clean this morning in anticipation of inviting me over tonight?"

He met my half-hearted punch to his bicep with a low chuckle.

"This is how my room always looks, you jerk."

Glancing around the small space, his eyes fixed on the study lamp on my desk. "Huh. Not even a stray pair of panties here." His gaze found mine. "I'm disappointed, Island Girl." The naughty expression accompanying his words intensified the second he spied the recliner in the corner behind the door. "Exactly what do you get up to in this?" He stepped over to the chair and made himself comfortable in it.

My recliner was big enough for me to curl up in with a blanket and a book. When Callahan sat in it, his football-player-size frame dwarfed it.

"That's my reading chair."

"Of course it is." He waggled his brows, and I shook my head.

Tossing my backpack on the floor beside my desk, I spun my desk chair around to face him and sat down. His playful demeanor evanesced as he leaned forward and held my eyes with his. "You're a junior in college. Why are you still living in the dorms with all their rules and restrictions?" Turning his head, he glanced around the tiny space. "And no room for much of anything."

"One of the perks of being an RA is free room and board. It means I only have to work a few hours a week at the sweet shop to pay for incidentals so I can go to class and study the rest of the time."

"You're smart, Jamaica. You don't need to study during every waking hour of the day."

Before I realized what I'd done, I'd grabbed the seat of my chair on either side of my hips and rocked back and forth. Stopping mid-movement, I said, "I can't lose my scholarship."

His serious expression did little to eradicate the fears this conversation engendered. "That's not going to happen."

"It will if I don't stay on top of my classes." Staring into his eyes, I willed him to understand.

For a long minute, we didn't say anything. Then he extended his hands to me, palms up. Without thinking, I set my hands in his. His hands enveloped mine as he gently rubbed his thumbs over my skin, sending cascading shivers over my arms.

"It's called balance. I'll help you work on it."

A long beat passed. Then in one fluid movement, he was on his feet, tugging me up with him. Cupping my face in his palms, he said, "I have to be in the weight room at dark-thirty, so I'd better head out."

He lowered his head and butterflied a kiss over my mouth. Without my permission, my fingers slipped through the belt loops of his jeans and I held onto his hips. On the second pass, he mashed his lips to mine, the pressure exactly what I needed, yet I craved more. The faint outdoorsy scent of his shampoo tickled my nose. That fragrance drew me in, and I pulled him closer.

His tongue flicked out along the seam of my lips, asking for an invitation I was already desperate to give. Tiny moans and whimpers escaped my throat with the hot glide of his tongue over mine. For reasons I'd never figure out, this man's kisses turned me inside out.

He slid one hand into my hair at the back of my head, holding me where wanted me while his other hand trailed over my shoulder and down my spine to wrap around my back and hold me tight. My arms came around his waist, and I clung to him while his kiss sent my heartbeat into overdrive, a heavy rhythm that echoed low in my belly.

The whole world could have crashed around us in the space of that kiss, and I wouldn't have paid one second of attention to it. I couldn't make sense of how Callahan O'Reilly could make me forget everything I'd worked so hard, sacrificed so much, for. But when he slowly backed out of the kiss with tiny nips at my lower lip and hard little pecks across my mouth, I didn't want to stop.

"Yeah, I thought we'd enjoy our good-night kiss more in your room than in the lobby or on the street, and I was right." His eyes danced as he rested a hand on the back of my thigh.

Only then did I catch on that I'd started climbing him. Mortified, I slid off him fast, but when I attempted to step away, he held me close.

"Not so fast, Island Girl. Don't pretend you weren't as into that kiss as I was. I gave you exactly what you've been asking for all evening."

"*What* are you talking about?"

A grin tipped the corner of his too-gorgeous-for-my-own-good mouth. "You haven't been able to keep your eyes off my lips since I showed up at the Union."

"Watch yourself, Hotshot. Your ego is showing."

His grin widened. "You can tell your fibs to other people, but I saw where your eyes went."

Pushing against him, I tried to pull away, but he held me close. "It's okay, Jamaica. I couldn't stop looking at your pretty mouth either. As a matter of fact, I'm surprised we got any work done with how much I was thinking about kissing you." Leaning in, he stole another kiss, so I stole one from him.

"This"—he gestured between us—"is only starting, but I can tell we're going to have a good time."

"Nothing is starting between us. I don't date jocks."

Glancing down at where our bodies still touched with our arms wrapped around each other, he grinned. "Too late." He patted me on the ass. "We're already dating."

I stepped out of his arms. "We are *not* dating. We're study buddies because Dair's TA has a warped sense of humor. That's all."

"Study buddies." He snorted. "That totally explains the way we both go up in flames every time we kiss—"

I might have growled at him.

"—and you spending the night in my bed after our second date."

My eyes flew to the ceiling. "This is not happening."

"Sure it is. And it's going to be a fun ride." He opened the door to my room and reached back with his other hand to snag mine, lacing our fingers together. "I may have been thinking about other things today"—he waggled his brows—"and dropped some easy balls in practice. I need to be on time for weights in the morning. Come on and walk me out."

He tugged me through the door and into the hall, then he reached behind the door to make sure the knob remained unlocked. At my questioning raised brow, he said, "Wouldn't want you to have to call room service to get back in. Might be embarrassing, you being an RA and all."

I sent my eyes to heaven and shook my head. But I was secretly touched that he'd made sure to save me a second trip to the lobby for the master key to unlock my door.

A giggly group of freshmen girls burst through the front doors to the dorm right as we arrived in the lobby. Their titters abruptly stopped when they caught sight of Callahan, who didn't seem to notice them at all. He leaned in and whispered in my ear, "Bet you dream of me all night."

I snorted. "You are so full of yourself."

His eyes glittered over the top of my hand, which he'd raised to his lips. "Don't worry, babe. I'll be dreaming about you all night too." The lingering kiss he planted in the middle of my palm sent tingles straight up my arm. Letting me go, he said, "See you in the morning."

With athletic grace he easily stepped around the knot of staring freshmen and out into the night. I watched him walk away while his kiss remained warm on my skin.

As I turned to head back to my room, one of the freshmen broke from the group. "That was Callahan O'Reilly, wasn't it? He's even dreamier up close. Are you dating him?"

"I wouldn't say we're dating, exactly," I hedged.

"Oh, then you won't mind if I go after him." A feral gleam came into her eyes—a cattiness I'd seen in the expressions of too many mean girls in my life.

Out of nowhere, the green-eyed monster reared its ugly head, and before I could stop them, the words were out of my mouth. "Sorry, Emma. Callahan doesn't date freshmen."

"What do you mean he doesn't date freshmen?" She flipped a long blonde lock over her shoulder. "From what I hear, he likes all the girls."

I crossed my arms over my chest. "Nope. Not freshmen. Too much drama, he says."

I had no idea if he dated freshmen or not, and now I was

putting words in his mouth. What was wrong with me? Emma's narrow-eyed stare didn't help. "'Scuse me, girls. I have a quiz to study for." Turning on my heel, I headed back to my room. All the while, Callahan's kisses lingered on my hand and my lips.

Chapter Seventeen

Callahan

AFTER FRIDAY'S PRACTICE, I powered through a shower, threw on my jeans and hoodie, and raced from the locker room. Finn caught up with me as I jogged across the parking lot to my truck.

"Hey, 'Han, what set your pants on fire?"

"I'm meeting Jamaica and some of her friends at Stromboli's before we head over to the bonfire." My duffel bag landed in the back seat with a thump.

Finn's bag landed on top of mine as he climbed in the passenger side.

"Sure, Finn, why don't you join us?" The sarcasm in my tone was completely lost on my roommate.

"Thanks, man." He settled into his seat and patted the dash in a "let's go" gesture. "Are Jamaica's friends as hot as she is?"

A laugh snorted out of me as we wheeled out of the parking lot. "Axel and Drake are into each other." I glanced over at him. "They're not exactly your type."

He crossed his arms over his chest and pouted. "Figures. On your advice, I gave up the jersey chasers—who, by the way, are always a sure thing—and now I'm literally the fifth wheel."

"I did you a solid with that advice. And you're the one who invited yourself to join us."

"Whatever."

As usual on a Friday night, Stromboli's was packed. But somehow Axel and Drake had snagged the football team's regular booth in the back. Jamaica sat between Axel and a blonde I didn't recognize. Drake held down the other side of the table. If I didn't know better, they were making sure my girl didn't bolt before I arrived.

With a relieved smile, I slipped a pair of game tickets into Axel's hand when he stood to open a space for me. "Thanks for making sure Jamaica didn't bail on me tonight." I glanced past him to where she chatted with her friend. "I know this isn't her thing, but seriously, dude, she can't go through college without experiencing the awesomeness that is Homecoming."

"Preaching to the choir, my man. I've tried to talk her into coming out with us for the bonfire for the past two years, and she always turned me down." He slanted a speculative grin my way. "Can't imagine what's changed this year."

Waggling my brows, I grinned at him.

"Hello, Callahan. What's the big deal about this bonfire tonight?" she asked as I slid into the spot Axel vacated.

"It's part of the celebration." I bumped her shoulder. "And it's fun." It had only been hours since I'd sat next to her in class, but I let my smile show her how happy I was to see her twice in the same day. "Hello, Jamaica. Who's your friend?"

A loud throat-clearing beside me reminded me I'd brought along a guest too.

"Sorry, Finn." Indicating the opposite side of the booth with

Axel and Drake, I said, "Have a seat. Axel, Drake, this is my roommate, Finn McCabe."

As they made room for him, Drake said with a grin, "Yeah, we know who he is."

Finn's brows shot up like a cartoon character.

Drake continued. "Only one of the best defensive ends MSC has ever recruited." He stuck his hand out. "Great to meet you."

Axel shook his hand next and smirked at Jamaica. "I truly love being your best friend. You introduce us to the most interesting people."

Her eye roll was impressive. "You're too easily entertained, Axel Benson."

For her ears only, I whispered, "I'd like to entertain you privately later."

She rewarded me with a full-body shiver that shot straight to my cock, leaving me half-hard. Distracting myself, I said, "Your turn. Who's your friend?"

"This is my other best friend, Chessly Clarke. She's the RA on third floor in our dorm." Turning to her friend, she said, "Chess, this is Callahan O'Reilly, and that's his roommate Finn."

Chess reminded me of a porcelain doll with her golden blonde hair, deep blue eyes, and perfect skin. Then she opened her mouth and shot that image straight to hell. Her gaze was directed at my roommate. "You're the one who hangs out with Tory Miller and her posse of mean girls, huh?" Turning to me, she said, "Did you get to pick your roommate, or does the coach do that for you?"

A dull red tinged Finn's cheeks, and I couldn't help but give him an I-told-you-so stare.

"Nice to meet you, Chessly." With a chuckle at Finn's expense, I added, "No, we aren't assigned roommates. But if you have attitude about this one, wait till you meet Bax."

As though I'd conjured him with his name, Bax sidled up to

our booth. Ignoring the fact six people already sat at a table for six, he said, "Hey, Finn, 'Han. Make some room, wouldja?"

"Nice shirt, Bax," Jamaica said.

After three years of living with the guy, I'd stopped paying attention to his T-shirts, but my lady's sardonic tone had me reading this one: "Dating apps should be like Carfax: you should get to consult the previous owner."

Bax glanced at his shirt and shrugged. "The truth is what it is." Seeming to clue in that the booth wasn't full of our teammates, his face lit up when he spied Chessly. "Hey, I'm Bax." He started to reach across Jamaica and me, remembered some manners, and waved instead. "Wyatt Baxter. And you are?"

"Not on dating apps," Chessly said.

Everyone but Bax cracked up.

Sliding my arm across Jamaica's shoulders, I said, "I like your friend already."

Finn took pity on Bax. "Pull up a chair and join us."

Bax grabbed an empty chair from a nearby table and took up the whole end of the booth with his broad shoulders and manspread. I shook my head. At this rate, he was going to need a lot more than a dating app to meet a girl.

Two servers arrived with two pitchers of beer and a mounded basket of wings. "Pizza is on the way. Anything else we can get you?"

Glancing at my uninvited roommates, I said, "Probably better double that pizza order. And we'll need another pitcher with that."

"On it."

I let my arm slide across the cushion to rest on Jamaica's shoulders and relaxed when a tiny sigh escaped her. She may pretend my action irritated her, but the way she melted a little into my side told a different story. Determined to stay in her good graces, I addressed her friend. "Chessly. That's a cool name. What's your major?"

She set her glass on the table and daintily wiped some beer foam from her lip with her napkin. "Physics."

"Oooh, you're hanging out with the smarties," Finn teased me.

"After having breakfast every morning with you Neanderthals"—I included Bax in my description—"I need mental stimulation."

"Is that what the kids are calling it these days?" Finn asked with a pointed glance at where my arm wrapped around Jamaica.

"What are you studying, Finn?" Chessly's question implied she thought he might be a basket-weaving major.

His eyes dropped to his plate of wings as he mumbled, "Bio-chem."

Bax slapped him on the shoulder. "Yeah, ole Finnegan here is going to discover the definitive cure for cancer."

I laughed. "Definitive, Bax? Did you just learn that word?"

Bax flipped me the bird, and Finn and I cracked up.

Axel rescued him. "What's your major, Bax?"

Drake answered for him. "Graphic design." Axel shot an incredulous stare at his boyfriend who shrugged and added, "He's in a few of my classes."

Bax nodded sagely. "I thought you looked familiar."

In the few minutes of our conversation, the mound of wings on the table had disappeared. With perfect timing, the pizzas arrived to replace them along with another pitcher of beer. As we enjoyed our meal, I whispered in Jamaica's ear. "You're uncharacteristically quiet."

Tilting her head, she side-eyed me. "So are you."

I squeezed her shoulder and reached for the nearest pitcher to refill our glasses. When I set hers back in front of her, I caught Chessly shooting Finn a narrow-eyed glare. That was when I heard the unwelcome pitch of Tory Miller's voice.

"Finn. You didn't say you'd be at Stromboli's before the bonfire."

Dark red tinged his cheeks as his shoulders tried to cover his ears. If he slunk any lower in the booth, he'd slide right off the seat.

"Oh, hi, Bax," she added as an afterthought.

He nodded. "Tory."

Then she spotted me, and her voice changed pitch again. Why some women thought the high giggly thing attracted men, I'd never understand. It grated like dragging a dead branch over glass. "Callahan. I've missed you at the library this week." She stuck out her hip and twirled a lock of her hair. This girl was such a cliché.

Beside me, Jamaica's soft body turned to granite.

At that moment, Tory caught sight of Jamaica then her eyes slid to Chessly. I stared in fascination as her entire demeanor changed from consummate flirt to catty bitch in a nanosecond.

"What in the world are you guys doing with this truck-stop trash?" she demanded.

Six pairs of eyes stared at her. The first person to recover was Chessly, but she spoke to the server who had arrived in the middle of the drama with our next pizza. "You might want to save your bouncer a fine and escort this person"—Chessly shot a glance past Tory to the group of girls standing behind her—"and her friends out of here before someone calls the cops on you guys for letting underage people in here."

Tory sputtered, "What are you talking about? We're all"—she gestured to her posse—"twenty-one. The bouncer checked our IDs." Her voice climbed an octave, and it was all I could do not to cover my ears.

Bax pushed his chair closer to Finn who was now crowding Axel who had Drake pushed into the corner.

Chessly's attention remained on the server. "Their IDs are all fake. Two of those girls live in our dorm, and I know for a fact they're freshmen. This one"—she pointed to Tory—"is a sophomore. Don't let the layers of makeup fool you. I don't think she's even twenty yet."

If looks could kill, the lasers of Tory's eyes would have crisped Chessly to a cinder.

"Chess," Jamaica hissed out of the side of her mouth.

I glanced at Finn who stared at Chessly with a stunned expression. When she remained calm in the face of Tory's fury, that expression turned to something that looked a whole lot like interest.

The group of four or five girls behind Tory blocked the servers trying to work the tables across from our booth. With their focus on their leader, they didn't move when someone asked them to. Like the sound of an avalanche rolling downhill, the grumbling increased to loud complaints from the people sitting at the blocked tables, but the girls didn't budge. It only took a couple of minutes for the bouncer to arrive and discover the problem.

When the server shook his head and didn't out Tory and her buddies, Chessly, said, "Hey, Steve. These girls are all underage no matter what their IDs say. Trust me."

"Is that right?" the bouncer drawled.

"She's stirring up trouble because she's jealous that the boys here"—Tory glanced around at my roommates and me—"would rather sit with my friends and me."

The bouncer wasn't convinced. "I need to see your ID, Miss."

Tory snorted a breath, tossed back her hair, and reached into the tiny purse hanging by a thin strap from her shoulder. Now that I thought about it, that purse was a tell. The women we spent time with—present company included—didn't generally carry purses. Freshmen, and apparently some sophomores, carried them though.

The bouncer pulled a penlight from his back pocket and shined it on Tory's ID. After turning it this way and that, he pushed at an edge with his fingernail and started peeling up the plastic. Huh. Next came a layer of paper with her vitals on it. Beneath that was another layer with her photo.

"You bought one of those overseas IDs, I see. Is your name actually Tory Miller?" the bouncer asked.

She tried to jerk her ID from his hand, but he raised it over his head and out of her reach. "You have no right to damage my property like that," she screeched as she pulled on his arm, which didn't move at all.

Unfazed by her antics, the guy said, "Miss, you and your friends will have to leave the bar immediately."

"But you can't—"

One of the bartenders joined the scene playing out in front of our booth. "Need some help, Steve?"

"I don't usually call the cops on women, but this banshee might change my mind."

Tory screeched again and stomped her feet in a tantrum. The sounds of people drinking, eating, and conversing stopped abruptly. A second later, so did her hissy fit. "You'll pay for this, Chessly Clarke. So will you, Jamaica Winslow. No one makes a fool of me and gets away with it."

With patronizing patience, Chessly said, "No one made a fool of you, Tory. You did that all by yourself."

"Miss," the bouncer said.

With a final toss of her hair, Tory flounced out of the bar. The eyes of every girl in her posse were the size of dinner plates as they stared at the bouncer, back at our table, and finally at her before they fell into step and followed her outside.

"Thanks for the heads-up, Chessly. I can't afford a seven-hundred-dollar fine for letting underage kids past the door." The bouncer gave her a tiny salute.

Chessly nodded back at him. "Anytime, Steve. See you in class on Monday."

A few minutes later, the server returned with a fresh pitcher. "On the house," he said as he set it in the middle of our table.

When he left, I stared hard at Finn. "Did you text her or something?"

He put his hands up. "No, I swear I didn't. I've been taking your advice and keeping my distance this last week." His eyes slid back to Chessly.

I leaned my forearms on the table. "So how did she know we were here? Especially since you invited yourself to join us."

Bax cleared his throat. "I might have responded to her text after I got here."

Cuffing him along the back of his head, I said, "Dumbass. All fall I've been telling you guys that girl and her friends are jailbait. Now do you believe me?" Both of them dropped their eyes to the table. Turning to Jamaica and Chessly, I asked, "How do you know her?"

"I was her RA last year. What a nightmare." Chessly sighed. "Growing up with her dad's money did that one no favors." She nudged Jamaica and grinned. "Your idea to glue her door shut with her in her room would have saved us all kinds of grief."

Giving her the big eyes, I said, "Whoa, Jamaica. I had no idea you had that in you."

"She has great ideas," Axel chimed in, "but she's smart enough not to implement them—anymore."

"Axel… " Jamaica warned.

"Especially after that time we filled Mrs. Stoker's desk drawer with exploding spiders sophomore year."

"What's this? You pranked your teacher? Now you have to tell us the story," I insisted.

Instead, she stuffed a massive bite of pizza in her mouth and chewed slowly.

Axel laughed. "Mrs. Stoker was only good at 'teaching' kids who already knew the material," he said with air quotes. "She was a rich girl who was 'giving back,' but she had nothing for those who struggled. Of course, that pissed J right off, so she started a little tutoring group during lunch."

"You instigated that as much as I did," Jamaica protested.

Axel ignored her. "After Stoker found out, she nitpicked every little thing Jamaica did in class. Somehow, we found out she was scared of spiders, so… ."

Jamaica glared at Axel.

"You can't leave us hanging like this," Bax whined.

"We were suspended for two days. But Stoker left our school and never came back, so it was worth it." Axel's eyes danced.

"You rebel, you." I grinned at my girl.

She shook her head. "Nope. I learned my lesson." To Chessly, she added, "But maybe we should have floured her room on some random Friday afternoon. It would have kept her busy cleaning it for the weekend at least." An impish grin played over her mouth as she reached for her beer.

I took the opportunity to whisper in her ear. "I like you even more now that I know what devious thoughts you have."

"Maybe you should be terrified," she shot back.

Oh yeah. I liked this girl.

CHAPTER EIGHTEEN

Jamaica

BY THE TIME we arrived at the field behind the stadium, the bonfire pep rally was in full swing. The cheerleaders and dance team performed to some pop song the band played. Behind them a giant bonfire lit up the night sky. Callahan made me promise to stick around long enough for him to meet back up with us after he did his football thing. But the night air had more winter than fall in it, and my leggings weren't keeping me warm.

Axel noticed me shivering and said, "Dancing with the band will warm you up." His eyes twinkled in the firelight.

"So will going back to the dorm and curling up in my recliner under a blanket," I muttered.

"I had the idea your boyfriend wants to you to stick around so he can warm you up." Drake smirked.

"I don't have a boyfriend," I insisted.

The three pairs of eyes staring back at me said I wasn't convincing.

Axel and Drake switched to Team Callahan after the first day he decided to crowd my space in class. But I couldn't believe Chessly had joined them.

"Et tu, Chess?"

"I spent the past hour sitting beside you in a crowded booth at Stromboli's while some football player drew patterns with his fingers on your shoulder, and you didn't shrug him off. That qualifies as something in my book," she said with a grin.

"You need to raise your standards, girlfriend," I huffed.

Yet I couldn't deny how even talking about Hotshot warmed me right up. Thoughts of his arm around me, such a casual, public claim, should have left me cold. But I couldn't lie to myself about how his body pressed along my side had me tingling all through dinner.

On some cue, the cheerleaders dropped out of their dance routine and disappeared behind the bonfire. A few minutes later, the drumline played a raucous cadence that had the band smartly forming into two lines. The cadence switched to the opening beats of the Wildcats fight song, and the cheerleaders ran up the middle of the line carrying a massive paper sign attached to a pair of two-by-fours. Someone in the art department spent more than a minute painting a perfect snarling Wildcat. Beneath it, stylized lettering read "Go! 'Cats! Go!"

When they reached the end of the line of band members—a pair of tuba players with the Wildcats logo stretched over the bells of their instruments—the cheerleaders stopped and held the sign taut. A massive cheer went up from the crowd as several members of the football team broke through the sign with the rest of the team behind them. One of the leaders carried a heavy-looking mallet painted gold, while three or four of the other leaders carried an effigy of a tiger painted in the colors of the Idaho Tigers, the Wildcats' opponents for the game.

The players wore their jerseys and raced for the stage set up in front of the roaring fire. Once the team filled the space, the coach stepped out in front of them. Even with a microphone, he had to encourage the crowd to quiet down in order to be heard.

"These boys have worked their asses to give you a good season," he shouted into the mic.

The crowd roared its approval.

"Now they need you to show up like you have been all year and cheer your hearts out." The crowd gave him a taste of tomorrow's excitement, which elicited a tiny grin from a man I had the notion didn't grin much. Then he sobered. "The Tigers are a tough program, and they're not going to roll over for us because it's our Homecoming. In fact, they'd like nothing better than to ruin our party. But we're not going to let that happen, are we, Wildcats?"

The players led the roars this time.

"That's right. What do you say, 'Cats fans?" he shouted.

"Go! 'Cats!" reverberated over the field behind the stadium.

He put a hand to his ear. "What did you say?"

"Go! 'Cats!"

Yelling into the mic, he asked again, "What did you say?"

"Go! 'Cats! Go!"

The chant went on and on until finally the players holding the effigy tossed it into the bonfire. When the flames engulfed the tiger, fireworks shot out of it. The crowd went bananas. As the cheerleaders and dance team took the stage to lead the crowd with their routines, the band played the fight song again. While they did their thing, the players exited the platform, and a minute later Callahan stood beside me.

"Admit it, Island Girl. This is fun." His eyes sparkled in the firelight.

"After all this fanfare, your team better deliver tomorrow, Hotshot."

His chin came up and his shoulders dropped back, his stance tall and proud. "Don't you worry about that, babe. How many touchdowns do you want me to score for you?"

"Cocky, much?" But I couldn't keep the grin off my face.

About then, Finn joined us, and I couldn't help but notice how he checked out Chessly who had her arm through Drake's to keep warm.

"You coming to the game tomorrow?" he asked us in general, but his focus keyed on my friend.

"We have tickets for great seats again, courtesy of your roommate." Axel's megawatt grin rivaled the light of the bonfire.

"You too?" he asked Chess.

"Nah. I took Jamaica's call weekend so she can leave the dorms to watch a certain player do his thing." She winked at me, and I wrinkled my nose back at her, eliciting a giggle at my expense.

Finn stuffed his hands in the pockets of his jeans. "That's a bummer. It's going to be a barnburner of a game. Shame you have to miss it."

She shrugged. "I can catch it on my computer if I feel like it."

The comical way he blinked at her said he couldn't believe she wouldn't "feel like" watching the Wildcats play.

The crowd surged around us and parted, letting a gust of frosty air swirl through. How Finn could stand there immune to the cold in nothing but his jersey and a pair of jeans was beyond me. I was already shivering, but that gust of wind made my teeth chatter. Callahan, who at least wore a long-sleeve shirt beneath his jersey, wrapped an arm around me and pulled me close to his side.

"I have an early curfew tonight. Can I give you a ride back to your place?"

"Axel and Drake have me covered."

Axel glanced up from his phone. "Actually, we're invited to a pregame party over at the Lambda House tonight. Wanna come with us?"

Neither Axel nor Drake was interested in participating in drag, but they loved to watch it. Usually, I had a good time with them when we went to a show, but tonight my frozen body craved a hot shower followed by a snuggle under a blanket in my recliner.

"I'm going to pass. But maybe you could drop me at the dorms on the way?"

"Stop playing hard to get, Island Girl," Callahan whispered in my ear. To my friends he said, "Don't worry. I'll give Jamaica a ride."

"Chessly too?" I asked.

He squeezed my waist, sending a shot of sensation straight to my core. "Sure."

"We'll pick you up at noon tomorrow, J," Axel said. "Wear warmer clothes." He shot a glance at my leggings and shook his head. Addressing Finn and Callahan, he added, "Good luck tomorrow, you two." He fist-bumped both of them. "Own the Tigers!"

Drake echoed him, and hand in hand the two of them took off for their party. Finn fell into step with us as we walked toward the stadium parking lot where Callahan had parked his truck. When we reached it, he said, "I can give you a ride if you want to avoid all the mush with these two, Chessly." He nodded toward Hotshot and me.

"That's all right—" I began but Chess talked over me.

"Thanks. Sounds like a plan."

Beside me, Hotshot snorted a laugh. I might have growled.

"There is no 'mush' between Callahan and me," I informed Finn.

He smirked. "Of course not. Which explains why you had breakfast with us last Sunday in the same clothes you had on Saturday night."

I threw up my hands. "For the last time, Finn McCabe. Nothing. Happened."

Chessly covered her mouth with her mittened hand, and I threw daggers at her with my eyes. At that she let her laughter out, the traitor.

Finn's noncommittal shrug could have meant anything.

Callahan tugged me toward the driver's side of his vehicle. "Hop in, Island Girl. I have a better idea for warming you up than smacking Finn around." He cleared his throat. "No matter how much he could use it."

"Hey!" Finn said.

Before I could respond, Callahan crowded me toward the open door of his ride and urged me to climb in. The console that separated us when he gave me a ride the last time was pushed up, leaving a bench seat. I slid all the way across to the passenger side. A long-suffering sigh escaped him, followed by a chuckle. I didn't give him the satisfaction of glaring at him for his blatant attempt to convince me to sit beside him. Instead, I watched out the window as Chessly climbed into the passenger side of Finn's truck and hugged the door.

"Your roommate is a gentleman, right? Because I'm entrusting someone important to him."

"After the way Chess took Tory down at Stromboli's tonight, I have no doubt she can handle Finn." He fired up his truck and set the heater to high. His eyes strayed to his hand where he fingered the curls that escaped my beanie. "You'll warm up faster if you slide over here, babe. Just sayin'." The low rumble of his voice sent a different kind of shiver through me.

He tugged lightly at my curls and smiled that naughty smile I was finding increasingly difficult to resist. Without meaning to, I inched closer to him.

"You know what I've been thinking about all day?"

I smirked. "Football?"

He tugged at my curls again, and again, I inched closer. "No. I've been thinking about an even more fun game."

Narrowing my eyes, I asked, "There's a game you like playing better than football?"

"Mm-hmm."

I was in the middle of the seat where the console should have been. Callahan slid his arm across the back of my shoulders and coaxed me over until my side was flush with his. At some point, he'd chewed some gum or something because the minty scent of his breath ghosted over me.

"What game do you like better than football?" With his eyes zeroed in on my lips the way they were, my question came out on a whisper.

"Tongue tag."

His warm lips covered mine, and I sighed into the soft pressure of his mouth. When his tongue slipped out to taste me, I opened for him, tasting him back. He shoved his hand into my hair, dislodging my beanie. Mimicking him, I slid my hand up the back of his neck beneath the brim of his backward cap, knocking it away as I tangled my fingers in the soft waves at the crown of his head.

As he deepened the kiss, I clutched at his hard shoulder. A moan slipped out, and he changed the angle, our tongues chasing and playing with each other. The tip of mine glided along the side of his, then the tip of his teased the underside of mine. On and on we played our "game" until Callahan groaned deep and let us up for air. He nibbled and kissed his way along my jaw and down my neck to the place where the collar of my jacket stopped his progress. Reversing course, he licked and kissed a trail to the spot beneath my ear. On a sigh I melted into him.

Somewhere in that endless kiss, I'd straddled him, our bodies smashed tightly together in the confined space of the front seat. My throbbing center was mashed up tight to the hard evidence of what my kisses did to him. Wild eyes stared into mine as we labored to catch our breath.

"Hottest. Kisses. Ever," he whispered. "Are you warm now?"

Needing to give my clit some relief, I rubbed against him. "You could say that," I rasped.

He clamped his hands on my hips, stopping my desperate movements. "You have no idea how bad I want this. Want you."

The storm of desire in his eyes gave me a clue, and I wondered if he could see an echoing need in mine.

"But I can't the night before a game."

"You don't really believe that old superstition about athletes abstaining from sex before a game, do you?" I ran my thumb along the thick column of his neck, enjoying the throbbing of his pulse beneath my touch.

"No," he croaked out. "But the first time I sex you up, I don't want to have a deadline."

Furrowing my brow, I asked, "What are you talking about?"

"I have to be at the field at ten, which would mean having to take you home before then."

I shrugged.

"In my fantasies of us together, we always enjoy a morning round or two of wrestling between the sheets before breakfast." At my wide-eyed stare, he grinned. "To be sure we're awake and all."

"Um—"

"We can't have that on game-day mornings unless we wake up while it's still dark outside. From your coffee addiction and the way you slide into class with fifteen seconds to spare, I have the idea you might be a grumpy morning person." He grinned and squeezed my hips again.

That's what alerted me to how insistently I'd been trying to use his hard length to relieve my wickedly excited clit. For a second I pressed into him. "You're right about me not being a morning person. But I might be persuaded to change my mind on occasion."

A laugh barked out of him followed by a sigh as he rested his forehead on mine. "You're killing me, Island Girl."

For a minute or two, we sat quietly. Then he pulled away. "Normally, I'd put out on a third date, but I truly do have to be out of the house early tomorrow morning." His eyes tracked his fingers as he pushed them into my hair, smoothing it away from my face. "Fitz is throwing the Homecoming after-party tomorrow night. Will you go with me?"

"I'm not a big party person."

"I've gathered that." He gave my hips a tiny squeeze. "We don't have to stay long. Drink a couple of beers, dance a little, go back to my place." He shifted beneath me, teasing a thrust of his length along my center.

"Okay."

"Okay, what?"

"I'll go with you to the party."

His eyes trailed his finger as he ghosted it across my lips. "As my girlfriend?"

The corner of my mouth inched up. "Is that how we're getting around the fact I don't date sports players? By calling me your girlfriend instead of your date?"

He maintained his focus on that maddening finger I wanted to bite. "We've already established you've made an exception for me." His eyes blazed into mine. "For the record, Jamaica, I'm not a player. I don't cheat. Ever."

I kissed the pad of that finger lingering on my mouth then pressed my lips to his. "I believe you."

CHAPTER NINETEEN

Jamaica

THE HOMECOMING GAME against the Tigers was even more of a contest than the one against the Bulldogs. Instead of focusing on the running game, though, the team's strategy changed to more passing. As promised, Callahan scored two touchdowns, and each time, he pointed the nose of the ball at me before he flipped it to the ref and enjoyed the congratulations of his teammates.

The defenders almost beat him to the ball on those passes, but he never let his quarterback down. It meant he sustained some hard tackles that had me covering my eyes, much to Axel and Drake's delight.

At one point after an especially jarring hit that took Hotshot a second to bounce up from, I yelled something irrational at the defense. Axel grinned and said, "You have it so bad for him, J," before he one-arm-hugged me. "About time."

"Agreed," Drake echoed.

"Since you two lovebirds found 'the one,' your little romantic hearts think everyone should. I cringe at all the tackles," I sniffed.

"You cringe harder when Callahan takes a hit."

I gave Axel the mother of all eye rolls and shook my head. "You're seeing things."

"Yep. I'm seeing you fall for the hottest player on the team." If I hadn't been wearing my beanie, I think he would have done the whole rubbing-the-top-of-my-hair thing. He settled for a shoulder bump instead. "Don't worry. He has it bad for you too."

The same as the previous week, we raced to Stromboli's after the game and grabbed the last four-top in the bar. We were on our second pitcher of beer and making a rather big dent in an extra-large pizza when Callahan arrived. He lowered himself gingerly into the open chair at our table and helped himself to my beer, draining half of it before he said hello.

"Um, are you sure you should be here?" I couldn't seem to keep the concern about whatever injuries he had from my voice.

His brow shot up. "As opposed to where?"

"I don't know. Your bed under a full-body heating pad?"

A grin split his face. "You're worried about me, Jamaica." Sliding his hand beneath the hair at the nape of my neck, he tugged me toward him. Against my lips he added, "Thank you." Though he kept his tongue in his mouth, the kiss lit me up like plugging a lamp into a hot socket.

When Hotshot let me go, Axel gifted me a knowing smile. The way his eyes danced, I could almost hear the "Jamaica's got a boyfriend" chant playing in his head. Mercifully, he switched his attention elsewhere.

"That was a close one today." Axel slid a slice onto a plate and passed it to Callahan. "Those touchdowns you scored for Jamaica"—he smirked—"were the difference, especially that second one."

"Nah. The difference was that timely interception Bax made when the Tigers were driving in the last minute. If he hadn't grabbed that pass, we wouldn't be celebrating tonight." He ate half his slice in one bite.

Impressive.

The other two nodded agreement, and the conversation plunged into the finer points of the game.

Signaling a passing server, I said, "We need another pizza." Shifting my attention to Hotshot, I asked, "What kind do you want?"

Indicating the remains of the one on the table, he said, "This is good."

"We need another chicken and artichoke pie. Thanks."

In short order, the second pizza and another pitcher of beer appeared then disappeared, mostly into Callahan, who was in much better form when we stood to leave the bar than when he'd arrived. We followed Axel and Drake outside where he invited my friends to Fitz's party. With a not-so-subtle brow waggle, Axel fist-bumped me, and the two of them ambled off to Drake's car.

Callahan slipped his arm around my waist and tugged me in the opposite direction. His truck was parked on a quiet tree-lined street behind the bar. After we hopped into it, he made a face when I went to buckle myself into the passenger seat.

"Seriously, Island Girl?" A wicked gleam lit up his gorgeous sea-blue eyes, and the next thing I knew, he was almost on top of me. "You're right. There's more room on this side without the steering wheel in the way." His gaze strayed to my lips. "I've been waiting all day for this."

His mouth crashed down on mine, going from "hello" to "you are the hottest thing in the universe" in half a breath. The chill of the evening evanesced as his big, warm body pressed me into the seat. Even through layers of sweater, jacket, and muffler (me) and Henley and hoodie (him), I could feel the deliciously hard planes of his pecs flattening my curves. Wrapping my arms around his neck, I pushed myself insistently into him, rubbing my achingly turgid nipples against his body.

It would have been so much better without the layers of clothes separating us. I'd missed him more than I wanted to admit since he'd dropped me off at my dorm with a chaste kiss on the cheek the night before. So I poured all that longing into the way I kissed him back, moaning in my throat at how crazy-awesome all that masculine power and heat covering my torso felt.

Callahan bumped his head on the ceiling when we both startled at a loud thump against the side of his truck. "Get a room!" Raucous male laughter followed the shout, and we glanced around at the fogged-up state of the truck's windows. No doubt my face matched the dazed expression in Hotshot's eyes. He blinked and grinned in pure challenge.

"Still want to sit way over here, or do you want to sit where you're supposed to?"

"Where I'm supposed to?" I challenged back.

He slid back over into the driver's seat. "In my experience, girlfriends sit next to their boyfriends whenever the opportunity presents itself." Glancing down at the open seat beside him, he said, "For instance, when the boyfriend drives a truck with a bench seat."

"You're ridiculous." I laughed.

"You're too far away," he countered.

I shook my head—and slid over beside him, buckling myself in with the shoulder harness attached to the back of the driver's seat.

When we arrived at Jeremiah Fitzgerald's house, we walked in on a celebration in full swing. Hip-hop thumped from a sound system in the corner of the living room, while people danced and shouted in conversation. Since we'd left our outerwear in the cab of the truck, I shivered, and Callahan stepped behind me to wrap me in his arms. As he slowly walked me forward, we swayed to the beat until we were in the middle of the rowdy crowd. Then he spun me around and leaned down to speak into my ear.

"Want something to drink?"

Nodding, I said, "Sure."

He slipped his hand in mine and led me to the kitchen. Apparently, these football parties ran on a protocol: dancing in the living room, alcohol in the kitchen, cornhole in the back yard. Since Fitz's house didn't have a dining room, the flip cup tournament filled the kitchen, which meant it took a bit of maneuvering to make our way to the keg. I guess the team didn't congratulate each other or something in the locker room after the game, because for the next twenty minutes, it seemed all the players at the party filed through the kitchen to tell Callahan how much they appreciated his play in the win.

The women who came over had an entirely different agenda. It didn't matter that he had one hand wrapped around a red cup and his other arm wrapped around me. They were walking their fake-nail fingertips up his bicep, leaning in close to his chest, and batting their fake lashes like something had fallen into their eyes.

I sipped my nasty keg beer and watched the circus.

Loud, attention-drawing laughter announced the arrival of Tory Miller and her entourage of freshmen mean girls a few seconds before they sauntered into the kitchen. It was enough time to let Callahan alert the player pouring cups from the keg. The guy nodded, and Callahan led me over to the side of the table, ostensibly to see how flip cup was going. From the way he positioned me between the door and him, I had the distinct impression I'd become a human shield. The idea that five-foot-six me could hide six-foot-five Hotshot was laughable. In fact, I think I might have let out a giggle when I saw what he'd done.

Over the rim of his cup, his glare morphed into a crinkly-eyed grin. His hand slipped around my waist, drawing me up flush with his side. Leaning down, he whispered, "This works better when you put your arm around me too, Island Girl."

"What does? Me hiding you from jersey chasers?" I teased.

"No, snuggling while we watch the game." He downed his beer and set the empty cup on the counter behind us. "I have a better idea for snuggling."

My brow went up in question.

"Let's dance."

As we sidled along the wall toward the door into the living room, one of Tory's girls caught sight of us, her wide-eyed surprise bouncing between Callahan and me. Before she could alert Tory, who appeared to be trying to wheedle beer from the player manning the keg, Hotshot dragged me through the door and into the heart of the crowd of dancers writhing and jumping in the living room. Beneath our feet the floor shuddered and vibrated as at least fifty people partied to the music.

While we danced, more people found us and fist-bumped or high-fived my date, which meant there was no snuggling. Oddly, that disappointed me. But he was subtly and steadily dancing us toward the front door. Right as we found the edge of the crowd, Tory Miller found us.

"Callahan! Callahan! Dance with me," she insisted as though he wasn't standing with his arm around me.

"I'm kinda busy, Tory," he said with a pointed glance in my direction.

Only then did she acknowledge my presence. "What are you doing with this loser?" she sniffed. Then she gifted him her biggest smile. "Winners should be with winners, don't you think?" The smile didn't reach her eyes. Instead, something ugly and calculating lurked in their sharklike depths.

"Exactly." Tugging me close to his side, he said, "Time for us to go, Jamaica."

"Do you even know who I am, Callahan?" she screeched.

Conversation in our vicinity stopped as people gathered around to watch the drama.

"A spoiled little rich girl who likes to sleep with the football team?" I asked with mock innocence.

Callahan dug his fingers into my side, letting me know I'd crossed a line. But contrary to the brat who went out of her way to make the rest of us feel small, I wasn't a loser.

"Come on, babe. Time for us to go." He tugged me toward the front door.

"Seriously? You'd rather slum it with this truck-stop trash?" She stuck out her hip, planting a manicured hand on it and showing off her super-short skirt. "Raise your standards, Callahan."

Though my mom had supported me until I graduated high school by waitressing at a truck stop, I wasn't truck-stop trash. Neither was my mom. I didn't grow up with Tory's opportunities, but I was still here, making good grades and apparently dating the guy she wanted.

"You know what, Tory? I absolutely love the sound you make when you shut up." With that parting shot, I allowed Hotshot to escort me outside.

"I know you said Tory lived in your dorm on Chessly's floor last year, but she's got it in for you. What's the deal?" he asked when he opened the driver's side door and gestured for me to climb in.

"I could ask you the same question. Looks like you two have a history—one she's not finished with, judging by the way she stalks you." The short walk from the house to his truck without my coat, combined with the adrenaline coursing through me, left my teeth chattering. Shrugging into my coat was awkward as hell, but I needed the warmth—and an extra layer of protection from my date.

He fired up the truck, and while it warmed up, he ran his hands through his hair and replaced his backward ball cap. Sliding his arm across the back of the seat, he faced me. "We made out in a hallway during a party at the Delta Nu house last spring."

My brows might have tried to disappear into my hairline.

"I walked out of the bathroom and she was waiting for me, it turns out, even though we hadn't met. She shoved me against the wall and had her tongue down my throat before I even knew what had hit me. I was smashed and horny, and I kissed her back."

Crossing my arms over my chest, I regarded him through narrowed eyes.

"Being stupid drunk is no excuse."

Callahan owned his behavior, raising my respect for him several notches higher.

"Fortunately, one of my teammates saw us and dragged my ass out of there."

"You wanted to keep making out with her?" To my utter horror, my voice cracked on the question.

"Babe, in the state I was in, I wasn't capable of making an intelligent decision. When I sobered up, I was mortified. Tory is capital B Bad News—something I've been trying to convince Finn of all semester." He tugged at one of my curls. "But her dad is a big-time donor to the school, especially to the football program, so I have to be polite and keep putting her off until she loses interest."

"I don't think that's happening anytime soon."

"As long as you don't lose interest, I'll be fine." His arms came around me, pulling me in close. "And I'm determined to keep you interested," he rumbled as he lowered his mouth to mine. "I know you're not a fan of these parties. Wanna go to my place and watch TV or something?"

"Watch TV? Okay. I'll think about the 'or something.'"

CHAPTER TWENTY

Jamaica

WHEN THE PERSON in the white mask and black hood loomed up from behind the kitchen counter, Callahan buried his face in the side of my neck and shivered.

I cracked up. "Seriously, you can't believe this is scary."

"It absolutely is scary," he protested. "It's even called *Scary Movie*."

Detecting a smirk in his tone, I leaned back and caught it. "Is this one of your signature moves?"

He blinked at me. "Signature moves?" The innocent act wasn't working with the naughty glint in his gorgeous eyes.

"Take a girl to your room, put on a horror movie, and wait for her to climb all over you to hide from the scary parts?"

"Obviously not since it's not working with you." He shifted on top of the comforter. "Why aren't you scared, Island Girl?" His hand slipped beneath my sweater, a ghost of a touch whispering over my skin.

I shivered and flinched, and he pounced. "You laugh at scary movies but fear a tickle? This hypothesis requires more testing."

With a shriek I tried to scoot away, but he was on me, his fingers finding every ticklish spot on my torso. I squeaked and squirmed, wiggled and pushed, but his busy fingers were relentless. Laughter (his) and indignant squeals (mine) filled the room as our wrestling match made a mess of the comforter atop his bed. At last, he straddled me, his hands holding mine above my head, and the mood shifted.

In the low light of his bedside lamp, I watched in fascination as his sea-blue eyes blazed down at me. His hands left mine to slip beneath my sweater again, his calloused fingertips grazing the sensitive skin of my belly, raising goose bumps in their wake. "I want you so bad, Jamaica. But if you're not ready yet, I can wait." His fingers stilled. "You're worth the wait."

The atmosphere in his bedroom crackled with the charged desire that had slowly built between us over the past couple of months. It was time to own my emotions.

"I want you too, Callahan. So much," I whispered.

His hands slid higher. His thumbs skimming along the undersides of my breasts sent shivers through me that had nothing to do with scary movies. My nipples puckered into aching peaks. Had I anticipated this when he invited me out tonight? Is that why I only wore a camisole and no bra beneath my sweater?

His nostrils flared—my only warning before my camisole and sweater lay somewhere on the floor of his room. He leaned back a bit where he straddled my legs and ran his eyes over me, his expression simultaneously raising the hairs on my skin and flashing flames through my blood.

"Oh, fuck, you're gorgeous, Island Girl."

He bent down and touched the tip of his tongue to one taut nipple. I would have surged right up off the bed at the exquisite contact of his skin on mine if his hand hadn't taken possession of my other breast. With a moan, I arched into his touch, which was all the encouragement he needed.

His lips closed over me, drawing me deep into his mouth while his thumb played over my other nipple. The twin sensations had me bucking and writhing beneath him. I plowed my hands into the silky waves of his hair and held on as my body did its own thing, undulating beneath him. I couldn't control the sighs and whimpers escaping my lips as he played me with his mouth and hands.

When he pulled off my nipple with a little kiss, his eyes found mine, and he smiled. "Do you have any idea how fucking sweet you are? Sugar and cherries." He ran his tongue over his lips and smacked them. "Delicious."

Before I could react to his description of me as dessert, he went to work on the other breast, suckling me in the sweetest way. His teasing tongue flicking over my sensitized flesh had me fisting his shirt over his broad shoulders, tugging and twisting until he took the hint. He sat up only long enough to drag it over his head and toss it somewhere off the bed, and then his mouth was on me again.

He kissed and nipped and licked his way down my belly. When he encountered the waistband of my leggings, he didn't stop kissing me. Instead, he curled his fingers over the fabric and tugged it down ahead of his hot mouth until he reached the natural barrier of curls covering my mound. Sliding backward down my thighs, he dragged my leggings and panties with him all the way off the bed.

Standing at the foot of the bed, he took his time cataloguing my body with his gaze. "Fu-uck, Jamaica. Undressing you is better than opening a lifetime supply of Christmas and birthday presents."

His response to my nakedness heated me from the inside out. Taking his time, his gentle hands mapped every contour and shadow, starting with my ankles, over the hearts of my calves, the sensitive creases behind my knees, and up the soft skin of my inner thighs. The sensation of his calloused fingertips on my body flooded my center already slick with desire from his attentions to my belly and breasts.

I couldn't stay still. "Please, Callahan."

I had no idea what I was begging for, only that I ached for him.

A wicked grin flitted over his mouth and he pushed my thighs wide and buried his face between them. When he closed his lips over my clit and tongued me, I would have shot off the bed without his forearm over my belly. Nothing in the world had ever delighted me like Callahan's mouth on my pussy. The growl deep in his throat could have meant anything as he flexed his hands on my thighs, holding me exactly where he wanted me.

Fisting my hands in the comforter, I held on as waves of pleasure crashed over me while his talented mouth went to work on my sensitive flesh. When one thick finger found its way inside me, my head thrashed from side to side on the pillow as my hips moved in rhythm with his hand. A second finger joined the first, curling perfectly, his tongue and fingers playing me in stereo. Without warning, the orgasm crashed through me like an avalanche. I speared my fingers into his hair and held on.

Days later when I floated back down from heaven, I blinked my eyes open to find him smiling up at me from his happy place between my legs. "You're amazing, Island Girl." Mischief danced in those sea-blue eyes as he stuck his two fingers in his mouth, sucking and licking my juices from them. "And delicious." With a flirty furrow of his brow, he asked, "Did I mention that already?"

Watching him enjoy me this way almost made me come again. Whatever he saw in my expression had him sliding off the bed and shucking his jeans and boxers in a whoosh. Involuntarily, my tongue slipped over my lips as I caught my first sight of his impressive shaft. Feeling it pressed against me through our clothes on more than one occasion should have given me a clue, but all that naked glory still surprised me.

And turned me on.

I wriggled into a seated position and reached for him, thoughts of returning the favor swirling through my head. But he had other ideas.

Sidestepping my reach, he opened a drawer in the nightstand and extracted a box of condoms. At the sight a dark thought rolled through me. "Are you always this prepared for 'movie night'?"

"I picked these up after your last overnight, babe. Had an idea we'd need them sooner rather than later."

I relaxed. "A whole box?"

The corner of his mouth quirked up. "Like I said, I had an idea we'd need them—all."

He plucked a foil packet from the box, tore it open, and smoothed the condom over himself, making sure I had a good view of what was on offer.

"I would have done that for you." I pouted.

A self-deprecating laugh huffed out of him. "I know, but I'm already a little worried about how long I'll last without feeling your hands on me just yet."

My brows shot up.

The bed sagged as he joined me on it. "You're so tight, Jamaica, and I've wanted you for so long." He crawled between my legs yet held himself away from me. "I want this to be so good for you that the only man you can ever feel is me."

I might have called him out on that, but right then, he pushed the head of his cock inside me, and I closed my eyes at the initial delicious stretch.

"Give me your eyes, Jamaica."

I fluttered my lids open and lost my breath. Desire and something deeper, stronger, intensified his blue eyes almost to black.

He laced his fingers through mine, our palms smashing together as he leaned into my hands on either side of my head.

"Stay with me," he commanded as he stepped right out of bounds.

Slowly, so excruciatingly slowly, he pushed all the way into me. I wanted a flag for unsportsmanlike conduct as that one move tore down every brick in the protective wall I'd built around my heart. Our bodies came together like two parts of one whole. The expression on his face said he'd reached the same conclusion, and more than anything I wanted to close my eyes and hide.

Reading me perfectly, he gave a slight shake of his head and pulled almost all the way out then he plunged back in all the way to his balls. My body clenched hard around his, and he hissed in a breath, pulled out and plunged in again.

"Fuck, Jamaica. Nothing in the world feels as good as you do." He leaned down and ghosted a kiss over my mouth, stopping to whisper against my lips, "Nothing has ever felt this good for you either."

Anticipating my reflexive protest, he stole it right out of my mouth when he thrust his tongue between my lips. His hips moved in rhythm with our tongues, his hardness driving and driving into my softness. Beneath him, my hips matched his, our bodies joining as though we'd danced this dance a hundred times rather than this being our first time together.

Tearing his mouth from mine, he came up on his knees. Grasping my thighs, he dragged my legs up, anchoring my ankles on his shoulders. The change in the angle combined with the increased speed of his thrusts left me begging for release.

"Callahan! Oh, my God, Callahan. Please." That last word stretched for two full measures as I tried to dig my nails into the rock-hard planes of his thighs.

"That's it, Island Girl. Give it to me." His eyes boring into mine, he ground out, "Let. Go."

For a second, the muscles low in my belly seized then released on an orgasm that had me thrusting my nipples to the ceiling and digging my ankles into Callahan's shoulders as I screamed his name. Waves and waves of sensation rolled through me as my climax crescendoed to a height I'd never known I could reach. I might have blacked out for a second, absolutely died the little death I'd read about in French literature. Then he was pounding into me. From his movements, his body was no longer his to control.

"Fuuuuck! Jamaica!" His shouts grew loud and raw as he emptied himself inside me. "Jamaica! Jamaica!" The expression on his face was pure shock.

I could relate.

For a few seconds, we held still, suspended in time. Then he thrust a couple more times, and a mini-orgasm had my inner muscles gripping him like a vise while he finished coming—or maybe came again. Our eyes locked, and I couldn't hide. Callahan O'Reilly had thoroughly wrecked me, and from the expression in those sea-blue depths, he knew it too.

At last, we both keyed in on the quivery state of my thighs. Gently, he lowered my limbs to the bed, following them down to rest his chest on mine. He leisurely kissed my mouth, my jaw, and down the side of my neck while the aftershocks continued to pulse through me into him. I let my fingertips roam the broad expanse of his back, reveling in the rippling of his skin beneath my touch. Good to know I got to him too.

"I don't ever want to move from right here," he whispered into the side of my neck. "But my arms are done, and I don't want to squash you."

Wrapping my arms around him, I held him close. "I like you right where you are."

With a chuckle, he shook his head. "You're killing me, Island Girl."

Cold air rushed over my heated skin when he rolled off me. He knotted the condom and slid off the bed. A minute later he reemerged from the en suite bathroom and walked over to turn off the TV. Until he'd left the bed, I'd forgotten it was still on.

"Hop up for a sec."

I dragged myself off the bed, and he threw back the comforter and blankets.

"Slide in, babe."

He followed me under the covers, positioning my head on his chest as he tugged me in close and wrapped his arms around me. Who would have guessed this big, tough football player was a cuddler?

"That was incredible, Jamaica." He lifted his head off the pillow to catch my eye. "You are incredible." A playful grin played over his features. "I can see already I'm going to need a case of condoms with you. Insatiable wench."

Indignation didn't work lying down, but when I tried to sit up to call him out, he laughed and tightened his arms around me. "The way I remember it, you started this."

"Nah, it was all you, Island Girl," he teased. "You laughed at my scary-movie moves, and the rest was history." Beneath my hand where it rested on his flat stomach, I sensed the change in his mood. "What happened here between us is special. You know that, right?"

His breath caught and held. I didn't want to acknowledge the truth of his words. Doing so meant I'd be giving up a part of myself, my autonomy. My control. Though I'd had sex before, everything with Hotshot was different. From the beginning, my experience with him had been different from anyone else I'd ever been with. Admitting—out loud—that sleeping with him was special was all kinds of dangerous.

But I couldn't deny it, not when my body lay flush against

his. I knew he'd be able to feel the lie on our skin. "What have we done, Hotshot?"

He relaxed. "We've become the poster kids for getting lucky." A chuckle followed his silly comment.

Except it wasn't truly silly. When he said lucky, every part of me touching him sensed that he meant it. He thought being with me was lucky. Exactly how long that would last was a whole different thing, especially after he discovered where I came from.

Chapter Twenty-One

Callahan

USUALLY, I PASS out pretty fast after sex. Especially when I have it at the end of a long day that began with playing a full four quarters of football and ended with drinking some beers. But while Jamaica snored softly in my arms, I remained wide-awake, my fingers unable to stay still with her silky skin beneath them.

She was such a live wire, sassing me, challenging me, driving me to distraction. I thought once we had sex, I'd have myself back under control. Considering the rest of our relationship, I should have known better. Sex with Island Girl was off. The. Charts.

Her inability to stay still as I sexed her up told me exactly how much I turned her on. Those fists clenched in the blankets, in my hair, and at her sides clued me in on how much she loved my hands and mouth on her. The breathy sighs and soul-deep moans that crescendoed into banshee-style screams, my name echoing off the walls of my room as I made her come, fired me up more than a stadium full of fans cheering my touchdowns on game day.

Yeah, I'd been with a few girls—not nearly as many as my reputation implied, but I knew what I was doing in the sack. This thing with Jamaica was on a stratospheric plane. She took me to a place I'd never been with a woman. A place I wanted to visit again and again. She turned me inside out, wrung every last ounce of desire from me, and left me more satiated and contented than I had ever experienced. Everything about her was real and honest and so fucking sexy it was ridiculous. Seriously, I should have been wiped out, but she shifted, throwing her thigh over mine, and my cock woke right back up.

I absolutely loved the riot of soft curls that covered her head. I also loved that she didn't try to tame them, other than with a headband sometimes to hold them off her face or to shove them into a messy bun they usually spilled out of. Sliding my hand up into the spirals of her hair, I tugged gently while shifting more to my side. The palm of my hand skimmed over the curve of her hip, then I feathered the tips of my fingers along the satiny skin of her thigh. She let go a sigh and reached for me.

A grin tugged at my mouth as I watched her puff out another sigh through pouty lips when I let my fingers roam up her side to the curve of her breast. When my thumb found her nipple, I discovered that while her brain might be resting, her body was thinking about more playtime. Leaning in, I brushed my lips over hers and whispered her name.

"Mmm, is it morning already?" she mumbled.

"The clock hasn't even struck midnight yet, Cinderella. The ball is still in full swing." I chuckled at my innuendo, and she groaned.

"That was so bad." She blinked one eye open. "Full swing, huh?" Her hand found my cock, which her raspy sleep voice and soft skin had enticed into a salute. Her eyes blinked wide-open. "Oh, I'll say. Definitely full swing." A wicked little smile slid over her lips before her tongue slipped out and toured them.

With no other warning, she vanished beneath the covers, and the next thing I knew, her warm, wet mouth was sheathing my dick while she explored my balls with her fingertips.

"Fu-uck, Jamaica. What—"

I lost all coherent thought when her tongue went to work, the tip of it teasing along my shaft on the upstroke, the flat of it rubbing my length on the downstroke. All the while she played with my balls. The twin sensations of her hands and mouth on me had me fisting the sheets as I desperately tried to control my urgent need to thrust into her mouth. When she sucked hard on the head with her hand jacking the shaft, I couldn't hold back. Tugging on that mass of curls, I urged her to climb up my body.

"You're killing me, babe. Come here."

Her answer came with the flat of her hand splayed across my abs, pushing me back down onto the mattress. She only stopped sucking me long enough to sass, "You had your fun with me. Now it's my turn. Lie back and take it like a man."

I flipped the covers back so I could at least watch and then wondered at myself when the naughty gleam in her dark green eyes found mine. She took me deep, held me suspended for a second, and then went to town. Her head bobbed as her hands played me. That wildly talented tongue teased and tasted, licked and sucked my dick until I thought I might lose my ever-loving mind.

"Jamaica, babe, I'm gonna come," I warned, my voice raw.

She hummed along my shaft and that was it. A galaxy of green stars burst behind my eyes, and my ears rang with my own shouts. My hips did their own thing, and she took it—she took it all. When she pulled off me, we were both breathing hard. Then she positively rocked me when she ran her tongue over her swollen lips and smacked them together as if she'd just tasted ambrosia.

Slowly, she kissed and licked her way up my abs, over my pecs, and along the column of my neck, her lips and tongue leaving a trail of fire over my skin. When she found my mouth with hers, I flipped her onto her back and dove in, kissing her breathless.

At last, I let her up for air. "Island Girl, you've ruined me."

Her brow shot up.

"Yep. I hope you're proud of yourself. I'm completely ruined for anyone else now." I smiled at her deer-in-the-headlights stare. "No one has ever done that to me before."

She smirked. "You expect me to believe you've never had a blow job?"

"Not one that made me see stars." Sobering, I said, "Thank you." This time the kiss was slow, gentle, and sweet. I wrapped her in my arms and took my time exploring her mouth with mine.

It wasn't long, though, before she stared moving, rubbing her gorgeous full tits along my chest, sliding her heel along the back of my calf and up to dig into my hamstring. While I tangled my tongue with hers, I let my hand drift down between us, slipping my fingers through the curls guarding her entrance. Finding her slick and hot fired me right back up.

"Mmm, hold that thought," I said as I reached over to the nightstand for a condom.

Before I could tear open the packet, she snatched it from my hand. "My turn."

Taking her sweet-ass time, she unrolled the latex along my length, giving me a squeeze that made my breath hitch. She didn't let me go until she had me positioned exactly where she wanted me, the impish grin dancing in her eyes telling me who was in charge.

Uh-huh.

The second she let me go, I pushed back and flipped her. "On your hands and knees, babe."

She hesitated, and for a second I worried I might have pushed too hard too soon. Then she languidly rose up into position and shot me a sultry, sexy smile over her shoulder that had me grasping her hips and pushing inside her with far less finesse than I'd intended. A tiny "Oh!" escaped her, and then she was moving with me, our bodies slapping out a rhythm that built and built and built.

When the orgasm barreled down my spine, I slid my hand around her, the pad of my finger zeroing in on her clit. "Come, Jamaica. I need you to come. Now," I growled.

Burying her face in the pillow, she pushed hard back into me, her pussy pulsing around my cock in the out-of-control rhythm of her climax. Her muffled screams sounded like my name, and in two quick thrusts, the shock waves of the mother of all orgasms crashed through me. Time stopped as sensations I'd never known echoed through me into her and back again.

When her legs went out from under her, I went down too, my body covering hers. I wanted the aftershocks to go on forever. I wanted her sass and her fire all to myself. I wanted to stay inside her in every way and never let her go. Somewhere along the line when I thought we were only teasing each other, Jamaica Winslow snuck into my heart and made a space for herself there. And that happened *before* the spectacular sex. A sneaky voice in the back of my mind said I should maybe be worried, but I was too happy to pay it much attention.

As the aftershocks gentled down into tiny pulses, she shifted beneath me, alerting me to the fact she probably needed to breathe. I pulled out, rolled off her, and dragged my ass to the head to dispose of the condom. When I returned to bed, she remained face down in the pillow, and I sat beside her, mapping the long lines of her back and the sexy contours of her ass, down and up, down and up. Her skin rippled beneath my touch, and she buried a moan of pleasure in the pillow.

Smiling at her lazy response, I climbed over her and stretched out beside her. Gathering her close, I said, "You're fucking incredible, you know that?" I kissed her hair and tightened my arms around her. "By the way, after tonight, there is absolutely no question you're my girlfriend." I lifted my head to catch the question in her eyes. "We're exclusive, Jamaica. You're mine." This time I kissed her pretty pouty mouth. "And I'm yours."

For a minute she tensed, and my stomach did a scary somersault. When her body relaxed in my arms, I dropped my head back on my pillow and closed my eyes. It seemed I'd barely fallen asleep when a raucous pounding on my door startled both of us upright in my bed.

"O'Reilly! Get your ass up! Breakfast is on the table," Bax shouted through the door.

"Fuck," I mumbled when I checked the time on my phone. "I had plans for how I wanted to wake you this morning, Island Girl. But I have to be at film in half an hour."

She stretched her arms over her head, thrusting her gorgeous rack out, and I threw myself back onto the mattress with a groan of frustration.

"Mmm, your bed is so comfy. I've never overslept like I seem to do whenever I sleep in it."

"You sure it's the bed that has you so relaxed?" I waggled my brows at her.

"Positive." She shot me an impish smirk. "I can't imagine what else would do it."

Before I could grab her and remind her exactly why she'd slept so well, she hopped out of bed with a laugh and headed to the bathroom. A few minutes later she walked out in all her naked glory and started gathering up her clothes. Fascinated, I watched as she slipped her camisole over her head and smoothed it down her body then shimmied into her panties. Nothing about her plain white underwear was especially sexy on its own, but when it covered her delectable curves, I couldn't remember seeing anything sexier. Then she ruined the view by dropping her oversize sweater over herself. Not bothering to hide my morning wood, I rolled out of bed and walked to the bathroom, deliberately taking a tiny detour to run my hand across her ass and give her a squeeze.

"Callahan," she warned. "You're gonna be late."

With a frustrated growl, I headed into the shower, setting it on full cold. Two minutes later, I was relatively clean and definitely less turned-on. Jamaica was sitting on the side of the bed, scrolling through her phone when I stepped over to my dresser and pulled out a fresh pair of boxers and my favorite sweats. After hustling into my clothes, I slipped my hand in hers and tugged her up from the bed. Unable to resist a minute more, I wrapped her in my arms and kissed her like I meant it—because I did. When she melted in my arms and kissed me back, I seriously considered skipping film and taking the consequences tomorrow afternoon in practice.

As though she'd read my mind, she pulled away. "I'm not going to cause trouble for you with your coach. Axel can pick me up and take me home."

Like I'd let that happen, let some other guy take my lady home after she'd spent the night with me. "The dorms are only a couple minutes' jog out of the way to the stadium. I'll take you home." Taking her hand, I led her downstairs.

"Morning, sunshine. Too much Homecoming party last night?" Finn asked with a smirk. Then he caught sight of my girl and color flooded his cheeks. "Sorry, Jamaica. I didn't know you were here."

Bax glanced up from stuffing his face. "Breakfast burritos are in the oven." He swallowed and added, "Good thing I made extra."

Danny glanced up from his food with a sly grin and waved. Apparently, he spent last night after the game at home. *Huh. Can't imagine how I missed that.* I grinned to myself.

"Good morning, guys. Great game yesterday."

I gave Jamaica's hand a squeeze and headed over to fill my

thermos mug with coffee. While I prepared our burritos to go, wrapping them in tin foil and napkins, Jamaica said, "I don't know much about the game, but it looked to me like you were the hero, Bax."

"You hear that, 'Han? Your girlfriend thinks I'm a hero."

"Now you've done it." Danny groaned. "We won't hear the end of this until next week at least."

She shrugged, but I saw a smirk ghost over her features. The look I shot her told her there would be punishments for encouraging Bax even if what she said was true, and every man in the room knew it. I handed her a burrito and slid the other one into the front pocket of my hoodie.

Snagging my coffee mug with one hand, I wrapped the other around my girl. "See you guys at the facility," I said to my roommates as I led her out the door.

Before she could buckle herself in, I pounced on her in the cab of my truck. "You did that on purpose, didn't you?" I asked against her lips.

"Did what?" she breathed.

"Gave Bax a big head."

"You're the one who called him a hero," she sassed with a grin.

I kissed that grin right off her mouth, tangling my tongue with hers as I speared my fingers through her hair. A long time later, we came up for air when we heard the front door of the house bang shut behind my roommates.

"If you drop me off now, you're going to be late." Worry flashed in those deep green eyes I'd never tire of looking into.

"Not if we don't see a cop."

I fired up my truck and roared out of the driveway.

After dropping Jamaica off, I made it to practice with thirty seconds to spare.

Chapter Twenty-Two

Jamaica

"THANKS AGAIN FOR covering for me this weekend," I said as Chessly and I walked to the dorm supervisor's apartment for our weekly RA meeting. "I had no idea Homecoming was such a big deal."

My friend shot me an "are you for real?" side-eye, but all she said was, "You're welcome." We walked a bit in silence, then "How was the after-party?"

"Pretty much the same as the one last week at Callahan's. Loud music and dancing in the living room, nasty keg beer and a flip cup tournament in the kitchen, cornhole in the back yard."

"I heard something this morning at breakfast about Tory Miller causing a scene with you. You wanna be careful with that girl, Jamaica," Chess warned.

"He shut her down, and we left before she could start in again." I sighed. "But you're right." I decided I needed her perspective. "She has a thing for Callahan—one he's never reciprocated."

With a tilt of her head, Chess gazed at me from beneath her brows. "As far as you know."

"He told me she stalked him at a frat party last spring. They kissed in a hallway for a few minutes—she initiated it—and one of the other football players intervened and hauled him out of there." I shifted my notebook to my other hand. "From the way he acts around her now, I believe him."

"It's not him I'm worried about."

"So, sweetheart, did you have the best time at Homecoming?" Across the table in the union for our usual coffee date, Axel grinned his cheekiest grin. "The way Callahan couldn't quit sneaking glances at you all during class this morning, I have the idea he had a good time."

"Quit fishing, you old gossip." I sipped my latte with a serenity I was far from feeling.

Feeling Hotshot's warm body pressed along mine for as much as the seats in the lecture hall allowed had thrown me right off my game this morning. I had so many questions for Dr. Dair concerning the reading I spent all of yesterday afternoon doing, and I forgot them all when my pussy went into happy Kegels from Callahan's nearness. Between that and Chessly's warnings about a certain mean girl, I barely even took any notes during Dair's lecture.

"You make a striking pair, what with your dark hair to his light, your toned curves to his hard football player body." He pulled at the collar of his shirt, fanning himself. "Seriously, J. You two walk into a room and everyone stares."

I slumped in my chair. "You're such a drama queen, Axel. I don't know why I put up with you sometimes."

Reaching across the table, he covered my hand with his. "Because I'm your oldest and bestest friend. And because you know I'm always on your team." Giving my hand a tiny squeeze, he added, "Now we're friends with benefits." At my raised brow, he clarified. "I have the added benefit of hanging out with the big men on campus—and the best seats in the house on game day. You have a wingman who makes sure you understand your man's game and who's watching your back at parties."

I snorted. "Like you did last week when you and Drake ditched me and left me to spend the night at Callahan's place?"

His shrug was not apologetic. "He was going out of his way to make it obvious to you and everyone else that he has a thing for you. Drake and I agreed you needed a nudge to stop being so stubborn and acknowledge it." He smirked. "Seems like it worked. You two barely spent any time at all at Fitz's party the other night before Callahan dragged you out the door. From what Chess says, you didn't come home until midmorning yesterday." Clearing his throat, he added, "She saw you kissing in the front of Callahan's truck. You sported a satisfied smile on your face and didn't even say hello as you walked through the lobby to your room."

I wrinkled my nose at my friend. "Add spying to gossiping. I should speak to Drake about keeping you more occupied."

His rich laughter flowed over me. "Don't you worry your pretty little head about that, J. Drake keeps me plenty busy." Then he sobered. "I want that for you too, Jamaica. Of all the people I know, you most deserve that kind of happiness."

A cloud fell over his features.

"What?" I asked, alarm and suspicion warring for the front of the line of my emotions.

"After you guys left Fitz's party after that little scene Tory Miller tried to start, that girl said some choice words about you. Finn and Bax shut her down before she could do any serious damage with the other players on the team, but she's a snake." After a thoughtful sip of his coffee, he added, "Drake and I always have your back. Now it seems Callahan's roommates do too. But you still need to pay attention. From what I saw, she's posting some nasty shit about you. Stay far away from that girl."

"Can we talk about something more pleasant, like your notes from Dr. Dair's class today? I seem to have zoned out a bit and missed a few things." My face grew hot at the admission.

Mercifully, Axel only smirked without commentary as he passed his iPad across the table. When I pulled out my notebook, to my horror, I saw that I only had about a fifth of the information in my notes that he had in his.

"Shall I walk you through those?"

I might have snarled at the oh-so-innocent batting of his eyes, yet I had no choice but to accept his help since none of the information in front of me was familiar at all. Obviously, I sat in class this morning, but it was as though I'd skipped it from what I got out of it.

"I can't decide which part is more fun—you needing to hear the basics of the lecture again or remembering the funny looks Dair kept throwing at you every time he left a tiny pause for your questions that never came." His grin was pure evil. "You've got it bad, Jamaica Winslow. About time you met someone who makes you forget the rest of the world exists."

"Gah! It's not like that. It's not like when you met Drake." With a sigh, I nodded toward his notes. "Can we go over these, please? I have to be at the sweet shop in half an hour."

"It's exactly like when I met Drake."

I wrinkled my nose and he roared with laughter. Crossing my arms over my chest, I gave him a long-suffering glare, which only made him laugh harder.

"Would you knock it off? People are staring."

Swiping at his eyes, he giggled a bit more and finally wrestled himself under control enough to talk me through what I'd missed in class.

Work was slower than a typical late Monday afternoon, which gave me lots of opportunity to work on homework. If only my mind would stop straying to a certain football player and what I'd been doing with him all through Saturday night… When I returned to the dorms after I finished my shift, I looked at my calendar and saw I'd wasted a chance to read ahead to be better prepared for Dr. Dair on Wednesday.

Then as I reread a passage of *Pride and Prejudice* for the third or fourth time, Axel's words came back to bite me on the ass. *"About time you met someone who makes you forget the rest of the world exists."* The way I saw it, the timing couldn't be worse. Meeting that someone after I became an established lawyer fit right into my plans. Meeting him when I was a junior in college who needed top grades to qualify for law-school scholarships? Not so much.

"We're only fooling around," I whispered to myself. "It's nothing serious."

Needing to give my mind a break, I grabbed a stack of sheet music from the cubby on the side of my desk and headed to the piano room in the basement of the dorm. At least I could work through some homework for the piano class I adored. Plus, concentrating on the music would take my mind away from the incredible night I'd shared with Hotshot.

As usual, I lost myself in the music the minute I sat down at the keyboard. After warming up with a few arpeggios and scales, I set to work on the Rachmaninoff piece I was working on. For the most part, I had it down, but there were a couple of tricky passages I wanted to perfect before my next class. Pulling a pencil from behind my ear, I marked some notes and nearly tore a hole in the page when the deep rumble of Callahan's voice interrupted my concentration.

"Hotshot?" I squeaked. "How the hell are you here?"

"We finished practice early, so I dropped by to see if you wanted to go out for ice cream." He looked lickable with his backward hat, his casual hoodie, and his hands stuffed in the pockets of his jeans.

I was still trying to force my breathing back under control. "The desk clerk didn't just let you roam around until you found me here," I accused.

"Nah." He grinned. "Chessly saw you headed this way and walked me here."

"How long have you been standing there?" I stuffed my pencil back behind my ear and turned sideways on the bench.

"Long enough to hear you've hidden some things about yourself from me." Stepping closer to the piano, he asked, "How is it you're majoring in English and pre-law rather than music? You're fucking *talented.*"

My face heated at his compliment. "In high school I took music classes and briefly entertained a music career until I remembered I didn't want to work multiple low-wage jobs in order to eat while I followed my muse."

"That's a damn shame. I don't know much about music, but I know what sounds good. Your playing is stunning. Will you play me something?"

For some reason, the idea of playing privately for Callahan made my stomach fizz with nerves. Several times in my life I'd played recitals in front of a hundred people, yet I never wanted to impress any of them as much I wanted to impress him. With a nod followed by a deep breath, I returned to the piece in front of me and began to play.

After a few bars, I somehow managed to forget he was in the room as the music carried me into a romantic fantasy of sound I could never describe in words. It was only as I held down the last note, letting the sustain pedal drag it out into the ether, that

Callahan's clean, masculine scent washed over me, alerting me to the fact he stood directly behind me.

"Jesus, Jamaica," he whispered. "I've never heard anything so beautiful in my life." He stood beside the bench and pointed to the open space beside me. "May I?"

With a ghost of a shrug I said, "Sure."

He took up more than half the bench, the heat of his body warming my entire left side and reminding me of the dearth of heat in the mostly forgotten room.

"How long have you been playing?"

"Since second grade."

"Impressive. My sister started lessons in second grade too, but she's not even close to your league." The expression in his eyes was one of sincerity—and something like pride.

I have no idea what possessed me to blurt out my life story, but before I could stop myself, it came pouring out. "I grew up with a single mom who worked long shifts in the truck-stop diner, which meant I learned early on how to entertain myself." I plucked at a few keys. "It also meant I spent long days at school. One day, my elementary music teacher caught me trying to work out a song on the piano when I should have been in the after-school program. Instead of escorting me back, he sat down beside me and started teaching me."

"Guess he saw your talent early," Callahan said with a smile.

When he didn't judge me, I continued. "By the end of sixth grade, I could play Beethoven and Bach with proficiency. Mr. Munari even invited me to play solos during our music programs for our parents. Mom couldn't afford lessons, of course, but Mr. Munari said someone with my talent and interest shouldn't be denied a chance to learn based on money." Sneaking a glance at him from the corner of my eye, I noted he still had that smile on his face—one that said he was enjoying himself.

"The wonderful thing I discovered about attending a liberal arts college was that I could pick up general credits in any field, which meant more piano lessons that my academic scholarship pays for. Spending hours at the piano is necessary rather than recreational."

He frowned. "Why do you have to justify it? As good as you are, you should play all the time if you want."

Snorting out a laugh, I said, "Indulging my hobby won't get me into law school, Hotshot." I gathered up my music, stacking it neatly, and closed the lid on the piano. "I think you mentioned something about ice cream?"

The disappointment on his face was almost comical. "You're done? Are you sure you don't need to practice something else? I promise I'll sit so quietly you won't even know I'm here."

"What time is it?"

He checked his phone. "Quarter after nine."

"I've been down here for two hours already. That's enough for today." Rising from the bench, I indicated he should stand too, and I pushed it into place beneath the keyboard.

When we reached my room, I turned to him before I unlocked the door. "You came over to take me out for ice cream. There will be no shenanigans. Understood?"

He saluted me with one hand. "Scout's honor."

But I noticed his other hand behind his back, and I could almost see his crossed fingers. With narrowed eyes, I unlocked my door and walked into my room. "I'll just grab a sweatshirt—"

In one quick move, he pushed me against the wall and cut off my words when he sealed his mouth to mine. Damn. The man's mouth was pure magic, stealing all my strength and good intentions with a single press of his firm lips on mine. Of their own volition, my arms twined around his thick neck, and I mashed my front to the rock-hard planes of his chest as I sank into his kiss. Before long, our tongues tangled, our breathing labored, and my ankle anchored over his hip as he squeezed and kneaded my ass.

At last, I tore my mouth from his. Panting, I said, "I thought we established there would be no shenanigans."

"Correction, that was your idea."

"But you saluted."

His grin was positively wicked. "I had my fingers crossed."

I pushed at his chest. "I knew it! I saw how you kept one hand behind your back."

Sliding out from beneath his arms where he'd caged me in by the wall, I snagged my hoodie off the chair and tugged it over my head. Fluffing out my hair, I said, "You promised ice cream."

He smirked. "I'd rather lick you."

My knees snapped together as heat flooded my core. "You are unbelievable."

"Believe me, Island Girl." His eyes darkened. "I know how delicious you are."

The desire in his eyes was almost palpable, and I sucked in a breath. "Ice cream."

"Yeah, all right." He made a show of adjusting the front of his jeans. "I did promise you ice cream."

As I watched him, I might have whimpered, and he shot me a sexy, knowing leer. I grabbed my phone and stuffed it in my pocket along with my wallet and headed for the door.

The ice-cream shop was only a block down the street from my dorm. We walked the distance in silence, though we kept stealing glances and bumping shoulders and slipping each other little grins. When we arrived, Callahan shot me the naughtiest of all naughty smirks and ordered a double cherry vanilla cone, which he made a show of licking long and slow, followed by shallow little touches of his tongue to the treat. With superhuman effort, I suppressed the moan that tried to escape as he carried on with his antics. But I couldn't stop myself from crossing my legs, clamping them together hard as a mini-orgasm threatened low in my belly.

At last, he gave me a reprieve. Kinda. Instead of teasing me with his tongue on his ice cream, he asked, "Do you ever play concerts?"

I snorted a laugh. "Hardly. When I was in high school, I played some recitals." Spooning a bite of pistachio deliciousness, I swallowed and added, "As part of my current class, I have to work something up for a recital as my piano final."

"Yeah? Is it public? Can anyone attend?"

Ducking my chin, I frowned. "Are you saying you want to attend a piano recital?"

His brows went up. "After I gave you tickets to watch me play football, are you saying you won't invite me to watch your recital?" Though his tone was playful, I thought I detected a touch of hurt edging it.

"All music recitals are public." I gave him a cheeky smile. "And they're free, but you have to arrive early if you want good seats."

"I'll keep that in mind." In two large bites, he finished off his cone. "Do you have a piano at home?"

"Single mom. Waitresses in a diner, remember?" Not wanting to see his judgment, I stared at my spoon as I scraped the last taste of ice cream from the paper cup.

"So how do you play in the summer?"

Of all the people I didn't want to judge me, the gorgeous man in front of me topped the list. When I glanced up, I saw only genuine curiosity in his expression.

As though it were no big deal, I shrugged even as my heart raced in my chest. "One of my piano instructors helped me land a position as a counselor at a summer music camp for teens. It sure as hell beat working split shifts as a barista at a coffee kiosk and desk-clerking at a local hotel like I'd done through the summers in high school." I caught his raised brow. "My mom wouldn't let me work at the diner." I wiped my mouth with my napkin and enjoyed the way his eyes tracked my motion.

"Why wouldn't your mom let you work at the diner?"

"Didn't want me to end up like her, I guess."

"Meaning what?"

Glancing out the window, I said, "Working at the summer camp is fun. The kids are all super-talented, so I hear a ton of great music. Plus, the camp counselors put on a concert at the end, and that's always a blast."

He peered at me through narrowed eyes. "Are the other counselors all girls too?"

I kind of choke-snorted at his obvious fishing. "It's a co-ed camp, Hotshot, so that would be a no."

Running the pad of his index finger over the top of my hand, he asked, "Did you date any of them?"

"Did you date any of the jersey chasers who follow you around like it's their job?"

"You already know the answer to that. No." All four fingers rubbed up and down the back of my hand.

"The first summer, I had a thing with one of them." Remembering that bad experience soured my ice cream.

"From the look on your face, he wasn't me."

Callahan's cockiness cracked me up. "No, he wasn't." Sobering, I added, "His problem was he liked all the counselors. Turns out he was sleeping with me, another girl from a cabin across the camp, and his roommate."

"Was his roommate a guy?"

"Yep. A real drama queen who outed him to both of us girls. The other girl was fine with it."

"But you weren't."

My eyes caught his and held. "Fidelity matters to me."

We were quiet for a long moment, then I stood and walked my trash over to the trash can near the door of the shop. Though the place only had five tables in it, we were the last people left.

From the looks the guy behind the counter kept throwing us, it was time for us to go.

When we headed back to my place, Hotshot slipped his arm around me and tugged me close to his side. "For the record, I don't cheat. Ever."

"Good to know." I smiled. "Thanks for the ice cream."

"Thanks for the mini-concert." He squeezed me closer. "You gonna invite me in?"

CHAPTER TWENTY-THREE

Callahan

AS WE NEARED the doors to Jamaica's dorm, I slipped my hand beneath her sweatshirt and teased my fingers along her side, reveling in the goose bumps I raised on her skin. As hard as she pretended I didn't get to her, her body gave her away every time. While I truly hadn't come over to her place with the idea of repeating Saturday night, watching her eat ice cream, her pink tongue licking the spoon the way I wanted her to lick me, changed my mind.

"It's a school night," she hedged even as she pressed closer to my side.

"Only for a minute, Island Girl," I coaxed.

She glanced at my other hand, and I laughed. "No, I don't have my fingers crossed."

"Okay, but only for a minute. I have a nine o'clock class in the morning."

"I lift at six."

When she relaxed into me, I didn't bother to tell her that on a few occasions, I'd partied all night on a Thursday and still made a six o'clock lift session on Friday morning. What I was thinking about doing with her was far easier on my body, even if it was a workout.

She keyed us into her room, and I tossed my snapback onto her desk and pulled my hoodie over my head, dropping it over the back of her recliner. That chair had given me all kinds of ideas the first time I'd seen it. As I lowered myself into it, those ideas crashed into the forefront of my thoughts.

"A leather recliner isn't standard dorm furniture."

Careful to hold her shirt down with one hand—damn it— she peeled her hoodie over her head and hung it on a peg on the back of the door. "It's my one indulgence and the only piece of furniture I own."

Somehow she managed to skirt my legs and seat herself on the edge of her single bed. The revelation about her recliner changed my plans. I didn't want us to break it if we got too rambunctious in it, which with the current state of my cock was a distinct possibility.

"It's comfy. And big enough for two if you sit on my lap."

"Callahan," she warned.

Running my hands over the butter-soft leather, I said, "Yeah, you're right. We should take care of your one piece of furniture, especially with how much it helps you read every book five or six times," I teased.

Crossing her arms over her pretty rack, she harrumphed. "Not all of us were born with an eidetic memory, smart-ass."

That harrumph was cute as hell.

"For the sake of your academic needs, we'll spare the chair." In one quick move, I pinned her to her mattress. "But dorm furniture is fair game."

The first quarter in the piano room showed me yet another attractive side to my girl. The flirting in the second quarter at the ice cream shop revealed we were on the same page when it came to exclusivity. The third quarter was touch and go until she invited me inside. Fourth quarters were always about winning. I intended for both of us to win. She squeaked my name and squirmed beneath me. Then we locked eyes, and the game changed.

Taking my time, I lowered myself along her side, careful not to squish her, and ran my nose along her jaw, dropping a kiss on her chin and nibbling my way to her lips. The kiss began slow and gentle until she shifted to press her front to my front. Fisting her hands in my shirt, she urged me closer, and I accepted her silent invitation.

I slid my hand beneath her shirt, smoothing my way along her satiny skin until I found the clasp of her bra. As I deepened the kiss, I unclasped her bra and let my hand roam until I found my prize. Cupping her firm breast, I discovered her taut nipple. Unable to resist such a gorgeous find, I worried it with my thumb and index finger and enjoyed hearing the whimpers coming from the back of her throat.

Her fingers tangled in my hair, tugging it the way I liked when I planted my face between her thighs. Our tongues tangled, mimicking the rhythms and motions I wanted to do with other parts of our bodies. When at last I needed air, I tore my mouth from hers and sat up, pulling Jamaica up with me.

The dazed expression on her face mirrored my own feelings. Kissing this girl was the hottest experience of my life and one I knew I'd never tire of even if I was lucky enough to have it every day. Gathering my shirt at the back of my collar, I dragged it over my head and tossed it in the seat of the recliner. When she didn't immediately follow my lead, I pushed her shirt and bra up her sides and over her head to join mine in the chair.

"Mmm." I licked my lips as I stared at the tight little buds of her nipples. "Cherries and cream. Did I mention that's my favorite?"

She answered with a heavy-lidded expression I had no trouble deciphering. Easing her back onto the mattress, I went to work pleasuring one pretty nipple with my lips, tongue, and teeth while plucking and petting the other. Writhing and moaning beneath me, she speared her fingers into my hair and held me to her, telling me exactly how much she enjoyed my attentions to her beautiful breasts.

I played with her chest until she pushed me away. "It's too much, Callahan. I can't take it," she pleaded.

Yeah, she could, but I gave her a break as I licked and kissed my way to the waistband of her leggings. God, I loved how she filled out a pair of them. Hooking my fingers in the elastic, I tugged them down ahead of my mouth until she had to lift her hips to let me ease them off her. Though I gave her gorgeous tits a rest, that didn't mean I'd be taking it easy on her pretty pussy. Burying my face between her thighs, I kissed her once as a warning before I went to town licking and sucking her clit. Her sweet taste fired me up, and I hummed my appreciation against her skin.

Sliding my fingers into her wet channel, I pumped in rhythm with my tongue. She rewarded my efforts by moving her hips with me. Her head thrashed on the pillow as she tugged my hair hard. Fuck, I loved how she didn't hold back, showing me how much she enjoyed what I did to her. The whimpers and moans and oh-God-Callahans that escaped her lips spurred me on. She covered her mouth with both hands, her muffled screams telling me she was about to tip over the edge. When she clamped those luscious thighs around my head, her body going rigid with her release, I sucked her clit hard, my fingers pumping steadily in and out.

And she lost it.

Her body arched, her hips lifting us up off the bed as my name echoed around the walls of her room.

That was what I was after.

As she settled back onto the mattress, I sat up on my knees between her legs. Deliberately capturing her eyes, I licked and sucked her sweetness from my fingers and enjoyed the hitch in her breathing, the involuntary squeeze of her thighs against mine.

"You're better than ice cream, babe."

"Oh," came out on a croak. She swallowed a couple of times and said, "I can't believe we just did that. In my room."

I bounced up off the bed, shucked my jeans and boxers, and pulled a condom from my wallet. Jacking myself a couple of times, I asked, "You want to do the honors?"

"Um."

Her uncertain glance at her bed drew a chuckle. "Babe, we only need room for one." Nodding toward her precious recliner, I said, "We could even enjoy this in your favorite chair."

When she narrowed her eyes at my suggestion, I grinned and knelt between her legs again, rubbing the pad of my finger over her still-hard clit. Surging up to meet my touch, she cried out and snatched the foil packet from my fingers. With stunning alacrity she suited me up and lay back, taking me down with her. She guided me to her pussy, and I didn't have to be asked twice.

This girl. Fuck. I'd never wanted anyone as much as I wanted Jamaica Winslow.

Still, I took my time and filled her slowly, inch by inch, until I was balls-deep inside her. The green of her eyes deepened to black as she clawed at my shoulders and wrapped her endless legs around me, urging me deeper. Her slick, tight heat was heaven on earth, and I wanted nothing more than to pound into her—hard. Instead, I leaned down and took her mouth, ravaging her lips and tongue, sucking and biting and tasting until she started writhing and squirming beneath me. Only then did I start to move.

Her soft body molded perfectly to mine as she matched my leisurely rhythms. But those didn't last—not with how much she'd been on my mind, especially after Saturday night. Especially after learning more about her tonight. I pushed up onto my knees and lifted her knees, pushing them up on either side of her head as I pounded into her. Digging her nails into the backs of my hands, she held on, her eyes blazing green fire into mine. Then she threw her head back and opened her mouth in a silent scream, and that was it. Lightning barreled down my spine as the orgasm tore through me. Her name left my throat on a shout as her inner muscles clamped around me, milking every last drop of life out of me.

At last, I let go of her thighs, and her feet hit the mattress on either side of my hips as I collapsed on her, my face buried in the pillow above her shoulder. Long minutes later I sensed her fingertips gliding up and down my sweaty back, sending shivers over my skin. I groaned and wished I could stay right here, joined to her, for the rest of my life. But since I outweighed my lady by about a hundred pounds, I knew I had to move and let her breathe.

Carefully, I pulled out and disposed of the condom in the trash can beside the desk. Then I tugged the covers out from under her and slid in beside her, urging her onto her side so we could both fit on her narrow bed. With our faces mere inches from each other on the pillow, I studied her even as she studied me. I smiled as I tangled my fingers in the soft curls our playtime had dislodged from her headband.

"You're really something, Island Girl."

Her full, pouty lips begged for a kiss, which I was only too happy to steal from her.

"For the record, my only goal for coming over here tonight was to take you out for ice cream." I fingered a curl then dropped my palm to her cheek and ran my thumb along her jaw. "But the way you savored your treat gave me other ideas."

"Which totally explains how you came prepared with a condom in your wallet." She smirked as she traced the tat on my chest with her fingertips.

"After what went down between us on Saturday night, I

thought it was wise to be prepared." I smiled. "After tonight, I'm always going to have two in my wallet."

"You are entirely too cocky, Hotshot." The way she touched me, tracing the football tat on my skin, took all the heat out of her chastisement.

"You are entirely too tempting, Island Girl."

Even in the low light coming from her desk lamp, I caught the pink that stained her cheeks at my compliment. Jamaica was such a contradiction. Single-mindedly focused on her pre-law classes, totally no-nonsense when it came to school, yet funny, musically gifted, and the hottest woman I'd ever had in the sack. She blew my mind. When she was out in public, nothing and no one—except for Dr. Dair—fazed her. But in private whenever I gave her a genuine compliment, she colored up or ducked her head or deflected. I had the sense she didn't see in herself anything other people could easily see. That kind of humility drew me to her as much as her kick-ass brain and gorgeous body.

The quiet sigh that puffed over my chest told me my girl was about to drop off. It seemed to be a pattern with her: I sexed her up, she blew my mind, and then she crashed. But I couldn't spend the night in her narrow bed and still be functional in the weight room in the morning.

"Hey, babe. Don't fall asleep."

"Huh? What?" She already sounded incoherent.

Sliding my hand down, I gave her ass a spank. With a squeak, she arched into me and nearly knocked me off the bed. "What was that for?" Indignation replaced incoherence, and I grinned.

"Women's dorm. You need to walk me out."

"Ugh!" She flopped back down on the bed. Then she walked her fingers up my abs and over my chest, shooting me a coy expression from beneath her brows. "You could stay here."

"Sorry, babe. Your bed is too small for the two of us all night." I covered her wandering hand with mine, pinning it to my skin.

"Plus, I only brought one condom. No way would I be able to spend all night with you without waking you up at least once for another round. I'm not tough enough to have you this close for hours and not want to be inside you."

Her eyes sparkled. "There's a condom machine in the community bathroom in the lobby."

"You still have to get up and either go there yourself or escort me there." I laughed at her grimace. "No matter how you try to avoid it, you have to get up, put on some clothes, and escort me out."

"Fine," she huffed.

This close to midnight on a Monday, the lobby was deserted. She walked me to the front door where I pulled her in close. "We're still on for a study session tomorrow night, right?"

She tossed me a look. "Of course."

Clearing my throat, I said, "Do we have to meet in the library or the Union?"

Furrowing her brow in consternation, she asked, "Where else would we meet?"

"After practice, I could pick you up from work and drive you to my place. There's plenty of room there, and no one else will be home."

"I don't know, Hotshot."

Pulling out my ace, I said, "Absolutely zero chance of interruptions from jersey chasers."

As I'd hoped, that grabbed her attention. "I have to admit, that's a plus."

Lowering my head, I whispered against her lips, "I'll pick you up at eight-ish. Maybe you should put your toothbrush and a change of clothes in your backpack."

"Callahan—"

I kissed her half-hearted protest right out of her head. When I looked back from the sidewalk a few minutes later, she was watching me with a sweet little smile on her face.

Chapter Twenty-Four

Jamaica

"YOU GOT LUCKY last night, didn't you, girl?" Axel's eyes danced over the rim of his latte.

"Keep your voice down, wouldja?" I hissed.

A group of girls at a nearby table were sneaking glances our way and being conspicuously quiet. I thought I recognized two of them as members of Tory Miller's posse. When one of them stood up and walked slowly past our table on her way to dropping her empty cup in the trash, I noticed a Wildcats jersey beneath her jacket, confirming my suspicions.

Axel utterly ignored my hiss. "Deets, darling."

"I don't ask you that," I countered.

The epic eye roll included his entire head. "I live with my man. It goes without saying I get lucky on the regular."

"Then why do you feel the need to pry into my love life?" I pushed at my bangs, gave up, and readjusted my headband.

"Because you're living my fantasy and sleeping with Callahan O'Reilly." He grinned and sipped his coffee.

Relief washed over me when I slid a surreptitious glance at the jersey chasers and found them whispering with each other. Nodding in the direction of their table, I said, "I'd rather not discuss this with an audience who are even more interested in my answers than you are. But for the record, he took me out for ice cream."

"You want me to believe ice cream is all you licked?" He smirked.

"Axel! Jesus. Knock it off." I sat back in my chair and almost scalded the roof of my mouth when I hid behind a massive swig of my flat white.

"Confirmed. You licked more than ice cream." Reaching across the table, he offered his fist to bump.

I left him hanging. "Sometimes I wonder how we're friends."

Merrily unoffended, he shot me a cheeky grin. "The best of friends. Because we watch out for each other and share our own gossip." He leaned both forearms on the table, his tone conspiratorial. "He's not selfish in bed, is he?"

"Will you let up? Please?" It wasn't only the eavesdroppers at the next table that kept me quiet about Callahan: for some reason, sharing my private experiences with Hotshot felt like I was betraying him—us—somehow.

Raising a finger to his lips, Axel nodded as if he were my therapist or something. "So that's how it is." A genuine smile spread over his mouth. "This isn't a fling. You're serious about him, aren't you?"

I sighed. "I guess? I don't exactly know."

"BS. You *do* know." A cloud fell over his features. "And I know you. Don't you dare screw up a good thing by being scared."

It was my turn to lean forward. "Axel, he's a *player*. With a reputation he didn't deny when I asked."

"I've seen the way he looks at you, how he can't stop touching you whenever he has the chance." He reached across the table and squeezed my forearm. "I'm a guy. Trust me when I say he might have been a player in the past, but he's not playing now."

My friend's words ran on repeat in my head hours later when I was closing down the sweet shop. As I jammed my homework into my backpack, a movement outside the door caught my attention. Hotshot waved through the glass then stuffed his hands in his pockets and rocked on his heels as he waited for me to finish.

After I locked the door, he caught me by the shoulders, leaned down, and brushed a kiss over my cheek. "Hello, Island Girl."

His warm smile washed over me like a balmy breeze, which was a gift considering the blustery day we were headed into. So I returned it.

"Hello, Hotshot." He smelled clean and fresh as though he'd come directly from the shower. "Did you come straight from practice?"

With a nod, he dropped an arm across my shoulders and guided me toward the stairs. "I didn't want you to have to wait for me."

Tilting my head at him, I said, "So you haven't had dinner?"

The rumbling of his stomach answered my question before he did. "I had a protein shake at the end of practice."

"We can study in a café if you want. That way you can grab dinner."

"Nah. I have it covered." At my raised brow, he clarified, "Before I left home this morning, I put stew in the Crock-Pot. It should be perfect when we arrive."

"Unless your roommates raided it." I smirked.

An enigmatic grin ghosted over his features. "There's enough."

After we reached his place and walked into the kitchen, I understood what he meant. I had no idea regular people could buy industrial-size appliances. The Crock-Pot was big enough to hold a five-pound bag of potatoes, a ten-pound roast at least, and a myriad of additional vegetables. Even though I'd grabbed a bite before my shift at the store, the savory smell of meat and veg roasting in gravy had my stomach rumbling.

"We can eat in about fifteen minutes."

My brows came together. "Didn't you say your dinner's been cooking all day?"

"Yeah. But you can't eat stew without biscuits." The "duh" in his tone had me tucking my chin.

By the time I'd shrugged out of my jacket, hung it on a peg by the door, and set my backpack down by the couch, he'd whipped up a batch of drop biscuits and was sliding them into the oven. After he set the timer, he stalked over to me, stopping an inch in front of me.

"How do you suppose we're going to distract ourselves from how hungry we are for the next ten minutes?" His eyes followed his fingers rubbing one of my curls between them.

"We could make a plan for our study session," I teased, grinning from beneath my brows.

Those gorgeous blue eyes blazed. "Or we could say hello properly."

He slid his fingers beneath my hair at the back of my neck and lowered his lips to mine. The kiss began as "hello," but then his other hand squeezed my hip and pulled me into him. I wrapped my arms around his neck, holding on as "hello" morphed into "all I've thought about for the past twenty-four hours is what happened in your bed last night." Our lips fused to each other as our tongues tangled and chased. His hard length pressed into my belly and flooded my core with heat. Of their own volition my hips moved, and I shamelessly rubbed myself against him. When the buzzer on the oven blared that our dinner was ready, I'd forgotten all about stew and biscuits and that I was at his place to prepare for Dr. Dair's class.

For a couple of seconds he rested his forehead on mine as we caught our breath. With a rueful smile, he slowly let me go and sauntered over to the oven to retrieve the biscuits before they burned. I watched in fascination as he expertly slid them into a bowl he'd lined with a tea towel and covered them before setting them on the table. As he set out butter and silverware, I asked, "What can I do to help?"

"Nothing. Just sit your pretty ass in a chair."

A minute later he carried two steaming bowls of savory-smelling stew to the table, setting one in front of me. He returned with two small plates for our biscuits and pulled out the chair beside me.

The second I dug my fork into my dinner, his three roommates appeared as if by magic.

"Hey, Jamaica. Didn't know you'd be over tonight," Finn said as he filled a bowl to the brim with stew and carried it to the table as though it contained liquid gold.

"Hi, Jamaica. Bet you had no idea your boyfriend could cook," Bax said as he stepped in behind Finn for his share of food.

"Had a bad day today, Bax?" I asked with a nod to his T-shirt, which read "What in the capital F?"

The third roommate I hadn't met yet laughed and said, "Nah, that's Bax's default state." Seeing that my hands were occupied, he contented himself with a wave. "Nice to meet you finally. I'm Danny Chambers, the adult among this band of reprobates."

I smiled. "Nice to meet you too." As advertised, something about Danny gave him the appearance of a man several years older than the rest of the crew even though Callahan said they were about the same age.

Callahan leaned in to whisper in my ear, "Grab two biscuits now, babe."

"Two? Why?" I whispered back.

"You'll figure it out after your first bite. But if you wait to taste the first one before you grab the second one you won't get it."

Gazing around at the half ton of male perfection filling the room, I decided to do as he suggested. Though the table seated six normal people, after Danny filled his bowl and joined us, the space became rather crowded. As Hotshot had warned, the two dozen biscuits he'd whipped up only minutes before disappeared at an alarming speed as the guys tucked into their meals. In short order, each of them was on seconds while half of my firsts remained in my bowl.

"May I have the butter, please?" I asked Finn who was hoarding it across the table.

"May I have half of your biscuit?" he asked.

I blinked and Callahan laughed. Then I glanced into the biscuit bowl and discovered it was empty.

"You were right, Callahan. These biscuits are to die for."

He grinned at my compliment.

Turning my attention back to Finn, I added, "I can eat this whole thing"—I held my treat in my hand—"without butter just fine. But I'd rather not."

He pulled the pot of butter closer to his bowl. "You have something I want. I have something you want. I learned in my government class that when that happens, both sides have to compromise." His grin was triumphant.

I tore my remaining biscuit in half, letting a bit of buttery-smelling steam escape, and held onto one half while I dipped the other in the stew gravy. "Mmm, that's even better than butter," I said after swallowing a bite. After dipping my biscuit in my stew again, I bit into it slowly, teasing Finn with my eyes, then I chewed, swallowed, and licked my lips. "Yep. I've always kinda been a fan of biscuits and gravy, but Callahan's are my new favorite."

Beside me, I sensed him tense with my little show of defiance to his roommate, but the compliment reminded him he always had my attention. The other two guys watched in avid fascination, probably because they were hoping for a shot at the last half of biscuit too.

With ill grace, Finn slid the butter across the table. "You're evil, Jamaica. Pure evil." Shifting his attention to Callahan, he said, "You're a nice guy, 'Han. How did you end up with such a wicked woman?"

The pout on his face cracked me up as I liberally slathered butter on the remaining half of the biscuit and took a normal, human-size bite as opposed to eating half a biscuit in one football-player-size bite like every guy at the table. No wonder two dozen biscuits disappeared in a blink.

Callahan slipped his hand beneath the table and rested it high enough on my thigh to make me squirm. "Lucky, I guess."

Right as I finished my dinner, I slapped a hand over my mouth as an unladylike belch escaped. Callahan squeezed my thigh while three pairs of eyes snapped to me. Then the entire table erupted in laughter.

Ducking my head, I excused myself, stood, and started gathering empty bowls.

"No need to be embarrassed, Jamaica. That qualifies as a compliment to the chef at our house," Bax said, his eyes dancing.

"You don't have to clean up, girl. 'Han cooked, so it's Finn's turn to do dishes," Danny added.

I set the bowls in the sink and returned to the table for plates and utensils. "My mama raised me to help, especially when someone else does the cooking."

"That's our division of labor too, Island Girl. You've done half of Finn's work for him, which makes up for that biscuit, huh, buddy?" Callahan grinned at Finn who flipped him the bird. "Come on, let's go do some homework." He reached a hand to me, and without thinking, I slipped my hand in his.

A speculative gleam came into Danny's eyes. "Work, huh?

I've never considered swappin' spit work." Leaning back in his chair, he chortled at his own joke.

With the glance Callahan slanted my way he must have picked up on my heated cheeks. "*Homework*, dumbass. Jamaica and I have a project to finish for a class we have together. Get your mind out of the gutter."

Danny shot an eloquent stare at where Callahan's arm now encircled my waist, but he kept his mouth shut.

Sliding out from beneath his arm, I walked to the door and snagged my backpack. "I thought you said your roommates weren't going to be home tonight."

Blowing out a breath, he said, "They weren't—until Finn forgot something and had to come home before practice. He sent out the all-call on our group text, alerting the other guys that I'd made stew in the Crock-Pot." He ran a hand through his hair and replaced his backward ball cap. "Guess that changed their plans."

"Guess that changes ours too."

"What do you mean? We have to work on *Emma*, and I'm out of town this weekend. We're leaving early Friday morning."

"I didn't mean about our study plans. I meant about the other plans—the ones that included you asking me to pack my toothbrush." I patted my bag.

A feral gleam lit his eyes. "I have the master. It's as close to soundproof as you can get outside of a music studio or something." Stepping into me, he added, "We're far less likely to be heard in my room than in yours." He gave me some room. "Just sayin'."

Taking my hand again, he led me up the stairs.

CHAPTER TWENTY-FIVE

Callahan

"MISS WINSLOW, DID you have a question?" Dr. Dair stared over the top of his glasses at my girl—no mean feat considering we sat at least ten rows up from the dais where he stood behind his lectern.

"I don't see Emma as a feminist at all. She runs her father's house because he's a widower. That was common for unmarried young women at the time." The professor dialed up his stare, and Jamaica sat a touch straighter in her seat. "She spends all her free time matchmaking everyone in her acquaintance. Preoccupation with marriage was also common at the time. Austen is making fun of that in the book for sure, but I'm having trouble seeing Emma as anything more than a caricature of Regency women."

"You don't believe inherent feminism plays into trying to supersede the wishes of a father or guardian when it came to the determination of whom a young woman was to wed?" he asked.

"Wives and mothers held a great deal of influence over who their husbands chose for their daughters. Austen herself is an example of an independent woman for the time considering she turned down a marriage proposal her father had approved," Jamaica countered.

"Emma has convinced her father to let her make her own choices as well, true?"

"It benefited him to indulge her. She ran his home and kept up his social calendar so he didn't have to think about either. Even though the story focuses on the titular character, most of the events in it benefited the male characters, which is what Austen is criticizing."

"I'll be interested in how you address these ideas in your project." The tone of his voice hinted more at criticism than interest, and in spite of myself I bristled. His attitude toward Jamaica annoyed me enough, but now it seemed it threatened me too since our project was half mine. Or maybe he thought she was carrying all the weight since I was majoring in sports marketing rather than English.

When Dr. Dair directed his attention to the suck-ups in the front row, I sensed my girl deflate beside me, and I leaned into her. "You're the most independent and exciting woman I've ever met. When it comes to feminism, that man is a clueless wonder."

"Clueless or not, he holds the key to my future," she whispered.

I rubbed my hand over her knee, giving her an encouraging squeeze. As always when I touched her anywhere on her legs, she rewarded me with a tiny squirm, telling me how my touch affected her. Suddenly my mind was on the night before when we'd started out with her sitting at my desk, me propped against the headboard on my bed, and ended up with both of us tangled in the sheets.

Now I was squirming in my seat.

As usual, Axel missed none of it, smirking at the two of us and shaking his head.

After class as I walked her to Huffine Hall, her mood hovered somewhere near the sidewalk. "I'm not trying to be contrary with him, but he brings it out in me. I honestly don't care if he wants Emma to be a feminist. The argument has nothing to do with our approach to the text anyway." She hitched her backpack higher on her shoulder.

Catching her free hand, I brought it to my lips and brushed a kiss over it. "I was proud of you in class today."

"You were?"

"Dair was an ass. But you held your own without being snarky or disrespectful. The way he tried to look down his nose at you and then dismissed you in that tone…" I threaded my fingers through hers. "I wanted to sack his ass, drive him right into the turf."

She snorted. "Have you noticed that all your metaphors are football-related?"

"Can't imagine why," I said drily.

Her giggle was exactly what I needed.

When we reached the intersection in the sidewalk that took her to class and me to the gym, I pulled her aside and shoved my fingers into her endlessly fascinating curls. Sliding my other arm around her waist, I tugged her close enough to rub my nose along hers. "I can't see you tomorrow night, but I have an hour or so after practice tonight."

"I have a staff meeting that'll probably go until nine or nine-thirty." Her tone was glum again.

At least this time she was sad about not seeing me rather than upset about our jackass prof.

"I'll be in the lobby of your dorm, say 9:15 p.m.?"

She hesitated for a fraction of a second, but after all these weeks I'd figured out her tells. Yes, she wanted to see me tonight. No, she thought she shouldn't see me tonight after spending last night in my bed. Sealing my lips to hers, I helped her make the correct decision.

Fuck, I loved kissing this girl. Those plush, soft lips were made to mold to mine. When I slipped her some tongue, she got right with the program and tangled hers with mine. Tilting my head, I changed the angle and deepened the kiss. She dug her fingers into my shoulders and smashed her delicious rack against my chest. The moan in the back of her throat vibrated into mine, and I held her closer. Desire throbbed through my veins, hot and insistent, and I forgot all about where we were and what we were supposed to be doing.

The shrill, unwelcome voice of Tory Miller interrupting our fun reminded me. "Callahan O'Reilly! What do you think you're doing?"

With a lingering press of my lips to Jamaica's, I slowly surfaced back to the real world and out of my fantasy of skipping the rest of the day and heading directly for her narrow bed. Tory and her posse practically surrounded us, all of them glaring mostly at Jamaica.

"Until you rudely interrupted, I was kissing my girlfriend." The snark slipped out before I could remember who I was talking to and what kind of damage she could do.

Tory planted her hands on her hips. "You couldn't possibly mean that this"—she wrinkled her nose in disgust as she gave Jamaica the once-over—"*person* is your girlfriend. Especially after what happened between us last spring."

In my arms Jamaica's body went rigid.

The choice between potential damage from Tory and the best thing that ever happened to me walking away was a no-brainer. "I don't know what you've been smoking, but nothing happened between us last spring—or ever." My words were as much for the woman in my arms as for the skank in front of me.

Something vicious crossed Tory's features before she schooled her lips into a pout. "That's not true, and you know it."

"It is true, and *you* know it. Now, if you'll excuse us, ladies, we're headed to class." I tightened my arm around Jamaica's waist and stepped through two of the freshmen who didn't fuss about letting us pass.

"Don't you walk away from me, Callahan," Tory warned. "We're not done here."

Ignoring her, I walked Jamaica to her building. I was going to be late for film, which meant Coach would probably punish me with extra drills in practice. Worth it for the pleasant interlude with my girl—not so much for the confrontation with a spoiled bitch trying to impress her little gang of wannabes.

The way Jamaica reacted to Tory made me want to look out for her. I had no doubt she could hold her own with that group of nasties, but I didn't see the point of walking away and leaving her to it when I was already right there.

"Um, Callahan—"

"Nothing happened, babe. I drunk-kissed her once for a minute in a hallway at a frat party, and I've stayed far away from her since." We stood in front of her building. "I'll see you tonight." I grinned. "And I plan on kissing you for a lot longer than a minute." For emphasis, I brushed a kiss over her lips. Then I turned her toward the door and patted her on the ass.

She shot me a narrow-eyed glare over her shoulder. "You're going to pay for that, Hotshot."

"I'm counting on it, Island Girl."

I'm pretty sure I heard her laugh as she opened the door and disappeared inside the building.

Taking a seat in a deep leather chair in a corner of the lobby of Jamaica's dorm, I flipped the bill of my hat forward and scrolled through my phone. I was going for inconspicuous as I waited for my girl to finish her meeting. Too bad Tory's posse had radar or tracking devices or something when it came to guys on the team.

"Callahan?"

I made the mistake of glancing up to a voice that wasn't my girl's.

"It is you. What are you doing here? Shouldn't you be at the library tonight?"

"Huh?" *Smooth, O'Reilly. But, what the ever-lovin' fuck?*

"I thought you studied at the library after evening practice."

With a raised brow I stared hard at her, and the girl fidgeted from foot to foot. Good. She should be uncomfortable keeping track of my schedule. It was bad enough the university posted the players' academic schedules online to make sure people knew we were actually student athletes or some shit. Now I had jersey chasers bird-dogging my off hours too? Jesus.

"Um, Tory and the other girls are at the library. I wasn't feeling well, so I stayed home. I can text them you're here." She reached toward the pocket of her sweats.

"Don't bother."

Her hand hovered above her pocket, a stunned expression on her face. Conversation carried up the stairwell in the middle of the lobby. A familiar snort-laugh followed it. Without another word for the jersey chaser, I stood and headed for the stairs. Leaning against the railing at the top, I smiled as Jamaica laughed again at something Chessly said.

This girl.

I'd never admit it to any of my buddies, but I had it so bad for her.

As if she sensed my thoughts, she glanced up, her laughter dying on her lips only to be replaced with the most gorgeous smile in the world.

"Hey, Hotshot."

"Hey, Island Girl."

"Hello, Callahan," Chessly said. With a smirk in Jamaica's

direction, she added, "You were pretty patient with Liana's endless questions tonight considering who was waiting for you."

"Jamaica warned me her meeting could run late." I caught her hand when she joined me at the top of the stairs. "But waiting even five minutes is forever." Tugging her hand to my lips, I brushed a kiss over the back of it and let my eyes tell her exactly why.

Her whisper of a gasp told me she understood me perfectly.

Apparently, so did Chessly. "I'll leave you two lovebirds to it." She smirked. "See you tomorrow, J. Have a nice evening." The way she emphasized "nice evening" had me smirking back at her.

"You two done with all your innuendo?" Jamaica huffed.

Her attitude didn't faze her friend. "He doesn't have his backpack," she stage-whispered. "Kind of a dead giveaway."

"Chess!" Jamaica hissed.

Her friend's laughter rang out as she hopped away from the friendly slap Jamaica tried to land on her ass. She chuckled as she walked in the opposite direction of my lady's room.

"So." I raised a brow while simultaneously stroking my thumb over the soft skin of her hand, which meant I didn't miss the tiny shiver that went through her at my touch.

She started walking, tugging me along until I fell into step with her. Out of the corner of my eye, I caught the jersey chaser furiously texting. Maybe now it was obvious I had a girlfriend, they'd forget about my schedule and stop following me around campus.

Keeping my voice low, I said, "Do you want to hear my plan for tonight's study session?"

Jamaica shot me a side-eye.

"It involves making sure you miss me when I'm gone this weekend as much as I'm going to miss you."

"You are so full of yourself."

Those were her words, but she skip-hopped a couple of steps, increasing her pace as we walked to her room. I hid a grin when I saw her hands tremble as she unlocked the door and let us into her private space. Then I put both of us out of our misery.

Pinning her to the back of her door with my body, I said, "Hello, gorgeous. I've been waiting for this part all day." I set my mouth on the soft skin in the corner of her jaw and nibbled my way to her plump lips. She slipped her hands around my waist, fisting my hoodie along my back and tugging me closer.

Fireworks exploded behind my eyelids as the kiss I meant as a slow seduction morphed into desperation when she pushed her tongue into my mouth. She gave mine a suck, and that was it. Flames licked through my veins at the press-and-tease, slide-and-glide game of tongue tag we played. When she rubbed her belly against my rock-hard fly, I reached behind her and grabbed two handfuls of her ass, encouraging her to wrap her lovely long legs around my waist.

Without breaking the kiss, I turned and took the three steps across her room to her bed and tumbled the two of us down on it. Only then did we come up for air.

"You've been looking forward to this today too, yeah?" I grinned.

She responded by wrapping a hand around the back of my neck and pulling me down to her mouth. Against my lips she whispered, "Yes," and kissed me out of my mind.

Clothes started coming off then. First my hoodie and T-shirt, then her sweater and bra. I worked her nipple with my lips and tongue while I pushed her yoga pants down over her hips. Kissing my way down the center of her belly, I reveled in her moans and the arch of her back, aiding me in my task of undressing her. When I started to kiss my way along the smooth muscles of her calves, she sat up, her eyes green fire as she stared into mine.

"Stand up."

I did as she commanded, and her busy fingers made short

work of the fly of my jeans. My cock sprang free right in her face as she pushed the rest of my clothes down my body. A naughty grin lit up her features, and my jeans and boxers stopped their downward progress at my knees. Starting at the base of my dick, she ran her tongue along my length. The incredible sensation of that touch shuddered through me from the top of my head to the soles of my feet. When she closed those gorgeous plump lips over the head, I speared my hands in her curls and held on as my knees threatened to buckle.

Then all my plans for seducing her went right off the rails as she kissed and licked and sucked me, long downstrokes that took me all the way in and pulled me hard as she hollowed her cheeks on the upstrokes. When her hands joined the fun, jacking me and massaging my balls, I saw stars.

"Jamaica." Her name came out on a groan. "Babe, if you don't stop, I'm gonna—" Lightning raced down my spine. "Too late," I gritted through my teeth before I shouted her name and came down her throat.

Taking her time, she let me go, those green eyes glittering up at me in triumph. Exaggerating the motion, she ran her tongue all around her gorgeous, swollen pink lips. "Mmm. You kind of taste like the sea." With a smile she inched back on the bed. "For the record, you're not the only one who enjoys giving oral."

It took me several tries to clear my throat. "You made that obvious just now." I smiled. "Lucky, lucky me." She left me so unsteady on my feet I had to hold onto the edge of her desk to finish kicking off my jeans and boxers. I fished a condom from my pocket and set it on the desk before joining her on her narrow bed.

I bent my elbow and propped my head up on my hand as I faced her. "I never know what to expect with you." Grinning, I tugged a curl and enjoyed the spring. "I kind of like it."

She grinned back. "No one's ever accused me of being boring."

Savoring the satin of her skin beneath my hand, I ran my palm over her shoulder, down her arm to her elbow, before finding her waist. I continued my tour to her hip, giving it a squeeze on my way to her luscious round ass. "Since you want to be in charge tonight, how about I take the mattress and you take me?" As I asked the question, I simultaneously slid onto my back and rolled her on top of me.

Resting her chin on her hands stacked on my chest, she narrowed her eyes, pretending to contemplate my suggestion. "Hmm. Sounds to me like you want me to do all the work."

I watched my fingers as I played with her hair. "Well, I do have a big game this weekend—"

"And you need to keep your strength up for pushing defenders into the turf?" Saccharine dripped from her tone.

"For someone who didn't start out as a football fan, you're a quick study, Island Girl."

She pushed up to straddle me. With all kinds of fanfare, she lifted her arms over her head and stretched, offering her gorgeous tits. Of course, I took that offer, sliding my hands up the sides of her waist and cupping and squeezing those pretty globes. From the way she wiggled on my lap, my touch excited her, and my dick perked right up. Her smile lit me up, and I shifted beneath her, encouraging her to move.

One hand held my hands to her breasts while she reached for the condom. Her eyes didn't leave mine as she tore it open with her teeth and took her sweet time suiting me up. I slid my hands around her hips but otherwise let her do her thing as she pleasured herself rubbing up and down my length. Right as I was about to start begging, she grabbed hold of me and positioned me where we both wanted me most. When she impaled herself, taking me in all the way to the base, I gritted my teeth against surging up into her—hard. Jesus, she felt sublime wrapped tight around me.

Glancing down at my hands, she said, "I thought I was in charge this evening."

"I'm holding on. That's all," I said in my defense.

She curled her fingers around my hands, prying them from her hips only to reposition them on her breasts. "If you need to hold on, hold on here."

Oh, hell yes! I thought. What I said was, "Great idea."

Gripping me with her inner muscles, she slowly—so damn slowly—lifted off me and equally slowly, slid back down. You would have thought that after that mind-blowing blow job she started off with, I'd be up for super slow-motion sex. You would be wrong. I did my best not to fist her perfect tits as I fought to keep from pumping inside her. Instead I pushed my head hard into the pillow even as my thighs and hips tightened in anticipation of taking over. Still, she rode me slow, the mischief dancing in the depths of her mesmerizing green eyes telling me she absolutely knew she held me on the razor's edge of losing my mind.

Shifting forward, she rested her hands on my shoulders. "You can put your hands on my hips now." Her couching the command as an invitation made me grin.

"Oh, I can, can I?" Turning the tables, I teased her with plucking and pinching her hard nipples.

With a gasp, she clamped down on me and increased her rhythm.

I laughed and tweaked her breasts again. "Looks like I found the speed dials."

"Callahan!"

Her narrow-eyed stare didn't deter me in the least. Instead of doing as I was told, I continued to play at her breasts as she ramped up the friction building between us. At last, I needed more speed than she could give me on her own. Dropping my hands to her hips, I squeezed her flesh and held her in place as I drove up into her. The bite of her nails digging into the skin of my shoulders egged me on, and soon we were both chasing our release.

A storm of incredible intensity gathered at the base of my spine. "Jamaica, babe. I'm so close. You have to come. You have to come right now."

I covered her perfect little clit with the pad of my finger and rubbed her in tandem with my rhythms. She clinched around me hard as her back bowed and she screamed my name to the ceiling. Two strokes later I followed her right off the cliff. Her body pulsing around me sent a second mini-climax through me, and I thought I might die from the pleasure. But what a way to go.

When she floated down to rest on my chest, it took a minute for our hearts hammering against each other to settle down to something less than a full-out sprint. I drew lazy patterns up and down her back and over her ass, enjoying the shivers rippling over her skin beneath my touch. Her breathing evened out, telling me my lady was about to drop off to sleep with me still inside her.

Giving her ass a love tap, I said, "Not yet, Island Girl."

She grumbled something into my neck, and I grinned.

"Come on, babe. You have to sit up, let me take care of a few things."

"Now?" she whined.

"Yes." I chuckled.

With exaggerated care she dragged herself off me and slid into the space on her narrow bed between me and the wall. After I slipped the condom off, I tied it off and dropped it in the trash while she watched me with a hooded expression.

"You have to leave, don't you?" She pouted.

"Yeah, but not for a while." I slid back into bed beside her, tugging the covers up over us. There wasn't enough for two, of course, so my ass hung out in the cold, but I didn't care. Dropping a kiss on those lips I couldn't get enough of, I snuggled her into me. "You gonna watch me play on TV on Saturday?"

"Maybe." Playfully, she dragged the word out against the hollow of my throat and kissed me.

"Jamaica," I said sternly. "It's your job as my girlfriend to watch my game." Tightening my arm around her, I added, "I'll know if you don't."

Rearing back, she caught my eye. "Yeah? How will you know?"

"I'll feel it. Right here." I tugged her hand to my chest and laid it over my heart.

She smirked. "Has anyone ever pointed out what a drama queen you are?"

I stuck my nose in the air. "There's nothing dramatic about an athlete needing his lady to cheer for him."

Both of us burst out laughing.

"Okay, Hotshot, I promise I'll watch your game this weekend."

We enjoyed the afterglow in silence until a tiny snore slipped from her. "Hey, babe. Wake up. You need to walk me out." I slid from beneath the covers and dressed while she made up her mind about waking up. After I gave her lip a nip when I kissed her, she sat up, her curls a wild halo around her head as she blinked herself awake.

Two minutes later she'd slipped on a pair of leggings—without panties, which was so unfair—and a hoodie also without a bra beneath it. Again, monumentally unfair.

"You did that on purpose," I accused.

Her grin was positively naughty. "Giving you something to think about during your long bus rides tomorrow and Saturday evening." She wrapped a headband over her wild hair. "By the way, you're welcome."

"For—?"

"For giving you a fantasy to keep you going through the weekend."

I hauled her up tight and kissed her senseless. When I let her go, her eyes remained closed as she sighed.

"That's to tide you over until Sunday night when you come over to my place."

"I'm coming over to your place?" Her brow shot up.

"It's my turn to cook Sunday dinner. Get your mind out of the gutter, woman. Jeez."

Her eyes took a turn around their sockets as she grabbed my hand and led me to the lobby.

Since it was cold outside, we said our final goodbyes near the front desk. "I'm serious, babe. I want you to come over for Sunday dinner. We can study or grab a movie or whatever afterward."

"Does 'whatever' involve me bringing my toothbrush?"

I pretended to think about it. "Probably. See you Sunday."

Her eyes twinkled, and I swooped in for another kiss. When I came up, I caught a flash of a camera out of the corner of my eye. The hairs on the back of my neck stood at attention, and I glanced over to the couches near the doors to catch Tory's spy tucking her phone in her pocket.

Shit. That couldn't be good.

Chapter Twenty-Six

Jamaica

WHEN I MET her in the Union for coffee Thursday afternoon, Chessly asked, "This thing between you and Callahan O'Reilly is heating up into something serious, isn't it?"

Blowing at a curl that had escaped my headband, I sighed. "I was *not* looking for this. Especially not with a football player." I blew on my flat white and took a sip. "But he wouldn't let up pursuing me."

Chess's brow lifted, a knowing expression on her face.

"It doesn't help that he's so hot and smart and fun. To be honest, he's done as much or more of the heavy lifting on our project for Dair's class as I have."

She smirked. "You say that like you're surprised."

Shaking my head, I huffed out a sigh. "That's because I am surprised." I slumped back in my chair. "Which is so unfair to him. I'm embarrassed to admit I stereotyped him right out of the gate. Fortunately for me and our project, he called me out on it but didn't hold it against me."

"Because he'd rather be holding you against him." Chess laughed uproariously at her own joke.

Even as I tossed my friend a half-hearted obscene gesture, visions of Callahan and me in my bed the night before swirled through my head and sizzled through my blood.

Her eyes sparkled as Chessly finally pulled herself together. "Judging from those pink cheeks, you like that part. Not that I blame you. If I was dating someone as fine as O'Reilly, I'd enjoy being held against him too." For a second, she wrinkled her nose as though she'd thought of something nasty.

The juxtaposition of her expression with her words had me gripping my coffee cup. "Okay, out with it. Is there something about him I should know?"

With a shake of her head, her expression cleared. "I was thinking about someone else for a second there. Sorry."

"Who has you looking like you sniffed something sour?"

All of a sudden her chai tea held great fascination. "No one." Squaring her shoulders, she said, "No one special anyway."

"You know ever since Homecoming when Finn drove you home, you've acted weird. Did something happen?"

I couldn't imagine Callahan's bumbling roommate would be capable of anything awful, but growing up the way I did taught me looks could be deceiving.

"Nothing happened. It was fine." The shortness of her tone meant that part of the conversation was over.

Not that it mattered when a shadow fell over me seconds before its owner opened her whiny mouth and ruined our coffee date.

"Well, if it isn't Little Miss Truck-Stop Trash and her stick-up-her-ass friend."

"Luckily for all of us, you don't live in the dorms anymore, Tory. So you can keep moving." A person could have frozen to death in the ice of Chessly's voice.

"You need to set your sights lower, Jamaica. Look for someone more on your level," Tory sneered.

"Fortunately for me, Chess thinks I am on her level, which means I don't have to stoop to being friends with you." Even though I remained seated and Tory loomed over me, I still managed to look down my nose at her and her pack of freshmen. Each of her sycophants' eyes saucered at me even daring to call out their leader.

"I'm not talking about this person." She waved dismissively in Chessly's direction. "I'm talking about Callahan O'Reilly. He deserves someone who's at least in his league."

Glancing around at the assembled group of fashionista wannabes, I said, "Which is obviously why he's dating me instead of one of you."

Tory planted her hands on her hips. Her eyes spit fire. "I don't know who you think you are, but I saw him first. You need to back off."

Chessly and I exchanged looks. "No matter how much money your daddy has, you can't call dibs on a *person*, Tory." Crossing my arms over my chest, I added, "Then there's your little problem of him not wanting a single thing to do with you, which, as I understand it, he made clear right after he met you."

"He comes from a good family. I know things about you, Jamaica. Things that will make his good family want him to stay far away from you." Her snide tone raised my hackles.

Under the table, Chessly pressed down on the top of my foot. Hard.

Batting my eyes at Tory, I asked, "Is that a threat?"

"My family has influence. For his sake as well as yours, you need to pull your claws out of him." With a toss of her poufy hair, she flounced away. Her pack of four or five wannabes echoed her flounce like the good little toadies they were, and I sat back in my chair with a sigh.

Once the adrenaline from that unpleasant encounter wore off, I sipped my tepid coffee, eyeing my friend over the rim of my cup. "Well. That was fun."

"She's such bad news, Jamaica," Chessly said, unhappiness written all over her face.

"As I recall, her family's 'influence' didn't result in your expulsion from school. Hell, you even kept your RA job, so I'm not too worried about Tory Miller's 'threats,'" I said with air quotes.

"I don't know, Jamaica. My issues with her were rules-related, something the dorm and the university could back me on. Yours have to do with a guy—a football player, no less." She crossed her arms and leaned on the table. "You do know her dad is one of the biggest donors to the team, don't you?"

"I didn't know that." I tried to infuse my tone with far more confidence than I felt. "But just because he gives money to the team doesn't mean he can decide who the players date."

She shrugged. "Let's hope not. Otherwise your guy might be stuck with that bitch, which would truly be a tragedy."

For the rest of the day, I brooded over my run-in with Tory Miller and Chessly's revelations in its aftermath. I was raised by a single mom who worked in a truck-stop diner. So what? Callahan didn't seem to care when I told him. If he was as close to his family as Tory implied, then perhaps they shared his attitude.

My dad drove an over-the-road eighteen-wheeler on an interstate route that sometimes took him through our small town. But he hadn't been through in over five years. The last time I saw him was at the end of my junior year of high school. He promised he'd help me pay for college if I kept up my grades. Then he disappeared. I thought he might show up when I graduated valedictorian from my class, but Mom was the only person seated in my designated family section.

Mom had his number, but it came with strict instructions never to call it unless it was a dire emergency. High-school graduation and lack of funds for attending college didn't qualify as an emergency, since Mom refused to call him even when I begged.

In the end a combination of scholarships and saving every penny from working multiple jobs kept me in school while Mom's money paid the mortgage that kept a modest roof over our heads and food on the table. If Callahan's family had a problem with women who worked hard for what we had, well then, perhaps he wasn't the guy for me.

Another thought struck me. What if he needed Tory's dad's backing to get into the pros? Though his focus remained on the Wildcats, he'd mentioned on more than one occasion that he and all his roommates—well, he wasn't sure about Danny but Bax and Finn—wanted to go pro after college. If Tory's dad was such a big-time donor to the team, maybe Chessly was right about him demanding Callahan break up with me in order to achieve his goals. Maybe courting favor with Tory's dad was the reason Finn spent so much time entertaining the jersey chasers.

I snuggled down into my comforter, pulled the footrest up on my recliner, and stared at *Persuasion*, willing myself to concentrate on the words on the page rather than on the words swirling around in my head. When my phone pinged with an incoming text, I almost kissed it for taking my thoughts somewhere else.

Then I saw the name on the text and actually did kiss the screen before I opened it.

Hotshot: Answer your phone.

Me: Maybe.

Hotshot: Answer your phone.

Before I could respond my phone started ringing in my hand, his handsome face filling the screen.

"Hello, Hotshot."

"Hello, Gorgeous."

"Aren't you supposed to be doing football things?"

"We practiced as soon as we stepped off the bus. I'm gonna be honest. I'm not a fan of Friday night games, especially Friday night away games." His eyes danced. "Let's talk about something important. What are you wearing?"

"A blanket." I smirked.

His expression turned intense and his voice dropped an octave. "Is that all?" In the screen, I could see him swallowing hard.

Chuckling, I said, "You wish."

"You have no idea how hard I'm wishing." When he shifted to sit up higher on the bed, I noticed the generic hotel backboard that didn't look all that comfortable to rest against. "Will you show me?"

Tugging my favorite fleece blanket to my chin, I said, "You've seen this draped over my chair every time you've been in my room."

Clearing his throat, he said, "I meant, will you show me what's beneath it?"

Only then did I catch on that I was the only one playing. Callahan was intently serious. Of course, that meant I had to ramp it up. With excruciating slowness I tugged the blanket down. His eyes darkened to a midnight sea as I revealed my décolletage. Then with one fierce jerk, the blanket fell to my waist, revealing my braless state in my low-cut tank top.

Covering my mouth, I tried not to laugh at the thought he might have concussed himself with how violently he banged his head against that solid headboard.

"Jamaica. That was mean."

"Since I didn't know you were going to call me tonight, you can't blame me for being unprepared." My tone was prim even as I suppressed another laugh.

His expression turned roguish. "If you'd known I was calling, would you be naked under that soft blanket?"

"Probably—I'd be wearing two layers and a hoodie." I giggled at his narrow-eyed stare.

Then the grin he shot me lit up the screen. "You're saying that if you'd known ahead of time you'd have given me a striptease?" He pumped his fist in the air. "Fuckin' A, Island Girl!"

For a second I dropped the screen into my lap.

The blanket muffled Hotshot's words. "Hey! It's not a striptease if I don't get to watch."

Returning my face to my phone, it was my turn to be serious. "You'll have to use your imagination. There will be no strip shows or any photos of choice naked parts of me on your phone."

"Babe," he whined. "It would only be for me."

"Until one of your buddies swipes your phone and shares it with the class. No thank you." I pulled my blanket back over my chest. "You'll have to rely on your overactive imagination."

"Or memories. Take last night, for example. Watching your pretty titties bounce while you rode me filled my spank bank right up." His grin was positively wicked.

My face heated. "You might be the naughtiest man I have ever met," I huffed.

"Admit it, Island Girl. You like it. You like me."

I shrugged. "Maybe." A pause. "A little bit."

His rich laughter filled my room as though he were sitting in it with me rather than reclining on a bed in a hotel a state away.

Thoughts of our night together played in my mind, and fire flashed through me, arrowing directly to my center. I slid my hand between my crossed my legs, holding onto sensations as I remembered the intensity of Callahan's eyes as he'd stared into mine while I took charge.

"Now you're the one with naughty thoughts." The expression on his face only added to those thoughts.

A door slammed and Finn's voice interrupted our conversation right as it was starting to sizzle. "Jesus, fuck, O'Reilly! Get your hand out of your pants!"

Callahan pulled the phone into his chest, and I heard a muffled, "Fuck you, Finn!"

When he returned to the screen, he blew out a breath, a sheepish expression on his handsome face as he changed the subject. "You're going to watch the game tomorrow night, aren't you?"

"Wait." My brow shot up. "Were you jacking yourself a minute ago."

"Jamaica."

The idea that he'd been getting himself off as we talked about my state of dress left me hot. "You were." I flashed him a smile. "Put your phone up to your ear."

His brow knitted, but he did as I asked.

"If you must know, I was touching myself too," I whispered.

"You truly are trying to kill me here, aren't you, Island Girl?" A pained expression accompanied his words when his face filled my screen once again.

I shrugged. "You started it."

"Seriously, fucking killing me." He shifted on the bed. "You haven't answered my question. Are you going to watch the game tomorrow night?"

"Axel, Drake, and I will be sitting at our usual table in Stromboli's, eating pizza, drinking beer, and maybe glancing up at the TV occasionally while the game is on," I teased.

"You are a cruel, cruel woman, Jamaica Winslow. How can you wound me like that?" He exaggerated covering his heart with his hand, and all I wanted to do was kiss that spot on his chest.

Giving him a pouty moue, I said, "You poor thing. Only twenty or thirty thousand fans are going to cheer for you tomorrow. However can you stand it?"

His eyes dialed up the intensity. "I only care about one."

I stopped playing with him. "I doubt I'll hear anything my buddies say except maybe at halftime."

"Because—"

The side of my mouth tugged up. "Because I'll be too busy watching you pancake opposing linemen and catching passes and making touchdowns. Satisfied?"

"Not even close." His lips twisted. "But it'll do until I see you again on Saturday night."

"You're seeing me on Saturday night? Did we have a date?"

"I'm making it now."

Giving him narrowed eyes, I waited for the ask.

"We'll get back to town midafternoon, go to film immediately after we arrive, and then I have the rest of the weekend free." Clearing his throat, he said, "I'd like to spend that time with you. Would you like to go out for dinner Saturday night?"

I pretended to check my calendar and Callahan shot me an "are you kidding me?" stare from beneath his brows. The corner of my mouth kicked up at his response to my antics, but what I said was, "Yes. I'd like that very much."

Chapter Twenty-Seven

Callahan

THE GAME AGAINST the Arizona Red Devils kicked my ass. In fact, on my ass is where I spent too much of that game. I swear their defensive coordinator had one scheme: blitz, blitz, and blitz. Forget about blocking. It was all I could do to put myself in the way of their linebackers as they blew through our O-line and into our backfield almost before Dally dropped the ball in Patterson's hands after Patty called "Hike!"

In the second half, I managed to run a couple of clean routes and even caught a pass for a teeder, but the final score showed that we played flat while the Devils brought their A game. At 42-35 it wasn't a thrashing, and we were in it until the last two minutes, but as Coach reminded us in the locker room, on the bus, and again in film, a loss is a loss. One point or one hundred points, it doesn't matter on our record. The loss dropped us from sole possession of first in our conference to tied with our rivals, the Eastern Idaho Panthers.

It didn't take a genius to know I'd be spending a fair amount of time in practice with the blocking sleds. Clearly, I also needed to up my game in the weight room. At 6'5" and 240, I'm not a small man. But the way Arizona's linebackers manhandled me, I may as well have been a guy half my size. Walking into the locker room after the final whistle pissed off and more than a little embarrassed was not an experience I cared to repeat.

But when I parked my truck and discovered Jamaica waiting for me in the lobby of her dorm, all that anger and disappointment melted away.

"Hello, Hotshot. How are you?"

"I feel human."

She arched a brow. "As opposed to what?"

"A walking ouch." I reached my hand out to snag hers. "Come here."

Wrapping my other arm around her, I hauled her in for the kiss I'd needed since I'd walked out of her dorm three nights before. As always, those pouty lips molded perfectly to mine, her greedy little tongue licking and sucking mine in that hot, passionate way that set my body on fire. The sizzling way she kissed me told me she'd missed me too.

Nearby someone cleared their throat, and with a groan, I pulled out with a series of soft presses of my lips to hers. Past Jamaica's shoulder, the desk clerk winked and nodded in the direction of a group of girls openly watching me with my woman.

"Sorry, Callahan. I might have been carried away for a minute." She put a sliver of daylight between us. "Even though you said you feel human, after that game, I'm sure you're sore."

Lowering my voice for her ears only, I said, "That groan was for a different pain, Island Girl." In case she misunderstood, I waggled my brows for clarification.

"It's only been three days," she hissed.

"Judging by that kiss, it's been three weeks for you too." The side of my mouth tugged up at her contrary snort. "Come on, babe. We can talk about how much you missed me over dinner. I'm starving."

Before she could shoot me a snarky retort, I headed for the glass double doors with her hand still grasped firmly in mine. Opening the driver's door on my truck parked in the circular drive in front of her dorm, I gestured for her to hop in. She was still sliding across the bench seat when I climbed in behind her. Slipping my hand beneath the curls at the nape of her neck, I stilled her for another kiss I couldn't resist.

When at last I let us up, her unfocused gaze told me all about how my kisses affected her too. A couple of blinks returned those gorgeous greens to the present from the wonderland of her kissing me back. "Um, I thought you were starving."

"I was, so I enjoyed an appetizer." It took work to keep my face impassive as I turned the key and fired up my truck.

As she clipped her seat belt on, she clarified, "Starving for dinner."

"I'm starving for that too." This time I couldn't keep the smirk in check. But in the rearview I caught her secret smile.

Deciding to take care of the unpleasant part of the evening on the drive to the restaurant, I asked, "What did you think of the game?"

"You mean other than the final score sucked?"

"Yeah."

She rested her hand on my thigh, giving me the barest squeeze. "I'm still learning the game, but it looked like you were overwhelmed by their double teams."

Beneath her touch my muscles went rigid.

Lightly running her palm down and up my thigh, she added, "But then you'd break free and run a perfect route and catch a pass. That touchdown you made was epic."

I relaxed. "For someone who's still learning the game, you talk football pretty damn well, Island Girl."

With a shrug, she said, "It's a big part of who you are. If I want to figure you out, I need to learn about what takes up the majority of your time."

I tossed her a side-eye. "You want to figure me out?"

She kind of slid down in the seat. "Maybe."

"I'm an open book, babe. Anything important you want to know about me, you already know."

"Is that right?" she drawled.

"I enjoy school, and like you, I'm good at it. I love football, and I'm good at that too." I covered her wandering hand with mine, mostly because I didn't want to earn a driving award for speeding. "When it comes to dating you, I'm all in."

"What about your family?"

"What about them?"

"You haven't told me much. I'm curious."

Letting go of her hand, I wheeled us into the parking lot of the fancy steakhouse where I'd made our reservations. As we climbed out of the truck, I laced my fingers with hers and led her to the door when she acted like she wanted to drag her feet.

The hostess smiled as we entered. "Hello, Mr. O'Reilly. Let me show you to your table."

Jamaica's brows went up. "Mr. O'Reilly?" she mouthed.

Grinning, I ushered her in front of me to follow the hostess to a quiet booth near the back.

Once we were seated with our menus, she said, "Is the hostess knowing you on sight one of the perks of playing for a winning team?"

"That and I do ads for this place, which means you don't have to hold back on what you order. Choose whatever you want."

"So you're not some Richie Rich whose family can afford dinner at a place like this." It was a statement rather than a question as she toured our opulent surroundings with her eyes.

Answering the implied question, I said, "Standard family.

Dad, Mom, my younger sisters Cassie and Cora, and my older brother Callum. Oh, and Archie, our cat who's the size of a small car, and Theo, our rescue mutt who thinks it's his job to make sure Archie exercises every day." I chuckled.

Following her lead, I glanced around the room, catching the understated dove-gray of the walls that set off the deep burgundy in the thick, patterned upholstery of the booths and the pads of the heavy wooden chairs at the tables. The quiet elegance of crystal and china place settings waiting on reserved tables reflected the soft glow of candlelight with a quiet elegance.

"If not for my ad deal with this place, I'd probably never step foot in it except if we won a championship or something. Then my dad would probably suck it up and make a couple of credit card payments to bring the family here."

Her shoulders dropped slightly from her ears. "Not rich then."

"Solidly middle class, babe. Dad owns a plumbing company and Mom takes care of his books."

She continued her perusal of our surroundings. "I've never stepped foot in a place like this." Glancing down at herself, she whispered, "I'm not even close to dressed for it."

When I'd texted to let her know what time I'd pick her up, I'd asked her to wear a dress. The clingy long-sleeve number that stopped a touch above her knees looked stunning on her. The riot of colors in its floral design was pure Jamaica. Paired with thin black leggings and a sweet pair of black ankle boots, she looked sophisticated and hot. I clocked more than one guy eyeing her as we wound our way through the tables to our booth.

"You look gorgeous." I slid around to sit beside her. "Trust me. You fit in here just fine." Beneath the white tablecloth I slid my palm along her thigh, giving her an encouraging squeeze. With my other hand I flipped open the heavy leather-bound menu. "I'm in the mood for steak tonight with prawns on the side. Unless the special is truly special. What looks good to you?"

"Callahan," she whispered. "The appetizers cost more than I make in a shift at the sweet shop."

Giving her thigh another soft squeeze, I said, "Don't worry about the prices. Like I said, I get a deal."

Her downturned expression worried me.

Sliding my fingertips beneath her chin, I drew her attention to my face. "I brought you here to impress you. Dinner tonight is one hundred percent my treat. I'm not loaded, but no matter what you order, I promise you won't break the bank. Not even close." For a long minute I held her eyes with mine. "Please, babe. Let me impress you. Relax and enjoy yourself."

She gave me a tiny nod. From the little she'd shared with me, Jamaica didn't come from much, which was why I wanted to treat her to the fanciest restaurant in town. I thought it would make her happy. Instead I'd made her self-conscious. Fuck.

When the server arrived to take our order, she killed me when she asked for water instead of a drink and ordered the chicken pasta—the least expensive item on the menu. But I let it go and ordered the steak and prawns—my favorite—and a beer. At least she relaxed a bit once the server had taken the menus away.

"Um, not to rub salt in the wound, but you guys lost the game last night. What are we celebrating?" she asked.

I slid my arm around her shoulders. "I have a Saturday night and a full Sunday completely free. That's always a reason to celebrate."

With a thoughtful tilt of her head, she said, "With your schedule I guess you would want to celebrate the odd Sunday off." The side of her mouth tipped up. "It's good your open weekend happened to fall on my one open weekend of the month."

"See? You get it, what with your on-call responsibilities and whatnot."

"Kinda. Strangers don't recognize me on sight and want to sleep with me because I'm an RA."

"What are you talking about?"

"The hostess." She bumped her shoulder into my chest. "Come on, Hotshot, don't tell me you didn't notice the way she devoured you with her eyes when we walked in."

"You mean like the way half the men in this place were undressing you with theirs when we walked through?"

Bubbling her lips, she blew off my comment. "Everyone in this place was watching you." Her gorgeous greens teased me. "With your size and your athletic grace, you command a room. But that's not news to you."

"With your sassy walk and gorgeous curves and all that luscious hair, you draw all the attention." I ran a finger along her jaw and would have stolen a kiss if the server hadn't chosen that exact minute to deliver our food.

As we enjoyed our dinner, I finally took the hint at the way she kept stealing glances at my prawns and offered her one. Though her expression was both mischievous and adorable when I forked one onto her plate, the way she took her time savoring it broke my heart. My girl truly wasn't used to such luxury as an expertly cooked meal.

"You said it's only you and your mom. Any cousins, grandparents, aunts and uncles?"

Her focus studiously remained on her plate as she slowly chewed and swallowed a bite of shrimp, chasing it down with a sip of water. "No. My grandparents pretty much disowned my mom when she dropped out of college after one year to have me. She has two older brothers, but she doesn't talk about them, and I've never met them."

"Fuck, Jamaica. That sucks." Thoughts of my own extended family with fifteen cousins and two sets of grandparents who called after every game to tell me how proud of me they were flashed through my head.

"It's no big deal. Mom made sure I had everything I need,

and she never passes up an opportunity to tell me how much she loves me." She shrugged. "Besides, it's hard to miss what you never had."

In the past couple of months since we'd started dating, I'd figured out most of her tells. When she slipped into that shell of feigned indifference, I knew not to press.

After signaling the server over to our table, I asked for a dessert menu.

"Seriously?" Her laughter washed over me like a summer rain. "You ate half a cow, and you still have room for dessert?"

Shooting her a look from beneath my brows, I said, "What part of 'college athlete' did you miss? It takes *calories* to keep my motor running, Island Girl."

When the server returned with the menu, I laid it on the table between us. "What looks delicious to you?"

Her eyes saucered, and it didn't take a genius to figure out why. Slapping my hand on the menu, I covered up the prices.

"Now, answer the question. What would you like for dessert?"

"I'm pretty full."

"No one is too full for dessert."

When the server returned, Jamaica still hadn't decided. Deliberately, I suspected. So I took care of it for her.

"We'll have the chocolate-hazelnut mousse and the cherry cheesecake. And two glasses of dessert wine," I said as I handed the menu back to the guy who'd had trouble keeping his eyes off my girl every time he arrived at our table.

"Callahan—"

"This is only first dessert." Leaning in, I whispered in her ear, "We'll have second dessert in private." Then I brushed a kiss over the corner of her jaw and grinned at the tiny shiver that rippled through her at my touch.

"You're incorrigible."

"You're delicious."

I brushed a second kiss over her jaw as I idly played with the curls at the back of her neck.

"We're in public. In a ritzy place, no less," she hissed.

"I'm keeping it PG when all I want to do right now is slide my hands under your dress and run my fingertips all over your satiny skin." Caging her in my arms, I ran my nose along her jaw while I toyed with the hem of her dress across the top of her thigh and delighted in the way she clamped her thighs together.

She remained still as though if she even took a breath we might lapse into an R-rated make-out session. Considering the half-hard state of my cock at the moment, that wasn't entirely out of the question.

A throat clearing beside the table alerted me the server was waiting with our dessert. With one last peck on her cheek, I let her go and gestured for the server to set the mousse in front of her and the cheesecake in front of me. In the end, we traded bites of our treats, sharing them down to the last scrapes of syrup on our plates.

When the check came, I turned my back to her to keep her from seeing the tab, slid my credit card in the wallet, and tipped the server for the full price of the meal rather than for the forty percent charge that was my discount. With my hand at the base of her spine, I ushered her ahead of me out of the restaurant and did my best to ignore the appreciative stares of some of the male patrons—until one in particular caught my eye.

Tory's dad, Cecil "Buzz" Miller, sat at a table in the corner behind the hostess stand. He was an alumni donor, nothing more, no matter how much control he thought his money commanded over the guys playing for the Wildcats. Still, his narrow-eyed glare at Jamaica as we walked by soured the lingering taste of dessert in my mouth.

CHAPTER TWENTY-EIGHT

Jamaica

CALLAHAN WAS WEIRDLY subdued on the drive over to his place after dinner. But he perked up when we stepped through the front door and walked in on a beer pong tournament in the dining room between his roommates and some other players on the team.

"'Han! You're exactly who we need," Bax called out.

"Sorry, man. I have other plans for the evening," Hotshot said, tugging me beneath his arm.

"Oh, hey, Jamaica. I didn't see you there," Bax apologized. Then he grinned. "You could play with us too. We're down two games to one and need reinforcements bad." He glanced over at one of the guys on his team who had a distinct sheen of sweat shining on his mahogany skin. From the way he was swaying, he was about two seconds from racing outside.

Two.

One.

He made it to the sink in the kitchen. The rest of the guys' laughter mostly drowned out the sound of retching, but I could still hear him. I covered my stomach with my free hand and tried to concentrate on not joining him.

"You okay, babe?" Callahan's quiet voice penetrated the awful sounds coming from the kitchen.

"Um, I was."

"We'll catch you all later. Try not to join Tarvi if you can avoid it," he said, addressing his teammates. A grin bloomed over his face. "Or not. It's your week to clean up the kitchen, Bax." He chuckled at Bax's groan and spun me toward the living room and the stairs to his bedroom. "Come on. Let's watch a movie.

"I heard about this cool indie flick, something about a kick-ass black ops agent carrying a secret virus with the ability to save the world. *Aesop: Matti Baker,* I think it's called. When I saw the trailer, I thought of you."

My eyebrows hit my hairline.

"Because you're such a badass, babe." The side of his mouth came up.

Shrugging out of my jacket, I said, "An action flick?"

"From the trailer I watched on TikTok, I think it's a thriller and comedy mix."

"Let's check it out." I draped my jacket over the back of his desk chair and slipped off my short boots. Crawling up on the mattress, I plumped the pillows and sat against them, tugging my dress down my thighs even though I wore a pair of tights beneath it.

Callahan busied himself cuing up the movie. While the opening credits rolled, he tossed his jacket over mine and toed off his dress shoes. He stepped over to his closet and dropped his pants, which took my mind completely off the movie. Not one ounce of fat clung to his long, muscular legs. Seriously, his body was a work of art. He slipped a pair of sweats over his boxer-briefs, shielding his perfect ass from my view, and unbuttoned his dress shirt and replaced it with a sweatshirt. Still, that short glimpse of his marvelously sculpted back made my mouth water.

When he bounced onto the bed, he took one look at me and said, "Get your mind out of the gutter, Island Girl. We're watching a movie."

I crossed my arms over my chest. "Then maybe you should have changed in the bathroom."

A laugh barked out of him. "Maybe you should keep your eyes to yourself."

"Uh-huh. You remember that the next time you drop by the dorm and I need to change for whatever adventure you decide we're having," I huffed.

He laughed again and slipped his arm around me, pulling me tight to his side. "Watch the movie, Jamaica."

I snuggled in close, resting my head on his chest, and surprisingly, we watched the entire movie. When we weren't laughing at the antics of Matti's sidekick and best friend Bethany, I was crawling up on his lap in terrified suspense as the bad guys surrounded Matti's house, leaving her no way out. From the way Callahan wrapped me in his arms, I had the idea me ending up in his lap was his goal with watching this flick.

As the final credits rolled, he ran his palm up and down my thigh. "I bought an extra toothbrush." Clearing his throat, he added, "And that body wash you like, the kind that smells like cherries—like you."

"Are you asking me to stay over?"

He tugged at one of my curls. "I was hoping you'd want to."

Putting a finger to my lips, I pretended to think about it. The trouble was, it had been three days since we'd seen each other last, and to my everlasting shock, I was becoming addicted to him. As though he read my mind, he'd tugged my hand to his face and leaned in, capturing my lips with his.

An evil gleam shone in those blue eyes I could drown in.

Before I knew it, he had me on my back and was tickling me like a demon.

Shrieking, I chased his hands with mine as I attempted to stop the madness. His deep, rich laughter filled the room as he teased me. Then suddenly the game changed as he pushed his fingers beneath the waistband of my tights and pulled them down my thighs. Two seconds later he stood at the end of his giant bed holding my panties and tights while I lay naked and panting in the middle of it. He whipped off the rest of his clothes and rummaged in the nightstand, setting one condom on top of it while tearing another open.

After he sheathed himself he stared down at me, his head tilted to one side. Before I could ask what devious plan he had in mind, he reached a hand toward me. "Pretty sure this will work."

I slowly swung my legs over the edge of the bed to stand in front of him. "What are you up to?"

"Getting you off. Turn around." He wrapped one arm loosely around me, put the palm of his other hand on my shoulder, and bent me over the bed. "Stretch your arms in front of you and spread your legs for me."

Excitement coursed through me as I did what he wanted. He planted his hands on my ass and spread me open more. When the head of his cock found my pussy, I nearly wept in anticipation of that first thrust. Gripping me hard enough to leave marks, he filled me full in one hard thrust.

A grunt slipped from my throat, and he growled, "That's it. Take it. Take it all, Jamaica."

He pulled out only to thrust hard again. I fisted the comforter and pushed back, silently begging for more. Nothing about what we were doing was sweet or easy. Somewhere along the line, he'd decided to mark me as his. In my wildest imagination, I never thought I'd want this, but I couldn't get enough.

"Harder, Callahan. Harder," I demanded.

"Jamaica," he shouted. "Oh, sweet Jesus, babe. You"—thrust—"are"—thrust—"killing me."

Then the only sounds were our bodies slapping together, our breaths sawing in and out, and the protests of the box springs as he pounded into me. When I came apart, I buried my face in the comforter to muffle my screams. Behind me Callahan stiffened, followed by a couple of thrusts and my name echoing from wall to wall in his room.

When the wild ride was over, he rested his front on my back, pressing me into the mattress as both of us labored to breathe normally again. My body pulsed around his, the aftershocks almost intense enough to make me come again.

At last, he pulled out, and I heard him pad across the room to the bathroom. When he returned a few minutes later I still hadn't moved. I couldn't be sure my jelly legs had it in them to climb up onto the bed.

"That is a gorgeous sight, babe. Your pretty ass up high in the air like that gives me ideas." He smoothed his warm palm over my skin.

Turning my head to the side, I said, "I thought we just experienced your idea."

He chuckled and slapped my ass.

Rearing up, I rolled to my side and glared at him. "What was that for?"

"It was too tempting to pass up." His grin held no apologies.

Standing on unsteady legs, I noted the mess I'd made of his blankets with my grasping fingers. There was nothing for it but to pull them down and crawl in beneath them. Apparently, that had been his idea when he gave me that spank because he wasted no time sliding in beside me.

Gathering me into his arms, he buried his face in my hair, kissed my head, and said, "Babe. That was the most intense sex I've ever had. You're incredible, you know that?"

"Mmm, you're incredible."

His fingertips lightly traced a pattern over the skin on my shoulder. "Does this mean you're spending the night?"

"Depends. Are you making me breakfast in the morning?"

"It's Finn's turn." He huffed out a sigh. "If he remembers. If he even manages to get up before noon tomorrow since we don't have film in the morning."

"This does not sound promising," I teased.

"I would have thought the promise of another round of blow-your-mind sex would be enough, but if you have to have a breakfast guarantee, I'll cook your breakfast too, Island Girl." For emphasis he tugged one of my curls and laughed as it bounced back.

"Then I'll spend the night with you, Hotshot."

Out of nowhere I yawned hard enough to pop my jaw.

Beneath my cheek his chest rumbled with laughter. "Wore you out, did I?"

Snuggling in closer, I threw my leg over his, yawned again, and let myself drop to sleep.

Somewhere in the middle of the night Callahan woke me for round two. This time he took it slow and gentle, seducing me one kiss, one touch, at time. When he brought me to orgasm, I saw a galaxy of sea-blue stars behind my eyes, and I knew I was in trouble. Unlike earlier when I fell into a deep, dreamless sleep, the second time I listened to his soft snores until the first light of dawn sneaked beneath the curtains. The sleep I managed to snag then was filled with dreams of him walking into a fancy restaurant while I remained stranded in a cracked and weedy truck-stop parking lot.

I woke up the second time far less rested—physically and emotionally. Hotshot no longer shared the bed, but I heard the shower running and was he singing? As I listened more intently, I caught the words to "Pour Some Sugar on Me" and covered the giggle that threatened at his off-key rendition.

The man was hotter than sin, super-smart, and gifted in the sack and on the football field. What he was not was a singer. What he lacked in skill he made up for in enthusiasm. After another minute or two of his impromptu concert, I heard the shower shut off and with it his singing.

I was thinking I might have to dress and use the bathroom down the hall when he stepped through the door, steam swirling in the room behind him. My mouth watered at the way he wore a towel slung low on his waist. With his wet hair slicked back and his jaw clean-shaven, he was every woman's fantasy.

"Do you have any idea how gorgeous you look lying there in my bed with nothing on?" he asked.

"I'm covered from chin to toes with blankets. How do you know I'm naked?"

He chuckled. "Because that's the way I left you a little while ago when I woke up and you were softly snoring beneath my arm."

"Uh-huh. Whatever." I had the urge to be contrary, but unfortunately I had a more pressing urge as well.

His laughter said he wasn't buying my sass.

"Um, I need to use the bathroom."

With a grand gesture he stepped away from the door, and I raced past him before he could check to be certain I lacked clothes. Once I was tucked away inside the bathroom, I decided I needed a shower too, only mine wasn't coming with a soundtrack.

The fact that he'd stocked his bathroom with toiletries specifically for me touched me in a way I wasn't ready for. His thoughtfulness and the way he'd made love to me in the middle of the night had left me feeling simultaneously cherished and terrified. Sure, we were dating. Yes, we were exclusive. No, we

hadn't talked about the future past the next moment. For someone who planned everything because I had to, the uncertainty left
me unbalanced. If I gave in and let myself feel the feelings I was
holding back, he'd have all the power.

Probably, I'd end up like my mom.

Callahan had made no secret of his desire to move on to the
pros after graduation. I had a plan to go on to law school. Our
goals didn't exactly mesh. So what were we doing?

When I stepped out from the steam of the bathroom wrapped
in my own towel, I discovered Hotshot furiously texting. Though
his back was to me, the tension in the muscles bracketing his
spine was hard to miss. With an angry toss, his phone skidded
across his desk, while his hands found their way into his hair,
ruining his careful styling.

"Um, what's that all about?" I asked.

"Stupid shit."

"Can I help?"

Dropping his eyes to my towel and back up, he said, "As a
matter of fact, you can." He gathered me in his arms. "Exactly
how hungry are you?"

"Starving."

The sensation of his fingers tracing my spine above my towel
distracted me. That and the tip of his nose nuzzling along the
length of mine. The minty fragrance of his toothpaste wafted over
me. Against my lips he said, "Me too."

Cool air rushed over my skin as he whisked the towel from
my body. With a squeak I wrapped my arms tight around his
shoulders, clinging to his warmth.

Chuckling, he said, "That's better, yeah?"

"You're such a brat," I said into his chest.

"Brat? That's a sissy term. You want to rethink it?" he asked
as he walked me back toward the bed.

"Mmm, nope."

"You sure?"

"Callahan, what are you—?"

I landed in the middle of the bed with a shriek. A second later he landed beside me, sans towel, and started tickling me. "Take it back, Jamaica."

Through peals of laughter, I chanted, "Brat. Brat. Brat," even as I tried to fight back against his lightning-quick hands. Before long we were tangled up in the sheets, blankets, and each other. With some kind of wrestling move or something, he had me flat on my back while he straddled me and pinned my hands to the pillow on either side of my head.

As he gazed down at me with an expression I'm sure he used on opposing linemen in games, he said, "You meant to say 'stud,' correct?"

The corner of my mouth turned up even as I batted my lashes at him. "Mmm, no. I said what I meant. Brat." Clearing my throat, I added, "Stud."

In a flash, sea-blue eyes turned cobalt. When his lips crashed over mine, we weren't playing anymore.

CHAPTER TWENTY-NINE

Callahan

"WELL, FUCK, 'HAN. That's the shits," Finn said as we rolled into the gym at dark-thirty for our regular Monday morning lift.

"Ya think?" I dropped my duffel on the floor in front of a bench by the door and pulled out my lifting shoes. As I laced them up, I said, "Maybe now you see the trouble those jersey chasers cause when you let them hang around."

"Aw, Jesus, I'm sorry." His tone was glum. "I thought they liked me. And I liked the attention."

"Understandable. I imagine more than one of those freshmen does like you, fine specimen that you are."

That perked my friend up a bit.

"Unfortunately, they're learning the ropes from that viper Tory Miller." I stood and stretched my torso from side to side. "After what went down with her sister and Freeman when we were freshmen, none of us should spend even five minutes with that girl." My pointed glare emphasized my meaning.

Finn stared dejectedly at his feet. "I didn't realize they were related."

I snorted and his head shot up with his hands.

"What? Miller is a common last name."

I cuffed him on the back of the head. "The seniors on the team warned us last year."

His eyes narrowed. "You didn't listen either. Didn't Stan catch you mackin' on her against a wall in Delta Nu last spring?"

Running my hands through my hair and down my face, I said, "Yeah. Except you got it backward. *She* pushed *me* against the wall and went to town. I was smashed and had no idea who she even was."

"Now you do."

"Before she makes an even bigger mess for anyone else or manages to actually date one of us, the whole team is going to know who she is." I headed over to a rack of barbells, loaded fifty pounds of weight each on two, and started warming up with a set of curls. "The steroid accusation Tory's sister made against Freeman was easily refutable with a drug test. Uncovering the truth about the abuse accusation only happened on accident. But she wouldn't have been able to level it at all if Freeman hadn't dated her."

Finn stepped over to the rack, loaded his own set of weights, and started his reps. "Coach is right about only taking out your aggression during practice and games."

"One hundred percent." A picture of Jamaica's soft skin flashed through my mind, and bile rose in my throat at the thought of putting a single bruise on it. "Which is why Celia Miller's accusations are still dogging Freeman in the pros even after they were proved unequivocally false. Fortunately, there are few entitled girls like her, but when you run into one you make sure not to tangle yourself up with her." Narrowing my eyes at him in the mirror, I added, "Or her sister."

"None of this solves your current problem," he reminded me.

I finished my set, racked the weights, stretched my arms over my head, and blew out a breath. "I know."

Grabbing the weights again, I finished another set of reps in silence, but inside I was seething. Where the fuck did Buzz Miller get off thinking he could blackmail me into dating his daughter? And why me? Sure, I was technically a college senior, but thanks to redshirting my freshman year, I still had a year of football eligibility left, and I planned to help the team to consecutive conference championships, maybe even a national championship. The NFL draft could wait. I wanted my senior year. So I wasn't a candidate for whatever NFL dream that dick was after by yoking some poor schmuck to one of his girls.

But my family wasn't rich. Comfortable, but not rich. Dad was already putting my younger sisters through school, so I not only needed my scholarship but also my sponsorship. Between classes, practice, and games, I didn't have time for a job to pay for little things—like food. Buzz Miller threatening to force the restaurant to drop me if I didn't drop Jamaica and start dating Tory made me want to throw the weights in my hands right through the wall.

Finn wiped down his weights and racked them. "You know, the other guys in the house can cover your groceries until you find another sponsor."

"Except who will sponsor me if Copper drops me?" My weights hit the rack with enough force to rattle it against the floor-to-ceiling mirrors. "'Cause you know they'll have to make up a reason, and no doubt that reason will be highly discrediting and difficult to refute."

I stomped over to the bench and started loading weights on the bar. "Spot me."

Positioning myself beneath the weights, I set my hands exactly as I liked them. Yes, I was mad as hell—and more than a little bit scared about the immediate future—but I wasn't an idiot. I paid attention to what I was doing. Still, I pushed the weight with more aggression than maybe was called for as I envisioned smashing every rep as an uppercut to a particular alumni donor's chin.

Hopping up from the bench, I gestured for my friend to take his turn right as Danny walked over to join us. "Hey, man. Heard you're in a spot with a donor."

Clearing my throat, I said, "Word travels fast."

He smirked. "We live in a small house."

"Who else knows?" I directed the question to Finn, who studiously blew out his breath with every rep.

When he racked the bar and sat up, he said, "Bax."

I glared at him.

His shoulders came up to his ears. "Like Danny said, we live in a small house."

"That's not what I meant, and you know it."

"I might have mentioned something to Fitz." He put his hands up in a defensive gesture. "But that's all."

I shook my head. "Why do I tell you anything?"

Across the room I saw Danny's brows go up, but he kept his mouth shut. As the new guy, he had a strong sense of when to stay quiet.

"Listen, Fitzy is pre-law. I thought he might know a way around your predicament. That's all." Finn took his place to spot my next set. "I mean unless you're going to give in and date Tory."

In the moment, I wished for that superpower where I could shoot fire from my eyes.

Finn blew out a breath. "Well, she is hot."

"She's a conniving, entitled bitch. She'd make a man's life a living hell twenty-four-seven." I shut up long enough to let him count out my reps, racked the bar, and sat up. "Anyone stupid enough to date her will probably end up like Freeman, a top pick who slides into free agency on account of her bullshit. No fucking thanks." I ran a hand through my hair. "Have you paid attention to my girlfriend? Tory could only wish she was as hot as Jamaica. Or as smart." A picture of my Island Girl wearing a wicked grin and nothing else as she climbed up my body to give me the ride of my life Sunday morning flashed through my head. "Or as much fun."

Danny stepped over to take his turn on the bench. Shooting Finn a side-eye, he said, "'Han's not wrong."

I fist-bumped him. "Thanks, man."

"Yeah, well, you're going to need some help fixing your problem with the Millers. That's all I'm saying."

As usual, my girl arrived about sixty seconds before Dr. Dair started class. Over the weekend, winter had decided to show up, which meant the morning breeze scattered her curls over her head. It cracked me up how in her focus on making it to her seat before the professor called us to order, she never caught sight of me waiting for her right inside the door to the lecture hall.

She sidestepped along the row to her seat beside Axel, who always grinned past her with a wink at me as I followed her in.

"How is it I never see you on the steps when I race up them, but you're always right behind me when I sit down?" she asked with accusatory eyes. "Do you apparate here or something?"

Leaning in, I brushed a kiss over the corner of her jaw. "Good morning to you too, Island Girl," I whispered in her ear.

The bonus of her full-body shiver at my touch improved my morning a hundredfold.

A grin ghosted over her lush mouth. "Seriously, Hotshot. Are you magic?"

"I thought we established that Saturday night."

"That's enough, you pretenses of scholarly pursuits," Dair

interrupted. "If you can tear yourselves away from flirting with each other"—his attention focused directly on Jamaica and me— "perhaps we can take care of some important housekeeping. If you checked your email over the weekend, you may have noticed the schedule for presentations. We'll be starting next week. Benson and Bond will have the honor of leading off." His eyes shifted to Axel and his partner on Jamaica's other side, and I heard both of them groan. "Since you're up first, you're allowed to earn full credit for a twenty-minute discussion. Those of you slated to go at the end are required to give us thirty minutes of scintillating information and commentary." Again, his focus shifted to Jamaica. "The extra time should ensure you don't bore us."

His tone implied he expected to be bored.

Asshole.

Jamaica's eyes glittered when she chanced a glance at me and whispered, "Challenge accepted," and I grinned and nodded. If Dair wanted scintillating, we were up for scintillating the hell out of him. I slid my palm over the top of her thigh and gave her a squeeze. Smiling at the hitch of her breath, I kept my hand on her thigh and my eyes on our instructor who narrowed his gaze in our direction before launching into the day's lecture.

As we made our way across campus after class, I bumped her shoulder. "You were on it in there today. I think you tortured him with no fewer than seven excellent questions." I held out my fist, and she smirked as she bumped hers to mine.

"Giving him a preview of the scintillation he can expect at the end of the semester."

"Thatta girl."

We sidestepped a group of high-school kids on a guided tour of campus.

"I have the feeling he baits you because he likes your questions though. Have you caught how his eyes sparkle for a second sometimes before he drops back into that bored delivery style he saves especially for you?"

"Sparkly eyes, my ass. Dair is a jerk."

Chuckling, I put my hands up. "Alrighty then. Tell us how you really feel, babe."

A lesser man might have crumbled at the disdain in the side-eye she slanted at me. I chuckled again and threw my arm across her shoulders, hauling her in close to my side. The secret grin she directed at the sidewalk told me she was over her snit with our professor.

"You work till ten tonight?"

She nodded.

"Who's buying candy at ten o'clock at night?" I asked, exasperation ringing in my voice. Seriously, couldn't people plan ahead for their sugar buzz and let me have my girl?

"Everyone who's studying in the Union after the cafeteria closes. Nine o'clock on Monday nights is rush hour."

"Well, it's dumb."

She snorted at my articulate observation.

"I'll pick you up at your place after practice tomorrow night. I made some scintillating notes in class today apropos our project—something that's going to blow Dair's doors off." I waggled my brows and she shook her head.

"Truly must be something if you're already practicing your vocabulary."

We'd reached the split in the sidewalk where she went to Huffine and I headed to the gym. My lips had barely brushed over hers when a strident voice interrupted my planned goodbye.

"Callahan. What are you still doing with her?" Tory Miller's whine grated on every one of my nerves.

I glared at her hard enough to singe her eyebrows. "Go find someone else to harass, Miller. I'm not for sale."

Thrusting her chest out and twirling a lock of her blonde

hair, she changed her tone. "Babe. You know steak is so much better for a star athlete like you than cheap burger." Staring down her nose, she gave Jamaica a derisive once-over.

"Did you actually just go there? Jesus, woman, have some self-respect." Angling my girl away from the witch and her posse, I was determined to walk Jamaica to class, burpees for being late to practice be damned.

"Don't you walk away from me, Callahan," Tory warned.

It was all I could do to stop myself from tossing her the bird over my head. Since one of her little friends was likely videoing the whole sordid encounter, I kept my composure and kept walking.

"What was that about?" Jamaica asked.

"Nothing important."

"It sounded like a threat," she insisted.

"Nothing I can't handle. See you tomorrow night."

Troubled eyes met mine. "You'd tell me, right?"

"Trust me, Island Girl. It's nothing." I shut up her protest with a smacking kiss. "Gotta go or Coach will have my ass." With a salute I turned and jogged across the grass to the gym, bypassing Tory Miller and the threats that left the remnants of my breakfast swimming in acid in my stomach.

CHAPTER THIRTY

Jamaica

ON TUESDAY AFTERNOON Chessly met me at our usual table in the Union, her indignation at my suspicions about Tory Miller blackmailing Callahan manifesting in her having to clean up sloshed latte from slamming her cup down.

"That be-otch! Where the hell does she get off?" The angry swipe of her handful of napkins lent emphasis to her words.

I appreciated how my friend didn't even question my suspicions, jumping directly into attack mode. Chessly Clarke was a great friend and a formidable enemy. Of course, when she'd been on the receiving end of Tory's BS last year, I'd remained staunchly in her corner too. When you were facing a barracuda who thought her daddy's money allowed her to do as she damn well pleased, it paid to have allies in possession of backbones.

Life had forced both of us to forge spines of steel.

As though our conversation had conjured her, Tory materialized beside our table. "Callahan O'Reilly is far too good for someone like you," she sneered.

"Hello, Tory. Looks like you're in bitch mode as usual," Chessly said as if she were remarking on the lovely autumn day outside the windows of the Union.

"Tell me something. Do you even attend classes or do you only spend your days stalking upperclassmen?" I asked in an equally pleasant voice.

"At least I earn my grades rather than blackmail a professor into giving me A's in order to keep me from airing his family's dirty laundry." She wrinkled her nose. "Or in your case, outing yourself as that dirty family secret."

I sat up in my chair so fast it screeched on the tile beneath me. "What the hell are you talking about?"

She twirled a strand of hair around her finger, and all I wanted to do was grab it and yank. "With one strategically placed word, a certain department head could lose his job over you. I bet he'd rather not do that, so he gives you A's." Her expression turned feral. "Of course, outing him will probably mean you're asked to leave the university too. What a bummer that would be, what with you being on scholarship and all."

At the mention of losing my scholarship, my chest constricted, and I gripped the sides of my chair to keep from clawing at the monster threatening me. "I don't have any idea what you're on about, Tory, but you'd better be careful about throwing around accusations of cheating and blackmail."

Her hand dropped to her hip. "There's an easy way around all the scandal. Stop seeing Callahan O'Reilly. Then you have nothing to worry about."

More than anything I wanted to slap the saccharine smile off her lips.

"If she chooses to keep lighting up Callahan's world?" Chessly asked.

"Then they both lose, along with a certain professor Jamaica knows all too well." Narrowing her eyes, she said, "Callahan's future in the NFL depends on you doing the right thing." Flipping her hair over her shoulder, she spun on her heel and flounced away. Only then did I pick up that she'd delivered her threats alone without her tiny army of sycophants surrounding her and tittering over her every word.

Chessly stared after her. "What was that all about?"

"I don't have the first clue." As the adrenaline wore off, I slumped back down in my chair. "But it sounds even more scary than that crap she pulled with you last year."

My friend reached across the table, and I laid my hand in hers. "We beat her then and we'll beat her now. She's a spoiled rich girl playing at street fighting. We're born street fighters. The odds are not in her favor."

"What about Hotshot?" I asked.

Tory's baseless accusations that I was related to some MSC professor who was handing me grades in return for keeping my mouth shut about him was as ludicrous as growing daisies on the far side of the moon. But whatever she had on Callahan could cost him the future he wanted more than anything. That wasn't something I was willing to risk.

Chessly's expression turned serious. "Sounds like you two have some things to discuss."

As I sat cross-legged in the middle of Callahan's giant bed, books and papers spread around me, Tory's threats rattled around in my head. He'd texted me that practice would probably go long because the game this weekend was the Wildcats' big rivalry with the Golden Bears. So I caught a ride with Axel over to Hotshot's house, let myself in with the spare key he'd given me a couple weeks ago, and made myself at home.

The aroma of the two extra-large sausage-and-hamburger pizzas I'd created from scratch drifted up the stairs and through the open door to his room. The timer on my phone said they had at least ten more minutes to bake, which was good. I wanted them hot and fresh from the oven when he arrived home. But in the half hour they'd been cooking, I should have finished the article I'd found on Regency manners, and I'd barely read two sentences of it.

All I could think about were the two nasty run-ins I'd had with Tory over the past two days. For most of the semester, she'd made a nuisance of herself at parties and any public space where Callahan tried to study. Until this week she'd confined herself to more outrageous—and frankly embarrassing—flirting. Then Callahan took me to dinner at that too-fancy-for-my-comfort restaurant, and now she was making threats to him and to me. It made no sense. With her family's money she could eat there three times a day if she wanted to, so why be jealous of my date taking me there? It was ridiculous.

But her threats were serious.

More than once as our relationship grew, Hotshot had mentioned the next step for him was going pro. He and his roomies watched film of themselves every Sunday morning and NFL games every Sunday afternoon and evening. They played Madden on their game console almost like a religion. Every one of them wanted to go pro.

I had absolutely no clue how me dating Callahan could interrupt that dream, but from the way he responded on the sidewalk outside Huffine Hall yesterday morning, he was worried about whatever it was Tory had on him.

The slamming of the front door followed by grumpy male voices alerted me the guys had finished practice. I pushed my books and papers aside—along with thoughts of Tory Miller—and headed downstairs.

"What is that heavenly smell?" Bax stood in the middle of the kitchen with his eyes closed, his nose in the air as though he were trying to inhale all the scent of delicious meat pie.

"Are you kidding me, Bax?" I asked when I caught sight of his latest T-shirt, which read "Overworked and Underfucked." "It's a mystery for the ages why you can't find anyone to date."

"What?" He glanced down at his black-and-white T-shirt and back at me with a grin. "It's stating facts."

Shaking my head, I pulled my phone from the pocket of my jeans and checked the timer. "Dinner is at least ten minutes away. Maybe you could put a hoodie over that or something."

"Seriously, Jamaica?"

With a shrug, I said, "Either that or I make fun of your pitiful status all through dinner."

"Jesus. You sound like my mom," he groused as he headed out of the kitchen and ran smack into Callahan. "Sorry, bro. Your lady here is being a hard-ass. You should talk to her about it."

Hotshot's eyes danced when he glanced at me over Bax's shoulder. "Let me guess. Jamaica's unimpressed with your thought for the day." He chuckled. "I do wonder why you proclaim your pathetic situation the way you do."

"Easy for you to say, seeing how you get some on the regular. With the hottest girl in the class." As Bax attempted to shoulder his way past Callahan, my guy stopped him with his words alone.

"You don't talk about Jamaica that way. Ever." The low menace in his voice had Bax putting his hands up in surrender.

"Sorry, Jamaica. I didn't mean to imply anything. I mean besides how lucky 'Han was to see you first."

The timer on my phone went off, and I shooed him out of the room. "Dinner in ten."

"Did someone say dinner?" Finn asked as he sidestepped Bax through the kitchen door.

"In ten." Callahan's eyes were on me.

Unlike Bax, Finn was observant today. Without a word, he spun on his heel and headed to another part of the house, likely his room considering he was still carrying his backpack.

Hotshot stepped over to me. "Hi, babe. When I asked you to meet me here, I didn't mean you had to cook for us." His hands found my hips, and he squeezed as he pulled me in close.

"I assumed you'd be hungry." My stomach rumbled. "Or maybe that was me." I grinned.

"Oh, I'm definitely hungry." His eyes darkened from a summer sea to cobalt in a blink.

Resting my palms on his chest, I threatened to push him away. "You invited me over to study, remember?" Smoothing my hands over his pecs, I said, "In fact, all my books and research are currently taking up most of your bed." His brow went up. "What? I had to do something while I waited for the pizza to cook and you to come home. Wait till you see my notes."

"I plan on seeing your notes—all of them." The corner of his mouth inched up. "But for now this will have to do."

He brushed his lips over mine, and I melted into him. In seconds, his ball cap hit the floor as I tunneled my hands through his hair. Powerful, sculpted arms wrapped around me, and I reveled in the sensation of being cocooned in his big, strong body. I could spend forever kissing him like this—a hot claiming that promised the closeness of love and trust that came in the private dark of his room.

Wait. *Love?*

The timer on my phone chimed again, interrupting our hello and probably saving our dinner. Definitely rescuing my sanity. *Love?* What a wild thought.

Pushing out of his arms, I waved in the direction of the oven and said, "Time to eat. There's a bowl of salad in the fridge along with fresh homemade ranch dressing. That bottled crap you had when I was over last week was awful, so I took care of that for you."

Stop babbling, Jamaica. He didn't hear your thoughts. I chanced a glance at his perfect ass as he bent down to scout the fridge for salad and dressing. *If he had, he'd have raced out of this kitchen and through the front door, leaving a trail of fire in his wake.*

"Homemade ranch, huh? You keep this up, you'll end up moving in." Shooting me a smirk, he said, "My roommates will insist."

"Ah, your roommates. Right. I'll keep that in mind," I said drily.

I know I should have expected it, but still, the speed with which the guys disappeared two extra-large pizzas and a bowl of salad half the diameter of the table shocked me. While I ate my first piece, Callahan made a point of adding a second to my plate. I tossed him a quizzical look, and his raised brow in response might have pissed me off if not for his nod at the empty pizza pan in the middle of the table. When I bit into my second slice, the other pizza was remnants of crust on Bax and Finn's plates. Only a few greens remained in the bottom of the salad bowl, but at least half the quart of ranch remained on the table.

Bax patted his stomach and with a hopeful expression asked, "Did you make dessert too?"

After a slow blink at the dinner carnage in front of me, I shook my head in the negative. "I didn't think about it. Sorry," I said with a regret-filled grimace.

"No brownies or cookies even?" he whined.

My shoulders went up. "Sorry."

Hotshot leaned in and whispered for my ears only, "You have cherries for me, though, yeah?"

My face heated and I stuffed my mouth with pizza. Which only served to draw attention to the fact part of one slice remained. Finn stared longingly at my dinner.

"You sure you're going to finish that?"

Callahan backhanded him on the bicep. "Let my lady eat in peace. Jesus."

"Do we have any ice cream left?" Bax asked.

"No. I finished it while I played COD with Fitz last night," Finn said.

"Guess we're making a dessert run since it was 'Han's turn to cook." Bax stood and walked his place setting to the sink. "Lucky bastard gets the prettiest girl. And she cooks," he muttered as he rinsed his plate and loaded it in the dishwasher.

Beside me Hotshot chuckled, his hand finding its way under the table to squeeze the top of my thigh.

"I took your cooking turn, huh? Guess you owe me," I said as I shifted on my chair, clamping my thighs together and trapping his wayward hand between them. Though he'd scolded Finn for eyeing my second slice of pizza, I didn't miss his designs on it as well. He was just sneakier by attempting to tease me out of it.

Giving him the smirk of all smirks, I stuffed my mouth full of meaty, cheesy goodness and angled what I couldn't eat yet away from him.

With a chuckle, he said, "Fine. Don't share that last bite." He tugged his hand from between my thighs, stood, and walked his place setting over to the sink, joining Bax and Finn as they loaded the dishwasher. Bax retrieved the pizza pans and the salad bowl from the table and took care of them. Guess it was his turn to clean up after dinner.

After our first study session at Callahan's house, it hadn't taken me long to discover the reason behind their compatibility as roommates. Their secret was teamwork. Everyone took turns doing chores, no one complained, and none of them ever took time off. They ran their house similarly to the way they performed on the field—as a unit with each man having the others' backs. I envied their closeness. They were like one big, tight-knit family.

Having grown up with only my mom, I handled most of the household responsibilities as I grew into them. By the time I graduated high school, I did all the cooking, cleaning, and grocery shopping. Moving into the dorms where I went to the cafeteria for my meals and was only responsible for keeping one room clean had been a vacation. But watching the camaraderie and the way the guys seamlessly divided household chores made me homesick for something I'd never even experienced.

After they cleaned the kitchen, Bax and Finn headed out for dessert and a study session at the library.

Hotshot and I headed up to his room.

"You weren't kidding about the state of my bed, babe," he chuckled. "Taking advantage of all that space, huh?"

My hands came up. "What can I say? I like to spread out."

The wicked gleam in his eyes called out my poor choice of words as he crowded me to the edge of the bed. "Do you now? How awesome is that?"

"Callahan!" I squeaked. "At least let me stack all my stuff first."

"Mmm, stacking. I like the sound of that too."

I scrambled backward onto the mattress and frantically started gathering my notebooks, papers, and laptop into something of a pile. I'd just set the whole works on the nightstand when a shirtless Hotshot pounced on me.

"I've waited all day for this, Island Girl."

"We need to study," I reminded him without any of the force I intended.

"We'll get to that, but if we don't take care of dessert first, my concentration will be fucking worthless." As he spoke, his hands moved up my sides, his fingertips feathering over my skin as my T-shirt and hoodie traveled up my body.

A second later he knelt in front of me, holding me steady with one strong hand while he tugged my jeans and panties off with the other. His eyes glittered as I stood in front of him in nothing but my plain, white bra.

"I've had cherries on my mind all fucking day. Open for me, Jamaica. Give me my dessert."

Without the nicety of a little kiss or a warning lick, his

mouth covered my center as he feasted with a hunger that proved I'd been on his mind all day. His hands on my hamstrings kept me from falling, even as I anchored mine in his hair and held on. Teasing and tasting, licking and sucking my clit, he held me on the brink of bliss. When his tongue speared in and out of my channel, my thighs began to quiver. Still, he worked me, adding one finger, then two as he returned to my clit with his talented mouth. Of their own volition, my hips moved in time with his fingers. A low growl of satisfaction rumbled through him when I came apart, his name torn from my throat on a scream.

A ghost of a nudge of his hands on the front of my thighs and I landed on my back on the bed. With seemingly superhuman speed he stood naked in front of me, the proof of his desire proud and erect as he tore open a condom packet and smoothed the protection over himself.

He tugged me to the edge of the mattress, pulled my ankles over his shoulders, and entered me on one long thrust.

Involuntarily, I clamped down on him and the delicious way he filled me full.

"Babe." The word stretched out on a growl.

When he started moving, each thrust was deeper, more forceful, more exciting than the last until both of us were out of control.

One of his long fingers found its way to my clit at the same moment he seated himself to his balls inside me, and I went off like a cannon shot. A series of explosions cascaded through me, lighting my entire body on fire even as a kaleidoscope of blue and green stars danced behind my tightly squeezed eyelids.

Another thrust and he stopped moving, his body rigid along the backs of my thighs as he howled my name. A few seconds later he dropped my thighs to his hips and collapsed over me, his chest heaving against mine.

An age later, we caught our breath and he pulled out and

FINDING THE END ZONE

padded to the bathroom. I didn't bother to open my eyes as the mattress sagged beside me. His fingers traced down the center of my body from collarbone to navel and back again, leaving heavenly sensations in their wake. I could have easily fallen asleep under that gentle movement.

In my super-satisfied, dozy state, I thought I heard him whisper, "I'd do anything for you, Jamaica. Anything."

Then he was up and moving around the room. A few minutes later, something soft landed on my belly.

"Put on some clothes, woman. We can't wow old Dr. Dair if we don't do some work. Jeez," he teased.

Reluctantly, I rolled over and discovered a jersey with his name on it. Shooting him a saucy grin, I tugged it over my head and went in search of my panties. A few minutes later, we were seated side by side against the headboard of his massive bed, our research stacked on either side of us, my laptop open on my lap, his iPad dialed up to our outline, the two of us working as if he hadn't just rocked my world with the best sex of my life.

I was cross-checking a topic on our outline when his iPad dinged an incoming notification. He jerked the device out of my hand, but not before I saw the text—and who sent it.

Chapter Thirty-One

Jamaica

MY HEART BEAT in my throat. "Why is Tory Miller's dad threatening you?" I asked as Callahan hastily switched the screen on his iPad.

His tightlipped response didn't make me feel better. "He's not. We have a difference of opinion is all."

"That's what the kids are calling it when a major alumni donor says 'You know what to do to keep your sponsorship,' huh?" I crossed my arms over my chest. "Sounds like a threat to me. What does he want you to do?"

"It doesn't matter because I'm not doing it." He pulled up a screen where we'd listed all the Regency manners we'd decided were relevant to our project. "That ass could do with learning a few of these," he muttered under his breath. Turning his attention to me with a brightness that sounded fake, he said, "I was thinking we could tell a marketing story about the necessity of good manners for keeping a society together. Something along the lines of the old 'Got Milk?' ads that ran in the nineties.

From what I've seen of the first presentations, doing something a bit out of the box will give us the 'wow factor' Dair dared us to show him. What do you think?"

"Callahan—"

He ran his hands through his hair and sighed. "There's nothing to talk about. Miller wants me to do something I refuse to do. That's it." Leveling me a look, he said, "Can we please work on our project? Our turn is coming up the week after next, so we need to settle on how we're presenting our research to give ourselves enough time to practice."

Though he was right about our project, he was wrong about whatever was going on with Buzz Miller. Something Tory had said when she flounced over to Chessly and me in the Union nudged the back of my brain, but Callahan was talking over my thoughts, and I had to let it go.

For now.

The next morning while Callahan showered, I wandered down to the kitchen in search of coffee. How the guys did these early mornings was a mystery for the ages. It wasn't normal to expect someone to roll out of bed and be ready to work out at a high level before the sun managed to peek over the horizon. It wasn't normal to expect someone to roll out of bed before sunrise, period.

When I caught sight of Finn pouring a cup of joe, I slapped my hand over my hippo-size yawn. "Good morning. What's that delicious smell?"

"Got breakfast burritos warming in the oven."

My eyes might have done that cartoon thing where they shot out of my head and snapped back like elastic. "You woke up in time to make breakfast?"

He chuckled. "'Han and Bax make 'em on the weekends and freeze 'em. All I have to do is put 'em in the oven to reheat."

"Nice." I blew across my cup of coffee and sipped, happy for the jolt of caffeinated energy.

He pulled his phone from his pocket, frowned at the text on the screen, and stuffed it back in his sweats. The action reminded me of Hotshot with his iPad the night before. "Um, Finn. Do you know anything about the threats Tory's dad is making to Callahan?"

Clearing his throat, he glanced away from me with a guilty expression. "Has he said something?"

"No. I saw something on his iPad before he pulled it away from me last night. What's going on?"

"Ah, Jesus. I don't want to get crossways with my roommate."

"Tory made some vague threats when she barged in on my conversation with Chessly in the Union yesterday, so I think I'm involved somehow." Raising my brow, I gave him my best "out with it" stare. "You have an obligation to tell me what you know."

He sort of danced from foot to foot and looked everywhere but at me.

"Finn." My tone demanded an answer.

"Tory's dad wants 'Han to dump you for her." Something like guilt lurked in his pained expression. "If he doesn't, Tory's dad is going to force Copper to drop their sponsorship for him."

My heart fell into my stomach. "That means—"

"'Han has to find another sponsor or a job that pays a shit-ton of money for very short hours so he can buy groceries."

I staggered against the countertop. "The sponsorship pays his rent?"

Finn looked as miserable as I felt. "It covers what he needs to stay in school and play football."

"Why? Why is her dad doing this?"

Finn shrugged. "He has a thing for hooking his daughters up

with players who have a real chance at the pros. Tory set her sights on 'Han last spring, and I guess she hasn't changed her mind."

Those words I thought I'd heard Hotshot say when I was half-asleep after the most intense sex of my life came back to me: *I'd do anything for you, Jamaica.* Was he talking about giving up a sponsorship that kept him on the field? *Was he talking about giving up his dream to play in the NFL?*

Oh, sweet Jesus. I couldn't stand in the way of him achieving his dream. Before I met him I didn't see the point of sports, couldn't understand why players were so dedicated. After watching most of a season's worth of games and Callahan in action, I saw the allure of playing the game. I marveled at an athlete's drive. Listening to his excitement as he broke down a series of plays with his buddies while they watched the pros on Sunday afternoons, I had no doubt he couldn't wait to have his turn playing in front of millions of fans.

After years of work and sacrifice, he deserved his dream. How could I live with myself if I let my feelings for him interfere with the one thing that drove him—the thing that made him who he was?

"You can't tell him I told you," Finn warned. "He told me he'd kick my ass if I did."

Shooting him an "are you kidding me?" stare, I said, "You outweigh him by at least fifty pounds. I doubt you're in any danger."

"No one on the team tangles with Callahan. He's a fun guy and all, but when he tells you not to cross him or he'll kick your ass, you'd better believe he will kick your ass." The imploring expression on his face might have been comical if the stakes weren't so high, the situation so serious. He held his palms together in front of his chest. "Please don't tell him I told you."

"Yeah, okay," I replied absently.

Callahan could lose his sponsorship. Because he was dating me. *Damn it.*

I'd started a relationship with a player—something I vowed I'd never do because it could only lead to heartache. Specifically, my heartache. It never occurred to me I could be the cause of someone losing everything that mattered to him. And double damn, not only had I started something with Callahan, but I didn't want it to end. As much as I'd lied to myself over the past several weeks, I couldn't lie anymore.

I was in love with Callahan O'Reilly.

Now, because I loved him, I had to give him up.

"What am I going to do, Ax?" I dropped my head on my arms resting on the table in the coffee shop at the edge of campus.

I'd called an emergency meeting with my best friend as soon as Hotshot dropped me at my dorm on his way to morning lift. Axel's expressions had morphed from sympathetic to downright pissed off to contemplative in the space of the twenty minutes since I'd spilled my bad news all over him.

He covered my wrist with his hand, giving me a reassuring squeeze. "Callahan has an agent for NIL sponsorships, doesn't he?"

"I don't know," I said into the table. "I don't have a clue how any of it works." Sitting up, I stared at where his hand remained on me, a sense of doom threatening to drown me. "Before he took me to dinner at Copper last week, I didn't even know someone sponsored him." Tilting my head, I asked, "NIL? Is that something else I'm in the way of for him?"

Axel grinned. "No, babe. NIL stands for 'Name Image Likeness.' It's what the sponsors pay for with athletes." With one last squeeze he sat back and sipped his latte. "Kids aren't going to bug their parents to shell out the big bucks for a jersey with Copper across the back, but they all want one with O'Reilly or Patterson or even Baxter's number on it. That's what the sponsors pay for.

Association with guys people want to be around. It's why they want him to have dinner there regularly, maybe sign a few autographs for patrons. Show up in a print or online ad."

"Which pays his rent," I said, not bothering to keep the sadness from my voice. I'd pretended with Hotshot from the minute he'd jogged down the stairs to grab his burrito until he dropped me back on campus. With my best friend I could be myself, let my fear and sorrow out.

"Have you talked about it with him?"

"I tried to when I saw a text from Tory's dad hit his iPad, but he tossed it aside and wouldn't let me in. From the way he tensed up, I know he's worried." I spun my cup around in my hands, making circles on the table with it. "Finn said something about how losing this sponsorship could impact Callahan's ability to obtain another one." After taking a fortifying drag of caffeine, I said the worst part—the part that hurt the most. "If he loses a sponsorship in college, it will lower his draft stock, make him less desirable to the NFL. Start his career under a cloud he might never step out from under." My eyes found my friend's. "I can't do that to him, Ax. I have to break up with him."

"But that's the last thing you want to do, isn't it?"

"Doesn't matter. Even if he thinks he will do anything for me"— Axel's brow shot up, but I plowed on—"there will come a time when he'll regret giving up so much of what he worked so hard for to be with a girl who brings nothing to the table." Closing my eyes, I sucked in air and willed the lump in my throat to go away. My voice came out as a croak anyway. "I can't face that. I just can't."

My friend sat up straight in his chair. "You're doing it again."

Furrowing my brow, I said, "Excuse me?"

"You're scared so you're making plans to run from the best thing that's ever happened to you." His censorious tone had me gripping my hands together in my lap. "Don't be a dumbass, Jamaica."

No doubt my nails were going to leave marks on my knuckles for days.

"This isn't about me, Axel. Don't you see? I can't be the reason Callahan loses everything he's worked for."

The screech of his chair along the linoleum made me cringe. That and the narrow-eyed glare he shot me as he stood up. "It's not your decision to make." He tapped the alarm on his watch, grabbed his empty cup, and chucked it in the trash as he reached the door. Glancing over his shoulder, he jacked a brow and said, "Are you coming?"

Slowly I dragged myself out of my chair, shouldered my backpack, and followed my friend out of the coffee shop. Though we walked across campus in silence, the vibes rolling off him told me all about his disappointment in me. But to make sure he didn't lose his chance at his dream, I had to walk away from this thing growing between Hotshot and me.

Because I was in love with him.

Chapter Thirty-Two

Callahan

"ARE YOU SERIOUS? We beat the Golden Bears. We won the conference championship. You have to come out and party with us, Island Girl." My voice sounded desperate to my own ears but damn. I was running on adrenaline and pure fucking excitement. I wanted—scratch that—I *needed* my girl with me to celebrate the biggest win of the season so far.

"I'm on call this weekend, Hotshot. I can't leave the dorms."

Even with the raucous party interfering with my hearing, something in her tone was off. In fact, her tone had been off since last Tuesday when she came over to work on our project—when she gave me the most incredible sex of my life. I swear, my body still hummed with what she did to me that night.

And hadn't done since.

She'd made some lame-ass excuse for not study-ing with me at my place, so we worked on our presentation in the Union on Thursday night. Friday was a travel day. We kicked some ass on

the field this afternoon and arrived home a few hours ago. The party at Fitzy's was in full swing almost before the bus had rolled to a stop in the parking lot at the field house. It was the biggest night of the year, and my girl wasn't spending it with me. What. The. Fuck?

Someone bumped my arm and almost jarred my phone from my hand.

"Whoops! Sorry." Tory's eyes glittered up at me, and she didn't look the least bit sorry.

With a narrow-eyed sneer, I turned my back on her. Redirecting my attention to the most important girl in the world, I said, "Can't you get someone to cover for you?"

"I already owed two of the other RAs for covering for me so I could see your games against the Trojans and the Miners. This weekend is me actually returning the favor. So, no. I can't get anyone to cover for me."

She was quiet for a minute.

Tory was not, her whine loud enough to be heard over the thumping bass of some hip-hop song the DJ played. "Callahan. Dance with me."

"You should probably go celebrate. Sounds like you're in demand."

"Hey, hey! What's going on, babe? Are you mad at me?" I stepped away from where Tory was grinding her ass against the back of my thighs.

The sigh on the other end of the call sounded exasperated. "It isn't about you, Callahan. I'm working all weekend, all right? Go have fun with your team—and whoever."

That last part came out so low I almost didn't catch it.

"Do you think I'm cheating on you? What the hell?" I demanded.

"Callahan," Tory sang my name from somewhere beside me. "Come play with me." She tugged on my arm, and I jerked away.

She let out a wail, her hand flying to her mouth. "Ouch! You split my lip! Look what you did!"

In horror, I saw a drop of blood on her mouth when she pulled her hand away.

"Shit. I have to go, Jamaica. I'll call you back in a while."

After pocketing my phone I clued in that the thumping music had suddenly stopped, and a crowd was surrounding Tory Miller and me. Massive crocodile tears dripped down her face as she stared at me. The corner of her bottom lip had turned puffy, and a weight the size of California dropped into the pit of my stomach.

"I can't believe you punched me," she said through sniffles.

"I didn't punch you. I was doing everything I could to move away from you."

"Then how do you explain this?" She pointed to her swelling lip.

"I might have accidentally caught you with my elbow when I tried to shrug you off me."

On the edge of the circle I clocked the grim expression on Fitzy's face as he shook his head, and I shut my mouth hard enough to crack a few teeth.

A calculating gleam hid behind her tears. "If you don't want my dad to find out about this, you should probably drive me home now," she said.

Finn and Bax stood beside Fitzy, twin expressions of horror on their faces. Fitzy frantically waved his hand beneath his chin in the universal gesture for "Cut!"

I stared hard into the viper's eyes. "The last thing I want is to be alone with you, Tory. Especially not in the cab of my truck."

"You hit me. Everyone saw it," she accused with slitted and suddenly dry eyes.

Two of the members of her girl group nodded enthusiastically when she turned her stare on them. The rest of the crowd around us wavered between prurient interest and worry depending on whether they were players or not.

"After ruining my night you need to be a gentleman and take me home."

My hands came up in front of me, warding her off when she took a step in my direction. "That makes no sense. Why would you want the guy you're accusing of hitting you to take you home?"

Her hands flexed at her sides, and her face assumed a mottled red hue. Then she stomped her feet in a classic tantrum. "You wait until I tell my dad how you hurt me and humiliated me in front of all these people. You had your chance. Now, you're gonna be sorry, Callahan O'Reilly."

Turning on her heel, she flounced out of the middle of the crowd as her entourage parted to allow her dramatic exit. As if on cue, the music cranked up again, and with the end of Tory's scene, everyone resumed dancing and drinking and laughing. Except for my friends and me.

Finn slung an arm over my shoulders and hauled me to the kitchen. Bax and Fitzy followed in our wake. We didn't stop until Finn handed me a beer.

"Looks like you dodged a bullet there, 'Han," he said.

Bax shook his head. "I don't think so, bro. I think the ugly is only about to begin."

Fitz clapped a hand on my shoulder. "Sorry, man. She wasn't invited. I didn't even know she was here until she started screamin' about you hitting her."

"I didn't hit her." Scrubbing a hand down my face, I blew a breath at the ceiling. "I was trying to talk to Jamaica on the phone, and Tory kept buzzing around me like a damn mosquito. When she grabbed my arm, I just reacted."

Bax's speculative stare made my skin crawl. His inappropriate T-shirts and lack of finesse with the ladies aside, the guy was brilliant, one of the smartest people I knew. Whatever he was thinking, I wasn't going to like hearing it.

"She set you up."

"What?"

"She set you up." Bax sipped his beer, ran his tongue over his foam mustache, and tipped his cup in my direction. "You said she was buzzing around you while you talked on the phone. Then she grabbed you and you reacted." Crossing his arms over his massive chest, he downed another pull from his beer. "She wanted you to push her off. Didn't her sister do something kinda like that with Freeman when she yelled assault and caused his draft stock to drop like a bomb?"

That weight in my stomach gained about a hundred pounds. "Yeah."

"Her dad is already threatening you with your sponsorship, so why would Tory pull this stunt?" Finn asked, his face a mask of confusion.

I shot him a "shut your fucking mouth" glare, and he hunched his shoulders and downed his beer.

"Her dad is threatening your sponsorship?" Fitz's tone was pure thunder. "What the fuck?"

"It's nothing. I'm handling it," I said through my teeth, my words directed at my loudmouth roommate who retreated a little further into his beer.

Speculation shone in the depths of Fitz's dark brown eyes. "That guy thinks his shit don't stink. It's about time someone proved to him that it does."

"I'm not starting anything with Buzz Miller," I warned.

"You don't have to. From the sounds of it, he started it with you," Fitz pointed out.

From the second Jamaica told me she wasn't coming out, my night had gone from sugar to shit. Though I had a plan for my sponsorship, it came with its own set of perils. Tipping my cup to my lips, I drained my beer and held it out to Bax for a refill. I couldn't do anything about anything tonight. Might as well get shit-faced and worry about it in the morning.

Something in my expression must have tipped him off to my mood. "Come on. Let's drink some beer, play some games, and celebrate kicking the shit out of the Bears," Bax said, refilling my cup. "Remind ourselves we're college athletes and fuckin' conference champs."

Beer sloshed over the rims of our cups as we toasted each other and downed them in one go. By some unspoken agreement, for the rest of the night, my roommates made sure my cup never ran dry. They also made sure I woke up alone in my own bed the next morning with no idea of how that had happened. Flashes of losing at beer pong then at cornhole in Fitz's back yard interplayed with off-color toasts and general fuckery. Judging from the wrecked state of my clothes—and the stench—I'd had one hell of a time.

Unfortunately, my stomach wasn't impressed. I should have known what to expect when I started my day praying to the porcelain god.

At film Coach rode our asses over how hungover we all were, which did nothing for my pounding head. Afterward, when I called Jamaica to invite her over for the afternoon—and hopefully the evening—she passed. She was still on call and had dorm meetings. Something about the way she turned me down sounded off, but she wouldn't stay on the phone long enough for me to pry it out of her. All of which meant Sunday sucked.

One would have thought that earning a by-week in the playoffs with our conference championship would mean a lighter day in the weight room Monday morning. One would have thought wrong. From the second we stepped into the gym, Coach Larkin barked at us to stop being candy asses and push that iron in the air, making it clear we were being punished for tying one on after our big win. Guess our idea of celebrating didn't mesh with his, though rumor had it, the coaching staff threw quite a rager after the game too.

When I arrived in class, Jamaica was already there, coffee in hand, and sitting *between* Axel and Jory. What. The. Fuck?

I stood beside Axel's seat. "Trade me."

He glanced up for a second and back down at his desk where it appeared he'd dumped out everything in his backpack—notebooks, pens, iPad. "I'm kinda settled in here, Callahan." His coffee balanced precariously at the edge of the tiny work space, almost daring me to knock it off out of spite.

"Jamaica?" I asked.

Sparing me a nanosecond of her attention, she shrugged. "Class is starting."

Dr. Dair's dry delivery interrupted our standoff. "Is there a debate back there, Mr. O'Reilly?"

"No, sir." I threw myself into the seat next to Axel, forcing him to scramble to grab his coffee before it spilled all over his jeans.

While Dair droned on for the next hour, I kept stealing glances at Jamaica who studiously avoided eye contact. When class ended, she lagged behind Axel until we were outside. Then she kicked it into gear, speed-walking away from me at a clip that would have grabbed the attention of every track coach in a five-hundred-mile radius.

Unfortunately for her, that foot difference in our heights favored me, and I caught her easily. "You mind telling me what's going on? Why have you been avoiding me since last week?"

"I don't normally have much time for social media."

"Which I like."

"Until it's shoved in my face. I couldn't go to the party so you were grinding on Tory Miller? What the hell, Callahan?" She stared hard at my hand where it lightly rested in the crook of her elbow.

When I let her go, she took off again and was halfway up the sidewalk before I caught her a second time.

"Are you going to believe what you think you saw on some blurry video or what I tell you is true?"

In seconds we'd reached the fork in the sidewalk where I went to the gym and she went to Huffine. "I don't want to be late for class."

"Jamaica."

"Please, Hotshot." The pain in those gorgeous green eyes gutted me. Then she ripped my heart right out of my chest. "Maybe we should take a break. You have so much going on with the team, your sponsorship. Tory Miller." The way she swallowed told me it hurt. "I need to step out of your way, give you a chance to do what you need to do to make sure you go high in the draft next year." For a second she closed her eyes tight, then she turned on her heel and ran to class.

Though the casual passerby probably wouldn't notice, I was bleeding out right there on the sidewalk. I had no idea how long I stared at the empty space where the woman who'd stolen my heart, torn it in half, and stomped on it had stood. A shout drew my attention to the doors of the gym where Finn was waving at me. Only then did it dawn on me that for once, Tory Miller and her giggling girl gang hadn't been waiting to interrupt me giving Jamaica her have-a-good-day kiss.

It was all I could do to drag my ass to film as the stone that dropped into my belly at Fitz's party Saturday night became a boulder.

CHAPTER THIRTY-THREE

Jamaica

THE PAST TEN days without seeing Callahan aside from in Dr. Dair's class had been excruciating. My concentration had lapsed into nonexistent. I'd dropped a quiz in my pre-law class that had landed me in my professor's office. I'd forgotten to follow up on a programming opportunity my supervisor had assigned me in last week's RA meeting, so I'd heard all about how our dorm missed out in this week's meeting. I even wandered into my Friday coffee date with Axel on autopilot twenty minutes late with no idea how I'd arrived or why I was there.

"You made a unilateral decision without knowing all the facts, J. Not a good move," he reprimanded me.

"Hello, Axel. Sorry I'm late. How was your day?" I said, my tone sweeter than the caramel syrup in my friend's latte.

"Callahan can't keep his eyes off you in class, and the look on his face is one of a seriously wounded man. You need to fix this before the Wildcats play their home playoff game next week."

"Is football all you can think about?" I blew on my coffee and tried to hide behind an outrage I didn't feel. "Besides, I did fix this. I made sure Buzz Miller doesn't take Callahan's sponsorship away from him."

Axel shook his head, his eyes going to the ceiling like he was praying for guidance. "You haven't heard? Callahan and Copper made a statement on Monday afternoon mutually severing their partnership. So your sacrificial martyrdom serves no purpose other than to make both of you miserable, which by extension makes all your friends miserable." That last part came with a censorious glare.

The news hit me like punch to the gut. Even after I broke it off with him, Callahan still lost his sponsorship? Now what was he going to do? Hunching my shoulders, I busied myself with rolling my hot cup between my freezing hands, letting the heat seep into my skin. "If you wanted to cancel today, you should have said so." I couldn't remember when I'd been so cold for so long.

"That's not what I meant"—he stared at me from beneath his brows—"and you know it. From what Finn says, Callahan's as big of a mess as you are."

My gaze flew to his. "Of course he is. Losing his sponsorship means he won't have enough money to buy groceries. Did Finn tell you that part too?" The pain of the past week sat on my chest like a ton of lead. Axel's news only served to steal even more of my breath.

He reached across the table, taking both of my hands in his. "Jesus, J. Your hands are like ice." For a few seconds, he rubbed his hands over mine. "I've never known you to have true feelings for anyone you ever dated—until now." With a squeeze he let me go. "But I gotta hand it to you, when you gave in, you gave in for someone who's worth it. Don't fuck it up now."

The alarm on my phone went off. Considering all the screw-ups I'd made in the past ten days, at least I'd had the good sense to remember to set an alarm for my meeting.

"What's that for?" my friend asked.

Slipping my hand into my backpack, I pulled out the envelope I'd received by special delivery yesterday afternoon. Since receiving it, I'd read and reread the formal letter from the dean over and over. For the life of me, I couldn't understand why I was being summoned to her office on a Friday afternoon.

"Maybe they're extending your scholarship," Axel said as he handed the letter back to me.

The ominous feeling that settled over me at the first sight of the dean's logo intensified. "That's not the vibe I'm sensing." I slid the envelope back into my backpack, stood, and shouldered it. Grabbing my coffee cup, I said, "I'll call you later."

I left my friend at the table with a troubled expression marring his handsome face.

"I-I'm sorry, but you're mistaken. Before I stepped into American Lit. 201 freshman year, I'd never even heard of Dr. Emil Dair. When I raised my hand to ask a question in that class, he took one look at me, and it was loathe at first sight. He's made it his mission to make my life hard ever since."

No doubt Dr. Steen thought I was a complete idiot with my babbling. But I was not related in any way to my nemesis in the English department, the pall of nepotism at least one heavy weight I wasn't carrying at the moment.

"As a matter of fact, he's gone out of his way this semester to make an example of me every day in class."

She started to speak, but I held up my finger.

"For instance, he assigned my partner and me to the end of the queue for our class presentations, requiring us to add minutes to our time with a heightened expectation of 'creativity and scholarship'—his words. It's one thing for him to do that to me because he does it all the time. I'm used to it. But I didn't think it was fair to raise such high expectations for my partner who's majoring in sports marketing. Yet Dair wouldn't even let me lodge a protest." I pulled in a breath and squared my shoulders. "Obviously, whoever told you I was related to Dr. Dair has me confused with someone else."

The dean pierced me with her gaze. "I'm afraid not, Miss Winslow. The information we have is solid. Emil Dair is your uncle."

Deflating against the back of the tasteful—yet super-hard—oak chair in front of her desk, I stared at her, dread churning my stomach like a sea in a hurricane. "I don't see how he can be. I know who my mother's brothers are. While we've never hung out with them, we all do have the same last name."

When she continued to peruse me with those sharp eagle eyes, I added, "Mom is the only girl in her family, so there are no brothers-in-law."

"What about your dad?"

Apparently we were moving on from the accusation round to the humiliation round. Terrific.

Sitting on my hands to keep from wringing them in my lap, I said, "He's a nonfactor. I haven't seen or heard from him since my junior year of high school. He never lived with us, only visited a couple of times a year." Pulling my lips between my teeth, I gathered my thoughts. "I've always had the idea he was married to someone but liked to spend time with my mom too." Too late, I figured out how that sounded. Putting my hands up, I hurried to clarify, "Please don't get the wrong idea. My mom's a faithful, hardworking person. The only man she's ever had in her life is my dad whenever he came to town."

"I see." She dragged the words out in a way that told me she didn't see. Not really.

Still, I ran with it. "Obviously, I have zero relationship to

Dr. Dair no matter what your sources told you. I've worked my ass off—pardon my language—in his classes. I've *earned* the A's I have in them."

"Please don't misunderstand, Miss Winslow. We aren't investigating you."

The way that came out implied she was investigating Dr. Dair. For what, I couldn't imagine. He was a curmudgeonly prick with a massive stick up his ass, but I'd learned a ton in his classes. As far as I knew, he was a fair grader even if he made me work harder than anyone else for my marks.

Glancing down at the report on her desk, she asked, "For the record, what is your father's name?"

"John Blackwood."

"And he lives—?"

"Wherever he does." Her brow shot up and I hurried to add, "I've never known where he lives. Couldn't even tell you which state. He drives an over-the-road truck—or he did the last time I saw him. He's not listed on my emergency contacts, and he stopped paying child support when I turned eighteen. I very much doubt he's in any way related to Dr. Dair."

Her expression turned soft, which left me more nervous than at any time during this bizarre interview.

"John Blackwood is married to Natasha Dair—Emil's sister. He owns Continental Trucking, the firm Dr. Dair's father started." She tugged a photo from the file in front of her. "Is this your father?"

A roar filled my ears as I stared at the man standing in the middle of a family photo, one arm around a beautiful blonde woman and the other arm around…*Holy shit.* There was my father all cozy with Dr. Dair. Three kids flanked the blonde, two boys and a girl. Two more kids flanked a plain brown-haired woman with a mischievous grin who stood on Dr. Dair's other side.

Swallowing hard, I nodded. My fingers hovered over the photo. "I think I'm going to be sick," I whispered.

"It's important for academic integrity that there is not even a hint of nepotism among students and professors. For this reason we'll have an independent panel of professors grading your presentation on Monday morning."

I managed to nod again.

"I will personally be reviewing your midterm exam and any other assignments you've completed for Dr. Dair's class."

Swallowing over the lump in my throat, I managed to croak out, "My other classes too? I don't know where all my assignments are."

"If your work in this class checks out, we will assume you have returned a similar standard in the other classes. If not, we'll have to figure out how to deal with that."

Willing the tears back, I said, "I'm here on a renewable academic scholarship. I've worked so hard to maintain my grades, ma'am. I swear I've never cheated. Never even thought about it."

"Yes, well, the problem is, while I'm convinced you had no idea until today that Dr. Dair is related to you—"

"But—"

She put up her palm. "No matter how peripheral that relationship is, from the outset he knew exactly who you were. He should have redirected you to other professors' classes, and he did not."

Was he deliberately trying to sabotage me? Because my dad had an affair on his sister? That was so screwed up.

"Therefore, we will take precautions to make sure you are not receiving nor can even be perceived as receiving special treatment." Dr. Steen returned the photo and papers to the file folder and stood. "Thank you for your cooperation and your candor. That will be all, Miss Winslow."

When she put out her hand, I shook it on autopilot. What the hell were we shaking on? The end of my college career because of something I didn't even know?

As I stumbled out of her office, my phone somehow appeared in my hand. Until I heard his voice on the other end of the call, I hadn't even been aware I'd dialed Callahan.

Chapter Thirty-Four

Callahan

FINN SLID INTO the passenger seat of my truck. "Man, you need to pull your head out of your ass before Coach runs all the muscle right off you."

He'd been waiting for a ride for at least twenty minutes while I did burpees until I thought I would puke. Coach was "helping" me remember how not to fuck up nearly every play I'd run in practice all week.

"What's going on with you? You let that sophomore on the scout team own you on the line on almost every down," he oh-so-helpfully pointed out.

"Leave it, Finn."

Muttering to himself, he ran a hand through his hair and stared out the window.

We'd rolled about five feet out of my parking spot when I slammed on the brakes. "What was that about Jamaica?"

He hunched down in his seat. "Nothing."

Jamming my truck into park, I turned in

my seat, facing him. "No, you said, 'I never should have said anything to Jamaica.' What did you say to her?" I demanded.

Finn blew a breath at the floor. "I was half-asleep when she came downstairs last week. I might have mentioned how she was the reason you could lose your sponsorship."

Before he could turtle down even further in his seat, I smacked him upside the head. "What the fuck, man? Can't you keep anything to yourself?" Glaring at him, I said, "She is *not* the reason for my problems with my sponsorship."

Holding his hands in front of him, he faced me. "Don't blame me. She saw a text on your iPad and asked me about it since you wouldn't be honest with her." He pulled his backpack up from the floor between his feet and set it on the seat between us. As barriers went it wasn't much, but it made his point.

I jerked my ball cap off my head, ran my hand through my hair, and tugged it back on. "Tory Miller is the reason for my sponsorship problem, which I'm handling. For the thousandth time, you don't need to worry your pretty little head about it. None of you will have to help me with groceries, all right?"

I put my ride back in gear and eased out of the parking lot at the field house. At least now I had a clue about why Jamaica had walked away from me last week, avoided me in class, and refused to return my texts or voice messages. My tough girl thought she was doing me a favor.

After we arrived home, I ignored Finn's invitation to dinner, ran upstairs to my room, and shut the door. Out of habit, I tossed my backpack on my desk, toed off my shoes, and threw myself on my bed. When I pulled out my phone to see if Jamaica had responded to any of my texts today, I almost fell off the bed to see a voicemail waiting in my inbox. Desperate to hear her voice, I jammed my finger on play and plastered my phone to my ear.

"Um, hi. I'm sorry. You must be in practice. I hate to bother you. Our project is in trouble with the dean. Um. Call me?"

Her voice sounded so distant, like she was barely hanging on. While her words made no sense, I couldn't miss the fear in her tone. Before I consciously knew what I was doing, I'd dropped down the stairs two at a time and slammed out the front door. As I fired up my truck, I hit speed dial. "Hello, Island Girl? Are you at your place?"

"Yes."

It killed me how small her voice sounded.

"Be there in ten."

It was all I could do to maintain the speed limit as I drove to her dorm. Whatever was going on, she was in trouble. That she'd reached out to me gave me hope. She'd shut me out when she thought she was saving me, but when she was in trouble, she'd come to me. I had no idea what that meant, but I clung to it like a raft in a storm.

The front desk clerk in her dorm had just called to let her know to come get me when Tory Miller appeared out of nowhere like a bad dream.

"Hello, Callahan. Have you come to your senses yet?" she asked as she sidled up to me.

This bitch was toxic, and I was done trying to play nice with her. "I wasn't aware I'd lost them."

"You lost your sponsorship with Copper. I would have thought you'd catch a clue."

"From what I've seen on the socials, after that stunt you pulled at Fitzy's party I would have thought *you'd* catch a clue," I countered.

Her little posse exchanged wide-eyed looks. The entourage flanking her was substantially diminished from the number of freshman following her every move earlier in the semester. Might have had something to do with one of them outing her for trying to set me up. That capsule of blood she popped when she smacked her hand to her mouth had me convinced I'd hurt her when I'd desperately been attempting to avoid her. I needed to find out who that girl was because I owed her a big one.

Of course, Tory hadn't been as patient or as smart as her sister. Pulling that stunt in the middle of a crowded party meant there were other witnesses too, which came out on the socials as well. Her grinding herself against me while I turned away from her as I talked on the phone to Jamaica. Her following me even as I sidestepped her and kept my hands to myself. Her poking and pushing at me until my conversation on the phone collided with her greedy hands and I swung around too fast with my elbow sticking out at the wrong height and angle. All of it ended up online with enough commentary to bury someone who wasn't Tory Miller. The girl had no shame and no boundaries whatsoever. Guess her daddy's money shielded her from what would send a normal person under a rock for the foreseeable future.

"Yeah, well, it won't be long before you won't have any reason to visit truck-stop trash in this dorm. Maybe then you'll wake up and come to me at the Delta Chi House." She twirled a blonde curl but the expression in her eyes was pure venom.

Dread filled my chest. "What are you talking about?"

"Ask her."

"Ask me what?" Jamaica asked as she walked into the lobby, her tone flat.

"Nepotism only works when you have the money to back it, Jamaica. Guess you'll learn the hard way." With that cryptic comment, Tory spun on her heel and headed toward the stairs, her girls obediently following in her wake.

"Jamaica?"

The bleakness in her eyes leached their vibrant green right out. "Let's have this conversation in private."

Without waiting to see if I followed, she headed back down the hallway to her room. After she keyed us in, she walked directly to the window and stared into the darkness beyond.

"Jamaica? What's wrong?"

My hands itched to touch her, to curl around her and pull her against me, wrap my arms around her and hold her tight. But the brittle set of her shoulders warned me she might shatter into a thousand shards if I laid a finger on her, so I stuffed my hands in my pockets and waited.

"I was summoned to the dean's office today." Her voice sounded hollow. "Turns out my father is married to Dr. Dair's sister. Dr. Dair has known who I was from the first class I took from him. It seems there's a question about the grades I've earned in his classes." She wrapped her arms around herself, her nails digging into the sides of her sweatshirt. "Because of this our project is on the line." In a whisper, she added, "My scholarship is on the line."

That did it. In one step, I was beside her, turning her and folding her into my chest. "Ah, babe. You didn't know?"

"Didn't have a single clue," she said into my hoodie. "I'm sorry I've dragged you into my mess. You already had enough on your plate."

"The only thing I have going on is helping you fix this." I pulled back enough to stare into the eyes I knew I'd dream about for the rest of my life. "What do we have to do for our presentation on Monday?"

"Not much. Only present the best project the entire college has ever seen." Tears filled her eyes, and she buried her face in my chest again.

Running my hands up and down her back, I said, "Is that all? Pssht. Child's play. The dean wants to see a kick-ass project? We are exactly the right pair to show her one." Then a thought occurred to me. "How does Tory Miller know about your relationship to Dr. Dair?"

Jamaica stilled. "That's a really good question."

My brow shot up. "Isn't it though? First her dad threatens me. Now the dean is threatening you. I don't think that's a coincidence."

"Axel said you lost your sponsorship."

The pain in her eyes killed me.

"It was a mutual decision. Copper was too high-class for me. None of my friends could afford to go there with me, so I usually had to eat there alone. That worked out great for the owner because I could give all my attention to the wealthy fans who showed up on my appointed nights." I pushed a wayward curl from her brow, fingering the softness of her hair. "But even with my discount, it was a big expense."

"You shouldn't have taken me there."

"I should take you there every weekend."

The massive eye roll she gifted me let me breathe fully for the first time in nearly two weeks. We'd been on hiatus, not broken up.

"What are you going to do?"

I grinned. "Make a commercial for Stromboli's tomorrow with Fitz and Bax and a couple of other players."

Her pouty lips formed an "O" I desperately wanted to kiss. "You have a new sponsorship?"

"I told you I was handling it." My tone might have been a bit harsh, but my girl needed to believe me when I said I could take care of things. "When Buzz Miller made his demands, I called my agent and asked her to work something out with Stromboli's. It doesn't pay as well as Copper, but it's more my kind of people— and there are no strings." Covering her hands resting on my chest with my own, I pulled them up around my neck. "I know you think you were helping me by walking away, but I've been a wreck without you."

It had been ten fucking long days since I'd had my lips on hers. Before I could work out the details of how to fix our academic dilemma, I needed her breath in me. I brushed my mouth over hers, once, twice, then pressed into her. Her arms tightened around my neck, her curves molding to my body. On a sigh she opened up and gave me the lifeline I needed. I took my time tasting and exploring her, imprinting her with my arms coiled around her.

Something like hours later, I rested my forehead on hers while we panted in air.

"I missed you so much, Hotshot. But I couldn't be responsible for you not going high in the draft because your sponsor dropped you." She sounded miserable—which after that kiss absolutely would not do.

"You had nothing to do with it, babe. No matter how her dad throws his money around, I wouldn't date Tory Miller if she was the last woman on earth." Pressing my lips to hers again, I said, "You're the only woman I want." One kiss morphed into four or five more. "I'm in love with you, Jamaica Winslow."

Burying her face in my neck, she squeezed me hard. "I never meant to date you."

Chuckling, I said, "I know."

She stared so deep into my eyes she had to have seen into my soul. "I never meant to fall in love with you, but I love you, Callahan O'Reilly. I love you so much."

I couldn't stop the smile that broke over my face. Her answering one was sunshine after a long, dark winter. For several minutes, we stood in the middle of her tiny dorm room smiling our asses off at each other and being in love and knowing that love was reciprocated.

Then sadness clouded her pretty green eyes again. "So what are we going to do if I'm kicked out of school?"

"Pack your bag for the weekend."

She blinked. "Excuse me?"

I let her go and looked around for her backpack. Spying it draped over her desk chair, I grabbed it and held it out to her. "Are you on call this weekend?"

"No…" There was a question in her tone.

"Right. Perfecting our presentation is going to take time, what with the ten days of catching up on touching you and making love to you I have to do."

A laugh snorted out of her. "Am I a chore then?"

"More of a reward." With a grin of pure happiness at having her back, I pushed her pack into her hands. "Get on it, babe. We don't have all night for you to pack."

A few minutes later, I'd shouldered her backpack and linked her hand with mine as we walked out to my truck.

While I showered and dressed for the commercial shoot, Jamaica slept. After we'd spent most of the night showing each other how much we'd missed each other, how much we loved each other, she'd passed out and hadn't moved. Her responses through the night left me feeling like Iron Man and Captain America wrapped into the superhero of all superheroes.

With a grin, I scrawled a note and propped it on the nightstand beside her phone. Silently, I let myself out of my room and headed downstairs.

Bax was leaning against the sink drinking coffee when I stepped into the kitchen. "You're back with your lady, huh?"

"Sure am." I didn't even bother to hold in my grin when I opened the cupboard beside him, pulled out my travel mug, and filled it with most of what was in the coffee pot.

"About damn time."

I shot him a look from beneath my brows.

"Now maybe you won't be such a bear to live with." He sipped his brew. "And such a fuckup in practice."

"Asshole."

He smirked. "You driving?"

"Don't I always?"

When we arrived at Stromboli's at 7 a.m., I was starved, but Bax had warned me not to eat because we'd be downing slices for as many takes as necessary to do the commercial. The heavenly aroma of fresh pizza greeted us at the door, along with a woman who directed us to a set of chairs where Fitz and Johnson were already being fussed over by a guy wielding a brush and a palette of makeup.

My stomach rumbled loud enough to be heard through the entire bar, and Fitz cracked a smile that had the makeup guy growling at him to remain still. We settled into our chairs, and as if by magic two more makeup artists appeared, throwing capes over our matching Stromboli's T-shirts and going to work to make us camera-ready.

This shoot was more fun than anything I'd ever done for Copper. First off, I was doing it with my guys. Second, we were selling pizza and beer, which didn't take any effort whatsoever. Third, the director made sure we all had a great time. By the time we wrapped up, six hours had passed in a blur, and it was time to eat lunch for real.

We'd commandeered our usual booth in the back and ordered a couple pitchers of beer when Bax stole all the good vibes by mentioning Buzz Miller. "At least he didn't wreck your career before it even started," he said as he poured a glass with a perfect head—his specialty—and handed it to me. "And you pulled your head out and made up with your girl, which is good for all of us." His comment included Fitz and Tarvarius Johnson, our star running back and the class clown for the shoot today.

When Bax mentioned Miller, though, all good humor left our friends' faces.

"You ready to do something about that dick-shine, 'Han? Don't get me wrong. I'm stoked you joined our crew to promote Stromboli's." Reaching a beefy brown fist across the table, Fitz bumped mine. "But that asshole has already ruined one guy's draft. He's trying to ruin yours. We all pay for it because he taints the team." Drawing down half a pint of beer in one pull, he wiped his thumb and forefinger along his mustache and continued. "I'm tired of some entitled white prick thinking he owns us—any of us. We aren't studs for his nasty daughters—or his ticket to an NFL party he'll never get invited to otherwise."

"He's not wrong, 'Han," Bax chimed in.

"I heard there's another daughter coming next year," Johnson added. "That puts all of us on the list for next year's draft in a fucking scary place—unless we do something about it now."

My gaze jumped between Fitz and Johnson. Beside me, Bax leaned back into the plush leather booth and sipped his beer. I didn't need to see his face to know he was on board with whatever our friends were thinking.

Tory's smug face when she'd mentioned nepotism last night in the lobby of Jamaica's dorm flashed through my mind. *Fuck!* That bitch was behind Jamaica's serious problem too. Jesus, how could one person be so fucking ugly?

"I'm in. What's your plan?"

CHAPTER THIRTY-FIVE

Jamaica

WHEN CALLAHAN RETURNED to his place after his morning NIL commercial for Stromboli's, I was deep into rearranging our research. As I worked my mind around the mess I'd found myself in, I'd decided to go for broke and make our presentation a referendum on the American class system dictated by money. From the looks of things, my dad had enough to send all his kids through college—including the one he'd abandoned—yet he'd let me struggle. His brother-in-law was perfectly happy to jeopardize that struggle. The kinship I currently felt with Fanny Price from *Mansfield Park* couldn't have been more acute.

After kissing me as though it had been ten days instead of ten hours since he'd kissed me last, Callahan snuggled in beside me on the bed to read over my notes.

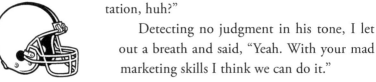

"Sooo, we're completely rearranging the presentation, huh?"

Detecting no judgment in his tone, I let out a breath and said, "Yeah. With your mad marketing skills I think we can do it."

He read a bit farther down the bullet-point outline, stopped, typed in a note, and continued. Occasionally, he added another note until he reached the end. Pointing at the screen on my laptop, he said, "We'll need a couple of new memes, but this is doable." His brilliant smile was all for me. "This is fantastic. You're a genius, Island Girl."

"You truly like it? Because we can practice what we already have. It's good too."

"Nope. We're going to rock Dr. Dair and the dean and whoever else they invite to the show. By the time our thirty minutes is up, they're all gonna go home to their mamas and apologize for being such poor students of how to treat people—literarily, of course." With a wink he fist-bumped me and I laughed.

"Literarily. Of course."

Finn knocked on the door and poked his head in. "What movie are you two watching? I could hear you laughing halfway down the stairs."

"Who said we had to be watching a movie?" Hotshot asked. "I could have been tickling the shit out of my naked girlfriend."

"Callahan!" I squeaked.

He smirked. "Point is, you don't knock and enter at the same time, Finnegan. But since you've invited yourself into my room, you can be our guinea pig." Turning to me, he asked, "How long do you think we'll need to practice?"

I shrugged. "Since we already have some of it down, I'd say two hours maybe?"

"Be here in two hours, Finn. Don't be late," Callahan directed.

Finn's confusion was comical as he backed out the door.

"I think he was hoping to catch us in a tickle and giggle. Pervert," I snorted.

"He needs pointers." Hotshot waggled his brows. At the look of horror I'm sure settled over my face, he patted my thigh and reassured me. "Don't worry, he's not getting them from us." In one lithe movement, he hopped off the bed. "Now, let's go to work creating our new memes to drop into the presentation."

For the next two hours, we worked seamlessly together. It was almost time for dinner when Callahan went in search of Finn, dinnertime making it easy to find him. Callahan pushed Finn ahead of him into the bedroom with Bax and Danny on their heels. Apparently, our audience had grown over the course of the afternoon.

Within seconds of our opening thesis, Hotshot's roommates were cracking up. By the three-minute mark they were all in. For the next twenty-seven minutes, at the appropriate points they alternately laughed or sat forward, chins on fists—or in Bax's case resting on his forearms on the back of the chair he sat on backward—their attention totally tuned in to what we shared. We finished to a standing ovation.

Admittedly, these were Callahan's roommates and friends, but none of them were lit majors, so keeping their attention the way we did meant we were on the right track. At least we'd nailed the entertainment portion of the assignment. Then they started asking pertinent questions, which continued all through dinner. At one point Callahan tugged me close, kissed the side of my head and whispered, "We got this, Island Girl. We got this."

Didn't mean I didn't work myself into a ball of nerves all day Sunday. Didn't mean I didn't insist we practice five or ten more times until Callahan put a stop to it with his talented hands and mouth, making good on that tickle and giggle he'd promised on Saturday afternoon.

Still, I slept poorly and woke up before him. After he dropped me at the dorm on his way to weight training, I spent far too much time stressing over my outfit for the presentation. At last I settled on a black-and-white sweater dress in a bold geometric style with black leggings and a fuchsia headband in a floral design to tame my curls. Gathering as much of my nerve as possible, along with my essentials for the day, I headed out of the dorm only to find Hotshot waiting in the lobby to walk me to class.

"Today's a big day. Thought we'd show up together," he said as he greeted me with a kiss. Eyeing my headband, he added, "Love that color. Glad you didn't do something conservative."

I touched my hair. "Like that's an option."

He laughed and grabbed my hand as we walked to Creston Hall.

"You skipped your nine o'clock today."

A serious undertone balanced the humor in his voice. "I had something more important to do than listen to marketing stats. I can catch up tomorrow."

When we entered the lecture hall, the place was buzzing with excitement and curiosity. My stomach bottomed out at seeing the usual group in the front row displaced with extra professors. Beside me Callahan stiffened for a second before following me to our usual spot. At least we had the familiarity of Axel and Jory seated where they belonged with our seats open beside them.

"What's up?" I whispered as we sat down and started unloading our backpacks.

"Coach Ellis is sitting beside Dean Steen. Looks like she pulled out all the stops for us."

"I might have mentioned to her how unfair all this is to you. Maybe she's making sure you have representation when that lot get together to render their verdict on our work."

On my other side, Axel handed me a coffee. "I had a feeling you might not stop today. But you need this, J."

"You are the very best, best friend," I said, my tone conveying my gratitude as I sipped the perfect brew.

"Are you sharing?" Hotshot asked, and I passed him the cup.

A second later, it seemed, Dr. Dair stood at his lectern glaring at our row over the top of his glasses. "If you can find a way to drop the volume down to a dull roar, we can move on with the final presentation for the semester. Miss Winslow? Mr. O'Reilly? The floor is yours."

Just like that we were on. We made our way to the front of the auditorium, hooked my laptop into the system, and in tandem breathed a sigh of relief when the screen behind us lit up with our title slide. Together, we slipped our hands into the straps on our iPads containing our notes. While I studiously avoided looking at my nemesis professor, I caught Callahan shoot a smirk in his direction. "Ready when you are, sir."

Thirty minutes later—on the dot—silence descended on the room. Then Axel and Jory shot to their feet, clapping wildly. A nanosecond later, the rest of the students in the auditorium joined them, their roar of applause deafening. In the front row I saw a ghost of a smile flit over Dr. Steen's lips while Coach Ellis openly applauded, his approval directed at Callahan. A couple of the other professors were nodding and talking among themselves.

Hotshot winked at me, and we disconnected my laptop and stepped off the stage together. The light brush of his hand on the small of my back as we returned to our seats was enough.

"Hot damn, J! You guys knocked it out of the park!" Axel gushed.

"Glad we didn't have to follow that," Jory added, his eyes wide.

"Thanks. Um, do you know where my coffee went?"

Axel handed me my cup, and I downed most of it in two swallows. Without asking, Callahan took it from me and finished it—the first indication I'd had that he'd experienced any nerves whatsoever.

As the noise in the lecture hall died down, Dr. Dair stood at his lectern. For the first time in three years he seemed small, unintimidating. Regular. Clearing his throat into his microphone, he said, "That will be all for today. Be prepared for the quiz on Wednesday. You're dismissed."

Axel and I exchanged incredulous glances. "Is he letting us out early?" we asked simultaneously.

Beside me Hotshot chuckled. "He has no choice after we entertained the hell out of the class today. Poor guy can't compete."

"Poor guy, my ass. He still holds my fate in his hands," I muttered as I stuffed my things into my backpack.

"I don't think so, Jamaica." Axel nodded toward the aisle where Dr. Steen and Coach Ellis were standing.

Hastily, I followed Hotshot out of the row.

"Impressive, you two. Though occasionally irreverent, your presentation showed thoughtful scholarship. If your sources hold up, I think you'll have nothing to worry about," Dr. Steen said.

"Two captains came to see me in my office this morning. I have an idea you already know what they wanted to discuss," Coach said, his tone stern as he stared Callahan down.

"I might."

"It's one hell of an ask, O'Reilly."

"It's for the good of the team, Coach." He gazed at me. "It's probably for the good of the school since it's related to the reason you were all here this morning."

"We'll discuss it at lunch." The coach's eyes crinkled the slightest bit as he spared me a glance then returned his attention to his star tight end. "Don't be late."

"Yes, sir."

As the two of them moved off, I closed my eyes and did a little dance, shaking out days of stress.

"We have half an hour till you have to be in your next class and I have to be at film. Let's find somewhere private to celebrate our win," Callahan whispered in my ear.

My brows met my hairline as blood rushed to my cheeks. "Are you nuts? We can't do that here."

"Not in the middle of the auditorium, no. But I think I know where. Come on." Mischief danced in his sea-blue eyes as he took my hand and walked purposefully up the aisle.

Heat flooded my core at the thought of how my guy wanted to celebrate our triumph. But as we neared the rear doors to the room, a tall, familiar figure materialized out of the back row and stopped me dead in my tracks.

"Dad?"

"Hello, Jamaica." He shoved his hands in his pockets as he looked me over. "It's been a while."

Adrenaline surged through me as I stared at the man in the designer jeans and perfectly tailored suit jacket. He'd left the top two buttons of his expensive-looking shirt open. The hair at his temples had started to gray, but his green eyes—the same ones he'd given me—remained soft, the way they always were when he looked at me. "I'd say four years is a while." I hid my hurt and surprise behind haughty sarcasm.

"Do you have a few minutes to talk?"

Callahan squeezed my hand.

Tilting my head, I said, "Not really, no."

He nodded and handed me a card. "I'll be in town until Wednesday. Perhaps we can have dinner together?"

I stared down at the card that held the one piece of information I'd always wanted and never thought I'd have: his phone number. Then I shoved it into a side pocket in my backpack. "I have work and classes. Plus, I'll be leaving early on Wednesday for Thanksgiving."

"I'd truly like to see you, Jamaica," he said quietly.

Callahan gave my fingers another tiny squeeze, and I relented. "I might have an hour for lunch tomorrow."

"You two did a great job up there," my dad said.

"Thanks," we said in unison.

"Right. Well. We have somewhere to be." I stepped around my father, Callahan in tow.

"Sir." He nodded to my father with perfect manners.

Once we were outside the lecture hall, Callahan said, "If that"—he nodded back toward the classroom—"wrecked the mood, we can celebrate at my place tonight."

"If you don't make good on your suggestion, I doubt I'll come over to your place tonight," I sassed.

His eyes heated to blue flames, and a second later, I was scrambling to keep up with him as he hustled us to a set of stairs. When we reached the top of the third floor, I was panting and laughing as I struggled to keep up with his long-legged stride. At the end of the hall opposite the stairs, he ushered me into a bathroom and locked the door. Our backpacks hit the floor simultaneously as he plastered the length of his body to mine and pinned me to the wall so his mouth could ravage my neck.

Bunching my dress in his hands, he hiked it to my waist. A second later, cool air wafted over me as he dragged my panties and leggings to the floor. I toed off my shoes, and then I was naked from the waist down. His busy fingers played along my calves, tickled the backs of my knees, and feathered over the skin of my inner thighs before they found their prize.

"Jesus, Island Girl. You're soaking wet." A feral grin crossed his features. "All for me."

I answered him by undoing the fly of his jeans and pushing his clothes down his powerful thighs to his knees. "I seem to recall you promising me a celebration."

He palmed the back of my thigh, dragging my leg up to hook my knee over his hip. "Don't you worry, babe. I'll deliver."

As if by magic a condom packet appeared in his hand. I snatched it from him, tore it open, and smoothed the protection over his impressive length. His eyes darkened almost to black as he watched me guide him to my entrance. When he pushed inside me, our gazes locked and happy smiles bloomed over our faces. Then my other knee found its way to his hip, and I locked my ankles together at the small of his back while he grabbed two handfuls of my ass and started a rhythm meant to drive me over the edge in seconds.

Sealing his mouth to mine, he swallowed my screams of pleasure as he thrust hard and deep inside me. Squeezing him tight with my arms around his neck, my thighs around his waist, and my inner muscles around his length, I came so hard, waves and waves of ecstasy crashing through me. Then Callahan went rigid in my embrace, and it was my turn to hold his shouts inside my mouth. After a couple of extra thrusts for more fun, he pulled out and gently lowered my feet to the floor.

As if sensing I couldn't stand on my own, he kept me pinned to the door with his body. When our breathing returned to something resembling normal, he stepped back and disposed of the condom.

"Congratulations on a job well done, Mr. O'Reilly," I said, my smile big enough to cover my face.

His smile mirrored mine. "Congratulations to you, Miss Winslow. You rocked everyone's world today—especially mine."

A few minutes later with our clothes righted and our faces a little less flushed, we exited the bathroom and hand in hand made our way back downstairs at more leisurely pace. Once we were outside the building, we noticed students hustling to classes. I checked my phone and said, "We have one minute less than usual to make it to our next assignments on time."

"I'm nothing if not a master of timing." He smirked.

When we reached the fork in the sidewalk that took me to Huffine Hall and him to the gym, he slid his hand beneath my curls, cupping the back of my neck. Against my lips, he said, "I'll pick you up at the sweet shop tonight after practice." He pressed his lips to mine, a quiet, lingering promise. "Make sure you're prepared to spend the night."

As I hurried into the building, it occurred to me Tory Miller and her entourage of freshmen mean girls hadn't interrupted us for once.

Odd.

Chapter Thirty-Six

Jamaica

"HE INVITED ME to Thanksgiving with his family," I fumed as I stomped back and forth across the rug in Callahan's bedroom. "Since the cat's out of the bag now, Dad wants me to meet his other kids. He said I'd be a great 'role model' for them." Sarcasm dripped from the phrase. "Is he going to tell his other kids he'll take care of their college expenses and then abandon them before they graduate too? I don't think so. Which means I'm not a role model whatsoever for his legitimate children."

Hotshot leaned against the pillows on his bed, his ankles casually crossed, his expression sympathetic while I paced and paced.

"If not for Tory Miller outing Dr. Dair's relationship to me, I doubt I would have seen John Blackwood ever again. Now he shows up out of the blue and wants to have a relationship with me? He's ridiculous."

"He's a businessman. You spoke his language when you blew his mind with your mad presentation skills, babe."

I threw my hands in the air. "Whatever. My mom gave up her family and her chance at achieving her dreams when she chose to have me. She's remained faithful to that man for over twenty years. How does he repay her? Asks me to abandon her on a holiday. Not. Gonna. Happen."

Callahan patted the mattress beside him. "Come here."

Shooting him a narrow-eyed stare, I said, "I'm too worked up for shenanigans right now, Hotshot."

"I can see that." He patted the mattress again. "Come here anyway."

Gingerly, I climbed onto the bed beside him. Sliding his arm around me, he tugged me in to rest on his broad chest. With his other hand he drew my hand across his waist and covered my arm with his own, cuddling me close.

"I'm proud of you."

Lifting my head, I stared hard into his eyes. "Why?"

"You're one of the most self-sufficient people I've ever met, yet when someone backed you into a corner, you didn't come out swinging. Instead, you reached out for help." He tangled his fingers in my curls. "Thank you for letting me back in. For letting me help you."

I settled down onto his chest.

"You also could have blown your dad off, skipped meeting him today, but you faced him head-on. No matter how angry"— he tipped his head up to catch my eye—"and hurt he made you, you gave him a chance to have his say. That makes you the bigger person." Tightening his hold on me, he whispered, "I'd do anything for you, Jamaica. You're the whole package." A chuckle escaped him. "Plus, you're fucking brilliant in the sack."

I smacked his flat stomach. "For a minute there you were doing so well." But I was laughing.

What began as a tease ended up with our clothes scattered on the floor. By the time Callahan had finished with me, I'd let go of all the negativity and fear of the past several days. Afterward, for the first time in weeks, I slept like a stone and woke up happy.

In the fork in the sidewalk between the gym and Huffine, we kissed each other goodbye for a couple of days. He'd still be in film when I finished with my last class before Axel picked me up and drove me home for the holiday. Since the team would be playing their first playoff game on Saturday, they'd be enjoying a team dinner for Thanksgiving courtesy of several football alums. When I asked if Buzz Miller would be among those involved, Hotshot said he doubted it. He met my follow-up why with an enigmatic smile and an admonition to be patient.

"You'll be at the game, right?" he asked after he finally let me up for air.

"After *someone* gifted Axel with prime seats, I imagine we'll be in the stands before you even suit up in the locker room." I added a massive eye roll for emphasis.

Without even a hint of apology he pecked a kiss on my mouth. "Whatever it takes." Then he sobered. "Call me when you get home, please."

I brushed a kiss over his lips. "I miss you already."

"Hey, that was my line." He kissed me again.

"O'Reilly! Get your ass in here!"

At the sound of Coach Ellis's voice, we broke apart. A quick check of my phone told me both of us were late.

The surprise of my life awaited me when I arrived home. Mom let me settle in, the two of us spending more than a minute catching up, mainly on my relationship with Callahan. She'd figured out there was someone special in my life almost before I did. The fact that she approved—and wanted to meet him—gave me more confidence than she could have imagined.

Then she dropped her bomb.

"Jamaica, I've been seeing someone too." Her lips stretched into a coy smile.

Clearing my throat, I said, "Wow. Tell me about him." What I meant was *Please don't let him be another over-the-road guy.*

"His name is Royal Smith-Greene, and he's the new principal at the high school." A dreamy expression erased ten years from her face. "We met at the library, which I know is so high-school." She giggled. "He makes me feel young again, like I have possibilities."

I'm not sure she even registered that she'd covered my hand with hers, squeezing tight as if she were willing me to like the guy before I'd even met him.

"Not trying to harsh your buzz, Mom, but he's single, right?"

"Divorced. A son in college." Another squeeze. "That was the first thing I asked when he asked me out."

"Just making sure after the fiasco that was John Blackwood." She tensed.

"I'm twenty-one, Mom. I have a right to my opinions."

"You have, but you should know the whole story first." With a sigh, she stood from the table to stare out the window above the sink into her postage-stamp-size back yard.

"Do you mean the part about where he was already married when he impregnated you with me? Or the part where he stayed married for personal gain and fathered my three half-siblings?"

Spinning on her heel, she faced me. "How do you know about that?"

"Long story, but the short version is his secrets nearly cost me my scholarship." Her eyes saucered as I plowed on with my story. "After I had to prove myself in front of the faculty of the College of Letters and Science, some of the professors from the School of Business, and the head football coach on Monday morning, he met me for lunch. Wanted me to spend Thanksgiving with his family, get to know my 'brothers and sister.'" The air quotes were not ironic. Shared DNA wasn't enough to make us family.

"Anyway, now he wants to make good on his promise to help me with school."

Her brows shot up.

"I passed."

"What? Why?" Shock dropped her jaw.

"For the past two and a half years, I've taken care of my bills by myself. I imagine I can make it work for another year and a half." Gesturing for her to sit again, I said, "I did ask him for something, though." I held my hands out to her across the table. "I told him if he truly wanted to do something good for us, he'd pay your tuition for the online business school that's bookmarked on your iPad."

"You did what?" She tried to tug away from me, but I held on.

I shrugged. "Turns out, Dad's brother-in-law is that jerk of a professor who's made my life miserable since freshman year."

I stopped as my brain processed something Mom had just said.

"Wait. You knew about Dad's other family?"

She sighed. "When he didn't show up for six months straight during your junior year, I called to make sure he was all right and hadn't been in an accident or something. He'd said his father-in-law had passed away and left the trucking company to him." Sad eyes met mine. "I think he stayed in that marriage because he wanted the company."

"And you didn't follow up when I asked about him helping me with college?" I was having trouble wrapping my head around Mom's revelations.

"He said he had to come clean with his wife first. He promised he would."

"Guess she wasn't in favor of spending her dad's money on her husband's accident."

Mom gasped. "You weren't planned but you were always wanted." She squeezed my hands so hard my bones rubbed together. "Things for your dad were…complicated." Letting me go, she stood and refilled her coffee mug. I forgave your dad long ago. For your own sake, you need to forgive him too."

"Even though his silence about his other family almost cost me everything?" No doubt my expression of incredulity bordered on nuts. "When the dean found out about my connection to Dad's brother-in-law, everything went to hell. But the outcome is that I asked dear old Dad to help you out since it was because of his selfishness that you lost all your opportunities and had to work your ass off to make sure I had a roof over my head."

"I don't need his money," she said quietly. "I won't take it. Royal is helping me with scholarship applications and grants. I have options."

A smile stretched over my lips. "I'm truly looking forward to meeting this guy."

Smoothing her hands down her thighs, she said, "I was hoping you'd say that. I invited him and his son to dinner tomorrow."

Though I worried about meeting Mom's new man—and she worried about me meeting him too—we were both silly. Royal's sarcastic sense of humor put me immediately at ease. His son Jamal was a sophomore at Wyoming, majoring in physics and football. He reminded me of Callahan's friend Jeremiah Fitzgerald, maybe because like Fitz, he played nose-tackle. Or maybe because he had an intensity to him that gave me a sense of safety with him.

When Jamal found out I was dating Callahan, the smile on his face could have lit up the entire house. Turns out he'd enjoyed knocking heads and exchanging wits with Hotshot during a pre-season exhibition game that I hadn't paid attention to, having not met the love of my life before then.

Who would have guessed football would bring so many wonderful connections into my life? Me, who'd made a career of steering clear of athletes?

After Thanksgiving dinner went so well, Royal and Jamal joined us again for dinner on Friday night. Jamal and I bonded over tag-team teasing our parents over the moony eyes neither could stop making at each other. During dish detail, we mutually determined Royal would put a ring on Sunny at Christmas, and both of us were fine with that.

"Seriously? You think your mom's gonna get married after all these years?" Axel asked as he drove us back to campus on Saturday morning.

"You should see them together. I swear they're as sappy as Drake and you."

My friend shot me a side-eye. "You mean they look at each other the way you and Callahan do?"

"We are not moony," I huffed.

His eyes danced. "You haven't seen yourself." Returning his attention to the road, he asked, "How many times did you text each other the past two days?"

"How many times did you text Drake?"

"Not enough."

I slumped into my seat. "Yeah, me too."

We grinned at each other like a pair of monkeys.

As I predicted, we arrived at the field forty-five minutes before kickoff. Stomping my feet to keep warm, I wrapped my mittens around my hot coffee and burned my tongue on it more than once as I drank it too fast. I couldn't wait to see Hotshot all suited up and looking menacing in his uniform and pads. When he exited the tunnel and ran out onto the field before the game, my heart actually fluttered like something I read once in one of Mom's romance novels.

With one quick scan he found me in the stands. He winked and mouthed, "I love you."

I blew him a kiss, and he grinned and returned his attention to the pep-up with his teammates.

The Spartans from the Southeast Division gave the Wildcats a game, going back and forth until the fourth quarter. Even though the game played on a holiday, it seemed the entire student body had shown up to cheer our guys to victory. The only touchdown Callahan scored came on a trick play on a faked punt with two minutes left in the game. We were down by three and had nothing to lose when the punter, who had played quarterback in high school, tossed a perfect spiral to my guy who caught it in stride, pushed off one defender, and raced to the end zone.

As always, he pointed the nose of the ball directly at me. I was jumping up and down in delight when Axel pointed at the scoreboard where my face filled the screen. Reflexively, I pulled my muffler over my mouth and nose, and the crowd went wild. That's when I remembered I was wearing my Wildcats scarf.

Mercifully the team swarmed Callahan, and the camera panned back to the celebration going on in the field. Beside me Axel chuckled. "Looks like you've been outed, J."

"Ugh!" But I couldn't truly be upset. Being Callahan's girlfriend was the best thing that had happened to me.

After the game Axel and I hustled to Stromboli's where we grabbed the team's booth in the back. Finn, Bax, Fitz, and Callahan walked into the bar together to a deafening cheer. Like magic pitchers of beer appeared on the table seconds before they made their way back to the booth.

While Axel congratulated the other guys, Callahan crowded me into the corner, leaned in, and kissed me stupid.

"Hello, Island Girl. Glad you could make the game," he said with a smile when he let me up.

"Hello, Hotshot. Glad you did your job." I smirked.

"We're all glad he pulled his head out of his ass," Bax said as he slid a full glass of beer across the table to my guy.

"Hey!" Callahan protested.

Finn said, "Yup. Your draft stock went way up with that teeder." Lifting his glass in the air, he said, "Go! 'Cats! Go!"

We all lifted our glasses and echoed the cheer that the entire bar took up. A pair of extra-large pizzas materialized in front of us, and the server said, "We'll keep these coming until you say when."

At his pronouncement, my eyes rounded, and Fitzy laughed his deep baritone laugh. "Way better perks than some snooty restaurant downtown, eh, 'Han?"

Hugging me close with the arm he'd wrapped around me when he arrived, Callahan replied, "You have no idea."

EPILOGUE

Callahan

WE MADE IT to the semifinals before we met our match. Playing—and losing—that game in the frozen tundra of North Dakota hurt on every single level.

But when I arrived home, I discovered the Christmas present to rival all Christmas presents. Jamaica was in my bed, and all the hurts faded like melting snow.

"Thought you were headed home Friday after the dorms closed for Christmas break," I said as I closed the door to my room.

"Someone gave me a key to his house and told me I was welcome to use it whenever I liked. I liked to use it Friday night." She shifted up on her elbow to rest her head on her hand. "I would have enjoyed watching the game on your big TV a whole lot more if the score had been reversed."

With a grunt, I tugged my hoodie over my head and tossed it over the chair. "I would have liked playing it a whole lot more if the score had been reversed." My jeans joined my hoodie while my boxers landed somewhere on the floor. "But finding you here makes everything better." Though I tried not to wince, when my back hit the sheets, it reminded me of the last series of brutal hits I took as both our coaching staff and the defense keyed on me.

"Where does it hurt?"

"Everywhere," I groaned.

She burrowed beneath the blankets, and my skin rippled beneath her lips as she started kissing her way up my body, beginning with my ankles. By the time she reached my cock, I'd forgotten all about football, hits, bruises, and a lost chance at a national championship. First, she took me with her mouth, demanding that I lie back and let her make me feel better. When I calmed down from the first climax, she started over with those soft kisses, and I thought I'd lose my mind with wanting her. When she climbed on top of me again, she demanded I let her do the work.

Afterward she collapsed on my chest and whispered into my neck, "I never expected to fall in love. Certainly not with a football player. But you had my attention from that first day in Dair's class when you opened with that cheesy line." I sensed her grin on my skin. "Win or lose, I love you, Callahan O'Reilly."

"When I met you, Jamaica Winslow, I scored the most important touchdown of my life." Wrapping my arms around her and cradling her close to my side, I said the words I knew I'd be saying to her for the rest of my life. "I love you."

Thanks so much for reading *Finding the End Zone*.

For a sneak peek at *Out of Bounds*, Wyatt "Bax" Baxter's story coming in January 2024, turn the page.

CHAPTER ONE

Piper

ON A THURSDAY night, one would have thought it would be easy to enjoy a drink in a bar in peace.

One would have thought wrong.

"The seat is taken," I said for about the hundredth time in the past half hour. The bar stool in question was home to my purse for the evening. Couldn't these guys see that?

Across the bar, the bartender winked and tipped his chin up. Whether his expressions were in solidarity with me or hitting on me too didn't matter. Either way, I couldn't care. As long as he let me nurse my lemon drop without hassling me to order another before I was ready, his opinions were none of my concern.

The big guy standing near the pool tables who kept catching my eye in the mirror behind the bar was a different story entirely. Tall, built, and sexy with a knowing upturn of the corner of his mouth, he struggled to keep his opinions to himself. Furrowed brow, a ghost of a wink, that hint of a grin told me all about what he thought of some of the guys coming onto me—and my responses to them. Something in the way he watched me hold that empty bar stool in the unexpectedly crowded bar both irritated and intrigued me. Especially since he seemed to be the only man in the place who hadn't made a run at it.

Until two months ago, it never occurred to me I'd have to endure the bar scene as a single person. On any other evening since the afternoon of The Fuckery, I'd have called Saylor or Chessly to come out with me. But after the day I'd had, all I wanted to do was have a quiet drink without the social pressure of checking out men and "putting myself back out there" as my friends had been harping on me to do since that awful day.

I wanted to unwind, process my failed stats quiz—a first for me that I had no idea how I'd let happen—and figure out next steps for salvaging my GPA. While Stromboli's would have been the obvious choice, I'd deliberately chosen an off-campus bar I never frequented to be sure I wouldn't run into anyone I knew. About two sips into my drink, that plan shot straight to hell when out of nowhere Charlie showed up and assumed he could park his ass on the seat beside me. I thought I'd sent him packing on his first attempt, but for some stupid reason, he was persistent.

"I've been watching since I tried to talk to you twenty minutes ago. At least six guys have asked to sit here, and you've waved them all off. Admit it, Pipes. You don't have a date tonight," Charlie said when he approached me again.

"My name is Piper, and I never said I had a date. I said the seat is taken." I stared straight ahead. "I would have thought the fact that I blocked your number and unfriended and unfollowed you everywhere on social media would have been your first clue that I have nothing to say to you."

"Piper," he whined. "Don't be like this. If you'd talk to me, let me explain, I know we could make things right again." When I wouldn't look directly at him, he transferred his attention to our reflections in the mirror behind the bar.

The glare I slanted him would have singed a normal person to a crisp. Apparently, Charlie had some superpower shamelessness as he stared back at me with his best wounded puppy eyes. Experience had taught me never to believe that expression again.

"Hey, babe. Sorry I'm late. Thanks for waiting for me," came the deep voice of the sexy giant who materialized beside me as if by magic. Casually picking up my purse, he handed it to me as he slid onto the empty bar stool. Glancing at my drink, now mostly ice cubes, he added, "Looks like you need a refill. Barkeep." He signaled the bartender and pointed at my glass. "While you're at it, grab me a stout. Thanks."

"Piper?" Surprise and something like worry sounded in Charlie's voice.

It was that plaintive note in his tone that did it. "Like I've been telling people since I arrived, this seat was taken."

Swinging his attention to my ex, the giant stuck out his beautifully formed yet weirdly scraped up and massive hand. "I'm Bax."

I hid a grin at the trepidation in Charlie's movements as he gingerly raised his hand to shake "Bax's."

"Charlie." They shook. "How do you know Piper?"

With satisfaction, I noted the way Charlie flexed his hand when he dropped it to his side.

"That stopped being your business when you did what you did." Resting my elbow on the back of my bar stool, I looked my former boyfriend full in the face for the first time since he'd started bothering me. "Goodbye, Charlie."

"But Piper," he whined again.

"This the one you were telling me about?" the big guy chimed in.

Playing along, I nodded.

"Dude, you blew it." Bax, if that truly was his name, casually rested his salad-plate-size palm on my thigh below the hem of my skirt. Tingles rippled over my skin, gathering at my center, pulsing and building pressure low in my belly. With super-human force of will, I managed to keep from clamping my thighs together at the unexpected onslaught of sensation from his touch. "Lucky for me." His nostrils flared as he swung a glance in my direction.

"You can't be serious," Charlie said as his eyes ping-ponged between Bax and me. "This guy isn't your type at all."

The striking contrast between Charlie's long, sinewy runner's body and the mounded muscles Bax's T-shirt could barely contain might have given him that impression. But it had never been about his body. Charlie's charm had drawn me to him, kept me around, convinced me my instincts were off when things started going south between us before The Fuckery.

Flicking my eyes between his pouty scowl and Bax's square-jawed hotness, I said, "You never truly knew me. If you had, you'd have known you were the anomaly. The guys I dated in high school were more like Bax."

At that comment, the smile Bax gifted me momentarily stopped my heart in a way Charlie's wounded expression couldn't touch.

Something in my face must have told him as much. Hunching his shoulders, he stuffed his hands in the pockets of his khakis. "If you're lucky, I'll still be around when you come back to your senses."

"I came to my senses at the beginning of the semester. That's why you're my past."

The bartender set a fresh drink in front of me and a beer in front of Bax, drawing my attention away from my ex's drama.

Bax lifted his beer to his lips, tipped some back, and gestured the bottle toward Charlie. "See you around, man." Though his tone was cordial, his dismissive demeanor had my ex backing up. Bax eyed him all the way to the door of the bar before he returned his attention to me.

"Bad breakup, huh?"

I nodded.

"His fault."

Not a question.

I nodded again.

"Dumbass. How the hell did he let a hottie like you get away?" That smile again. It did funny things to my insides. Offering his hand, he said, "Wyatt Baxter, but most people call me Bax."

"I'm Piper Maxwell—Wyatt." His warm hand swallowed mine in a way I weirdly liked.

"Darlin', you can call me anything you like as long as you call me." With a tiny squeeze, he let my hand go.

That cheesy line should have put me off. Instead, I heard myself laughing. Glancing over the rim of my glass, I said, "For the record, I was handling him fine." Wyatt's brow went up. "But your timely intervention speeded up the process. Thanks."

He held his beer up for a toast. "Nice to meet you."

I clinked my glass to his. "Nice to meet you, too."

We smiled at each other and drank.

"Do I detect a bit of the South in the way you talk?" I asked.

Turning his stool a quarter turn, he rested his elbow on the bar while his jeans-clad knee lightly brushed my bare one. "We moved around some as I was growing up, but I graduated high school in Kentucky."

"So how did you end up in the Great Northwest?"

The corners of his eyes crinkled in a way that said he laughed often. "Football."

With a nod, I said, "Of course."

"What's your story, Piper Maxwell? Why have you chosen to sit at the bar alone tonight?"

Super-hot and insightful proved an irresistible combination. Before I knew it, I'd shared my bad day with him. "There you have it. I'm a nerd who's never failed a test before. A quiet drink in a room full of strangers seemed like a good way to forget about screwing up for an evening." I sipped some vodka and lemon deliciousness. "I chose this bar because I'd never come here before. I didn't expect to see Charlie here." Wrinkling my nose in disgust, I said, "His appearance only reminded me this entire semester has been one massive screw-up."

"You have to let it sit with you for a minute, feel it, and know you never want to feel it again." For a second, his expression darkened. "Then you let it go."

"Sage advice from a man wearing a T-shirt that says 'For people who are bad at identifying things, there are a lot of UFOs out there.'" I laughed.

He glanced down at his shirt as though he'd forgotten about it, glanced back up, and grinned. "The thing is, I know how you feel. I fucking hate to lose. On the few occasions where we've done that, Coach has made us sit with it, feel that failure. The next time we go out on the field, we tear it up. Dump all that pent up frustration, anger, and disappointment on the next game." Tipping his beer up, he downed a long pull. "We play about a thousand times better then." He tapped his finger on my glass, encouraging me to take a sip. "Tonight, you feel your failure. Tomorrow, you kick some ass."

A warm glow radiated through me, his words instilling a confidence I'd let falter after The Fuckery.

Fingering my glass around the rim, I rolled it around, letting the ice clink and crash around the cherry on the bottom. "I take it you play for the Wildcats. What position?"

"Middle linebacker."

"Makes sense."

He snorted. "Because of the way I'm built?"

"No. Because of the way you sized up my situation and waited until I'd had enough before you stepped in. That and the scraped up state of your hands." At his wide-eyed blink, I said,

"Isn't that the job of the quarterback of the defense? To assess the formation, signal the other players on the line, and execute a play that stops the offense's progress?"

My breath caught at the way his face lit up. "You like football?"

I shrugged. "I've watched a game or two."

"You sure have." A slow sexy wink accompanied his words.

With someone else that move might have come off as kind of silly. Instead, that wink left me hot.

He signaled the bartender for another beer. "You want another—what are you drinking?"

"A lemon drop but I'm done. Two's my limit so I can drive myself home."

"The lady here will have a water please," he said when the bartender delivered his beer.

"Thank you." By not pushing me to keep drinking, the man scored major points and made me want to know more about him. With a tilt of my head, I studied him from beneath my brows. "What are you majoring in?"

"Art and graphic design."

The way he straightened his shoulders when he said that made me think someone had given him a hard time about his major. I had to admit, I'd expected something like kinesthetics or personal training, which was wildly stereotypical considering my punk rock style might have given someone the wrong idea about how seriously I took my business major.

Touring his sculpted arms with my eyes, I noted the absence of tats. "I thought art majors liked to decorate themselves."

"We do." His wolfish grin drew me closer. "But mine are private."

"Is that right? How private?"

It had been a while since I'd flirted with a stranger in a bar, but from the minute we locked gazes in the mirror not long after I sat down, I'd sensed a connection with this man.

His unusually light green eyes darkened to a mossy color that sent an arrow of sensation straight to my core. "Too private to show you in here."

"That's a bummer." Crunching on a cube of ice to cool myself off, I clocked his disappointment. "Maybe you can describe yours then."

He shifted, his inner thigh lightly brushing my outer thigh, subtly caging me in. The move sent a shiver through me in direct opposition to the expression of pure innocence on his handsome face. "I have two below the waistband of my boxers."

Blinking hard I asked, "Why?"

Deep velvety laughter enveloped me. "Not there, Piper. Jeez. Give me a little credit for a sense of self-preservation."

The corner of my mouth tipped up. "You play football and talk about self-preservation."

"I take very good care of myself." Those arresting eyes twinkled. "Certain parts most especially."

Delicately tracing the scrapes on his hand, I said, "I can see that."

I could also see how the hairs on his forearm stood to attention when I touched his skin. *Interesting.*

Glancing down at where I continued to explore his battle wounds, he grinned. "I've been told I have nice—hands."

"You're a funny guy, Wyatt Baxter." Signaling the bartender, I reached for my purse. "Thanks again for making my otherwise shitty day better."

"Wait. You're leaving?" The crestfallen expression on his face cracked me up. Pulling his phone from his back pocket, he checked the time. "It's only ten." Waggling his brows, he said, "You have hours before you turn into a pumpkin, Cinderella."

"Ha. Ha," I wrinkled my nose at him. "I have a nine o'clock lab, and I don't want to repeat today's fiasco."

Covering my hand holding my debit card, he sobered. "Hey,

I got this." When I raised a brow, he added, "No strings. No expectations."

He fished his wallet from the front pocket of his jeans. Beneath his touch, I relaxed, the gentle pressure of his hand more reassuring than commanding. The bartender's eyes darted between us, then he offered his card reader to Wyatt who paid our tab.

"Entertaining and generous." I smiled as I slid off my stool and held out my hand. "It truly was nice to meet you."

His eyes held mine even closer than our palms touching as we shook hands, and a frission of heat arced through me to throb between my thighs.

Slowly, reluctantly, he let me go. "How 'bout I walk you to your car?"

"Sure. Thanks," popped out of my mouth before I had time to think about it.

Of course, if I thought about it, I'd have to admit my intense attraction to this guy. The heat radiating from his hand on the small of my back puckered my nipples and pulsed my core as we walked out to the parking lot. After The Fuckery, I had no intention of becoming involved with anyone any time soon, but as we neared my car, I decided I wouldn't be opposed to a hook up with superhot football player.

ACKNOWLEDGEMENTS

A month before this book was due to my editor, I received a phone call no one wants: my editor had suffered an aneurysm and passed away a day before my last book, *Stay For Me*, released. The news staggered me. Nikki Busch and I had worked together for eight years on twelve books, several of which have won awards and all of which have earned four- and five-star reviews from readers like you. Her editing skills made me a stronger, better writer, and I will be forever grateful for her professionalism and expertise. Not to mention, she was an incredible person. I miss comparing notes on all the rock shows we'd seen and listening to her stories of playing guitar in a rock band.

After a month of wringing my hands and wishing I could ask her for a recommendation for her replacement, I finally moved on with the difficult task of auditioning a new editor, which is sort of how I imagine online dating works. Finally, I found Bryony Leah. Thanks for agreeing to take me on, Bryony, especially with the busy, busy summer you had marrying the love of your life, honeymooning on a Greek island, and coming home to the loss of your nana. Your plate was pretty full before the addition of editing *Finding the End Zone*.

Joni Blood, without your insistence that I write a football romance, I doubt I would have written this book. Thanks for the push. I loved writing Callahan and Jamaica's story so much that now theirs is the first book in the Game Time football romance series with at least three more books coming. You're welcome. ;)

Bri Weigel, you are a rock star. Every time I ask you to beta read for me, you never hesitate to say yes, even when you're chasing an active toddler around the house and teaching a full load at Casper College. I appreciate your insights so much. Thank you.

Coleene Torgerson, I'm so lucky to have you in my life. Thanks for your help with the blurb and for your endless support of my writing. Because you believed in me from the start when I sent that very first draft of *Talisman* to you, I have a career. I truly hit the best friend jackpot on the first day of first grade all those years ago.

Levi Meyer, I appreciate all the work you do to keep my website top notch. The revamp looks marvelous. Thank you.

Julia Goldhirsch, VA extraordinaire, I appreciate your tireless efforts to keep my books in front of readers. You always come up with fresh ideas and new places for me to connect with people. Without you, I'd be muddling around in the dark trying to figure out marketing and driving myself bonkers in the process.

My critique partners—JR Cobourn, KJ Gillenwater, Linda-Rae Sande, and Sara Vinduska—you're the best. Thanks so much for your comments and catches on the early drafts of this book. I'm so pleased you love this story. Our working dinners together are such fun. Cheers!

CruiserMan, you always believe in what I'm doing. Having that kind of support is a gift. Thank you. I love you.

I've saved the biggest thanks for you, Dear Reader. Without you, this writing dream is airy nothing. I love to connect with readers online, especially on Instagram and TikTok, so keep tuning in and commenting. I also love to see you on the reading sites where I check in regularly. Readers truly do influence what I write. If you haven't already done so, head on over to my website *www.tamderudderjackson.com* and subscribe to my newsletter. I always have something fun to share including free books, sales, discounts, sneak peeks, and bonus chapters. See you there.

ABOUT THE AUTHOR

Tam DeRudder Jackson's love of all things Celtic led her to write the Talisman Series. Steeped in Celtic mythology, these steamy, fated mates, fantasy romance adventures are set in the mountains of Tam's native Montana and the Highlands of Scotland. *Rogue*, the most recent book in the series, was named a best book read in 2022 by the *Independent Book Review*.

An avid fan of rock music, Tam never misses a chance to see a live show. Her love of rock music inspired her contemporary rock star Balefire Series, a sexy fun ride following the lives and loves of the members of a fictional mega-band. *Play For Me*, book one in the series, was a finalist for the 2023 Amor Book Awards.

Tam earned her BA in English from Montana State University and her M.Ed. in literacy from Lesley University. After a short teaching stint in Bath, England, she settled in the wilds of Wyoming where she taught adolescents all about the Celts and a bit about writing before she stepped out of the classroom to pursue her writing career full time.

When she's not writing, you can find Tam working her way through her mountainous TBR piles, alpine skiing, or traveling to some new place on her ever-expanding bucket list. To stay up to date on her adventures, connect with her on her website www. tamderudderjackson where you can subscribe to her newsletter and hang out with her on Instagram at https://instagram.com/ tamstales32.

Milton Keynes UK
Ingram Content Group UK Ltd.
UKHW040712201123
432908UK00001B/300